HOCKEY
NIGHT
IN THE DOMINION
OF CANADA

A NOVEL

HOCKEY NIGHT

IN THE DOMINION OF CANADA

ERIC ZWEIG

LESTER
PUBLISHING
LIMITED

Canadian Cataloguing in Publication Data

Zweig, Eric, 1963–
    Hockey night in the Dominion of Canada

ISBN 1-895555-07-8

I. Title.

PS8599.W43H56 1992   C813'.54   C92-094-240-7
PR9199.3.Z94H45 1992

Lester Publishing Limited
56 The Esplanade
Toronto, Ontario
M5E 1A7

Printed and bound in Canada.

92 93 94 95   5 4 3 2 1

To my parents, Stephen and Joyce, without whose love and support this would not have been possible,

And to my brothers, David and Jonathan, who, by their actions, encouraged me to take a chance too.

PART I
THE ARENA

I

The Ministers decided this afternoon to carry out an arrangement which had been arrived at through communication with the Imperial authorities. The Home Government agreed to receive into the army in South Africa a contingent composed of a number of units of 125 men each and certain officers, the highest to be a major, so that the units may on arrival be consolidated with the Imperial forces under Imperial officers. The movement is to be entirely a volunteer one. The number of officers and men determined on is 1000, which is a much larger number than that supplied by any other colony of the Empire.

Sir Wilfrid Laurier,
Prime Minister.
October 12, 1899

WHEN FREDDY WENT TO BED AT NIGHT, HIS LAST WAKING thoughts were of the Boer War. He dreamed about it while he slept. In the morning, he read newspaper reports on the war's progress. Freddy Taylor had the romantic vision of war so common among young boys. The Boer War brought to mind images of dashing, red-coated British soldiers marching off to fight for Queen and country. The horrors of armed conflict were unknown to him. The struggle in South Africa was more like an adventure story in a land far away. "Is it really summer there?" he asked himself. It seemed impossible that it could be summer anywhere when the Maitland River, and everything else around his home town of Listowel, Ontario, was frozen under a blanket of snow. "How do they celebrate Christmas?" he wondered. "With picnics at the beach?" Or maybe the Boers didn't celebrate Christmas. He wouldn't be surprised by anything that people foolish enough to take on the British Empire might do.

Freddy sighed as he flipped through the pages of his newspaper. He put his elbows on the table, tucked his thumbs under his ears, and rested his head in his hands. With a faraway look in his large, dark eyes, he thought about how he would behave if he were fighting a war. Heroically, he decided, setting his square jaw firmly like a brave British soldier.

The striking of the clock on the mantel snapped Freddy out of his daydream. News of the war was the only thing he found fascinating enough to divert his attention from his true love: hockey. Noticing the time, Freddy tucked the newspaper under his arm, grabbed his skates and stick, and headed for the Piggery.

The Piggery was where the poor kids in Listowel played hockey. The rich kids played in the new Listowel Arena. Freddy had been playing at the arena a lot himself lately. This was not because his family had come into any money, but because the tales of his skill as a hockey player had spread, and the local team had invited him out to play many times. Freddy loved performing before the crowds and enjoyed the honour of representing his home town in the big arena. But for sheer fun, you couldn't beat the games on the Piggery.

The Piggery was a pond formed by a sharp bend in the Maitland River. It came by its unusual name for the brutal reason that it was downwind from the local slaughterhouse. In summertime, the smells were so overpowering that the pond was usually left to itself, but in the winter the pungent aroma seemed to help the youngsters stay warm as they cut and slashed their way along the ice.

Freddy loved the walk down the path through the woods to the pond. As he got closer, he could hear the shouts of the other boys playing. Then, suddenly, the sight of the pond was upon him. The hard ice glistened in the sun and the snow-covered trees towered above it.

Freddy sat down on a stump that someone had dragged over to the frozen pond to use as a bench. He pulled off his heavy winter boots, rolled down his long socks, and stuffed in a few pages of newspaper to protect his shins. He rolled the tight socks back up to keep the newspaper in place, laced on his skates, grabbed his stick, and hit the ice.

"Here comes Freddy," called out one of the many boys who were already playing.

"Here comes Freddy!" another boy buzzed, as word of their friend's arrival was passed on among the players.

Freddy hit the ice with a game already in progress. The action continued while he made a couple of lightning-fast circles around the edge of the pond. He enjoyed no feeling more than the cold rush of air against his cheeks. No sound was better than the "swish, swish, swish" of his blades biting into the ice. By this time, everyone on the ice knew what was coming, but for Freddy that made it even more fun.

Freddy was doing more than limbering up as he circled around the other boys. He was studying the game, looking to see who had the puck. It was Bobby Thomson, a classmate of his. Freddy swooped in on the play, but Bobby knew what to do. He took off towards the far end of the rink.

"I'm gaining on you!" Freddy warned him, as he quickly closed the gap between Bobby and himself. The boy cut sharply to his left, trying to shake Freddy. When he wheeled back to the right, Freddy was upon him.

"Nice try," Freddy said with a smile, as he picked the puck cleanly off his classmate's stick. Bobby was now out of the game. For the next few minutes he would serve as a kind of referee.

When Freddy spun around after taking control of the puck, he found all of the other boys lined up against him. From the clunking sound as his own stick pushed the puck forward, Freddy knew that today the puck was really a chunk of wood. Sometimes the puck was a lump of coal, but coal was valuable, and besides, it tended to break apart as the game wore on. More often, a small piece of wood was used. It might be painted black, if someone had bothered to think about it during the week.

Cradling the wooden puck carefully with the blade of his stick, which he kept close to his body, Freddy sped towards the group of boys. There were maybe two dozen of them. A younger boy moved forward to oppose him. Freddy made eye contact with the red-cheeked youth. A knowing smile spread across his face.

Freddy bobbed his head to the left, then to the right. Because the young boy had been watching his eyes, and not concentrating on his body, he was completely fooled by the head fake. Freddy sped past him easily. "You're out of the game!" Bobby Thomson shouted to the boy. Once Freddy had beaten you, you couldn't play again until he was stopped.

Another boy emerged from the pack. Older and much larger than the first one, he was determined not to make the same mistake. Instead of staring into Freddy's eyes, he concentrated on the puck. Again Freddy smiled. He shifted the puck to the left. The burly boy leaned left. He moved it to the right. The boy moved his bulky body right. Then Freddy pushed the puck between the boy's legs. The boy nearly fell down trying to follow the puck this time. Freddy leaped out of the way as the boy's off-balance body blocked his path, then he scooped up the puck again and pushed on.

"You're out of the game!" Bobby hollered.

Freddy could usually keep the puck away from the other boys for several minutes. Today was no exception. Freddy was in top form, swerving in and around the other players, putting each boy he passed out of the game. When he sensed that the few remaining fellows might finally be catching up to him, he broke away from the pack. Streaking at full speed towards the goal, he slipped the puck between the two wooden posts.

"HAWHHHHH!" Freddy cheered, his hands covering his mouth so that the sound became a rough approximation of the 1200 fans who jammed the local arena. "Taylor scores for Listowel!"

"Get him!" shouted one of the boys, as Freddy turned around to face them. It was Richard Lawrence, his arm extended forward and upward like an army general giving the signal to charge.

Suddenly, the boys who had been put out of the game by Freddy's exploits buried him under a barrage of snowballs. But it was all just good-natured fun. Nobody really minded the way Freddy showed off. It was obvious to everyone that he was a far greater hockey player than anyone else they had ever seen. Still, Freddy feigned disappointment in his friends.

"A fine thing for you fellows to treat a friend this way," he said, shaking his head in mock sadness. "Especially," he continued, his voice much more animated, "when I brought you these!" Freddy emptied the pockets of his coat and tossed three real rubber pucks on the ice. They skittered away in three different directions.

"Wow! Where did you get them?" It was Richard Lawrence again.

Freddy looked around nervously, then waved his friends in closer to tell them his secret. "The last time I played for the team," he whispered, "I took them."

The boys at the Piggery regarded real rubber pucks as golden treasure. They were almost as rare. If a real puck was shot off the smooth pond into the deep snowbanks built up around the edges, games could break down for long stretches while the boys hunted for their lost possession.

Sometimes, somebody's dog would grab the puck, and the players would take off in hot pursuit. But the four-legged creatures had much better traction in the snow, and even if the boys caught the dog, there was no guarantee they'd ever retrieve the stolen puck. Usually the dog had dropped it somewhere before they could round him up. Then the puck was lost forever — or at least until the snow melted. The occasional puck hunt was about the only reason anyone would endure a summertime visit to the Piggery.

Pity the poor puppy, though, if Richard Lawrence was the one who caught up to him first. The boy was not above striking the animal with his hockey stick, and striking him hard. Once he'd stepped on a dog's tail with his skate.

Games on the Piggery could last for hours — sometimes, on warmer days, until after sundown. Nobody really bothered to keep score, but Freddy was often swapped from team to team to make sure the games stayed close. Lately, though, the games had been breaking up a little early. One of the boys would pick up his stick and aim it at somebody like a rifle. The others would quickly follow suit, and soon the hockey game was transformed into a re-enactment of the Boer War. It was tough to find a boy in Listowel who wanted to play a Boer, so the make-believe war usually didn't last long. As the boys walked back to town, they would discuss the latest news from the real war.

"Mind if I trek home with you?" Richard Lawrence asked Freddy. "Trek" was a South African word. All the boys were starting to use it and other South African phrases. "Trekking to the Pig-fontein" was the way most of the boys now referred to walking to the Piggery.

Richard Lawrence was taller than Freddy, but then most of Freddy's friends were taller than he was. Richard was taller then any of them, though, and unlike most other tall boys, he was not a gangly assortment of arms and legs. His young frame seemed much more mature, almost as if he were a boy inside a man's body. He had black hair that hung down so straight he didn't need a comb to keep it neat, and grey eyes that looked at people with too much intensity.

Though they seemed to spend a lot of time together, Freddy wasn't sure how he felt about Richard. The boy was a few years older than

Freddy, and two grades ahead of him in school, but since they were next door neighbours they made the "trek" home together often. Freddy didn't like the way Richard treated the dogs, but there was at least one good thing about him. His father worked for the local newspaper and Richard always seemed to get the news from the Boer War before anyone else.

Like most boys in small-town Ontario, Freddy and Richard were of British descent. The boys and their parents — and probably all the people of Listowel — were pleased that the Canadian government had decided to show its support for the Empire by sending troops to fight in South Africa, though they all wished Laurier had taken stronger action than committing a troop of volunteers. For his part, Laurier believed the British were right in going off to war in South Africa. He felt the Boer government was wrong in its treatment of its British subjects. Still, while the war made sense for the British, there appeared to be no reason for Canada to take part. Canadian interests were not threatened.

British Colonial Secretary Joseph Chamberlain had other ideas. Chamberlain saw the war in South Africa as a new rallying point for British Imperialism. He had pressured the Canadian Prime Minister to make a substantial military contribution. Laurier could have resisted such pressure from Britain, had it not been for the groundswell of support for the Empire from within English Canada. It was so great that it became politically impossible for Laurier to turn a deaf ear.

Freddy supported Queen and country because he had never known any other way. He sang "God Save the Queen" in school every morning; he read the Imperialist stories of Rudyard Kipling; and he adopted unquestioningly his father's Conservative ideology. Politics mattered little to Freddy, but war — that was a different story!

"Did you hear about the armoured train ambush?" Richard asked Freddy, as they walked home from the Piggery.

"No! What happened?"

"It's bad news." Richard shook his head, a frustrated look on his face. "Two companies of British soldiers were being transported on board an armoured train. A bunch of Boer soldiers appeared on a hill behind them, so the train sped up to get away. All of a sudden it hit something. Those bloody Boers had put a rock on the track! A whole lot of cars got derailed."

Freddy winced, his mind filling with images of twisted train cars, as Richard continued his report. Several soldiers had been killed in the train wreck; many others had been injured. Boer soldiers raced on horseback to the crash scene, shooting away at the crippled train and at the dazed British soldiers. About fifty of them were taken prisoner. Among the captured was a young journalist named Winston Churchill, who was covering the war for a British newspaper.

"Even though fifty-two men were captured," Richard told Freddy, "they say this Churchill fellow was a real hero."

Churchill had worked hard, under a hail of bullets, to clear the derailed train cars from the track. And, just before he was captured, he had helped load as many wounded soldiers as possible onto the engine, which was able to speed to safety. Churchill, stories would later confirm, had demanded that the Boers release him, since he was merely a newspaperman and not a soldier, but it wasn't often the Boers captured the son of an English lord, and they refused to let him go. Churchill had been marched off along with the others to the Boer capital in Pretoria, where he was being held as a prisoner of war at the State Model School.

"I hate the Boers!" Richard concluded passionately. "I wish I was old enough to volunteer. I'd show them a thing or two!"

"Me too," said Freddy, and he imagined himself fighting side by side with the British colonel who was heading up the army in South Africa. He even liked the sound of his name — Lord Robert Baden-Powell — a fighting man with a double-barrelled moniker like the heroes of his favourite adventure stories. What was the name of the journalist Richard had just told him about? Oh yes, Winston Churchill. Freddy liked the way that name sounded, too. He hoped Churchill would be all right.

Winston Churchill's name became very familiar to Freddy over the next five weeks. News of his capture made headlines around the world, but news of his escape caused an even greater sensation. Freddy scanned the newspapers day after day, as conflicting reports made their way into the world. Bulletins from Pretoria confirmed Churchill's escape, but boasted that it would be impossible for him to cross the border out of Boer territory. In fact, a reward of twenty-five pounds was offered for the return of Churchill to the Boer forces in Pretoria, dead or alive. Several reports in the next few days indicated that the young journalist had been recaptured.

Freddy was relieved to read, about two weeks later, that Churchill had arrived back in British territory, greeted in Durban with a hero's welcome. Now the full story of his escape was finally told. Freddy read it over and over, and each time he read it, it seemed better. Churchill had gone over the wall at the State Model School and concealed himself on a train bound for the coast. He jumped from the train before daybreak and spent several days hiding from the authorities in a small mining village. After that, Churchill hid away in a shipment of wool on a train headed for Portuguese territory. When he arrived at Delagoa Bay, he walked into the British Consulate, where he was given passage to Durban.

Churchill's story aroused in Freddy feelings of pride and awe that tingled up his spine and down his arms. It was the greatest story of courage he had ever read, and he wished he could have been among the crowd in Durban who greeted Churchill. He wished, in fact, that it could have been Freddy Taylor who was greeted upon his own heroic escape. He prayed that the Boer War wouldn't be over before he was old enough to volunteer for duty.

Despite the glorious news of Winston Churchill's escape, things were not going well for the British in South Africa. Only two weeks into the struggle, the Boers had inflicted a beating upon the British the likes of which had not been seen in over a century. The British had lost 38 soldiers killed and 100 more wounded in a battle outside Ladysmith. But, most humiliating of all, almost 1000 British soldiers had been marched away as prisoners of war. Ladysmith had fallen under Boer martial law and had remained that way for over 100 days.

Freddy was playing in the schoolyard with Bobby Thomson. A heavy snow was falling, and the boys were taking turns throwing snowballs at passing wagons when Richard Lawrence raced over.

"Did you hear the news?" Richard shouted, putting a large, strong hand on each of Freddy's shoulders and shaking him violently in his excitement. "Did you hear? Did you hear?"

The school bell rang before Richard Lawrence could tell Freddy his news. But it was not the dull, rhythmic clanging that usually called the children to school. It was a wild, jubilant crashing. Soon other bells could be heard, as the chimes in the town's church towers rang out in celebration. The sound of train whistles from the local station added to the din.

"Ladysmith!" Richard yelled. "The British have won back Lady-smith!"

News of the relief of Ladysmith set off huge celebrations all across the Empire. Although much of Ontario was blanketed by a snowstorm, towns like Listowel didn't let that spoil the fun. School was cancelled, and so was work, as men, women, and children gathered around huge bonfires, taunting the Boer leader by singing "We'll hang old Paul Kruger from a sour apple tree." Townsfolk ran the Union Jack up every flagpole. Freddy, Bobby, and Richard threw handfuls of snow in the air like confetti as they raced from the schoolyard to join in the rejoicing.

II

When I rejoined the South African Light Horse, the irregular brigade had begun to advance again. . . . Never shall I forget that ride. . . . The evening was deliciously cool. . . . The ground was rough with many stones, but we cared little for that. Beyond the next ridge, or the rise beyond that, or around the corner of the hill was Ladysmith — the goal of all our hopes and ambitions during weeks of ceaseless fighting. . . . Whatever victories the future may have in store, the defence and relief of Ladysmith, because they afford, perhaps, the most remarkable examples of national tenacity and perseverance which our later history contains, will not soon be forgotten by the British people, whether at home or in the colonies.

Winston S. Churchill,
War Correspondent.
March 9, 1900

IT WAS ALSO SNOWING WHEN NEWS OF THE RELIEF OF Ladysmith reached Montreal. Canada's decision to send volunteer troops to the Boer War had not been well received by French Canadians. Why help the British military crush the small Dutch population in South Africa, whose only mistake seemed to be a desire to live independent of British rule? Many Quebeckers could sympathize with that struggle, and many quietly supported the Boers.

Students at McGill, Montreal's English university, poured out of their classrooms when they learned of the relief of Ladysmith. The snow was almost knee-high, but, ignoring the nasty weather, the students paraded through the streets, singing "God Save the Queen" and "Rule Britannia."

As the McGill students marched by a nearby high school, waving Union Jacks tied to hockey sticks, some of the high school students ran outside to watch them. Among this younger group were a boy named Lester Patrick and his pal, Art Ross. As English Canadians growing up in Quebec, the boys had not been caught up in the war news in the same way as their Ontario counterparts. There was something about the McGill march, however, that captured the boys' imaginations.

"Hockey sticks!" Art cried.

Politics was something the boys had trouble understanding, but hockey wasn't. Along with some of their classmates, they picked up their own sticks and rushed off to join the crowd.

The throng headed downtown, cheering and waving their flags. They surged into the Montreal Board of Trade, where cheer after cheer rang through the hall as members forgot all about the price of wheat and barley. The Stock Exchange was the next stop, where trading had been halted and those on the floor joined in a rousing rendition of "God Save the Queen." The Stock Exchange was a small building, so little time was wasted there. "Up to St. James!" someone shouted from the front of the crowd. The growing mass of people was on its way again.

Lester and Art got caught up in the frenzy, waving their sticks and singing along, as the mob pushed on to the offices of the city's French-language newspapers. *La Patrie, Le Journal,* and *La Presse* had adjoining offices.

"Where is your flag?" challenged one of the McGill students. He wore a long knitted hat, coloured blue, white, and red like the Union Jack, and he appeared to be intoxicated by more than just the highly charged atmosphere.

"Hoist your flag!" chanted the mob, and within a few minutes *La Patrie* flung out a large banner. *Le Journal* was quick to follow suit.

"Now to *La Presse!*" shouted the student in the Union Jack hat. The mob roared its approval, but the newspaper's doors had been locked. Angrily, the students began pounding and kicking at the door. Snowballs rained down upon the awning. No one responded, though some of the employees could be seen scurrying for cover inside the office.

"Break in!" a voice thundered from within the mob. The crowd bellowed its agreement. A mighty heave against the door sent it crashing inward. Students tumbled on top of each other, as the force of their momentum carried them sprawling into the newspaper office. A *La Presse* reporter wrested a hockey stick from one of the fallen students and used it to fend off the on-rushing crowd. Two students broke away and dashed for the stairs. Making their way to a third-storey balcony, they hung two large flags from the railing. The crowd outside yelled itself hoarse when the flags were unfurled.

As the two students tried to make their way back outside, the *La Presse* reporter, blind with panic, heard the noise behind him and spun around wildly. His hockey stick smashed into the side of one student's head. A huge gash opened above the boy's ear. The reporter wheeled around again, and caught the other student flush on the nose. It splattered against the boy's face like one of the many snowballs against the window. Other students who witnessed the assault flew into a rage. They were shattering windows with their sticks and pounding violently against the walls as half a dozen police patrol wagons arrived.

Several officers entered the building, while others moved up and down the street, trying to clear it. The students hissed and hooted at the police. Many grabbed at the horses' bridles, trying to halt the wagons. One frightened horse reared up on its hind legs, snorting like a bronco, and kicked out at one of the students. The boy got his arms up in front of his face in time to ward off the horse's hooves. The loud crack as his wristbone snapped could be heard even through his thick winter coat. That sickening sound did more to persuade other students to back away from the wagon than the police had been able to achieve.

Soon the policemen who had entered the *La Presse* office made their way out with the reporter. He held his head high, staring at the crowd defiantly, and was pelted by snowballs as he was led away. A few minutes later, the two bloodied students were assisted out, both with their heads bandaged. They were cheered wildly.

Had Lester and Art witnessed the destruction outside the *La Presse* office, it would have been clear to them that, hockey sticks or not, this truly was not their kind of crowd. But they had already broken off with another large contingent of McGill students who were heading for City Hall.

"Flag! Flag! Flag!" shouted the students when they arrived at City Hall to find no Union Jack flying in celebration. Some of the students climbed the flagpole, where once again they unfurled their own Union Jack.

From City Hall, the mob waded through the snow to Laval, Montreal's French-language university. Again the students found no British flag and demanded that the Laval students hoist the colours. As the McGill students continued singing and chanting, the Laval students, who by this time had learned about the violence at the *La Presse* office, turned a fire hose on them. Now the crowd raged out of control. Cold, wet, and bewildered, Lester and Art looked on as the stick-swinging students around them smashed in windows and pounded on doors.

To Lester, it seemed the people around him were moving too quickly. It was a blur of confusion and panic. Suddenly, he heard shots as the police entered the fray once again, this time wielding clubs and firing in the air to disperse the crowd. He heard the crack of wood against bone as the police swung their clubs. People were running in all directions now, but Lester was too paralyzed with fear to take a step. He was unable to duck when he saw an elbow coming towards his face. The blow to his cheekbone caused his eye to puff up immediately. He felt waves of pain pounding through his head. Policemen continued to arrive until the mob was finally subdued. Large groups of students were rounded up and, young Lester and his pal Art among them, were taken away to jail.

Lester Patrick was born December 31, 1883, in Drummondville, Quebec, a small town about seventy miles outside Montreal. He grew up in a number of small Quebec towns, attending French schools because none of the places had enough English-speaking families to set up their own schools. Naturally, Lester learned to speak fluent French and he and his family blended well into Quebec's rural French culture.

Lester's father, Joe Patrick, owned a general store in a small village outside Drummondville, where the family moved when Lester was four. Carmel Hill was experiencing a boom because the Intercolonial Railway line linking Montreal to Halifax was being built through the area. Providing supplies for the railway gangs proved to be a lucrative endeavour, and when Joe Patrick and his partner sold the business in 1892, they split a profit of $10,000 between them. Joe Patrick used his $5000 to start a lumber company and build a mill in Daveluyville, where he soon relocated his family.

Daveluyville was a small town sixty miles west of Quebec City. It was situated in a thickly wooded area, which made it perfect for the lumber business. In fact, Joe Patrick's lumber company did so well that he soon set up an office in Montreal for the distribution and sale of lumber by-products. Within a year, the Patrick family moved again to Point St. Charles, a railway district of Montreal, so that Joe Patrick could manage his Montreal office.

Lester and his younger brother Frank received their first pairs of skates during the family's only Christmas in Daveluyville. They were little more than crude metal runners to be attached to the soles of ordinary shoes. Not until a year later, after the move to Montreal, were the Patrick brothers introduced to hockey.

"Why is everybody in such a hurry?" Lester asked the boy next to him, as he watched the other boys in his new neighbourhood run home from church one wintery Sunday morning. "Where are they all going?"

"Haven't you heard?"

Lester shook his head sheepishly.

"My father says the ice on the river is finally thick enough," Russ Hodges explained in a condescending tone. His father was the local fire chief, and thus the leading authority on all things concerning safety.

"Thick enough for what?" Frank asked innocently.

"Thick enough for what!" Russ repeated. He stared at the younger Patrick brother in amazement. "Thick enough for skating! Thick enough for us to play hockey!

"So go home and get your skates and stick," Russ continued. He spoke to Frank as if the boy were an infant, not an eight-year-old. "I'll meet you and your big brother at my house in ten minutes."

Frank looked up at his older brother. Lester could see that Frank was wondering the same thing he was, but just as Frank was about to open his mouth, Lester scowled at him, shutting him up. It was clear that Russ thought them strange enough already. Asking "What's hockey?" would only make things worse.

"We'll see you there, Russ," Lester said, in a voice that carried as much confidence as he could muster.

"Where are your hockey sticks?" Russ asked, when Frank and Lester appeared on the steps with nothing but their skates.

"We don't have any," Frank blurted.

Neither Frank nor Lester had been sure what Russ had meant when he instructed them to bring their skates and sticks. Frank had wanted to bring a broom stick, like the ones he'd seen men use when they went curling, but Lester talked him out of it. Better to bring nothing at all, he reasoned, than to show up with the wrong thing. He was right. If Frank and Lester had arrived with broom sticks, Russ Hodges would have laughed himself silly. To have no stick at all was not such a crime. All it usually meant was that you were too poor to own one.

"No sticks, eh?"

Lester shrugged apologetically, but Russ went around to the tool shed behind his house and grabbed a small axe. "Then we'll have to hack you a hockey stick out of a tree branch on the way to the river."

The hockey played on the river in Point St. Charles was far different from the game being played in the downtown arenas of Montreal, where that winter the Montreal Amateur Athletic Association team would claim the first Stanley Cup. As many as fifteen or twenty Point St. Charles boys might play on each team, and in no particular position. The puck was usually a block of wood, or sometimes a tin can. There were few rules in these crude hockey games, except perhaps for survival of the fittest. It was a rule that Frank and Lester learned the hard way.

The Patrick brothers were easy pickings for the other boys. Lester was just ten years old. He was quick to smile, and had bright, inquisitive eyes. His light brown hair had a slight wave to it as it flopped down around an angular face, which, despite his youth, already had sharp, well-defined features. Although he was tall for his age, most of the other boys on the river were bigger and older than he was. To them,

a young, good-looking boy — especially a newcomer to the neighbourhood — was nothing more than an obvious target.

"It's our rule," one of the older boys announced, "that the newest
kid has to take the first rush." The other boys were barely able to
contain their laughter as the tin-can puck was passed to Lester. He
scarcely had a moment to adjust to the added weight and the strange
new sensation of the puck against his stick when the game began. The
boys on the opposing team sped towards him. Lester had no idea what
to do.

"That way, Lester," Russ shouted, pointing to the wooden goal at
the far end of the snow-cleared patch of river they called a rink. "Put
the puck between the posts!"

Lester sped off, the shouts of encouragement from the boys on his
team filling his ears as he skated past the other players. It seemed so
easy! He pushed the puck forward and chased after it, moving carefully
around anyone who got in his way. But slowly, without his being aware
of it, the other boys were forcing him over to the rink's far side. When
Lester finally noticed the snowbank looming larger on his left, it was
too late. He was knocked off his feet and left flat on his back at the
river's edge. The game went on around him.

"I'm sorry, Lester," a voice said, between bursts of laughter. "I
should have warned you."

"Yeah, Russ," Lester said quietly, "I think you should have." But
Russ had already dashed off to rejoin the game. Lester sat in the snow
for a while, with only his younger brother to share his hurt feelings.

Frank wore a large winter coat, passed down from Lester, that he
still hadn't grown into. His long stocking cap hung halfway down his
back. His hair, much darker than Lester's, curled out from under his
cap. His face was rounder than Lester's and slightly pudgier too, and
he had sadder eyes than his brother's. Sadder still after what he'd just
seen.

Like his hat and coat, the stick Russ had cut for Frank was too
large, but as he stood there, going over on his ankles, he insisted on
holding the stick at the very top, so that his right arm was fully extended
and his mittened hand was high above his head.

"Frank," said Lester at last, "one day I'm going to be so good at
this game that these fellows will tell their children they used to play
with me."

"Me too," Frank said, in a voice which conveyed the fierce pride
and loyalty that only an eight-year-old boy can give his older brother.

The Patrick brothers continued to take their lumps, but they learned that when they were knocked down, they had to get right back up and in the action. Slowly, their skills developed. They learned how to control the puck, cradle it on their sticks, and snap their wrists to fire it at great speed. There was a vacant lot behind their house, and, when they could talk him into it, Russ's fireman father would come around with his hose and flood it for them. The backyard rink got plenty of use, as Lester and Frank tirelessly practised their new skills. By winter's end, they were as good as anyone playing on the river; better than most.

The Patrick brothers didn't stay long in Point St. Charles. Joe Patrick's business was expanding rapidly, as was his bank account. By 1895 the Patrick family had taken up residence in Westmount. The paved streets in the affluent Montreal suburb meant the boys could play hockey all year round: ice hockey in the winter, street shinny in the summer. Lester now played hockey in the neighbourhood leagues and at school, and he had become so adept at handling the puck that he was soon in demand all over the city as a "ringer," brought in for important matches. But it wasn't until the following winter that he saw his first big-league hockey game.

On his thirteenth birthday, Lester's father took him to a challenge match at the Victoria Arena between the Montreal Victorias and the Winnipeg Victorias. From his first glimpse of the arena's interior, Lester was spellbound.

The boards around the ice stood only about twelve inches high, with two rows of benches rising behind them, a few feet back from the playing surface. The spectators who stood along those benches faced hazards from flying pucks and bodies.

"Look, father," Lester gasped, as he stared up at the elaborately carved wooden posts that rose from the benches, every few feet all the way around the rectangular ice surface. They helped support the galleries above, which seated most of the patrons. "Look at the gold plaques!" The galleries were festooned with pleated bunting, gathered up by gold-edged plaques.

"Look up there, Lester," Joe Patrick said, pointing up above the galleries.

"Wow!" cried Lester, staring at the dazzling array of red flags and green ribbons which danced from the rafters.

The players themselves added to the arena's colourful atmosphere. The Winnipeg team appeared in bright scarlet uniforms with gold trim and a gold buffalo on the chest. Their goalie wore white cricket pads. The Montrealers wore maroon sweaters with white around the cuff and collar and a fancy white "V" on the front.

Lester was awed by the skill of the players he saw that night, and amazed at the reaction they could draw from the spectators. The full house of 1500 people was the biggest gathering he had ever seen. He loved the wild emotions displayed by the Montreal faithful: their cheering when the home team scored seemed to shake the building. The booing when the breaks went against their side vibrated through Lester's whole body. He was now more sure than ever that he wanted to be a hockey player.

Two years later, the hockey rink Lester had fallen in love with was gone. His infatuation with the game, however, was not diminished. Like the new 2500-seat Montreal rink, Lester's love of the game was bigger than ever. He quickly became a familiar figure at the new rink. His high school team got to practise there, and, even better than that, he sometimes got to work as a stick boy for the big-league teams visiting from other cities.

Soon, Lester found another way to profit from his time at the rink, when he and his pal Art Ross began a partnership as ticket hustlers. At a championship game between Montreal and Quebec in 1899, Lester and Art put their savings towards the purchase of thirty-five-cent reserved tickets, which they then resold for a dollar apiece. They collected nearly thirty dollars between them, but as they split up the money, Lester looked worried.

"What's the matter with you?" Art giggled. "You think I'm cheating you or something?"

"No," Lester answered. "It's nothing like that. It's just that I've never had this much money before. How am I going to spend it all without having to explain to my father?"

Until his family moved to Montreal, Lester Patrick had not even been aware of what some English Canadians called "the French problem." He learned about it first-hand during the riot that broke out after the relief of Ladysmith, when what he had perceived as high-spirited fun had, to his shock and horror, degenerated so quickly into an ugly confrontation between two distrustful cultures. Try as he might to block out the memory, Lester would never forget winding up in jail that night.

"What's going to happen to us, Art?" Lester asked miserably, as the two boys sat in their cell. "How long do you think they'll keep us here?"

"It could be a while," Art reasoned. "They arrested a lot of people. It'll take a long time to sort everything out. Then they'll have to call someone to come down and bail us out."

"They're going to call my father!" Lester gasped, panic-stricken as he realized it for the first time. How was his father going to react to having a son in jail? Oh, how he had let his father down! "Art," Lester moaned, staring at his friend, tears beginning to form. "He's going to kill me."

It was well past midnight when Joe Patrick came to bail out his son. They rode home in complete silence, with only the sounds of the horses that pulled their carriage filling the cold night air. For three days, Lester's father maintained that silence. For three days, Lester skulked around the house, full of apprehension about what his punishment would be. He did his best to avoid his father's stern gaze and was afraid even to look his mother in the eye, so filled with shame was he for having tarnished the family name. He spoke to no one except Frank.

"Have you heard anything from father?" Lester finally asked.

"I thought I heard him say something about military school," Frank replied seriously.

Lester went pale. He stared at his brother with a blank expression that slowly transformed into a look of terror.

"Sorry, Lester," Frank said, shaking his head at how easily he had taken in his older brother. "I thought you'd know I was only joking."

Lester was too relieved to be angry.

"I haven't heard anything," Frank assured him.

On the fourth day after Lester's arrest, the uneasy silence in the Patrick family home was broken. Joe Patrick simply approached his son and stated, "You'll never do anything like this again."

"No, father." The incident was never mentioned after that.

Joe Patrick knew he could never find a worse punishment for his eldest son than what the boy was already feeling. Lester had grown up embracing the French culture of rural Quebec and he certainly wasn't anti-French. The Patricks, in fact, were of Irish descent, but as Protestants from the north of Ireland they were not anti-English, either. Still, Lester felt like an outsider in his own province, unsure where he fit in. The next few years would be very difficult for him.

III

Of the French Canadians it may safely be said that nine-tenths had no wish to participate in the [Boer] War. But the Minister who took us into the war was a French Canadian, and he drew with him the French politicians in the Parliament of the Dominion. The sentiment of French Canada was thus veiled or misrepresented.

Goldwin Smith,
Historian/Journalist.
Summer of 1902

"BUT WHY WOULD YOU WANT TO FIGHT IN THE WAR?" the young boy asked the man as they walked home from the ice rink, skates hanging by their laces from the sticks they carried over their shoulders. The man and the boy spoke in French, for though their home town of Cornwall had been founded by United Empire Loyalists back in 1784 — and was still populated mostly by those who traced their roots back to the British Isles — it had, as it prospered, attracted many families from across the nearby Quebec–Ontario border.

Like many other boys his age, Edouard Lalonde, the boy who had posed the question, could see the romantic attraction of marching off to battle in a distant land, but his enthusiasm was tempered by the debate between French and English Canadians the war had sparked.

He was well aware that many prominent French Canadians were speaking out against Canada's participation in the Boer War. Edouard was not quite thirteen years old, but he already had a part-time job in a local newsprint factory. Because of his ties to the print media, tenuous though they might be, he had taken to reading many newspapers and reading them thoroughly. He knew the English newspapers were branding those who were against the war as disloyal, stopping just short of calling the French traitors for objecting to any action that strengthened the bonds uniting Britain and Canada. He also knew what the French papers said. "Canada is for us the whole world," observed *La Presse*, "but the English Canadians have two countries, one here and one across the sea."

"Why do you want to fight for England, Uncle Bernie?" the boy asked.

"Sit down, Newsy," Bernie Savard instructed, calling the boy by the nickname he had coined for him. He brushed the snow off a tree stump with a gloved hand, then tapped it gently as he spoke again. "Sit down with me and I'll try to explain."

Bernie Savard was not really Newsy's uncle, though the two could not have been closer had they been blood relatives. Bernie had not had much luck in the adult world, bouncing around from job to job in the ten years or so since he had left high school. Only when he was with children did he feel as if he fitted in, and so he had set up a sports club for the young French boys in Cornwall, coaching lacrosse in the summer and teaching hockey in winter. That was how Bernie had met Newsy. The young boy had become by far the best lacrosse player in the club during the past summer. Bernie felt sure Newsy would show equal talent on the ice — so much so that he even managed to scrape together a few dollars to buy the boy his first pair of skates.

"I have something for you," Bernie told Newsy on a cold winter's night, as they sat together in the sports clubhouse. He held out a package for him, wrapped in white paper with a red ribbon that was tied in a bow.

Newsy struggled, at first, to loosen the ribbon, but youthful impatience got the better of him and he tore into the wrapping.

"Skates!"

They were the most wonderful he had ever seen. The leather boots were shiny black — not scratched and faded like the skates other boys wore. The steel blades glistened as they reflected the room's incandescent light. Newsy held the skates out in front of him for a moment and gazed in speechless delight.

"Well, don't just sit there staring at them," Bernie said. "Try them on!"

Newsy kicked off his heavy winter boots and pulled on his new skates. They were a little big, but that was all right. He would grow into them. Bernie helped him lace them up.

The whole winter long, every morning before school and all day after church on Sundays, Newsy and his "uncle" skated on the old open-air rink outside the local curling club. The youngster would cut and slash across the ice, his black hair blowing in the wind, his dark eyes opened wide, his puffy cheeks red with cold — but with excitement as well — and his lips curled upward in a wide, happy smile. Newsy would skate around and between the two large trees that jutted out at the far end of the frozen surface, firing pucks off the eight-inch boards that surrounded the playing area, while Bernie Savard chased behind him, shouting words of encouragement. And words of criticism.

"Don't smile when you carry the puck!" he told Newsy over and over again. "You should snarl. I want you to look mean when you play. A hockey player should have no friends on the ice!" No matter how many times he was told this, Newsy couldn't help but smile. The game was just so much fun. But the war changed everything.

"I don't know if it's right or wrong for Canada to be fighting in this war," Bernie told the boy, "but I do know that Laurier has asked for more volunteers."

Bernie had not enlisted when the first call went out in October, because he had thought the British army would have no real need for him. Almost everyone had expected the war to be short. Early British military setbacks, like the armoured train ambush and the capture of Ladysmith, had shown that England was indeed in need of support from the colonies. Again the call to arms had gone up in Canada, and this time Bernie had responded.

"I've given it a lot of thought, Newsy," Bernie said, rubbing one boot on the snow until it formed a smooth, icy patch. "I know as well as you what people think of this war, but I think my place is with the fighting men."

"No!" the boy shouted. "This is not our war! Let the English fight it." He leaped from the stump where he and Bernie had been sitting, knocking his stick and skates to the ground. Leaving his hockey equipment lying in the snow, he raced home, choking back bitter tears.

"What's wrong, Edouard?" his mother asked (she was fast becoming the only person who still called him by his given name) as the boy burst into her kitchen. "Have the older boys been teasing you again?"

Growing up French in Ontario was not easy at the turn of the century, even in an integrated town like Cornwall, and the tension generated by the Boer War had made it even harder. Newsy was shorter than most boys his age, and even in a town with a large French population, his accent when speaking English stood out as surprisingly thick. Picked on by the English kids because of his small frame and poor speech, he had been coming home dejected quite often of late.

"No, *maman*," the boy blurted. "It's Uncle Bernie! He's signing up for the army!"

Newsy's mother nodded her head knowingly. She was aware of the pressure on able-bodied men of Bernie's age to join in the war effort. She did not support the war in South Africa, but neither would she condemn her son's hero for his decision.

"Wipe that scowl off your face," she scolded her son. "Do you not think this was a very hard choice for Bernie? Do you not think that now more than ever he needs to know you believe in him?"

The boy was silent.

"When you see him again, I want you to tell him you'll be praying for him while he's fighting in South Africa."

No sooner had she spoken than there was a knock at the door.

"Newsy?" a voice called. It was Bernie. "You left your skates and stick at the rink." He walked into the kitchen and held the hockey gear out to the boy.

"Edouard," his mother said, in a tone of voice that let him know what was coming next. "Don't you have something to say to your Uncle Bernie?"

"Thank you," he mumbled, his voice barely above a whisper.

"That's not what I meant."

The boy looked at his mother. A white apron hung down from her neck and spread out over her wide waist and hips. Beneath it, she wore a plain dress with a simple floral pattern. It was the dress she always wore when she was baking, and for the first time Newsy noticed that the kitchen was filled with the aroma of fresh bread. The sudden realization made him smile, but when he looked at Bernie the smile vanished.

Tears welled up in Newsy's eyes. "I hate you!" he yelled, as he ran crying from the kitchen.

Newsy's mother watched her boy leave. "I'm sorry," she told Bernie. He nodded his head sadly, then turned and walked away.

Bernie Savard was posted to the "A" Squadron of Mounted Rifles, assigned to the First Battalion of Canada's second contingent of Boer War soldiers, and sent to South Africa. There he was caught up in one of the worst British bungles of the war.

After hard-fought victories in the towns of Paardeberg and Bloemfontein, the British army, including its brigade of Canadian soldiers, prepared to march on Pretoria. A small patrol group had been sent out to scout the area, but had failed to notice some 350 Boer soldiers carefully camouflaged on the steep banks of a small valley. Wagons filled with supplies would have to pass through this valley one at a time, making it the perfect spot for an ambush.

As the first British wagon went down the slope, the Boers seized the driver. A Boer soldier was put in his place, guiding the team of horses that pulled the wagon, and when the vehicle emerged on the far side of the slope, all appeared well to the British troops watching from the other side. Wagon after wagon rode into the same trap. They were all captured without a single shot fired. Then came the foot soldiers. Almost 200 were either disarmed or slaughtered before they knew what was happening. Among the dead was Bernie Savard.

News of Bernie's death reached home a few days later. A charity hockey game to raise money for the war effort was about to be played between a group of French and English children's hockey clubs. The game was to take place in the Victoria Rink, the rambling frame structure that gave Cornwall claim to having one of the country's largest indoor ice rinks. The game would be Newsy's first inside his city's showpiece arena.

As the French youngsters were receiving their final words of encouragement and instruction from their coach, the door to the dressing room opened and a French Catholic priest slowly entered. The priest took the coach aside and whispered something in the man's ear. In an instant, all colour drained from the coach's face. He turned away from the boys, hoping to hide from them the fact that something terrible had happened.

Newsy could sense what it was. He had read many accounts of the British debacle outside Bloemfontein. He also knew Bernie had been in the area. Bernie had been sending him letters almost every day since he left for South Africa, but Newsy had not responded. And now he would always have to remember what his last words to Bernie had been. He would never forgive himself for that.

The coach and the priest decided to wait until after the evening's contest to tell the players about the death of the man who had taught most of them how to play the game. But when Newsy skated onto the ice, he was already sure that he had lost the best friend he had ever known. As he skated to centre ice to begin the game, his eyes burned with tears. He tried hard not to cry, but a single tear trickled down his cheek.

"Hey, look at the Frenchie," teased the centre of the English boys' club. " 'e iz cryING," the boy said, mocking a French accent. "Whatsa matter, Frenchie," he taunted, "we haven't even beat you yet!"

Suddenly Newsy no longer felt sad. Instead he was filled with a rage so intense that it felt as if his body were being consumed by fire. He had never before felt such anger. Seconds later, when the referee put the puck in play, Newsy Lalonde did not swing his stick at the tiny piece of rubber. Instead, he snarled and jammed his stick into the English boy's stomach.

IV

With the largest number of passengers ever brought to [Canada], the Bulgaria arrived early this morning. . . . She brought 2692 immigrants, of whom 1718 are for the Canadian Northwest. The trip was uneventful, the weather was good, and fine progress was made. Two deaths occurred on the

passage (two children). The passengers represent all
nationalities. . . . It was indeed an unique sight to see those
people all huddled together near the bow of the steamer as she
drew into the wharf this morning, all straining their eyes to
catch a glimpse of the landing point. A vast majority of the
new settlers are men and boys, there being but few women.
The men look superior to those brought here in the past . . .
there being very few sheepskins among them.

Newspaper Report,
The Globe, Toronto.
May 1, 1902

ANTON PETROVIC STOOD ALONE ON THE CROWDED DECK,
leaning against the rail, staring out at the ocean. He watched the sun
rise over the unfamiliar coastline, which was now clearly visible. "The
ship will arrive in port sometime tomorrow," Petrovic thought. "I've
come a long way." He smiled as he realized the double meaning. It
was true, he had travelled many miles in making the trip to Canada,
but he had come even further in changing the direction of his life.

Anton Petrovic was seventeen years old. Had he not chosen to flee
his native country, he would have been forced to serve three years in
the army after his next birthday. But he had known that he could
never be a soldier. He had seen what soldiers did. The way they treated
the women of his village. The way the eyes of the old men filled with
fear whenever they heard the hoofbeats of the soldiers' horses. No,
he could never be a soldier. And so he had left.

Petrovic had been forced to sell almost all of the little he owned to
finance his trip to Canada. There was nothing much he could have
taken with him anyway, since his flight to freedom had forced him to
travel light. Because he was, in effect, running away from the army,
he had felt safest when travelling at night. Under cover of darkness he
had walked across his homeland, saying goodbye to it. Once he had

gotten safely out of the country, Petrovic bought a train ticket to Vienna. A cousin lived there and Petrovic had written to him before leaving home, saying he would be coming to stay with him for a short time. He had said only that he was on his way to Canada. He had not explained that he was running away. He didn't have to. His cousin would understand.

Petrovic stayed with his cousin for about a week, and then they left together for Belgium.

"Passport check," the border guard shouted as he boarded the train at the station in Antwerp. "Get your papers ready for inspection."

The man spoke German. Petrovic did not understand. His cousin explained.

Petrovic did not have a passport. He had never been outside his village before and had had no idea how many borders he would have to cross on this journey. Besides, fear had prevented him from keeping any papers from his own country. But Petrovic's cousin knew about passports, and he had thought up a plan before they left Vienna.

"Passports, please," the border guard said to Petrovic and his cousin.

The cousin produced his papers. The guard flipped through the pages, nodded his head, then handed them back.

"And where are your papers?" he asked, turning to Petrovic.

"My cousin speaks no German. He is from Russia," Petrovic's cousin lied, "and he lost his papers while fleeing the country."

The border guard eyed Petrovic suspiciously. He was about to call out for his superiors when the cousin spoke again.

"The socialists will be taking over," he said. "My cousin does not wish to live that way. He does not want to stay in Russia with the socialists coming. He lost all his papers when he ran away."

The guard nodded his head grudgingly. "Passports," he said to the man and woman in the next row of seats.

"Thank you, cousin," Petrovic whispered.

Anton Petrovic said goodbye to his cousin at the harbour in Antwerp. After a short boat ride across the Channel, Petrovic was in England. After another train trip he was in Liverpool, where, after stops in Ireland and Scotland, the big ships left for the voyage to the New World.

Petrovic had only been able to afford the least expensive ticket aboard the ocean liner, and was crammed into the steerage section several levels below the main deck with hundreds of other passengers. They were almost all young people like himself, mostly unmarried youths and a few young women. They slept six to a room, the beds hammock-like cots that hung from straps off dirty grey walls. There was one room with a water closet and sinks at the end of a long passageway that was shared by fifty men. A similar room at the other end was used by the women. The dining room for the steerage section was on another level of the ship. There were three long wooden tables, each with equally long wooden benches on either side. Breakfast, lunch, and dinner generally consisted of a bowlful of a thick soup or porridge. Sometimes there was a piece of fruit.

To pass away the monotonous hours aboard ship, Petrovic had taken to spending time with the young people who had come on board in Scotland and Ireland, hoping to pick up some words of English before he arrived in Canada. A girl named Meaghan became his closest friend. She was a redhead. Petrovic had never seen red hair before. He was fascinated by her, and often sat with her at mealtimes, pointing at various objects to learn what they were called.

He tugged at his pant leg. "How do you say?"

"Those are trousers," she told him.

"TRROWzerrs," Petrovic repeated.

He pointed at his feet next.

"Boots," she explained.

"BUUtz," he said.

One day, when Petrovic was having lunch with his young Irish friend, a strange looking piece of fruit accompanied the bowl of soup. It was about six inches long, with a slight hook in it. Most of this fruit was yellow, but parts were also a dullish brown. Petrovic had never seen anything like it. He picked up the strange new food, turning it over in his hands. Squeezing it gently. It felt soft.

"It's a banana," Meaghan told him. "You eat it," she said, pointing to her open mouth.

Petrovic took a bite. Then spat it out.

"Oh, Anton!" the girl said between giggles. "You're supposed to peel it first!"

Not all of the situations Petrovic encountered on the passage to Canada were as pleasant as his English lessons with Meaghan. With so many people crowded into such a small space for so long, problems were inevitable.

One night somewhere in the middle of the ocean, Petrovic dreamed he heard the hoofbeats of the soldiers approaching his village, and awoke in a cold sweat. The next afternoon, Petrovic heard the terrifying thundering again. "I must be hallucinating," he told himself. He clamped his hands against his ears and closed his eyelids hard, trying to block out the horrible noise. But it wasn't a hallucination. Petrovic was hearing the sounds of human feet. Running wild among the passageways of the ship's lower levels, many of the older, stronger boys would bully the younger children or harass the women.

Petrovic feared the hooligans. They were too much like the soldiers he had left home to escape. He would never take part in such rough-housing — and yet he never spoke out against it, either.

One morning at breakfast, a tough-looking youth with three of his friends approached their table and grabbed Meaghan's arm. Petrovic did not understand what the boy said to her, but he could get the idea from the way the colour rose in her cheeks, and her spirited words as she struggled to free her arm. Feeling helpless, he could only look away. But Meaghan was lucky. The boys were in the mood for nothing more than practical jokes and she ended up with only a lapful of porridge for her troubles.

It made Petrovic feel terribly guilty that he did nothing to protect Meaghan, nor any of those being tormented, but he had been conditioned all of his young life to turn silently away from such things. Those who opposed the soldiers received a rifle butt in the stomach, or a kick in the groin, or worse. Petrovic prayed for the ship to make fast passage to Canada and bring an end to his life of fear.

The ocean liner that carried Anton Petrovic to Canada arrived in port at Quebec City sixteen days after leaving Europe. Before Petrovic and his fellow passengers were permitted to leave the ship, they had to be inspected by doctors for any sign of disease. Petrovic looked forward to trying out his limited English vocabulary on his first Canadian citizen.

"Hello," Petrovic said with a heavy accent. "How are you?"

The doctor merely grunted his response. He had dozens of people to inspect and no time to waste speaking broken English to an immigrant.

"Stick out your tongue," the doctor ordered.

Petrovic stared at him, his dark, deep-set eyes showing no sign of understanding.

"Your tongue," the doctor repeated impatiently. "Stick . . . out . . . your . . . tongue." He stuck out his own. "Ahh!" he droned, by way of example.

"Ahh," Petrovic mimicked.

The doctor pressed down with his tongue depressor. He inspected Petrovic's eyes and ears as well. Everything appeared to be fine.

"Take off your shirt," the doctor instructed.

"Shirt" was a word Petrovic knew. He pointed to the dull grey flannel shirt he was wearing. It had been white when he left his home.

"Yes," the doctor said, surprised that Petrovic had shown any understanding. "Take it off," he repeated, miming the movements.

When Petrovic had stripped to the waist, the doctor poked and prodded him. Petrovic had reached his full adult height — about three inches below six feet — but his large hands, wide elbows, and broad shoulders indicated that he still had some filling out to do. He had straight sandy-blond hair, framing a face that was neither very handsome nor terribly ugly. His bushy eyebrows were a few shades darker than the hair on his head. Beneath them, his eyes were so dark brown they were almost black.

"This one's fine," the doctor told the immigration official who was waiting for his prognosis. "He's got a few fleas in his hair, but nothing that won't wash out if he ever gets a bath."

Free to enter the country now, Petrovic took a final look at the giant ship that had transported him across the ocean, then raced down the gangplank.

Three days after he arrived in Canada, Anton Petrovic stepped off a train in Winnipeg. He carried with him his most treasured possession, a creased and soiled slip of paper with the name and address of an uncle he had never met; an uncle who had gone to Winnipeg five years before. He had come to regard this paper as his passport to freedom in the new world. Winnipeg was the city where his uncle lived. So Winnipeg would be Petrovic's new home.

Petrovic's first few nights in the bustling city were spent in the Dominion Immigration Building, crowded into the two-storey structure with hundreds of other newly arrived immigrants. It was the same introduction to Winnipeg that greeted most foreigners. In hopes of finding his family, he spent his days wandering the streets of the city's North End, showing the address on his precious piece of paper to anyone he thought had a friendly face.

The North End, to Winnipeggers, meant more than simply a direction on the map. The "foreign quarter," as the North End was sometimes called disparagingly, was practically a district apart from the city. In the earliest years of Winnipeg's history, the area had been among the city's most prestigious. Ironically, it was the decision to build the main line of the Canadian Pacific Railway through the city, a decision that changed Winnipeg almost overnight from a quiet prairie community into the most important city in the West, that destroyed the social standing of the North End.

By the time Anton Petrovic searched its streets, the North End had become a working-class area. The construction of a large railway station, locomotive shops, power houses, metal-working facilities, and scrap yards had seen to that. The huge CPR facilities dominated the landscape of the North End, and no one who entered that section of the city could help but notice the maze of buildings and tracks, or the noises of the railway, or its dirt and smell.

Petrovic certainly noticed the sights and sounds of the North End, but for him these did not yet carry any negative connotations. "Things move so fast here," he thought to himself, as he navigated the district on foot. In the old country people walked more slowly. In his village, if he had wanted to stop in the middle of the street to give thought to some matter, he could have done so. Here, he feared he might be knocked down, and maybe even crushed — it was that crowded. Buildings had been constructed so close to the road and so close to each other. Petrovic was amazed and impressed by this at first. Later he would learn it was not such a good thing.

As Petrovic made his way through the North End, still wearing the now-grey flannel shirt he had worn on the boat, baggy pants and felt cap, and boots so battered with age that they no longer had any rise in their heels, he noticed something strange. Almost all the other people were dressed like him. Dressed like peasants. Where were the wealthy people in this rich new land? This, too, was something that Petrovic would learn soon enough. The rich did not come to Winnipeg's North

End. Nor did the poor very often get out. He did not know this yet, and again he saw these clothes, like the crowded streets, as a good thing. If this was how the people of Winnipeg dressed, he would fit right in!

A level railway crossing intersecting Main Street cut off the North End from the rest of the city. Passenger trains were constantly pulling into the CPR station, as were hundreds of freight trains. Petrovic, once again, saw only good in this. The city was alive! It was thriving! He did not yet see what others saw: that the trains choked the tracks to such an extent that traffic on Main Street was almost always blocked, sometimes for hours at a time; and that streetcars did not cross the tracks, forcing passengers for the North End to transfer at the level railway crossing, often with long waits in all sorts of weather before they could get across. "Those who locate north of the tracks," the saying went, "are not of a desirable class."

Why had Anton Petrovic's uncle chosen to settle in the North End? It was likely he had no choice at all. Winnipeg was still a young city, lacking old, cheap housing in its rapidly growing central core. Instead, the city's developers and real estate speculators bought up large tracts of railway land in the North End, on which they built homes to sell to the newcomers. These were little more than one-room shacks comprising four thin walls and a roof. Less than half of them were connected with the city's waterworks. None had any heating beyond their small cast-iron stoves. Still, it wasn't uncommon for several immigrant families to share the same tiny dwelling, since few newcomers could afford a house of their own. Scrap lumber was often used to build shelters for extra people.

Anton Petrovic, as yet, understood none of this. Winnipeg, as he saw it, was truly the land of opportunity. He wandered the streets of the North End in awe, searching for his uncle.

"Do you know this name?" Petrovic asked of strangers in the street, speaking the language of his old country. "Do you know this address?"

Those who did not understand the words he spoke merely shrugged their shoulders. A child offered to help if Petrovic gave him a nickel.

"But I have no money," Petrovic explained.

The boy ran away.

Finally, a shopkeeper who spoke his language, or at least understood enough of it to give adequate directions, recognized the name on Petrovic's slip of paper and guided him to the proper address.

"You are Gregor Zlatte?" Petrovic asked, after knocking on the door to which the shopkeeper had directed him. He was confused. The man who stood before him now appeared to be about his own age.

"Yes," the man answered cautiously. His uncle, it turned out, was little older than Anton. Petrovic's grandfather had had so many brothers and sisters that his descendants were often confused by relatives of similar ages who were actually of a preceding generation. "Who are you?"

"I am Petrovic. Anton Petrovic. I am your sister Sasha's oldest boy." Tears filled the eyes of both men.

Petrovic's uncle had no family in Canada. Like Petrovic, he had come to the New World alone. He had first settled in a farm community north of Winnipeg, but hampered by the rocky terrain and short growing season — as well as his lack of experience as a farmer — he had not been able to make a go of it. After two years, he gave up and moved to the city.

Uncle Gregor now lived alone in a tiny room in the back of an apartment owned by an elderly Jewish man who ran the shop below. He worked in the store Monday to Friday in exchange for the room. On weekends, he tried to pick up employment at the railyard to earn some money. It was a difficult existence, "but with hard work," he told Petrovic, "I'm getting by." He would be crowded by taking in a relative, but the thought of turning away his nephew never crossed his mind. "But now that you are here," Gregor said, "we will have to find you a job."

Petrovic had acquired no formal skills during his youth, but that would not be a great hindrance in his hunt for a job, Gregor assured him. Despite the heavy annual flow of immigrants into Canada, labour was constantly in short supply in the West. Railway construction, farming operations, and the construction of homes, public buildings, and other facilities required in new western communities involved a demand for labour that was never satisfied. As the metropolis of the West, Winnipeg was the great labour market of the region.

"This is where one goes to find a job?" Petrovic asked. He stared in disbelief at the tiny shack of a building before him. "I need only to go in here and they will give me work? Truly this is a great country."

Gregor didn't answer. There was a great deal of work to be found, but it wasn't as simple as that. "Straighten your tie," was all he told his nephew.

Petrovic pulled at his collar. "How do I look?" he asked.

"Like a greenhorn," his uncle laughed.

It was true. Anyone who looked at Petrovic would know he was fresh off the boat. Gregor had loaned him a clean white shirt, and given him the use for the day of his only jacket and tie, but the clothes, while an improvement on the rags he had been wearing, did not fit him well.

Petrovic entered the employment office. He took off his cap, twisting it nervously in his hands while he waited in the short line.

"I am needing job," Petrovic said to the men in charge, once he had reached the front of the line.

"Oh, jeez," laughed one of the men. "Listen to this guy!" He gave a sly smile to the man beside him. "You are needing job, eh?" he said to Petrovic, mocking his accent. "Well, that's good," he added. "We are having jobs."

"Sign this," the other man said. He produced a work contract. "You can write your name, can't you?"

Anton Petrovic had signed up for a job in the railyard, unloading sacks of wheat from trains that pulled in from the Prairies. The sacks from western farms had to be removed from the railcars in Winnipeg so that the grain could be weighed, inspected, and graded before being packed back on the trains and carted to the Lakehead. There it would be loaded on ships for the rest of its voyage to eastern Canada and beyond. When he wasn't unloading wheat destined for eastern markets, Petrovic loaded farm supplies onto westbound trains. He worked from seven o'clock in the morning to seven o'clock at night in a seventy-two-hour work week that stretched from Monday to Saturday. He was paid just under six cents an hour, taking home $4.25 at the end of his long week. Petrovic didn't mind the hard work. Nor did he mind the meagre wages. He was in the New World now. Anyone could get ahead in the New World. If only he worked hard enough.

V

WINNIPEG, ANTON PETROVIC'S NEW HOME, WAS KNOWN
as the "Bull's Eye of the Dominion" and the "Gateway to the West."
In the decade following 1900, the population of Winnipeg more than
tripled. With over 130,000 citizens, it became the third-largest Canadian city — and the fastest-growing one. But rapid growth puts strains
on a city: serious problems with public health, shortcomings in the
public school system. Winnipeg had these problems in abundance, and
every problem the city faced was made greater by the bigotry between
its earlier inhabitants, most of whom were English-speaking Protestants
from Ontario and Britain, and its newer immigrants from Eastern Europe. Many of the Anglo-Protestants saw the Jews and Slavs of Eastern
Europe as a threat to their values.

As an immigrant labourer, one of thousands off whose backs the
city's more established citizens reaped their profits, Anton Petrovic
benefited little from his tedious, painful work on the railway loading
platform. The discrepancy between his paycheck and the earnings of
those who relied on his work for their money was illustrated by the
difference between the North End and the South End of the city.

On Sundays during the early months after his arrival in Winnipeg,
Petrovic would endure the long wait to cross the tracks at Main Street
and pay the two-penny fare to ride the streetcar from the North End
to the South. He gazed in awe at the stately homes along the broad,
tree-lined streets of South Winnipeg. Their huge lots, with neatly
trimmed hedges and rose gardens, would easily accommodate a dozen
homes or more in the North End. But the houses here were nothing
like the ones where Petrovic lived. No scrap lumber was used in South
Winnipeg. Only the best building materials would suffice: limestone,
wrought iron, beautifully carved wooden posts and beams, and leaded
glass windows. With their high, pointed roofs and decorative terra
cotta shingles, these three-storey mansions looked more like castles
than houses. They answered with solid stone the prayers of a young
immigrant worker like Anton Petrovic, who still believed that anyone
who worked hard might some day own such a house.

"The homes there are so wonderful!" Petrovic exclaimed to Gregor,
who had never ventured that far from the North End. "Like palaces!
Nobody lives like that in the old country. Only kings and queens could
live there!"

"You just be careful," Gregor warned him, but it was not a lesson that could be taught. It could only be learned.

"What are you doing here?" a young man about his age demanded of Petrovic on one of his day trips to South Winnipeg. The man was apparently acting as a spokesman for a group of about four or five others. "This isn't the first time we've seen you. What do you want?"

"I am wanting nothing," Petrovic explained carefully, in his awkward, accented English. "I am just liking to look at things."

Some of the other men laughed. "We don't like your kind to 'look at things' in this neighbourhood," said one of the others.

"I am doing nothing wrong," Petrovic protested.

The young men formed a circle around him. Petrovic looked about nervously as the taunting man spoke again.

"We think you are," the young man said. He took a step forward, and, staring Petrovic straight in the eye, put a hand on his chest and shoved him.

"What's your name?"

"Petrovic." His voice cracked with apprehension. "Anton Petrovic."

"Get out of here, Petro-vick," the first man said, intervening only slightly on Anton's behalf. "Before you get hurt."

Petrovic left and did not come back. In time, he even stopped dreaming about the homes in South Winnipeg. As he continued to struggle over the years, barely making a living amidst the squalor of the North End, the remembered splendour of the homes to the South served only as a reminder that the rich got richer off the fruits of his labour. He grew to despise them. The homes there housed enemies who laughed at the strange sound of his name, mocked his accent, and ridiculed his ragged clothes.

As his first few years in Winnipeg passed, Anton Petrovic was forced to abandon his belief that hard work alone could achieve success and happiness in his new land. He had come to Canada with almost no knowledge of the English language, but he had worked hard to become competent in the tricky new tongue. He had worked hard at his job.

It was not enough. The dreams the young immigrant boy had brought to his new country were slowly crushed under the weight of a city that was not only divided along ethnic lines but was rapidly becoming polarized into labour and management camps as well.

Winnipeg had a long history of union activities. The importance of the railway in Winnipeg's economic structure had assured the growth of organized labour in the city, since railway workers were among the very first to seek collective protection. Several local unions had been organized as far back as the 1880s, and the trade union movement began to gain momentum in Winnipeg during the 1890s. By 1900, conflicts between workers and employers began to break out with increasing regularity. Major strikes were occurring by 1906.

In March of that year, the motormen and coachmen of the Winnipeg Electric Railway Company — the city's streetcar drivers and mechanics — went on strike. When the company tried to maintain service with strikebreakers (imported from eastern Canada), most citizens refused to go along for the ride. Anton Petrovic was among thousands of Winnipeggers who travelled to work on foot the day the strike started, sporting a "We Walk" tag on his lapel to show his solidarity with the strikers.

Soon crowds of strike sympathizers were jamming downtown streets, blocking streetcar routes and heckling the strikebreakers with taunts of "Scab!" Still, the men continued to drive their streetcars through the mob at top speed. When one car, manned by an axe-wielding strikebreaker, roared towards the crowd, a gang of strike supporters surrounded it and smashed its windows and fenders, putting it out of service. Throngs of men, women, and children chased other cars through the streets. When two streetcars broke down in front of City Hall, they were first rocked off their tracks by a gang of men, then smashed and burned. By early afternoon, the system was shut down.

When the Electric Railway Company sent out a fleet of streetcars manned by scabs the next morning, a swelling mob of strike sympathizers once again converged on downtown. By mid-afternoon, the situation threatened to get out of hand. In an effort to maintain order, Mayor Thomas Sharpe decided to call out the troops of the Royal Canadian Mounted Rifles, stationed at nearby Fort Osborne.

Anton Petrovic was among the crowd watching a gang throw rocks at a stalled streetcar and cheering on those who were attempting to dump it over into the roadway, when he caught sight of the soldiers marching down Main Street. Seized by a terror he had not felt since he was a child, Petrovic was overcome by the urge to run away. But he couldn't. Not at first. He was too frightened to move. Others didn't share Petrovic's fear, and as Mayor Sharpe followed the soldiers in his motorcar, the gang continued to attack the crippled streetcar while the rest of the crowd went on cheering.

"Silence!" the Mayor called out. He was standing, ashen-faced, on the seat of his car. Few paid attention.

"Silence, please," the Mayor pleaded again, removing his hat with trembling hands. "I have something to say."

Shouting now to make himself heard, Mayor Thomas Sharpe read the Riot Act to those who continued to resist both police and soldiers.

> Our Sovereign Lord the King charges and commands all
> persons being assembled immediately to disperse and peaceably
> to depart to their habitations or to their lawful business, upon
> the pain of being guilty of an offence on conviction of which
> they may be sentenced to imprisonment for life.
> God Save the King.

Mayor Sharpe's plea fell on deaf ears. As the disturbance around the streetcar persisted, the Mayor turned slowly to the troop commander. "Lieutenant-Colonel Cameron," he said in a voice that, while stern, was nonetheless filled with anxiety, "prepare your men."

"Ready arms!" the Lieutenant-Colonel barked.

The soldiers, whose rifles had rested on their shoulders, brought their guns forward.

The crowd fell silent.

"Load ball cartridges!"

The rifles clicked once in unison as the soldiers pulled back the bolt, then again as the ammunition was loaded into the breech and pushed into the bore.

The attack on the stalled streetcar ceased.

"Prepare to charge on my command!"

The soldiers moved their rifles into position and awaited the call to charge.

Though the order to fire never came, the mob scattered like game birds before a hunter. They raced up side streets, staying close to buildings for added protection and taking cover in the open doors of stores. No one ran faster than Petrovic.

The turbulent year of 1906 did much to change Anton Petrovic. Until that year he had been so beaten down by the circumstances of his life in Winnipeg that he had lost the will to try and change them. Petrovic had come to believe that he would always be poor and unaccepted and that there was nothing he could do about it. After all, he was not of British descent, and somewhere deep in his mind he had simply resigned himself to the fact that this cruel stroke of nature had sealed his fate.

The decision of Winnipeg's civic leaders to call out troops to put down the streetcar strike demonstrations could easily have reinforced Petrovic's attitude. Instead, the action freed him of such beliefs. Such persecution had forced him to leave home. He might be poor in Canada, just as he had been in his homeland. He might be uneducated. He might live with the bitter hostility of a deeply prejudiced ruling class. But in Winnipeg, he was free! He had not known freedom until now, and he could not stand aside if events such as those he had witnessed in his homeland were taking place in his new country. Here, he was free to form his own opinions, and free to speak out in defence of them. Petrovic knew he would have to find a means of expression.

PART II
PREGAME

VI

*Mr. Speaker, I move for leave to introduce a bill to provide
for the construction of a National Transcontinental
Railway. . . . We ask Parliament to assent to this policy because
we believe — nay, we feel certain and certain beyond a doubt
— that in so doing, we give voice and expression to a
sentiment, a latent but deep sentiment, which is today in the
mind, and still more the heart, of every Canadian, that a
railway to extend from the shores of the Atlantic Ocean to the
shores of the Pacific Ocean, and to be, every inch of it, on
Canadian soil, is a national as well as commercial necessity.*

Sir Wilfrid Laurier,
Prime Minister.
July 30, 1903

AMBROSE O'BRIEN SAT IN THE LOBBY OF THE WINDSOR
Hotel, awaiting his chance to speak to the delegates of the Eastern
Canada Hockey Association. It was November 25, 1909. Ambrose had
been in Montreal for a few days, lobbying the various hockey owners
for their support in gaining a franchise for his home town of Renfrew.
So far, all he knew for sure was that he could count on the support
of the Montreal Wanderers.

Ambrose checked his pocket watch again. It was now a little after
half past nine in the evening. The meeting had been going on for over
an hour and a half. Many would have considered Ambrose O'Brien
much too young, at just twenty-four, to be given the responsibility of
wooing professional hockey's most powerful owners, but those people
didn't know Ambrose O'Brien. He went over and over in his mind all
the points he hoped to make, then checked his watch again. A quarter
to ten. The flow of people in and out of the hotel lobby had slowed
to a trickle. It probably wouldn't pick up again until after midnight,

when people began to return from their evenings out. Ambrose was glad the people were gone. He was tired of returning their curious gazes with a polite smile or a solemn nod.

By now, Ambrose was beginning to suspect what had actually been the case all along. The other hockey owners had no intention of inviting him in to address their meeting. Ambrose was about to return to his room when Jimmy Gardner of the Montreal Wanderers stormed out of the meeting.

"Those sons of bitches! Those bloody bastards! How dare they do this to us!"

Jimmy Gardner's face was red all the way from his shirt collar on up, and the veins on the sides of his forehead were bulging. He was punching his right fist into his left palm as he spat out profanities, his face contorting as he struggled to get the words out. After a few minutes of venting his anger, he sat down heavily in the chair Ambrose had vacated, still cussing under his breath. Suddenly he looked up.

"O'Brien," he barked, "doesn't your father own a couple of hockey teams up north? In Cobalt and Haileybury?"

Ambrose nodded.

"Listen. You've got Cobalt, Haileybury, and Renfrew. We've got the Wanderers. Why don't we make our own bloody hockey league? That would really show those bastards."

Ambrose O'Brien was nodding. Slowly at first. Then a wide grin spread across his face. Ambrose liked the idea, and the O'Brien clan was used to getting what it wanted.

Michael John O'Brien was born in Nova Scotia in 1851. A few months before his fifteenth birthday, he landed his first job — as a water boy on the railway line being built between Truro and Pictou. He was paid ten cents for every pail of water he carried to the men working on the line.

The work was finished just a few weeks before Confederation. It was considered the most efficient major railway construction job ever completed in Canada. With Confederation came the job of extending local railways all across the country in order to link the new Canadian provinces, and young O'Brien had caught the railway bug.

With the money he made as a water boy, Michael O'Brien was able to buy a horse and some tools and get a job with the men who cleared the land. Shortly thereafter, he bought another horse and more equipment and hired a man to work for him. By the age of eighteen, he was a foreman, and in another year, he was picking up work as a contractor, buying up parcels of land and building railways on them.

Railway work soon brought O'Brien to Ontario, where he contracted to build the North Shore Line of the Canadian Pacific Railway between Montreal and Ottawa. Upon the completion of the North Shore Line, he contracted for a job that would change the course of his life.

Jim Barry was working with a team of horses on his father's farm along the shore of Calabogie Lake. As he approached the thick woods at the back of the field, the horses pricked up their ears. The closer Jim drove the horses towards the woods, the more nervous they became.

"What's the matter, fella?" Jim asked, gently rubbing the neck of the lead horse. Then he heard a sound from somewhere within the woods. As the crashing noise came closer and closer, Jim wished he had brought his rifle with him. Now all he could do was hope. Hope that the bear, or whatever it was, would continue on past, or that if it lumbered out from the woods in front of him, the animal would be startled by the sight of a man and a team of horses and duck back into the forest.

Now Jim could see something moving in the darkness of the trees. His heart was beating so hard that he thought his chest might explode. Finally, the last branch protecting him and the horses from whatever it was parted — and a man walked out.

The tall, bearded stranger looked up, as shocked to see Jim as Jim was to see him. The man was carrying a small pack on his back and was wearing rough bush clothing. He had a large sickle in his right hand which he'd been using to clear a path. He approached Jim and stuck out his hand.

"Michael John O'Brien," he said, by way of introduction.

"James Barry," Jim said slowly, staring at the sharp object in the bearded man's hand.

O'Brien sensed Jim's apprehension, but didn't know why the man seemed so nervous. Then he began to laugh as he realized he still held the sickle.

"Perhaps I should explain," he said, putting the sickle down. "I'm a railway contractor, and I'm thinking about taking on the job of completing the Kingston and Pembroke Railway. I wanted to see first-hand what kind of terrain we would encounter. I have walked here from Lanark, which is where the line ends now." It was, in fact, where the last contractor had gone broke.

"My God!" Jim exclaimed, his apprehension suddenly replaced with amazement. "Lanark's got to be at least thirty miles away. You've hiked all that way through the bush today?"

O'Brien nodded. He hadn't realized it had been so far.

"You must be exhausted. Why don't you head up to the farmhouse and get yourself cleaned up and rested. You can join us for dinner. My folks will be glad to see you."

Jim pointed him in the proper direction, and O'Brien was off. After a short walk, he came upon the rectangular log farmhouse. O'Brien could see no one moving in or around the house, so he made his way around back. There he found the most beautiful girl he had ever beheld. She had dark brown eyes and thick, dark hair that framed a round, cheerful face, tanned by long hours of farm work in the sun. Her long, slender arms were also quite dark. She was sitting on a low stool with her skirt pulled up above her knees, washing the day's dirt from her feet. Jennie Barry saw Michael O'Brien just a moment after he had first seen her, and she leaped to her feet, confused and embarrassed. He introduced himself.

"I'm sorry to startle you. My name is Michael John O'Brien. I have come here from Lanark to survey the land for the railway. The gentleman I met at the edge of the forest, James, said I would find his parents here. He mentioned nothing of such a lovely girl."

Jennie blushed and dropped her head, but not before O'Brien caught a glimpse of her shy smile "Jim is my brother," she replied quietly, slowly regaining her composure. She went to find her father. O'Brien repeated his story to Mr. Barry, and was invited in. He stayed for two days.

Michael John O'Brien took on the job of finishing the Kingston and Pembroke Railway. The Barry farm was just a few hundred yards away from where the railway plans called for a causeway to be built across Calabogie Lake. The rock-cutting work that had to be done in order to build the causeway quickly became the talk of the countryside, and

O'Brien soon became a familiar figure in the area. He also began making regular visits to the Barry farm.

O'Brien was eleven years older than Jennie Barry. He was older than her brothers. Even her father, who soon went into partnership with O'Brien, buying and selling farms in the area, deferred to him because he was a man familiar with the big cities of Kingston, Montreal, and Halifax. It was this exotic quality, his air of having seen so much of life beyond the farm, that attracted Jennie Barry to Michael John O'Brien. They were married in December of 1883. Nine months later, the first train chugged out along the newly completed final leg of the Kingston and Pembroke Railway. Not until nine months after that did they have their first child, Ambrose.

Jennie knew that her husband was a railway man. He had come into her life only because a railway was being built through the area. And she knew that other railways in other places would constantly be taking him away from her. If her husband was going to be gone so much of the time, Jennie wished to make her home somewhere where she would have friends and family close at hand, so the O'Briens settled in nearby Renfrew.

Michael John O'Brien — M.J. O'Brien as he was now becoming widely known — saw little of the town of Renfrew in the early years of his marriage. He spent most of his time in Montreal and Ottawa, where he conducted most of his ever-growing railway business.

"A good railway man can't afford politics," he was fond of saying. By this he meant that, since railway contracts came from governments, there was no point in playing favourites among political parties. O'Brien was often urged to run for office, both provincially and federally, but always turned down the opportunities. He did, however, give financial support to both Liberals and Conservatives from time to time. For, while he couldn't afford political affiliation, he also couldn't afford to be without friends in high places. O'Brien became so skilled at his own particular brand of non-party politics that he was often accused by Liberals of being in cahoots with the Tories, and accused by Conservatives of having more than a working relationship with the Grits. Accusations such as these always amused O'Brien. "I must be doing something right," he would say with a smile.

In 1901, Ontario's Liberal government appointed O'Brien commissioner of the Timiskaming and Northern Ontario Railway. The line currently ended in North Bay, and O'Brien was brought in to extend it northward. It was during construction on the T.&N.O. that M.J.

O'Brien made the jump from being a highly successful railroad contractor to becoming one of the richest men in the world.

One day early in the summer of 1903, lumberjacks James McKinley and Ernest Darragh were exploring the shores of Lake Timiskaming, looking for timber for the Timiskaming and Northern Ontario Railway.

"That's a strange colour in them rocks on the beach," McKinley said to Darragh. "I'm gonna take a closer look."

They began collecting the loose pieces of rock and washing them off in the lake.

"Look at the way these bright coloured bits flake off!" McKinley said excitedly. "You can bend 'em like metal."

Darragh placed one of the flakes between his teeth and bit down on it. It marked easily. The loggers had discovered silver.

On a warm night in September, blacksmith Fred LaRose was doing construction work on the railway with a young apprentice.

"You see that fox over there?" LaRose said, with a hint of mischief in his voice.

"No," responded the apprentice, without even looking up.

"Look over there." LaRose waved his arm in the direction of a small depression in the side of the hill across the tracks. "Can't you see his eyes glittering?" The young man still wasn't paying much attention. "Betcha I can hit him with my hammer," LaRose bragged.

His throw came up short, but close enough that it should have sent the fox scurrying for cover. Yet for some reason, the fox didn't run away. LaRose could still see the eyes sparkling.

LaRose walked across the tracks to investigate. It turned out that the glittering he had seen was something in the rock. Silver! He began digging in the dirt with the back end of the hammer. More silver! LaRose had uncovered what would turn out to be the richest silver vein the world had ever seen. Soon afterwards, prospectors began streaming into Northern Ontario to seek their fortune.

Neil King was one of those prospectors. He staked a claim in the rich silver region and travelled to Toronto looking to sell. King came from a town near Renfrew and when he heard that M.J. O'Brien was also in Toronto, he paid a visit to the wealthy railroad man. O'Brien was holding a business meeting in his hotel room when King found him. He knew the prospector and didn't much care for him. O'Brien assumed that King was after money and told him to come back after the meeting, but King insisted on seeing him immediately. Reluctantly, O'Brien agreed. King showed him some samples of his silver ore.

"These are from my stakes in Cobalt," King explained. Cobalt was at the centre of the silver rush. The town had gotten its name from the presence of cobalt in the silver ore. "I want to sell them to you."

O'Brien sighed. He'd been right. King wanted money. "How much do you need?" O'Brien asked.

King was annoyed at the suggestion he'd come begging, but he tried not to show it. He didn't want to get on O'Brien's bad side. "No, Mr. O'Brien, you've got it wrong. I want to sell you my stake. I'm asking $5000."

"Well, quite frankly, Mr. King, I don't think it's worth $5000."

"I'll let you have it for $4000, then." King wasn't asking for a hand-out, but he did need money.

O'Brien agreed.

Within one year, the land he had purchased was valued at $10 million. A few years later, the O'Brien mine was shipping out silver ore valued at more than $1 million a year.

Both directly and indirectly, the railway business made Michael John O'Brien a very rich man, but he paid a price for it. He had been away from home so much that he barely knew his own family. O'Brien was closest to his two eldest children, John Ambrose and Mary Stella, who had been born early in his marriage to Jennie, when business consumed less of his time. While the relationship with his first-born might not have seemed warm to those outside the family — O'Brien was a father who would gladly back his son in practical matters, but not one in whom a child was likely to confide his personal thoughts — a strong bond developed between M.J. and Ambrose.

Ambrose O'Brien had his own horse, a gift from his often-absent father, and learned on his own to became a skilled rider. He also liked tennis, competing in his high school years at Renfrew Collegiate, but never in the presence of his father. Although the senior O'Brien was proud that his son would never know poverty, he made sure that not all of Ambrose O'Brien's boyhood days were devoted to schoolwork and leisure.

When he was in high school, Ambrose would rise at five o'clock every morning to deliver milk from his father's farm. He would transport the milk cans on a cart in the summer and with a sleigh in winter, along a delivery route that meandered all over Renfrew. He would arrive home at about eight o'clock to a scene more in keeping with his family's wealth. His three younger sisters and baby brother would be up by then, and his mother would be supervising their dressing while the cooks prepared breakfast. Breakfast usually consisted of fresh fruit and porridge, followed by large platters of eggs with bacon or ham, and toast with marmalade. Jennie O'Brien always insisted on making the porridge herself, no matter how many servants she came to have.

Breakfast was generally a noisy affair: servants bringing trays in and out, the younger children crying, the older girls chattering about school or teasing each other over the boys they liked, or the ones who liked them. Except when father was present. Breakfasts were much quieter then. O'Brien was a fair man, and a more attentive father when home than might have been expected, but he was very stern with his young children and one look from him could quickly silence the girls' giggling.

Sometimes when his father was home, Ambrose would play cards with him late into the night, usually a two-handed version of euchre. The games were fast and exciting: the man and the boy slapping down cards, delighting in trumping one another and taking the trick. They played for a penny per point, with an extra penny going to the winner. When they were done, it was Ambrose who got to tally the financial score.

"You're ahead, father," Ambrose said dejectedly. "I owe you six cents. Can't we play one more game? Please!"

"You know the rules," O'Brien said sternly. "No one will give you a second chance in the business world."

Nodding his head, Ambrose gave the coins to his father, his pocket money gone but a valuable lesson learned.

Win or lose, Ambrose treasured those card games. It was the only time while he was growing up that he really felt close to his father. During their card games, O'Brien would often discuss his business dealings. From an early age, Ambrose had understood that when he was old enough he would participate in his father's affairs. In fact,

Ambrose was away on railway business when officials from his home town contacted him and asked him to attend the Eastern Canada Hockey Association meetings in Montreal to see about getting a franchise for Renfrew.

VII

HOCKEY HAD BEEN A WINTERTIME PASSION FOR THE BOYS of Renfrew for many years. The Bonnechere River ran right through the town, and in winter it became a giant skating rink. With the cold weather sometimes lasting all the way into April, there was plenty of opportunity for the boys to play hockey, and many became skilled at the game. By 1896, the best hockey players in town had formed a team and were playing against other Ottawa Valley towns. The Upper Ottawa Valley Hockey League was formed the following year, with teams in Almonte, Arnprior, Carleton Place, Pembroke, and Renfrew. It was strictly amateur.

Over the next ten years, the team from Renfrew proved time and again to be the best in the league, and the locals began dreaming of the Stanley Cup. By 1907, officials with the Renfrew hockey club felt that their team was ready for a Stanley Cup challenge. After all, the team had won the Upper Ottawa Valley league title again and had gone on to defeat Vankleek Hill of the Lower Ottawa Valley Hockey League to claim the championship of the entire region. Not only that, but the Renfrew team had defeated the mighty Ottawa Silver Seven 9–5 in an exhibition game that year. Ottawa had virtually owned the Stanley Cup in the first half of the decade, and was still among the top teams in the game. Renfrew now intended to challenge the Montreal Wanderers for the coveted trophy.

The Stanley Cup had been donated in 1893 by the Governor General of Canada, Lord Stanley of Preston. The terms of the donation allowed any team in the Dominion to submit a challenge for the trophy. A board of trustees became responsible for accepting or rejecting challenges for the Stanley Cup. If a challenge was accepted, a series of games was arranged between the challenger and the current holder of the Cup. Preferably, these series would be held in the spring, after the regular season. Sometimes, however, warmer weather would cause natural ice surfaces to become unplayable, and a Stanley Cup series would have to be held over until the next season.

Many small-town teams had challenged for the Stanley Cup over the years. Kenora had even beaten the Wanderers to win the trophy earlier in the year, before Montreal won it back in a challenge rematch. Yet the big-city press snickered at Renfrew's bid.

"And now Renfrew talks of challenging for the Stanley Cup," a Toronto newspaper mocked in the spring of 1907. "All because they have won a fence-corner league." The paper went further, sarcastically advising its readers not to laugh at the Renfrew challenge: "If you never lived in a country town you don't know how seriously these people take themselves."

Much to the dismay of the people in Renfrew, the Stanley Cup trustees agreed with the assessment of the Toronto newspapers. "The level of hockey played in the Ottawa Valley is not of a high enough calibre for us to accept the challenge from Renfrew," the trustees declared.

With their Stanley Cup dreams dashed, Renfrew returned to the Upper Ottawa Valley Hockey League and easily outclassed the other teams while breezing to yet another championship. The league disbanded the following year, after the other valley teams refused to play against the powerful Renfrew outfit. Rather than let this new turn of events put an end to their Stanley Cup hopes, Renfrew hockey officials made a bold move. They decided to pay their hockey players and enter a professional hockey league.

In need of financial backing, the Renfrew hockey officials turned to their town's most prominent citizen, Michael John O'Brien. O'Brien was already backing hockey teams in the mining towns of Cobalt and Haileybury, where miners yearned for tough entertainment. Newly rich prospectors looking for a way to spend their fortunes were known to bet heavily on the outcomes. O'Brien could hardly turn down his adopted home town, and he agreed to put up the money for Renfrew's professional team. Ambrose O'Brien, who had played hockey while attending the University of Toronto and had inherited much of his father's business sense, was elected an executive member of the hockey club.

Renfrew entered the Federal League for the 1909 hockey season, joining Smiths Falls, Cornwall, and a team from Ottawa on the professional circuit. The Renfrew team swept the league, having no trouble winning yet another championship, but was denied again in its bid for a Stanley Cup challenge. Disappointed, the team disbanded, and Ambrose O'Brien returned to the railway business.

Later that year, Ambrose was in La Tuque, Quebec, headquarters of his railway contracting partnership, when he was contacted again by Renfrew hockey officials.

"There's going to be a meeting in Montreal on the 25th of November," Ambrose was told. "They're going to form a new hockey league. It's supposed to be the best anyone's ever seen. This is our chance, Ambrose! If we can get into that league there's no way anyone can deny us a chance at the Stanley Cup! Can you get down to Montreal and see if you can get Renfrew in?"

Ambrose did go to Montreal. He spent a few days before the meeting lobbying the various hockey owners for their support in gaining a franchise. He got firm support from the Montreal Wanderers, but what he didn't know was that this team was not in the good graces of the other clubs in the Eastern Canada Hockey Association.

The Wanderers had been sold just a few months before to P.J. Doran and a group of associates that included hockey star Jimmy Gardner, who would act as a team spokesman at league meetings. Doran owned the Jubilee Rink in the east end of Montreal, and was going to move his new hockey team there. The other hockey owners weren't happy with the planned move. The Jubilee Rink was much smaller than the Wanderers' previous home, the Wood Avenue Arena, and therefore the visiting team's forty percent share of the gate would be much smaller. The other hockey owners had taken the opportunity of the delegates' meeting in Montreal to teach Doran and Gardner a lesson.

Form our own league, Ambrose thought. He liked the idea, but he wanted to know more. "Jimmy, why don't we go on up to my room and discuss this concept of yours over dinner? But before we even get started, I want to know something. What exactly happened in that meeting that's got you so angry? Obviously there's more to your suggestion of forming our own league than just getting a franchise for Renfrew."

"You're bloody well right there is!" snapped Gardner, who was on his feet again and pacing the lobby, still fuming and not in the mood for any more discussion.

Ambrose decided not to push him just yet, and led the way up to his hotel room. He ordered a roast beef dinner from room service, then produced a bottle of scotch. Ambrose wasn't much of a drinker, but he liked to keep some liquor around when he travelled. He poured a small drink for himself, and a much larger shot for his guest. Gardner drank it at once, exhaling contentedly. He was starting to calm down. Ambrose decided to ask him again. "Well, Jimmy, what went on?"

"First of all," Gardner began, "the Ottawa guys nixed your bid right away. I was ready to fight for you, Ambrose, I really was, but they didn't even allow a discussion on it. Typical of those fucking fat cats. . . . Whoops! Excuse my French," Gardner laughed.

"Anyway, we spend the next hour or so discussing all sorts of bullshit issues. Roster sizes, some rule changes. Crap like that." He was starting to get angry again. "So now that we've got all that stuff sorted out, they hit us with this: 'The Eastern Canada Hockey Association will disband,' they say, 'and in its place we will form the Canadian Hockey Association.'

"Dammit, Ambrose, I'm sitting in there and I'm starting to wonder just exactly what the hell is going on. Why had no one told me about this! I'm representing the Montreal Wanderers, for Chrissakes. Then the bastards start reading out the list of teams who'll make up their new fucking league: the Ottawa Senators, the Quebec Bulldogs, the Montreal Shamrocks, the Montreal Nationals, and a new team called All-Montreal.

"It took a bit of time before I realized they hadn't read out the Wanderers. You know, I was still angry about not knowing about this new league business. Then everything got real quiet. Everyone was just sucking on their fucking cigars. The smoke was so damn thick in there it looked like a fucking cookout! Then it dawned on me. 'What the hell are you bastards trying to pull?' I say. 'Jimmy,' says one of the Ottawa guys, 'your new rink doesn't come up to league specifications.' Then the son of a bitch showed me this list of bylaws.

"That's when I put the whole thing together. These guys are freezing us out! And this wasn't just some spur-of-the-moment thing, either. No, sir. The bastards had been planning it ever since Doran bought the team a few months back.

"Well, I got so angry at those sons of bitches I couldn't see straight. Then I stormed out."

Ambrose had sat down by now and was shaking his head back and forth. The look on his face was a mixture of disgust and disappointment. He couldn't believe what he'd just been told. "They cut you out," he finally said. "Just like that?"

"Just like that. Now what are we going to do about it?"

"Well, I'll tell you right away, Jimmy, I like the thought of our own league," Ambrose began, "but it does present a couple of problems. Renfrew's bids for the Stanley Cup have already been laughed off by the Cup trustees and the big-city papers. The leagues we've formed up till now have always been looked on as small-time. Now I realize, Jimmy, that the Montreal Wanderers are a first-rate operation, but Renfrew, Cobalt, and Haileybury are all going to have a difficult time being taken seriously in most hockey circles. We're going to need something more, if this idea is really going to help either of us."

Gardner had already considered that. "You're right, Ambrose. No doubt about it. So here's what I propose. First of all, we line up a team in Toronto. That should take care of the criticism there. And I think if a team of all Frenchmen was formed in Montreal, it would be a real draw."

"I don't know about that," said Ambrose. "Won't Quebeckers resent the idea of a group of English businessmen trying to sell them a French hockey team? It even sounds a little bit peculiar to me."

"This is hockey, not politics," Gardner shot back excitedly. "The pea-soupers will eat it up. We could give the team a real French Canadian name. It'll be a gold mine!"

Ambrose and Gardner kicked the idea around for a while, and Ambrose slowly came around to Gardner's way of thinking.

"OK, Jimmy. I'll finance the club, but under two conditions. First, that I can gain my father's support for the new league. And second, that the operation of the team be turned over to French Canadian businessmen as soon as it's practical to do so."

"Sure, Ambrose. Whatever you say. After all, it's your money."

After some more discussion, they decided to call the team Les Canadiens.

As soon as his meeting with Jimmy Gardner ended, Ambrose telephoned Renfrew. He told the hockey officials there the bad news first: the new Canadian Hockey Association had refused the town's application. "But there's some good news too," Ambrose advised. "I don't want to say too much yet, but Jimmy Gardner of the Montreal Wanderers and I are discussing a new league and it looks promising."

Ambrose then telegraphed up to Haileybury and Cobalt to urge their team representatives to come to Montreal for a meeting as soon as possible.

Ambrose was joined at the quickly convened meeting by Renfrew hockey officials George Martel and Jim Barnet. Jim was the son of Renfrew's other famous millionaire, lumber baron Alexander Barnet, who had also provided some financial backing for the town's hockey ventures. The Wanderers were represented by Jimmy Gardner. Thomas Hare was there from Cobalt and Noah Timmins from Haileybury. They had been looking after the O'Brien hockey interests in the silver region from the beginning. Jean-Baptiste Laviolette, better known to most simply as Jack, was a hockey player and businessman from Montreal, recruited by Ambrose to run the new team, Les Canadiens. E.J. McCafferty represented the Toronto interests, though it was clear from the start that he wouldn't be able to put a team together by January, when the 1910 hockey season was to begin. McCafferty was given permission to hold onto his franchise without having to take part in the inaugural season.

Among the decisions made that day was the name for the new league: the National Hockey Association. At Gardner's urging, the NHA decided that instead of going to the trouble of drawing up a new constitution for their league, they would simply adopt the constitution and bylaws of the Eastern Canada Hockey Association, which had been legislated out of existence only days before by Gardner's former cohorts. "That'll really show those bastards," Gardner cackled.

The Renfrew delegation went home after the meeting, pleased with what had transpired. Ambrose, accompanied by Barnet and Martel, at once laid out the plans for his father. "Boys," said M.J. O'Brien expansively, "if we're going to do this, let's do it right. Ambrose, I want you to assemble for Renfrew the greatest hockey team ever seen! Spare no expense in bringing the Stanley Cup to our home town. Now who's available?"

"I don't think Lester Patrick has signed with anyone yet," answered George Martel.

VIII

*The best way you can help the manufacturers of Canada is to
fill up the prairie regions of Manitoba and the Northwest with
a prosperous and contented people. . . . Let us hold out the
hand of encouragement to these people who come in and open
up new homes in that land.*

William S. Fielding,
Finance Minister.
April 16, 1903

IN 1901, A YEAR AFTER THE BOER WAR RIOT, LESTER
Patrick enrolled as a student at McGill University. Joe Patrick was
pleased with the prospect of turning out the family's first college grad-
uate. His son, however, seemed less enthusiastic. Lester displayed a
greater interest in school sports than in his studies, and his father took
him out of McGill after his first year and put him to work in the
family business. Lester began as an office boy, but was soon promoted
by his father to manage one of the branch offices. The war in South
Africa was over by then, and cultural tensions were easing, yet Lester
still had many unanswered questions. Though not all of them stemmed
from French-English issues, they could all be traced, in one way or
another, to the day of the Boer War riot.

Joe Patrick had always been careful, both in his professional and
personal life, to remain as neutral as was possible with regard to "the
French problem." Lester's arrest had been a great embarrassment to
Joe, and the incident had created an unspoken air of tension between
them. Lester had seen the bare, ugly emotions of the cultural conflict
too closely to be as impartial as his father was, and could not yet come
to terms with them. This, in turn, made it even more difficult for
Lester as he also tried to face the fact that he did not want to work
for his father, nor live in the proper social world of Westmount. Hoping

that getting out of Montreal would help him resolve his personal problems, nineteen-year-old Lester Patrick announced that he was heading west in the spring of 1903.

Lester went to Calgary. The booming frontier town in the foothills of the Rocky Mountains, at the heart of the Alberta district of the Northwest Territories, was filling up with new citizens. Poles, Ukrainians, and other Eastern European immigrants, as well as Asians, and even some Americans, were coming to the Canadian West as the Laurier government opened up the region. Knowing that cattle ranching was the biggest economic activity in the area, Lester decided to find a job as a ranch hand. It was as far removed from his life in Montreal as he could think of.

"You ever ride a horse?" the Alberta rancher asked, looking Lester over. The man was probably only a few years older than Lester, but he already had deep lines around his eyes, and his face looked cracked and dark from years of wind and sun. The skin on his hands was like old leather.

"No," said Lester. "I've never ridden a horse, but surely I can learn." The rancher shook his head. Lester had been through this before, and he was getting tired of it. Some ranchers had asked before he got a chance to introduce himself. "We can't use you," he'd been told over and over. Lester thought about lying, but knew the lie would be exposed as soon as anyone saw him on horseback. He just remained hopeful that someone would be willing to give him a chance

"Look," said the rancher, "I've only got one job available. It pays twenty dollars a month. We work in the saddle from sunrise to sunset and it ain't gonna be any easier on you if you can't ride a horse."

It was obvious the man didn't want to hire him. Lester was fed up, and decided to abandon the impractical notion of becoming a cowboy. Instead he took a dreary job with the Canadian Pacific Railway, working on a survey gang. He stayed until late in the fall when the gang was frozen out by the cold weather, and then decided to return home.

Lester felt defeated by his trip to Calgary. He had fled Montreal hoping to recapture the carefree days he had known as a boy — before the Boer War riot had opened his eyes to realities he was still not ready to face. He had found no quick answers. No easy solutions. He realized now there probably weren't any.

As his train rolled east across the Prairies, Lester read about the upcoming season in the Manitoba Northwest Hockey League. As he read, it dawned on him how much he missed the game. It had been over a year since he had last played. His thoughts drifted back to his boyhood days. He thought about the first time he had played hockey in Point St. Charles. He thought about playing with his brother Frank and Art Ross and the boys from Westmount. He remembered back to the first game his father had taken him to, and he smiled. It was, he realized, the first time in a very long while that he had smiled. Lester made a decision right then and there. When the train reached Brandon, he got off.

"Son, my name's Harold Reese. I manage the Wheat Kings. We're the top team here in Brandon. Best in the city — but I think we could find a spot for you, my boy! What do ya say to that?"

"Well, it sure has felt good to get back out on the ice again," Lester admitted to Reese.

Lester had been in Brandon only a few days. He had taken a room in a local boarding house, and was spending his afternoons skating with the other young hopefuls who were trying to win a spot on one of the city's teams. Lester's job in Calgary — clearing land for the railway — had kept him in pretty good shape, but still his muscles had ached for his first few workouts. He'd felt stiff when he began to skate, but slowly the fluidity came back to his legs. Soon he was moving with the long, graceful strides that made his motion look so effortless. Thanks to the railway work, his wrists and forearms were stronger than ever, and he shot the puck with power and precision.

"How is it we didn't catch on to you sooner?" Reese asked. "I thought I'd seen all the best talent 'round these parts."

"Well, sir, I've been away from the game awhile," Lester said. "And I'm not from around here."

"That would explain it," said Reese, nodding. "But you didn't answer my first question," he exclaimed suddenly. "How'd ya like a spot with the Wheat Kings, kid? We need a cover point. You'd play with Lorne Hanna. He's the best point man in Manitoba. Your strong skating and smart play would go great with Hanna's loft shot and solid hitting."

"Cover point, eh?" Lester said thoughtfully. "I used to play rover back home."

"Rover, cover point, whatsa difference? It's all hockey, ain't it kid? All's I'm sayin' is a guy with your talent could play anywhere."

Lester dropped his head, embarrassed to hear the man heaping praise on him.

"Listen, kid," said Reese, his voice suddenly harsh, "I haven't got all day. Do ya want the job or don'tcha?"

The change in the man's tone caused Lester to look up. He still had a trace of embarrassment on his face, which Reese misinterpreted.

"Don't worry, kid, I know what you're thinkin'. It's an amateur league up here so we can't pay ya. No problem. The team provides ya with free room and board." He lowered his voice and looked around before continuing. "And don't be surprised if you find twenty-five bucks on your pillow at the end of each month."

Lester had not even considered the financial benefits of playing hockey. He had merely wanted to test his boyhood skills against adult competition. Now he could do that and be paid for it, too.

"You've got yourself a cover point, Mr. Reese."

Because he was new to the position of cover point, Lester looked to his partner, Lorne Hanna, for advice on playing a defensive position. It was the job of the defencemen, in the era of seven-man hockey, to protect their goaltender at all times and clear the puck out of their end. The point and cover point, as the defencemen were called, were expected to loft long backhand shots high up into the rafters and into the opponent's end. Up ice, the forwards — the centre, left winger, right winger and rover — would circle the ice furiously, trying to get into position under the spot where the puck would come down. There were no lines on the ice to differentiate zones, and forward passing was not allowed. In fact, any player up ice from the puck carrier was considered offside until the puck had been brought past him. Since there was no forward passing, the offensive players couldn't receive the long loft shots and had to get into position to try and chase the puck down or get it back from the opposing players.

Once a forward got hold of the puck, it became a game of possession. A player would skate with the puck for as long as he could, stickhandling around the opposition. Forwards would stickhandle and drop-pass until they got in position for a shot on goal. When a clear shot was lined up, the goaltender, in keeping with the rules, would have to remain standing at all times as he tried to make the save. If he stopped the shot, he would clear the puck back to a point man, who would then loft it up ice. If the rover had hustled back on defence, the goalie might leave the puck for him. The rover would then try to rush the length of the ice.

Lester and Hanna became good friends during the season, and often talked about the fine points of the game. "Lorne," said Lester one day, "why do you suppose defencemen don't carry the puck?" This had been bothering Lester for some time, since he was used to carrying the offensive load from his rover position.

"Why would you want your point men to be carrying the puck?" Hanna asked. "You've got a rover to lug it up ice and three other forwards for him to work with. Everybody plays their own position. That's how it works. If your point men are rushing all over the ice, who's going to take care of your own end?"

Lester respected Hanna's opinion. He just didn't agree with it. After all, it wasn't as if a defenceman had never carried the puck before. As a boy, he'd seen Mike Grant rush the puck on defence with the Montreal Victorias. Lester always wondered why the move hadn't caught on, why it had been discouraged. He brought up the question with other Brandon players, and always received a similar answer to Lorne Hanna's. All the same, he wasn't convinced.

"If the game doesn't change, it can't move ahead," Lester reasoned. "It's not good enough to say 'this is the way it is' and not question it. If the game can be made better, we owe it to everyone involved to make it better."

Lester's comments generally resulted in blank stares from his teammates. Although they were all skilled hockey players, Lester also possessed a sharp eye and a keen mind. One day, he might revolutionize the sport. Meantime, he took small steps. The first came in a game against Winnipeg, when he rushed the length of the ice to score a spectacular goal. The tactic broke the unwritten law stating that a defenceman should never abandon his spot in front of the goaltender. It went against conventional thinking. It went against what his teammates had told him — and the fans loved it. Lester received a loud and long ovation for his brilliant goal.

Lester's innovative play helped lead Brandon to the Northwest League championship. The Wheat Kings then challenged Ottawa for the Stanley Cup. The challenge was accepted, and a two-game, total-goal series was scheduled in the nation's capital. Lester was going east again.

The team Brandon came east to face in its Stanley Cup series, the 1904 edition of the Ottawa Silver Seven, was led by a scoring machine named Frank McGee. McGee had lost the sight in one eye before his arrival in Ottawa, yet was still the outstanding player of the day. He combined exciting speed with extraordinary stickhandling to average almost three goals per game during his hockey career. Ottawa accepted four Stanley Cup challenges during the 1904 season, and with McGee leading the way, they were winners every time. McGee scored twenty-one goals in those eight Stanley Cup games. Eight of these goals were scored against the overmatched Brandon team, as the Silver Seven beat the Wheat Kings by scores of 6–3 and 9–3.

Despite Brandon's lopsided loss, Lester received praise for his play in the series, though he was criticized by some hockey experts for "his tendency to wander off down the ice away from his position," as one newspaper reporter put it. The Ottawa fans, though, like the fans in Brandon, were quite taken by the new tactic. Soon cover points all over the country were rushing the puck on offence, then hustling back to their defensive position.

Lester did not return to Brandon after the Stanley Cup series. After almost a full year in the West, he missed his family and went home to Montreal. Frank met him at the train station. Lester greeted his brother with his right arm extended.

"I'm afraid a handshake's just not going to do it," Frank said, as he hugged his brother, slapping him hard but affectionately on the back. "How are you, Lester?"

"I feel great, Frank." His smile was evidence of that. Hockey had put joy back in his life. "Of course, I would be feeling even better if we'd won!"

Frank laughed. Then became serious. "Have you worked everything out?"

This time it was Lester who laughed. "Well, no. Not really," he admitted with a shrug. He hadn't found an alternative to his father's Westmount lifestyle, but at least now he knew that he wanted hockey to be a part of it.

"Come on," said Frank. "I'll take you home."

Lester went back to work with his father. But this time things were different, for he had also signed on with his pal Art Ross to play for his old neighbourhood on the Montreal Westmount club in the new Canadian Amateur Hockey Association. Lester went back to playing rover, while Art Ross played cover point. Later in the season, Frank was enlisted to help out on defence, but weak goaltending doomed the Westmount team to a disappointing year. Following the season, the Patrick brothers went their separate ways again. Lester took a job with the Canadian Rubber Company, and later in the year, signed on to play with the Montreal Wanderers as well.

Frank attended McGill, where he captained the varsity hockey team. He played cover point, the same position Lester had played in Brandon, and he played it in the same innovative fashion. Frank was a strong skater, but put no one in mind of Lester's graceful style. Instead, he looked like a sprinter on ice, covering the frozen expanse in short, choppy strides. Still, he was able to bring the fans out of their seats with brilliant rink-long rushes. The highlight of Frank's 1906 season with McGill came in February, when the Montreal school took on Harvard University in Boston. A crowd of 700 was on hand in Harvard's new ice hockey rink, and though the Ivy Leaguers put up a good fight, they proved no match for the Canadians. The McGill team scored a convincing 8–2 victory. Frank had three goals.

While Frank was leading McGill to impressive victories, Lester had the Montreal Wanderers on the verge of their first-ever Stanley Cup. His quiet strength and ability to remain calm in the most hectic situations had quickly won him the respect of his new teammates, and though he was only a rookie, Lester had quickly become a team leader. The twenty-two-year-old rover kept his overachieving squad even with the mighty Ottawa Silver Seven all year long, and at the end of the season the standings in the newly formed Eastern Canada Amateur Hockey Association showed the two clubs deadlocked, with identical 9 and 1 records. A two-game, total-goal series was scheduled to settle the issue. Since Ottawa still held the Stanley Cup, the series would not only settle the league title but would determine the Cup champion as well.

Lester couldn't sleep the night before the series with the Silver Seven was set to start. True, he'd been involved in a Stanley Cup series just two years ago with Brandon, but this was different. The upstart team from Manitoba had been given no chance of defeating the powerful

Ottawa outfit, and for that reason there was very little pressure. Now he was a local celebrity representing his home town on a team that had a real chance at victory.

He wandered the streets alone for a while, lost in his thoughts. It had been a very good season for him. Lester, Ernie Russell, and Moose Johnson had all been newcomers to the team. They'd blended well with veteran Pud Glass to form an effective forward unit, but how would they stand up under intense pressure against longtime champions like the Smith brothers, Alf and Harry, and Frank McGee, and Rat Westwick?

"Westwick can be such a pest," Lester thought. Rat's real name was Harry, but his elusive style and small physique had led to the uncomplimentary nickname. Yet it was one Westwick relished. As the Ottawa rover, he was able to set up brilliant scoring chances for the rest of his linemates, especially Frank McGee. McGee's reputation had only grown stronger since he had almost single-handedly beaten Lester's Brandon team in 1904. The following season, McGee and the Silver Seven had defended the Stanley Cup by manhandling a team from Dawson City. Travelling by dogsled, boat, and train, the Klondikers made the 3000-mile trek to the capital, only to be crushed 9–2 and 23–2. McGee scored fourteen goals in the second game. No professional hockey player would ever score more in a single outing. McGee played just eight games during the 1906 season, but had poured in twenty-eight goals. His total was exceeded only by that of teammate Harry Smith, who had tallied a league-leading thirty-one goals in nine games. These were the legends Lester Patrick would be facing tomorrow night.

Before he knew it, Lester found himself in front of the Montreal Arena. He decided to go in. It was dark inside, but after a short time Lester's eyes adjusted to the dimness. How strange the arena looked in the dark. The pale ice appeared ghostlike.

Lester climbed up a few rows into the stands and took a seat behind the players' bench. Only one other man was inside — the rink manager, who had stayed late to make final preparations the night before the big game.

"When the place is this quiet," Lester said to the man, "it's hard to believe it can be so wild."

"Yup," said the rink manager. "You'd never know that tomorrow night there'll be screaming fans packed in all the way up to the rafters."

It was hard to imagine, yet, if he closed his eyes, Lester could almost hear them. He sat in silence for a while, leaning forward with his left hand on his hip and his right elbow on his knee. His right hand rested against his forehead, his thumb gently stroking the scar over his eyebrow. He'd been cut in a game a few weeks back and the gash had required twelve stitches to close. Thinking about it made him tired. It must have shown on his face.

"It's late, Lester," the rink manager said sympathetically. "You should go home and get some rest. You'll want to be at your best tomorrow."

The Ottawa team was already on the ice when the Montreal Wanderers left their dressing room for game one of the Stanley Cup series. The Silver Seven were an intimidating sight in their striped uniforms of black, white, and red. They oozed confidence as they skated circles in their own end of the rink. Ottawa had first won the Stanley Cup back in 1903, and had held off every challenge over the past three years. In fact, in just the last two weeks they had crushed teams from Queen's University and Smiths Falls which had dared to try and take away their trophy.

The game began at nine o'clock sharp when the referee placed the puck on the ice between the two opposing centres. "Play!" he shouted. The game was on.

Frank McGee beat Pud Glass to the puck, using his long reach to snatch the rubber and feed it back to Westwick. The Rat dashed off for the Montreal net. Ottawa had gone quickly to the attack, but the Wanderers were ready to respond, and Westwick was met by a stiff check from Montreal cover point Rod Kennedy. Kennedy's defence partner, Billy Strachan, pounced on the loose puck and lofted a high shot into the Ottawa end. The Wanderers forwards scrambled for position in front of the Silver Seven defence, as the puck came down in front of Ottawa cover point Harvey Pulford.

Pulford scooped up the puck and rushed towards Wanderers territory. He was gaining speed when he was dumped by a crushing body check from Moose Johnson. The crowd roared its approval as the Ottawa star fell. Pulford swung his stick at Johnson as he went down. He missed with his wild swing, but Frank McGee levelled Johnson with a vicious cross-check to the upper body that went undetected by the referee. When Johnson retaliated by tripping McGee, a penalty was called.

The fans groaned as Ottawa prepared to play with the man advantage, but the Wanderers proved equal to the task and killed off the three-minute penalty. Slowly the flow of the game turned in Montreal's favour. They peppered Ottawa goalie Billy Hague with shots. Eight minutes into the opening period, a puck bounced off Hague and into the corner behind him, to the right.

"I'm on it!" Lester called out to his teammates as he raced Pulford to the corner.

As Lester moved in, Pud Glass took up a position along the boards directly behind him. "Drop it back!" he shouted when he saw Lester beat Pulford to the puck. "Drop it back!"

Lester spun around, and, spotting Glass in the clear, he snapped off a pass. Pud played it cleanly and cut for the centre of the Ottawa end. Glass faked to his right, then moved to his left and slipped the puck between the legs of Ottawa point man Arthur Moore. Picking up the puck on the other side, Glass skated in alone on Hague and beat the goalie on a shot low to the stick side.

The Montreal Arena thundered with cheers. The Wanderers led 1–0. Two more Montreal shots beat Hague in the next eight minutes, as the Wanderers upped their advantage over the defending Stanley Cup champions to 3–0.

Play now raced from end to end as Ottawa tried desperately for the next goal, but the Silver Seven were clearly tired. They had played a lot of hockey in the past two weeks, finishing up the ECAHA season as well as facing two other Stanley Cup challenges. Unable to keep up with the more rested and younger Wanderers, Ottawa decided to become more physical. Pulford decked Moose Johnson with a high cross-check, opening a gash just below his eye, and was sent off for a penalty while Johnson retired to the dressing room to get patched up.

Working with the man advantage, Rod Kennedy, Lester Patrick, and Pud Glass moved the puck up ice. Glass finished off a magnificent rush with another swift deke around Arthur Moore before passing off to Ernie Russell, who bulged the twine to put the Wanderers ahead 4–0. That's where the score stood when the bell rang after thirty minutes of play to end the first half. The capacity crowd stood as one, ringing the arena with cheers, as the Wanderers skated off.

The Montreal players whooped it up as they made their way down the corridor under the stands to their dressing room. They laughed and shouted as they loosened their skates and towelled off, but Lester was not ready for a celebration.

"Gentlemen," he said, striking a dramatic tone, "we've not won anything yet. The team we are playing tonight did not get where they are by giving up after a difficult half. They'll not back down, and I suggest we not let up. None of you needs me to remind you how important this game is. It's what we've worked for all season. It's what most of us have worked for all our lives! A game is sixty minutes long, and to beat a team like the Silver Seven we've got to play hard for the full sixty minutes." Lester paused for a moment and gazed around the room, looking each player in the eye. The others knew that he was right. "Gentlemen, that's all I have to say."

The Silver Seven, indeed, did not back down. McGee won the draw to open the second half and played the puck back to Pulford, who carried it forward. Harry Smith circled behind Pulford and took a drop pass from him. Moving up ice, he shook off his check and, faking a pass over to Westwick, split the Wanderers' defence. He had a clear view of the Montreal net, and slammed a hard shot on goal. Wanderers netminder Howie Menard stretched as far as he could to his right and, kicking out his leg, made a difficult skate save.

Menard's magnificent effort sparked his teammates, who were all over Ottawa in the second half. The Wanderers took the play to the Silver Seven, setting their own quick pace on offence and swarming the Ottawa players on defence, wearing down the weary champions. It was evident that neither Westwick nor McGee could hang on to a swift cut pace, so most of the Ottawa puck carrying fell to the cover point, Harvey Pulford. He threw all his energy into initiating attacks and, as a result, he was often caught up ice. On too many occasions point man Arthur Moore was faced with trying to stop all four Montreal forwards on his own. He couldn't keep up. The Wanderers cruised through the second half and, when the final bell rang, they had scored a stunning 9–1 victory.

Wanderers fans spilled out of the stands and onto the ice, picking up the Montreal players and carrying them off on their shoulders. The Wanderers had beaten the Silver Seven in all phases of the game. Ernie Russell had led the onslaught with four goals, Pud Glass had added three, and Lester and Moose Johnson had banged in one goal apiece.

Montreal fans were confident that with an eight-goal lead in the total-goals series, the defending champs were about to be dethroned.

The teams had two days off before the final game of the 1906 Stanley Cup series took place in Ottawa's Dey Arena. With their team eight goals down, Silver Seven fans could have been forgiven for being down-hearted, yet interest in the game was at a fever pitch. It was sold out long before game day. Temporary bleachers were added behind each goal, and a riot almost broke out when those tickets went on sale. Hundreds of fans, many of whom had camped out all night, jammed the box office, and local law enforcement officials had to be called in to restore order.

The citizens of Ottawa were crazy about their hockey team. In fact, Ottawa residents had been wild about the game since long before Lord Frederick Arthur Stanley, Baron of Preston, had seen fit to donate his championship trophy in 1893. Hockey was already a passion in Ottawa when Lord Stanley was appointed Governor General in 1888, and he, an avid sportsman like a great many English noblemen of his time, quickly became a hockey fan.

When Lord Stanley's term as Governor General ended in 1893, he decided to make sure the game he had come to love would remember him always, by providing a challenge trophy which could be held from year to year by the leading hockey club in Canada.

Upon his return to England, Lord Stanley paid a visit to the best silversmith in London. For ten guineas, he ordered a silver bowl with an interior finish of gold, mounted on an ebony base. The Stanley Cup was born.

As champions of their league in 1893, and favourite team of the departed Governor General, the Ottawa hockey club laid claim to the Stanley Cup. Their claim, however, was denied by the trustees appointed to administer the Cup. The trustees ruled that as a challenge trophy the Stanley Cup must be won on the ice. They ordered a game between Ottawa and the Osgoode Hall team of Toronto to decide the issue, but the Ottawa club, maintaining the Cup should be theirs already, refused to play. Instead, the first Stanley Cup was awarded to the Montreal Amateur Athletic Association club, which had just won the Amateur Hockey Association title.

A year later, the Ottawa club was back to challenge Montreal for the trophy they considered rightfully theirs, but were beaten 3–1 in the first-ever Stanley Cup championship game. Ottawa vowed it would win the Stanley Cup the following year, but ten seasons passed before the Cup finally came to the capital.

The Silver Seven defeated the Montreal Victorias in 1903 to claim the coveted Cup, and turned back ten challengers over the next three years. The team now faced a huge uphill climb against the Wanderers to retain their prized possession, but their fans had not lost hope.

While Ottawa fans were hopeful, the Wanderers faithful were giddy with anticipation of their first Stanley Cup championship. After all, hockey had practically been born in Montreal. Though the real history of the sport was unclear, the game that fans had come to know traced its roots to Montreal in the mid-1870s.

James Creighton was credited with proposing the idea of playing hockey indoors in Montreal around 1874, after an indoor exhibition of lacrosse on ice proved to be a failure. Soon, members of the Victoria Skating Club were playing hockey regularly, and the first public display of indoor hockey was given at the Victoria Skating Rink in 1875. Two nine-man teams, one captained by Creighton, took part in the game. The arena where hockey was first played had only an eight-inch platform for fans to stand on. Because the spectators were so close to the action, it was decided that, for their protection, the regularly used rubber ball would be replaced with a flat, circular piece of wood — the first hockey puck.

Hockey's historic first public game ended in a 2–1 victory for Creighton's team. In the years that followed, Montreal hockey clubs dominated the sport. Nine of the first eleven Stanley Cup winners had come from there. Wanderers fans were anxious for their team to add its own chapter to Montreal's rich hockey history, as they descended on Ottawa in special trains scheduled for the Stanley Cup series. Just 200 tickets had been allotted to the Montreal fans, but more than 1000 people made the journey to Ottawa. Scalpers had a field day. The top two-dollar tickets were selling briskly at ten dollars apiece, with no guarantee they were the real thing. When the game started, 5400 fans — including the Earl and Lady Grey, the current Governor General of Canada and his wife — were stuffed into an arena designed to seat 3000. Hundreds more were left outside, hammering on the doors.

The Wanderers skated around their end of the ice, warming up for the championship game, awaiting the arrival of the Silver Seven.

"My God, Lester," Moose Johnson said, staring up at the stands incredulously, "have you ever seen such a sight in your life?"

He hadn't. The arena was simply a sea of people. With the temporary bleachers climbing the far sides of the building and a newly built press box hanging from the rafters, it appeared as if even the walls and ceiling were alive. Just when Lester thought the noise from the stands could get no louder, the Silver Seven hit the ice. A thunderous standing ovation greeted the home team as the players went through their warm-up routine.

There was one change in the Ottawa lineup. Percy Lesueur was now in goal, taking over from Billy Hague. Lesueur was the brilliant young goalie from the Smiths Falls team that Ottawa had beaten in a Stanley Cup Challenge just ten days before. While they may have been within their rights to do so, the Wanderers chose not to object to the late addition to the Ottawa roster. Bringing in ringers was not an uncommon practice; besides, how much damage could a new netminder do in trying to make up an eight-goal disadvantage?

The Silver Seven were fired up by the raucous reception they had been given. Frank McGee was certainly ready to play. He was lined up for the opening face-off well before Pud Glass, just itching to get started.

"Put your stick on the ice and get into position," McGee growled at the Wanderers centre. "Let's play some friggin' hockey."

McGee won the draw, and dropped the puck back to Rat Westwick. Westwick cut for the right side and swooped in on the Wanderers' end. He cut sharply around Moose Johnson and drove in on cover point Rod Kennedy. The small and elusive Ottawa rover faked to his right and tried to cut back into the middle of the ice, but Kennedy had not been fooled. His eyes had been riveted on Westwick's midsection and he caught him with a crunching body check, laying his shoulder in hard under Westwick's chin and bringing his stick up into the Ottawa player's stomach for good measure. The Rat groaned from the force of the blow, but he refused to fall down. The puck was lost, though, and Kennedy's defence partner, point man Billy Strachan, picked it up and lofted it back into the Ottawa end.

It was obvious early on that the Wanderers intended to play a defensive style, content to sit on an eight-goal lead, waiting for offensive chances rather than trying to create them. Still, it was the Wanderers who scored first, Pud Glass poking the puck from Pulford as he tried to return a Strachan lob shot, then feeding it to Lester who set up Moose Johnson for a goal. The Wanderers led 1–0; 10–1 for the series.

But Ottawa refused to back down. Frank McGee got the Silver Seven on the scoresheet with a rink-long individual rush, then Harry Smith further narrowed the margin with another goal. Just before the half, McGee struck again, and the Silver Seven went into their dressing room with a 3–1 lead in game two, still trailing in the series by six goals. The margin was cut in half within minutes after intermission, when the Smith brothers and Rat Westwick notched goals for Ottawa. With the score now 6–1 (10–7 Wanderers, total), the crowd became frantic.

Right after Westwick's goal, Lester dropped to a knee, bent over his skates and took his time readjusting the laces. As he re-tied the bow, his teammates gathered round for a quick strategy session. The screaming from the stands was so loud Lester could barely hear himself speak.

"Gentlemen," he said, "here's what we're going to do. Whenever the Silver Seven come down with the puck, all of us will form a barricade in front of the goal. When one of us gets possession, he'll flip the puck over the boards into the crowd." The ploy, while perhaps not sporting, was well within the rules of the day.

The Wanderers' tactics infuriated the Ottawa fans, whose booing shook the building itself, and baffled the Ottawa players, who stubbornly tried to crash through the human wall of Wanderers. Finally, a solution occurred to the Ottawa players.

"What we're gonna do is this," Alf Smith told his teammates. "I'm gonna carry the puck into their end and make it look like I'm trying to break through the line. But at the last second, I'll drop the puck to Harry."

"I get it," said the other Smith brother. "I use you as a screen and fire the puck through."

The play worked perfectly, as Harry blistered a hard shot low along the ice. He beat Menard before the goalie had even seen what happened, and the score for the series was cut to 10–8. Smith scored again two minutes later, and with ten minutes to go in the game the once huge Wanderers lead was down to a single goal.

The roar from the crowd was so loud now that the panicked Wanderers players could no longer hear each other as they tried to shout out instructions. The Ottawa squad sensed the kill, and bore down on the beleaguered Montreal outfit. Harry Smith was on the offensive again. He swept around Lester and was moving in on the Montreal goal. He had only Billy Strachan to beat, and he easily sidestepped the Wanderers point man.

"I got him!" shouted Rod Kennedy, as he raced back into the play, levelling Smith with a vicious cross-check that sent him crashing to the ice.

The crowd roared its disapproval of Kennedy's technique, while their club's top goal-scorer tumbled towards the Montreal net. But the mood changed instantly when the Ottawa winger slid into the net with the puck underneath him and the referee signalled a goal.

Pandemonium reigned! Hats, scarves, gloves, and galoshes poured from the stands as the fans littered the ice. The Governor General came down to the Ottawa players' bench to shake Smith's hand and congratulate him on his great performance. The Wanderers, meanwhile, stood behind their own net, heads hanging, while arena attendants cleared the playing surface.

The sudden realization that they were facing an unthinkable, humiliating defeat forced the Wanderers finally to open up their play, but had they waited too long? The Silver Seven, too, were on the attack, and the two teams took turns rushing the puck up and down the ice, only to be turned back again and again. At last, with under two minutes to play and Ottawa pressing for the go-ahead goal, the Wanderers got their chance. The Silver Seven defencemen had come too far into the Montreal end trying to join in the offensive push, and Lester flipped the puck across to Moose Johnson, who had a clear lane into the Ottawa end. Johnson and Lester sped towards the Ottawa goal, and Lester, taking a return pass from Johnson, rammed the puck past Lesueur.

A disappointed groan and then a sad silence fell over the Ottawa crowd. With just ninety seconds to play, the incredible comeback had fallen short. Lester administered the finishing touch when he scored again just before the final bell. The Stanley Cup returned to Montreal. Lester had led the Wanderers to their first championship. Barely.

IX

"LESTER, YOU'RE MAKING SEVENTY-FIVE DOLLARS A month with the rubber company. A new pair of shoes costs only two dollars. You can get a good meal in any restaurant for seventy-five cents. You pay no room and board to live in our family home. It would be un-Christian of you to accept money for playing hockey and, as your father, I won't allow it."

Professionalism officially came to Canadian hockey during the off-season after the Montreal Wanderers' 1906 Stanley Cup victory. The Wanderers had made two moves to shore up their defence. They signed goalie Riley Hern and point man Hod Stuart to professional contracts. Professionalism, both real and disguised, had been rapidly gaining ground in hockey. Professional leagues in the United States had been raiding the Canadian amateur ranks of their greatest players. To combat this, amateur teams had taken to paying their players directly, although under the table, or to landing them cushy, high-paying and low-working jobs during the off-season. The dispute over "salaries" came to a head at the league meetings in the fall of 1906.

"Clubs that pay their players should be thrown out of the league," bellowed Montreal Shamrocks president John McLaughlin. "They are parasites. We have never paid any of our players, and we don't intend to start now!"

McLaughlin's speech was met with much nodding of agreement, and shouts of "Hear! Hear!" — but not from everyone present.

"You, sir, are behind the times," shouted enraged Wanderers president Jim Strachan. "And not only that, you are a numbskull!"

After much discussion, it was decided to allow amateurs and professionals to play together on the same teams, as long as the clubs declared the status of each performer. When the Wanderers presented their players list, they noted newcomers Hern and Stuart as professionals, as well as veterans Pud Glass and Moose Johnson. Stuart, Glass, and Johnson were said to be making $2000 among them. It was these outrageous wages which had brought the whole issue to the forefront.

Professional sports was a bone of contention in the Patrick household as well, with Joe Patrick among those who believed that a person playing a game was doing just that, playing a game. It was wrong to expect financial compensation. Lester had heard the speech from his father many times, in which only his salary, and the shopping list of goods he could hypothetically buy with it, ever changed. He was twenty-three years old now, and a hero in his city. He no longer had to listen to his father, and yet he could not bring himself to defy him. When the Montreal Wanderers announced their amateur performers, Lester Patrick's name headed up a list of four.

With the issue of professionalism now dealt with, the way was cleared for the hockey season to begin. Fans were looking forward to the early season rematch between the Wanderers and Ottawa. The Silver Seven were now known as the Senators, and it became apparent early in the game that they had come to Montreal not so much to win, but to extract a measure of revenge for last spring's defeat.

Harry Smith set the tone early in the game when he attacked Moose Johnson away from the play, slamming him across the face with his stick and breaking his nose. Later, Harry's brother, Alf, got into the action with a similar shot to Hod Stuart's forehead, sending the big defenceman thudding to the ice, out cold.

Despite the physical beating they were taking, the Wanderers were winning on the scoreboard, and a late goal by Lester put them ahead 4-2. As he turned up ice to celebrate, Lester was levelled from behind with a blindside body check. Several Ottawa players had surrounded Lester, taunting him as he lay dazed on the ice, when Hod Stuart arrived on the scene. With blood still dripping from the hastily stitched gash on his forehead, Stuart attacked Lester's assailants. Lester was helped off the ice as a brawl broke out behind the Ottawa net. He wasn't aware of what had happened until told in the dressing room after the game.

When Lester learned of how Hod Stuart had come to his rescue, he sought out the big defenceman to thank him, finding him in the saloon of a hotel across the street from the hockey rink. The hotel bar was a favourite hangout for many hockey players.

"That's what I'm there for," Hod told Lester, shrugging off his teammate's gratitude as he sipped his beer. "Someone's gotta stick up for you amateurs!"

Lester laughed. "Well, at least let me do something to thank you," he insisted. "Bartender! Another beer for my friend. And bring me a ginger ale."

Lester had grown from a good-looking boy into a handsome young man. He was tall, with broad shoulders and a rugged physique. His angular face had sharp, well-defined features which had remained un-altered despite the stick work of many an opponent. Lester was polite to a fault, and his smooth and graceful playing style was merely an extension of his gentlemanly manner off the ice. Hod Stuart was a rugged defenceman, noted for his toughness and bulldog tenacity, who was not afraid to speak his mind no matter what the consequences. Despite their dissimilarities, Lester and Hod fast became friends, though Hod continued to tease Lester about being an amateur and encouraged him to stand up to his father.

"It's not a matter of standing up to my father," Lester protested, trying to convince himself as much as Hod. "It's more of a family obligation. He's worked hard for us all his life and I simply respect his wishes."

"Nah," scoffed Hod, wiping his mouth with the back of his hand after taking a swig of beer. "I think you just tell yourself that. I think you're really afraid of him. Stand up to him, Lester. I'm not telling you to rebel against everything he says or stands for, but jeez, a guy like you could make a fortune in this game and I don't see what's wrong with that. If you see something you want, you've got to go after it. Forget about what your old man thinks once in a while."

Lester just sighed.

A week after the Ottawa game, the Wanderers took time off from their regular schedule to face a Stanley Cup challenge from the Kenora Thistles. The small Ontario town near the Manitoba border had built a hockey powerhouse that had been running roughshod over the competition in the Manitoba leagues for a number of years. The Thistles had challenged for the Stanley Cup twice before, when the city was still known as Rat Portage, but had been beaten by Ottawa on both occasions. Their lineup included Si Griffis and Tommy Phillips, two of the fastest players in the game, and was bolstered for the Stanley Cup challenge by the addition of Art Ross. Following the example of his pal Lester, Art had gone west to Brandon where he had emerged as a star.

Art Ross got a warm reception from the large delegation of his Westmount friends on hand for the game, and the cheers had hardly died down when Tommy Phillips put the visitors ahead with an early goal. Phillips and Griffis rushed the puck whenever it came their way, and Riley Hern in the Montreal net was continually tested with hard drives. When the bell rang to end the first half, the score stood two-all, with Phillips and Ernie Russell netting a pair each. Phillips added two more goals in the second half as Kenora beat the Wanderers 4–2 in the opening game.

The second game was a rough one. The Wanderers decided that, with the exception of Lester, they were unable to keep up with the speedy Westerners, so they would have to try to slow them down with heavy, battering body checks. Phillips was knocked to the ice early in the game by Hod Stuart. He slashed the Montreal defenceman in the back of the leg as he went down.

"Try that again and I'll knock out your fucking teeth," Stuart growled at Phillips, as the Kenora player picked himself up off the ice.

Phillips flashed Stuart a gap-toothed grin. Obviously such threats were not new to him. The smile enraged Stuart, who started to go after Phillips, but Si Griffis intervened. At 195 pounds, Griffis was the largest man on the ice. He and Stuart sized each other up for a moment, then skated away to get back into the play.

Despite the rough play, the game proved to be more wide open than the first contest. Phillips netted three goals, but Lester kept pace for the Wanderers with three of his own. The score was even at 6–6 with just three minutes remaining, but the Wanderers were still down two goals on the round and were forced to open up their play. The strategy backfired. The Thistles poured in two late goals, and Kenora lifted the Stanley Cup.

Fuelled by a desire to win back their prized trophy, the Montreal Wanderers finished the year undefeated to win the league title. They promptly challenged the Kenora team to a Stanley Cup rematch. It was scheduled for late March. Because the rink in Kenora was much too small for such a big series, the Stanley Cup challenge was moved to Winnipeg.

Art Ross was no longer with the Thistles by this time, but two other familiar Wanderers rivals had been enticed to move west temporarily to help in the defence of the Stanley Cup: Alf Smith and Rat Westwick. No matter. The fired-up Wanderers dumped the Thistles 7–2 in the opening game, and though they lost the second contest by a narrow 6–5 margin, they had won back the Cup by a total score of 12–8.

Both the matches in Winnipeg attracted crowds of 6500, the largest ever to attend hockey games in Canada. Among the huge throng was Lester's father, Joe Patrick, who had made the long train trip from Vancouver.

"Son, I've just settled a deal for a large tract of timberland in the Slocan district of British Columbia. I'm planning to move the whole family out west immediately. Except Frank, of course. He'll join us next spring after he graduates from McGill."

Lester was dumbfounded. Not even a word about the hockey game. Just an announcement that the family was moving west. He'd gotten used to the constant moves when he was young, but he was no longer a child. His whole life was in Montreal. Hockey was in Montreal. "Father," Lester protested, "I can't just leave." Confused thoughts and emotions jostled in his mind, but he couldn't put them into words. "What about the team?" was all he could say.

"What about the team?" Joe Patrick demanded. "Lester, I've put up with this hobby of yours long enough. Did I complain when you announced you were going to Calgary? Did I complain when, instead of returning home where you were needed, you went to Brandon to play hockey? No! I know you've become quite skilled at the game, but what's left in it for you? You've proved your worth, won championships. I want you to quit hockey and come west with the family. You're my eldest son, Lester. I'm counting on you to help me run the business."

Lester couldn't believe what he was hearing. He didn't know how to respond. "Yes, father," he heard himself say.

"This is exactly the kind of thing I'm talking about, Lester," Hod Stuart roared. "You're letting your father run your whole life."

Lester was hardly listening. He stared out the train window, watching the countryside pass by. He'd been like that for the whole ride home, sitting by himself while his teammates celebrated the Stanley Cup victory. Finally, when he could stand it no longer, he'd told Hod what his father had said.

"You're not actually going to go, though, are you Lester?"

"What else can I do, Hod? My father's moving the whole family west. He says he needs me. What am I supposed to do? This is my family we're talking about."

"Shit, Lester, sometimes you make me so damn angry. 'This is my family we're talking about,'" Stuart mimicked. "'What am I supposed to do?'" He shook his head, his face contorted with disgust. Lester sat glumly, staring out the window again. No one spoke for a while.

"Look at you," Stuart finally said. "You'll never forgive yourself if you walk away from the game like this. Give yourself one more year at least. Hell, you can bring yourself to tell your father that, can't you? That you'd like to play just one more season before you leave the game? That way you can still do what he wants, but at least you can do it on your own terms. You owe it to yourself, Lester. Think about it."

Lester did think about it, and it made sense. When his family boarded the train for British Columbia in April of 1907, Lester stayed behind. Two months later, Hod Stuart dived into shallow water in a lake near Belleville, Ontario, and snapped his neck. He died instantly. Lester was devastated. With Hod gone, he quit his job in Montreal, resigned himself to giving up hockey and headed west for the new family home in Nelson.

As he travelled west, Lester made up his mind to hate life in Nelson. However, his resolve was tested with his very first glimpse of the city. Lester had taken the rail link from the CPR main line through the Rockies down to Kootenay Landing, at the south end of Kootenay Lake. There he had boarded the stern-wheeler for the run to Nelson, some twenty-odd miles north up the lake's west arm. He was leaning over the bow rail of the ship, listening to the rhythmic splashing of the paddle wheel, when he first caught a glimpse of his new home town. High mountains surrounding the city rose to the north, west, and east with the lake to the south. The setting sun was just beginning to paint the sky a soft rose and, in the distance, Lester could see the lights of the city begin to shine. It was a beautiful sight.

Watching the ships come in was a popular evening pastime in Nelson, and a large crowd had assembled at the dock when Lester arrived. As he walked down the gangplank, he spotted his father and shook his hand.

"I was sorry to hear about your friend," Joe Patrick said, hugging his eldest son, "but I am very glad you decided to come west."

The next morning, Lester was up early and decided to take himself on a tour of the town. Nelson was a strange mix of a city, populated by men who had struck it rich in silver and gold, and other less fortunate souls who had come to hunt for wealth but had not yet found it. There were those, like Joe Patrick, who were creating thriving businesses and establishing homes and others, like the many lumberjacks and miners drawn to the area, who lent a carefree and often crude edge to the town. Lester encountered all of it. As he made his way down to Lakeside Park, he passed luxurious homes and plush hotels.

The park was already crowded with people dressed in their Sunday best, and Lester sat down on a bench to take it all in. He nodded and smiled at the people who passed by, tipping his hat to the ladies and offering a friendly "good morning" to the gentlemen.

Leaving the park, he headed up Lake Street, a thoroughfare renowned locally for its sensuous pleasures. If he'd come by later in the day, Lester would have found any number of women smiling welcomingly from second-storey windows, but at this early hour the curtains were still drawn. As he walked on, he passed several taverns. They were empty now, but, he would soon learn, they did a booming business almost every night. He had to admit the quaint little town on the edge of the British Columbia wilderness was much more than he had expected.

Trying to forget about Hod and hockey, Lester settled down to work at the Patrick Lumber Company office. He supervised the arrival of twenty French Canadian lumberjacks his father had brought in from his former Quebec business, and, on weekends, he travelled to the mountain community of Slocan City to help construct the sawmill and set up logging camps. Later, he was put in charge of the company books.

Late in November, Lester was working in the company office when a group of visitors approached him.

"Mr. Patrick?" inquired one of the visitors.

"My father is Mr. Patrick," he said with a smile. "Call me Lester."

"Mr. Patrick, uh, Lester, we represent the Nelson hockey club. We have a team in the Kootenay League. We've all read about your exploits back east and, while we're certainly not the Montreal Wanderers, we'd be honoured if you would join us this season."

Lester smiled wistfully. He was going to tell the gentlemen thank you but no. He was trying to leave that part of his life behind. Then he thought about Hod Stuart. Hod would have been furious at him for turning down such an invitation.

"I'd be pleased to join your team," Lester told the visitors.

In the team's first game a few weeks later, Lester scored five times in a 5–0 victory. The calibre of hockey was better than he had expected, especially considering that he hadn't even known the sport was being played on the west coast — Easterners tended to look upon the game as something that belonged to them — though he had to tone down his play considerably. Local games in a city league were not as hard-fought as Stanley Cup clashes with the Silver Seven or the Kenora

Thistles. Still, he enjoyed getting back on the ice. Hockey, he realized, was still in his blood.

Back east, where he was finishing school, Frank was keeping the Patrick name in the hockey headlines. Just after the new year, he was named a member of the all-star team that would take on the Montreal Wanderers in the Hod Stuart Memorial Match. The proceeds of the game, $2000, were given to the Stuart family. The Wanderers won the game 10–7, and although Ernie Russell netted five goals for the winners, Frank potted a pair in a losing effort and was named the game's most outstanding player. The game was one of the first things Frank discussed with Lester when he came west to Nelson that spring. Lester listened with delight to the stories about his old teammates, but he also had news for Frank.

"I've been contacted by the hockey club in Edmonton and asked to join them in their challenge for the Stanley Cup. The team will be taking on the Wanderers in December."

Joe Patrick grudgingly gave his permission for Lester to take three weeks' leave of absence to travel to Montreal for Edmonton's Stanley Cup challenge. The meeting with the Wanderers was like a reunion. Most of his old teammates were still there. The Wanderers had replaced Hod by signing up his brother, Bruce Stuart. Lester's spot on the roster had been filled by his old pal, Art Ross. As for his new teammates, Lester was familiar with most of them too, but only because Edmonton officials had stacked their squad with ringers. Old rivals, like Tommy Phillips, had been added to the roster, as had other eastern stars Lester had once played against. In fact, only one member of the regular Edmonton outfit, rover Fred Whitcroft, wasn't replaced for the big series.

Although the challengers were loaded with talent, the all-stars from Edmonton didn't have enough time to learn to play together as a team. They proved no match for the Wanderers, who won the two-game set by scores of 7–6 and 7–3. For the second time in a little over a year, Lester headed west from Montreal believing he had seen the end of his big-time hockey career.

Life in Nelson wasn't so bad, Lester had to admit. His brother was there now, his studies completed, and that was good. The lumber business was booming and the Patrick Lumber Company was making the family wealthy. That was good, too. The local hockey team, with two Patricks now in the lineup, was beginning to make a name for itself. Nothing wrong with that, either. He'd even gotten a chance to meet the Governor General — an admirer of his ever since the Stanley Cup battle between the Wanderers and Ottawa back in 1906 — when the Royal representative had passed through town on a tour of the West. Best of all, there was a young woman named Grace Linn.

Lester had made his first official foray into Nelson society the spring before, at a community event staged to honour the hockey team, which he had led to its first Kootenay League Championship. He had been the life of the party at the community social. Stories about his hockey adventures back east captivated listeners. Comical renditions of light-hearted Quebec folk songs brought bursts of laughter, and his singing voice won him applause. Lester not only impressed the hockey fans of the area, but also made an impression on the local ladies. Still, Lester had not yet met a woman who made a lasting impression on him. Until he met Grace.

Lester first saw Grace at the opening hockey game during his second year in British Columbia. The game was the social event of the season. After playing the previous year in the rickety old outdoor arena, Lester had decided his new home town needed better hockey facilities and convinced his father that he should ante up the first $1000. Lester solicited the rest of the funds through public donations, and by the start of the next season a new 800-seat indoor arena had been constructed. Two Patricks in the lineup may have been enough in itself to draw large crowds to the opening game, but with the added attraction of the new rink, local society was out in force. None in attendance went home disappointed. Frank scored four goals and Lester added a pair as the Nelson squad downed the team from nearby Rossland 14–1.

As Frank and Lester walked home after the game, Lester asked his brother about the pretty young woman he had seen sitting a few rows above the home team's bench.

"Her name's Grace Linn," Frank told Lester. "She's visiting here from Nanaimo."

"How do you know her?" Lester asked, trying unsuccessfully to hide his disappointment at learning the woman was not from Nelson.

"You like her, don't you?"

Frank poked an elbow playfully into his brother's ribs. He arched his eyebrows knowingly, as a silly smile spread across his face. "Don't you?"

"I don't even know her, Frank," Lester said testily. He swatted away Frank's annoying elbow.

"Yeah, but you like her!"

Just as Frank had said, Grace Linn was a visitor in town, staying at the home of a prominent local doctor. Lester paid a visit to the doctor's home the next day.

"Good afternoon, Miss Linn," Lester stammered. "My name is Lester Patrick." He could feel himself blush as he found he was at a loss for words. He'd found himself in the company of beautiful women many times in the past — often, in fact, women had thrown themselves at him — but there was something about this woman. It suddenly seemed very important that she think well of him.

"I know who you are," Grace replied cheerfully. She sensed his anxiety, and was trying to make things easy for him. "I was at the hockey match last night. Allow me to commend you on your outstanding play."

"Thank you. I'm happy you were there — that is, I'm happy that you enjoyed the game — " Patrick, you're babbling, he thought, and broke off awkwardly.

Grace took charge of the situation. "It's a beautiful day, Mr. Patrick," she said. "I love a brisk, clear winter's day, don't you? I was planning to take a walk down to the park. Would you care to join me?"

Lester looked up, smiling, beginning to regain his composure. "I'd like that very much," he said.

At twenty, Grace was a few years younger than Lester, but not so many that the age difference mattered. She was of slightly less than average height — about an inch or two above five feet — and plump in a well-shaped, pleasing way. Her round face, framed by thick, dark hair, seemed only conventionally pretty, perhaps even bland, until she smiled. When Grace smiled, her whole face lit up.

Grace Linn had been raised in an affluent family. She was well educated and well read, and she was also the first woman Lester had ever met who appreciated his skill as a hockey player, not for the celebrity it bestowed upon him, but for the athletic ability it took to master it. Soon Lester felt completely at ease with Grace. The two saw a lot of each other over the few weeks that followed their walk in the park, and she decided to extend her visit to Nelson indefinitely.

Lester and Grace spent winter evenings together dancing or taking in a show at the Empire Theatre. When summer came, their days were spent on the lake, where rowboats could be rented for a nickel an hour.

One late summer's day, Lester paid for a rowboat and dragged it across the sand from the grassy hill behind the beach to the water's edge. He was dressed casually, with the sleeves of his white cotton shirt rolled above his elbows. A white straw boater's hat was perched on his head. The red band around the hat matched both the red bow tie he wore and his red suspenders. His cream-coloured flannel trousers were rolled up to just below his knees. His shoes and socks had been left on the hill.

Lester pushed the rowboat into the water until only the narrow bow was left on shore. "I'll hold it steady for you while you climb aboard," he told Grace.

Just before she sat down he rocked the boat playfully.

"Careful," he teased, as she fell to her seat.

But Grace could give as good as she got. She leaned over the side of the boat and splashed Lester with a handful of water. "Careful," she said, in the same mock-concerned tone. "You wouldn't want to get wet."

Lester pushed the rest of the boat into the water, then climbed aboard. "That's one for you," he said, licking his finger and pretending to tally up a score.

Lester rowed the boat about fifty feet offshore, then pulled in the oars so they could drift for a while. He thought Grace looked beautiful. She was wearing a white lawn dress with delicate pintucks and lace inserts on the bodice and sleeves, and edged with more lace at the collar and cuffs. A wide white bonnet was tied beneath her chin with a red ribbon, and she carried a lacy white parasol to keep the sun off her face.

Their knees were almost touching in the small boat. Lester looked lovingly at Grace. She returned his steady gaze, and it seemed to him that there was the slightest hint of a question in her eyes. As the silence stretched out until the air between them seemed to vibrate, Lester could stand it no longer. He leaned forward and kissed her mouth.

"Oh!" she gasped. "Not out here! Not with so many people on the beach. They can all see us!"

"I don't care who sees us," Lester said softly.

"In that case, Mr. Patrick," Grace said grandly, "you may kiss my hand."

She stretched out her left hand daintily, but when Lester leaned out to take it Grace made a playful gesture as if to slap his hand away. Her parasol shifted and the tip of one rib caught Lester just above the eye. He sat back abruptly, clapping a hand to his face.

"I'm so sorry!" Grace apologized, leaning forward anxiously. "Do take your hand away so I can see — is it bleeding?"

Lester shook his head, lowering his hand. Grace touched his forehead, gently tracing the red scratch above his eye, her face full of concern. Her fingers trailed down his cheekbone to the corner of his mouth, and then she kissed him. If anyone was watching from the beach, at that moment it no longer mattered to her.

"I've been blindsided on the ice, Grace," Lester teased her as they headed back to shore, "but never in a rowboat."

Frank had watched his older brother's romance unfold with some satisfaction, as his teasing comments about Lester's interest had proven to be prophetic.

"You like her!" Frank said.

"You're right, Frank," Lester agreed. "And I'll tell you something. I think I might just ask her to marry me."

But before Lester could propose to Grace, events unfolding back east took him away from her for a time. Back to his first love: hockey.

"What do you know about a fellow named O'Brien?" Lester asked Frank. He was holding a telegram from Renfrew.

The war between the Canadian Hockey Association and National Hockey Association had heated up. The teams in the NHA were in the process of upgrading their rosters, since most of them had previously been in less competitive circuits, while the teams from the re-aligned ECHA, now the CHA, were trying to hold on to their existing talent and plug up holes as players leaped to the rival league. The bidding wars left teams searching far and wide for new talent. A seasoned veteran like Lester Patrick was an enticing prospect.

Lester was receiving telegrams daily from teams all over Ontario and Quebec asking what it would take to lure him back east. Lester hid the telegrams from his father, but answered each one. He confided in Frank that he was demanding $3000 plus all expenses for the twelve-game season. It was more than he dreamed he could possibly get, far more than anyone else was getting, but he knew he held all the cards in this poker game.

"M.J. O'Brien?" Frank said. "The railroad tycoon?"

"That's the one!" Lester exclaimed. He had known the name was familiar, but he hadn't been able to remember from where.

"Yeah, I hear he's loaded. Maybe the richest guy in the country. You know he owns those silver mines up near Cobalt. Why do you ask?"

"He and his son Ambrose are the only ones who've agreed to meet my terms. Look at this telegram." He waved it at Frank. "They're willing to pay me $3000 to come to Renfrew in the National Hockey Association. No one else would go above $1800. Can you imagine being paid that much money just to play hockey!"

"Write them back and let them know I'll sign up too!" Frank laughed. "Hell, tell 'em I'll sign for two grand."

Frank had only been joking, but Lester did it anyway. Perhaps he was just stalling, knowing that eventually he'd have to face his father. A short time later, he received a reply.

"Frank, look at this. Remember when you said to tell Renfrew you'd sign up too? Well, they've agreed to it. They're going to pay you $2000!"

Like much of the hockey establishment, Lester had underestimated just how badly Renfrew wanted the Stanley Cup, and how committed M.J. O'Brien was to providing the best for his home town. Both Frank and Lester agreed that the offer was too generous to turn down. They would have to take up the matter with their father.

Joe Patrick was stunned. He didn't know if he was more upset that his sons were still obsessed with hockey, or that they were being offered such huge sums of money for playing what he thought was essentially a child's game. Still, he listened while Frank and Lester pleaded their case.

"Father, professional sports are here to stay," Lester argued. "Like it or not, it's a fact."

"But professional hockey players are such hooligans," Joe Patrick countered. "The cross-checking, the butt ends, the slashing. I used to worry about you boys every night when you played back east. And look at the way these players hop around from city to city and team to team, going wherever the money is best. Why, they're nothing more than paid hoodlums!"

"Father," Frank shot back, "Lester and I were professional hockey players in every way but name. Are you saying we're hoodlums?"

Joe Patrick was silent for a moment. Then he laughed. Lester looked up. Both he and Frank were surprised by their father's reaction.

"Boys," said Joe, "is this what you really want?"

They both nodded, still not quite sure what to make of their father's sudden change in mood and hoping not to do anything to spoil it.

"Well, then do it!" Joe Patrick said, throwing up his hands in a gesture of defeat. "I know how much the game means to you. I'm not so stubborn that I haven't noticed the way you boys light up whenever hockey is mentioned. Not many people get to do what they truly enjoy in life. If hockey is what you really want, then I won't stand in your way. Go to Renfrew. Go with my blessing."

It was a cold morning in early December when the Patricks' train pulled into Renfrew. Frank peered out the window.

"My God, Lester, you have to see this. It looks as though the station platform is alive. Look at all the people!"

"Jeez," Lester exclaimed, "I haven't seen a crowd like that since we brought the Stanley Cup back to Montreal after that game in Ottawa." It was their first glimpse of the people of Renfrew, a hockey-mad lot craving the respect of the big cities.

Frank and Lester, sporting stylish raccoon coats and derbies, stepped off the train to a roaring welcome. They were greeted by Ambrose O'Brien, Jim Barnet, and George Martel from the Renfrew hockey club, Mayor Arthur Gravelle, and local M.P. Thomas Low. The politicians made speeches, and then, before the large gathering, the Patricks signed their contracts.

Reporters from Toronto, Ottawa, and Montreal were on hand for the signing. The big money offers coming out of the small town were making news in all the hockey centres. "Renfrew is willing to pay $3000 for a hockey player," scoffed a Toronto reporter as Lester put his name on his contract. "Let's see, what does the average Renfrew schoolteacher get?" The other reporters laughed.

But the Renfrew spending spree was far from over. Ambrose was just getting started. Now that the Patricks were safely in the fold, he was ready to embark on his next project: bringing Fred Taylor to town.

X

Nobody would have supposed in 1837 that in a few years the two provinces of Canada would have been entrusted with powers of self-government, but the result of the action of the Imperial government at that time was to turn rebels into supporters of the government. The Roman Empire meant war. The British Empire means peace. I thank Providence I was born in Canada, but Canada's history is only commencing. As the nineteenth century was that of the United States, so I think the twentieth century shall be filled by Canada. For myself, I cannot see much of it, but when my eyes close I hope it will be on a United Canada cherishing an abundant hope for the future.

Sir Wilfrid Laurier,
Prime Minister.
January 18, 1904

DURING THE EARLY MONTHS OF 1904, THE FUTURE DIDN'T look bright for Fred Taylor. Just a short time before, he had had everything he wanted in life. Summers had been filled with lacrosse and baseball; winters had revolved around hockey or just skating for pleasure, with band music and no end to the girls wanting to be escorted across the ice by the town's top hockey star.

Freddy, as he was known then, had left the Piggery behind in 1901. As a full-fledged member of the Listowel Mintos hockey club, he had led the team to two straight championship seasons. Braving snowstorms and sub-zero temperatures, 1200 fans would pack the Listowel Arena for every game. They had come by foot, by sled, by train. The drafty arena provided little protection from the cold outdoors, but the fans bundled up in furs and mufflers and huddled under blankets and screamed themselves hoarse. Games consisted of two thirty-minute halves, with a ten-minute break between. The players got a chance to retreat to their dressing rooms, where a pot-bellied stove kept them warm. The fans got nothing more than a few sips of lukewarm coffee, which vendors sold for a nickel a cup. Why had they turned out? They loved hockey, and they loved to watch Fred Taylor perform. He never let them down. Taylor was small, and younger than most of his team-mates and opponents, but could he skate!

Hockey in Listowel was strictly amateur, but sometimes, after games, Fred would find a few dollars tucked into the toe of his shoe from some of his many admirers. The money had come in handy. Fred had quit school to work in the local piano factory, but times had continued to be tough for the Taylor family.

Taylor's on-ice speed and goal-scoring ability had become legend in the Listowel area. Soon the legend was to grow. Early in the winter of 1902-1903, Taylor was invited by some former Listowel teammates, now living in Detroit, to come south for an exhibition series against a hockey team from Houghton, Michigan. He went, and was the star player of the series. Tales of his exploits filled the pages of the local press; word of his outstanding play was picked up as far away as Toronto.

W.A. Hewitt, secretary of the Ontario Hockey Association, had long been receiving reports on the brilliant young star from Listowel, but hadn't given them much consideration until the Michigan series. Now he wanted Taylor as the star attraction in his league, and offered him a position with the Toronto Marlboros.

Taylor was flattered by Hewitt's offer. It was his chance to move up to big-time hockey. He told Hewitt he would come to Toronto. But then he got cold feet. His entire life was in Listowel, a town he loved. He was a small-town boy at heart, and suddenly Toronto seemed awfully big and too far away. He decided to stay put, and telephoned Hewitt to inform him of his decision.

Hewitt was stunned. As head of the powerful OHA, he was used to getting his way. "Taylor," he screamed, "if you don't come to Toronto and play for the Marlies, I'll see to it that you won't play anywhere!"

Taylor didn't know yet that Hewitt had the authority to make good on his threat. When he got an offer from the OHA team in nearby Thessalon, Taylor decided to report there. When he showed up for his first practice, however, he was told he'd been barred from playing anywhere in the province. Bitterly disappointed, Taylor went home, worried about his future in hockey.

Although his prospects seemed bleak in 1904, his fame had spread farther than he realized. In the summer of 1905, Taylor received a letter inviting him to play for the hockey team in Portage La Prairie of the Manitoba League. They offered him room and board plus twenty-five dollars a month "pocket money." The authority of William Hewitt and the Ontario Hockey Association did not cross provincial borders, and Taylor gladly accepted the Western offer. Not only was it a chance to play hockey again, but to play in a first-rate league against some of the best players in the country.

Fred Taylor arrived in the Manitoba town in November, and was met at the train station by officials of the team. "He's awfully small," Fred overheard one of the team officials say, but he just shook his head. Taylor had been hearing such comments ever since he first stepped on the ice.

Because he was so small and light, and because he had also been the best player on every team he played for, Taylor had become a marked man, with all the opposition players gunning for him. Speed and cunning had usually been enough for him to slip past the opposing checks, but not always. As a result, he had experimented with ways to give himself additional protection against injuries. Back in Listowel, Taylor had asked his mother to sew layers of felt into the shoulders, elbows, and lower back area of the long johns he wore under his uniform. He'd also had bone stays, like those used in a lady's corset, sewn into his canvas hockey pants to protect his thigh muscles. Taylor was ridiculed at first for his padded clothing, but as he continually proved to be the best player everywhere he went, the laughter subsided and the idea began to catch on.

Portage La Prairie was a small town of about 3000, a short way out of Winnipeg on the road to Brandon. It was not much bigger than

Listowel, and Taylor felt very much at home there. Clad in the green and white of his Portage La Prairie uniform, Taylor prepared for his first game in the Manitoba League, against the Winnipeg Victorias. He had worried about how he would play after a year away from the game, but once again there was no need for concern. His blazing speed brought oohs and aahs from the crowd each time he rushed the puck, and three times in the first half those rushes resulted in goals. He created numerous chances for his teammates in the second half and, by game's end, the Portage La Prairie team had skated away with an 11–8 victory.

Fred Taylor quickly became a fan favourite. But his stay in the Manitoba town proved to be a short one. Despite his presence, the Portage La Prairie team was weak and, as word of Taylor's immense talent spread, stronger teams, looking for an extra edge, began asking about his availability. As he made his way out of the rink one night, Taylor was met by a tall, muscular man he did not know.

"Come with me," said the stranger, clutching Taylor's arm.

"Where are we going?" he responded, more surprised than frightened. After all, what could happen in such a small town?

"You haven't had dinner, have you?" demanded the stranger.

"No."

"Then come with me."

It was a frosty January evening, and a gusting wind gave the night an additional chill. As they walked the streets, Taylor turned up the collar on his coat to ward off the cold. Finally, they turned into a downtown cafe, where they were met by a third man. He ordered ham and eggs for the three of them before he introduced himself.

"I'm Tommy Phillips," the man said, offering his hand in greeting. "This gentleman," he motioned towards the tall stranger, "is Si Griffis. We're with the Kenora Thistles. We saw you play tonight. Quite a performance."

"Well, thanks," Taylor said graciously, adding with a cocky smile, "I hear you two aren't bad yourselves."

"So you've heard of us," Tommy Phillips said.

"Good," added Griffis, who then came to the point of the mysterious rendezvous. "Taylor, we'd like you to join our team. We're heading down to Montreal after the season to challenge for the Stanley Cup. We've lost twice before in the past couple of years, but we think you would be a big help. Maybe push us over the top. Portage La Prairie isn't going anywhere and I'm sure they'd give you your release, if you asked. What do you say?"

By the end of the meal, a decision had been made. Taylor would ask for permission to join the Thistles. Just as Griffis had told him, there was no problem getting a release from his Portage La Prairie obligation, but Taylor never did make it to Kenora.

The day before he was supposed to leave Portage La Prairie to join the Thistles, Fred Taylor received a telephone call from a man named John McNamara. McNamara managed the Portage Lake team in Houghton, Michigan, which was a charter member of hockey's first professional league, formed shortly after Taylor's visit for the exhibition series two years back. The league had been started by Jack Gibson, who, like Taylor, was a refugee from the Ontario Hockey Association.

Jack Gibson, born in Berlin, Ontario, had played on an OHA intermediate championship team in 1897, but when he and his teammates had beaten rival Waterloo in a big game and each been rewarded with a $10 gold piece by their town's proud mayor, the entire team had been barred from the OHA for violating the league's amateur status. Gibson had left town in disgust and, after graduating from the Detroit Medical School, he'd set up a dental practice in Houghton, on the shores of Portage Lake in Michigan's northern peninsula.

"Doc" Gibson, as he was now known, had set up the Portage Lake team in 1902 with a group of Canadian players whom he paid to come to Houghton and play exhibition games against neighbouring towns. So thoroughly had the Portage Lake team dominated the local competition that soon other towns began signing stars of their own. Within two years, Gibson had organized the first officially recognized above-the-board professional hockey circuit in the world. The league boasted other Michigan teams in Calumet and Sault Ste. Marie, two teams in Pittsburgh, and a team in the Canadian Soo — hence it was called the International Pro Hockey League. The teams were made up almost entirely of Canadian players enticed south by the lure of big pay-cheques.

McNamara telephoned Taylor because the Portage Lake team was in need of an extra player, someone who could handle any position. "I'm told you're a man who could fit the bill," McNamara said. "We'd sign you to a professional contract."

"How much money are we talking about?" Taylor asked.

"Four hundred dollars for the rest of the season, plus expenses."

"Well, I'll have to think it over," Taylor told McNamara. The financial offer was impressive — more money, in fact, than he'd ever seen before.

Taylor was now faced with a difficult decision. He had the opportunity to join the Thistles and challenge for the Stanley Cup, or to sign on with Houghton for a chance to get paid to do what he'd always wanted to spend his life doing. He'd never really considered the possibility that he could make a living at the game he loved, so the offer was tempting. But Kenora also had its strong points. The Stanley Cup was the biggest prize in hockey. It was what all players dreamed of, and winning the Stanley Cup with Kenora would certainly offer fame, if not fortune.

The Houghton offer won out. After all, the arrangement with Kenora was simply to play through the Stanley Cup challenge, after which he would have to return to Portage La Prairie. Houghton offered security. Taylor could play there as long as he liked. He telephoned his regrets to the hockey officials in Kenora, and informed McNamara he would be heading south. The Houghton team sent him a train ticket and ten dollars in travelling money.

It was a bitterly cold morning when Fred Taylor caught the train for Houghton, Michigan. It was snowing lightly as he boarded, but the weather got worse as the train moved south. Taylor stared out into the whitened wilderness with an uneasy feeling in the pit of his stomach. A little over a year ago, he had refused to travel to Toronto because he didn't want to leave his own home town. Now he was travelling to another country, and he wasn't sure he had made the right decision.

The train pulled into the Houghton station just before noon the following day, and Fred Taylor stepped off. Two men walked up to greet him. The first man moved past him and as Taylor turned back he realized he'd forgotten to tip the porter. The man handed the railroad employee ten cents, then turned around to shake Fred's hand.

"I'm Bruce Stuart," he said with a smile. "You owe me a dime."

The other man, Taylor soon found out, was Riley Hern, the club's goaltender. As they walked him to a nearby hotel, Taylor noticed that for the first time in days he no longer had that queasy feeling in his

stomach. He felt great, and even chuckled to himself when he overheard Hern whisper to Stuart, "He's awfully short."

Houghton was a boom town at the heart of Michigan's copper mining
country. It was populated by rugged miners who lived hard and liked
to play hard. Hockey became their favourite pastime, and the Am-
phidrome ice rink was a favourite hangout. Several hundred fans brought
their lunch to the arena to watch the highly touted new Canadian work
out in his first practice with the team. Taylor was quick to impress
the fans — but it took a little longer to impress his Portage Lake
teammates.

Practice had already begun when Taylor skated onto the ice. Bruce
Stuart made his way over to the new recruit.

"We play what you might call a scientific game down here in the
International League," Stuart explained. "The emphasis is on combination play among the four forwards. Lots of skating. Lots of stickhandling. Lots of passing. From what I hear, that should suit you fine.
Of course that doesn't mean you won't get hit. You'll find the hockey
here a lot tougher than you've been used to. Line up at rover."

They hadn't scrimmaged for more than a few minutes when Stuart
skated over to Taylor again.

"Smarten up, pal! What good is speed if you haven't got brains?"

Taylor was crushed. "What the hell are you talking about?" he
demanded.

"You keep breaking ahead of the other forwards."

"So can I help it if you guys can't keep up with me?" Taylor shot
back. He was angry and determined not to let Stuart get the better of
him.

Stuart smiled, trying to lighten the mood. "No, no, no," he said.
"Listen, I'm not looking for a fight. I'm just stating a fact. When you
get the puck, great, take off as fast as you can. We'll keep up, or at
least we'll try," he laughed. "Hell, I don't think there's anyone who'll
be able to keep up with you. But anyway, if I've got the puck, or
Grindy Forrester or Joe Hall has it on one of the wings and you break
ahead of us, you're offside. We can't pass you the puck. That hurts
the line and it hurts you. Like I told you, we play a scientific game.
Combination play. That means you've got to be thinking all the time.
Lag back when you have to stay onside. I know it's going to be hard

for you at first, but trust me, it's going to make you a better player and that'll be good for all of us."

Taylor nodded. He could see the logic of what Stuart said.

"OK, Bruce," he said. "I'll work on it."

If there was any doubt in Taylor's mind about the importance of what Bruce Stuart had told him, it vanished in his debut with Portage Lake. Taylor scored two goals in the game's first few minutes, but both were called back. He'd been offside. Taylor improved as the game wore on, adjusting his speed to his new linemates, but rushing the puck whenever he could. He buzzed the enemy net all night and scored two goals, one on a brilliant individual rush that brought the miners in the stands to their feet, and one on a neat three-way combination play with Stuart and Joe Hall. Taylor was clearly the star of the game as Portage Lake humbled its rival, Calumet, 8–2.

Taylor's star continued to rise over the next few weeks. His dazzling speed, his crisp, clean passes, and his blistering shot attracted attention. "He is a whirlwind," a local newspaper enthused, "and has not a superior on any of the league teams." As he led Portage Lake to win after win, and as more and more praise was heaped upon him, opposing players began gunning for him, and none more aggressively than Newsy Lalonde.

Until Taylor arrived in Houghton, Lalonde had been the top player in the International League, but because his team in Sault Ste. Marie, Ontario, did not provide him with the strong supporting cast the Portage Lake team gave Taylor, he had never attracted the same attention from the sportswriters. Newsy Lalonde looked at Taylor as a personal challenge and was always trying to intimidate him.

Since leaving Cornwall, Newsy had taken the advice of his boyhood hero to the extreme. He had no friends on the ice. Newsy played with his face set in a snarl and his elbows high, ready to come at opponents with a stiff shoulder or quick fists. Taylor preferred to beat his tormentors by working them into a corner, stealing the puck, and leaving them standing there, looking foolish, while he took off on one of his brilliant rushes. But it was tough to make Lalonde look foolish in a battle of skills. He was no mere goon; his speed and puck-handling skills were equal to Taylor's.

Unable to beat his new rival in the style he preferred, Taylor had to fight. Lalonde would attack and Taylor would counter, never backing down from a challenge. Despite his desire to rely on his skill, when pushed, Taylor could shove. He had sharp elbows and was pretty handy with the butt end of his stick. And if things got out of hand, Taylor had his teammate Joe Hall to fall back on. "Bad Joe" they called him, and they meant it.

Joe Hall's temper was the stuff of legend, and his reputation for violence was well known. If anyone wanted to get at Fred Taylor, they had to go through Bad Joe Hall. Usually, after Lalonde and Taylor had both given as good as they'd got, they would settle down and get back to playing hockey, but when Joe Hall thought the aggressive opponent was taking too many liberties with Taylor, he would step in. Hall's scraps with Newsy could turn vicious, with the smaller French player often resorting to stick swinging or swiping his skate at some unprotected area. "That fucking Frog isn't happy," Hall would grumble, "unless he finishes a game leaving someone needing a doctor."

Taylor spent two seasons with Houghton in the International League, and left only because the loop collapsed. A recession hit the U.S. economy in the spring of 1907, and the copper region of northern Michigan was among the hardest hit. The recession, combined with the fact that the small arenas throughout the league could not generate enough money to offset increasing payroll and travelling expenses, led to the demise of hockey's first pro circuit.

In his two seasons in Houghton, Taylor won two league scoring titles, was twice chosen as an all-star, and led Portage Lake to two league championships. The scientific hockey in Houghton had sharpened his abundant skills, and the rough play had taught him how to take care of himself. He left Houghton not only knowing he could compete, but aware he could dominate.

The collapse of the International Pro Hockey League had the teams back in Canada battling for the many talented players that were suddenly available. As he returned home to Listowel, Fred Taylor's name topped everyone's wish list.

Fred Taylor was the biggest celebrity Listowel, Ontario, had ever produced, and he returned home in April of 1907 to a hero's welcome.

Everywhere he went, he was greeted with handshakes and slaps on the back from the gentlemen, and adoring smiles, sometimes even a kiss on the cheek, from the young ladies. Taylor basked in the glory. He didn't exactly seek out the attention, but he wasn't one to shy away from it, either. All he did was play hockey. Could he help it if he played with a style and flair unmatched by anyone else the game had ever seen? Could he help it if his skills just happened to have the ability to lift crowds of thousands to their feet shouting his name?

Taylor spent the summer in Listowel playing lacrosse, his second love, to stay in shape for the upcoming hockey season, and playing baseball just for the fun of it. He also sifted through the numerous offers he was getting from hockey teams everywhere. It was funny, he thought, that just two years ago, when he was a junior, he'd been barred from playing in the province, forced to leave home. Now he had the hockey establishment at his mercy, and it was he who could pick and choose where he wanted to go, and when.

W.A. Hewitt had no control over hockey at the professional level, and for that reason Taylor considered joining the new Toronto team in the Ontario Professional Hockey League, Canada's first official pro circuit. It would be gratifying to rub Hewitt's nose in it by going to Toronto now, but the team had just signed Newsy Lalonde, and Taylor had no intention of playing beside him. He also ruled out offers from Quebec City and the many top teams in Montreal, because he had no intention of playing in French Canada. Taylor didn't like French Canadians, although, with the exception of Lalonde, he really didn't know any. And he didn't know Lalonde well, either. But what little he had observed of Newsy only strengthened the negative image he had of French Canadians. They were troublemakers who hated the English, not too bright, and easily provoked. No, he wouldn't play in Quebec.

One offer that interested Taylor came from the hockey club in Cobalt. He knew that M.J. O'Brien had a stake in the hockey teams around there, and that there had been a lot of money to go around since the silver strike a few years back. But he also knew that the hockey played there wasn't of the calibre of the leagues in Eastern Canada. He suspected that accepting the Cobalt offer might be interpreted in some quarters as an admission on his part that the great star of the International League wasn't up to playing on the best Canadian teams. That ruled out Cobalt.

Late in August, the train from Ottawa pulled in to the Listowel station carrying Malcolm Brice, sports editor for the Ottawa *Free Press*. Brice had been sent by the Ottawa Senators to sign Fred Taylor. Taylor had heard the team was interested in him and was not surprised when Brice showed up at his family home. Brice came right to the point.

"Mr. Taylor, I've been authorized by the Ottawa hockey club to offer you $500 for the ten-game season. That's a top wage for players in the Eastern Canada Amateur Hockey Association, and I happen to know it's $100 more than you were making in Houghton. We've also arranged to provide you with a job. A government job in the civil service. You'd be given a spot in the Immigration Department."

Ottawa was one of the top teams in the game, a veteran squad just two seasons removed from its three-year reign as Stanley Cup champion. It was a team, Taylor reasoned, that needed only his youthful spark to become champions again. He was keen on the Ottawa offer, but he'd learned more than simply how to play the game during his two-year stint in professional hockey. He had also learned how to negotiate.

"Mr. Brice, that's an interesting offer. And I'll give it my most serious thought. Can I see you out?"

Brice was shocked. "Mr. Taylor," he said slowly, "I don't believe you're fully aware of just how good this offer is. I have no intention of leaving until you give me an answer."

But Taylor was aware. The $500 salary didn't impress him, since he'd been offered more to play elsewhere, but he was very much intrigued by the promise of a job with the federal government — even if it was a Liberal administration. He knew he couldn't play hockey forever, and the immigration position could turn into a permanent career. Yet he didn't want to appear too anxious. He'd been burned by the hockey establishment once, and never intended to let it happen again. He would not give Brice a firm answer simply because he chose not to. He did, however, promise that he would come up to Ottawa in the future to discuss the offer at greater length.

"All right, Mr. Taylor," Brice sighed. "We'll see you in Ottawa."

XI

FRED TAYLOR LEFT LISTOWEL FOR OTTAWA IN OCTOBER of 1907. Even before he reached the capital city, he was already the subject of a heated controversy. Word of the negotiations with Taylor had split the Ottawa hockey public. Senators fans were very loyal to their team, and to the veteran players who had brought them the Stanley Cup. Taylor was seen as an outsider, a brash young player touted as a speedy and spectacular individualist. Many fans doubted he would be able to fit in with Ottawa's highly disciplined, conservative team approach. Even some of the team's directors and older players felt it was wrong to tamper with the club's lineup.

But Taylor was not without his supporters. The Ottawa veterans were getting old. Frank McGee and Harry Smith had already retired. Alf Smith was thirty-four years old. Harvey Pulford was thirty-two, and slowing down after fourteen seasons. Rat Westwick was also showing his age after fourteen years of hockey. It was time for an injection of youth, this group argued. The debate raged on for weeks in the Ottawa newspapers, with the latter view finally prevailing. Tommy Phillips was brought in from Kenora, and Marty Walsh, another refugee from the International League, was also signed. And now Taylor was travelling to Ottawa to round out the youthful complement.

Taylor's appointment in Ottawa was with grocery store magnate Llewellyn Bate, who also happened to be an important man in the Ottawa Senators hierarchy. Taylor met Bate and some other team officials at Bate's office on Sparks Street. As they talked about the terms of the deal Malcolm Brice had presented back in August, Taylor overheard one of the men say, "I expected him to be a lot taller." He shook his head and smiled.

A contract was signed, and Bate and Taylor left for the Department of Immigration where Taylor had been promised a job. They travelled in a horse-drawn carriage, from which Taylor was given his first glimpse of the city.

"I prefer a carriage to these newfangled automobiles," Bate explained. "Don't you?"

Taylor didn't answer. He didn't want to admit that he'd never ridden in an automobile.

"They're so dirty and so noisy," Bate went on, "and they really aren't very reliable. You never know when one of them might leave you stranded someplace."

The carriage headed east along Sparks Street, the fashionable main street of the city's business district, known as "the Broadway of Ottawa." Taylor was impressed by the electric street lamps and large buildings, some towering five or six storeys, and all in the latest styles: handsome red, yellow or brown brick, with flat copper roofs. Overhead was a maze of wires — power, telephone, telegraph, and streetcar.

Leaving Sparks Street behind, the carriage turned south towards Laurier Avenue. Crossing the Rideau Canal on the Laurier Avenue Bridge, the party was soon in the city's prestigious Sandy Hill district.

"Do you see that yellow brick house on the end of this block?" Bate asked Taylor, pointing at a quirkily shaped three-storey building with a blue mansard roof. "That's where the Prime Minister lives."

From Laurier's house, the carriage made its way out of Sandy Hill, crossing the canal onto Wellington Street. Before long, Taylor got his first glimpse of the Parliament Buildings.

In the spring of 1860, a public competition had been held for the design of the Parliament Buildings. The competition had been won by Thomas Fuller, an Englishman recently arrived in Canada, who was considered to be North America's foremost expert on Gothic architecture. Fuller had presented a plan for a robust Gothic revival building featuring rugged stone carvings and pointed openings above the many large doors and windows. Until well into the 1890s, the beauty of the Parliament Buildings had been all Ottawa had to offer. The city Fred Taylor had just finished touring could now boast of many attractions, but the Parliament Buildings remained Ottawa's most impressive site.

The Centre Block, which housed the Senate and the House of Commons, was a striking three-storey structure of concrete and stone, with a steep slate roof whose dark blue-grey colour was lightened by bands of green slate throughout. From Taylor's first distant glimpse, it appeared as though the entire building had been chiselled out of one massive piece of stone; a gigantic grey rock flecked with veins of yellow, black, and red. As he got closer he could see that the building was, of course, actually made up of countless smaller stones, most of them grey, but many of them the other colours he'd been able to see.

The Centre Block spread some 500 feet across Parliament Hill, and extended over 200 feet in back. At either end were twin towers that extended another storey or so above the roof. But the most dramatic feature of the Centre Block was the central tower. Rising high above the rest of the structure, the tower boasted the Parliament Buildings' most intricate brickwork, topped by tall stone spires that ringed the tower's steeply sloping roof. The roof was capped with a dome, on which a flag pole displayed the Union Jack.

As Taylor entered the Parliament Buildings, he was overcome by feelings of pride such as he could not recall experiencing since he had read about the Boer War as a young boy. He smiled as he remembered how he had wanted to run off then, and fight to preserve the British Empire.

Taylor was snapped out of his reflective state when he realized that Bate was telling him about the Honourable Frank Oliver, Minister of the Interior and top man in the Immigration Department — the man Taylor was to see about his new job.

"He's rather blunt," Bate warned, "and he can be quite intimidating, but once you get to know him, you might like his no-nonsense approach. He gets things done because he gets right to the point. Just try not to let him scare you. I think he senses that sort of thing."

"I understand he has quite a way with words," Taylor said with a smile. Anyone who knew anything about politics knew the Minister had a well-earned reputation for swearing.

Bate laughed. "You know I once heard that when he was a young man in Edmonton his fiancee refused to marry him unless he promised never to swear again! I guess he broke that promise!"

Taylor and Bate arrived at the immigration office and were ushered into Oliver's chamber. The Minister of the Interior was seated behind a large oak desk. He eyed Taylor up and down and sat back, giving no indication of what he might be thinking.

"Sit down," he ordered, waving Taylor into the chair across from his desk.

Despite Bate's warning, Taylor was intimidated, though he tried hard not to show it. Fortunately, he didn't have to sit for long as, just as he'd been told, Oliver came right to the point.

"Let me see your papers," the Minister barked.

Taylor didn't know what the man was talking about. He had no papers. He glanced over at Bate uncertainly. Perhaps he had the papers. But Bate merely looked back at him with the same expectant stare the Minister had on his face. Taylor was confused.

"Don't tell me," the Minister growled, "that you don't have your papers!"

Taylor said nothing.

"Nobody gets a job in my department," the Minister continued, biting off each word in a deliberate, insulting manner, "unless he has first obtained the proper papers from his local Member of Parliament!"

By now, Taylor was no longer scared. He was angry. Angry that none of the Ottawa officials had told him he needed these papers, and angry that he was being blamed for something he didn't perceive to be his fault. But Taylor wasn't about to let a Liberal politician get the better of him.

"Well, Mr. Minister," Taylor began, his calm tone of voice not quite masking a growing animosity, "I'm afraid I don't have the papers you require. You see, our local M.P. is not a Tory. And I don't like to deal with Liberals."

Bate stared at Taylor in disbelief, as an uneasy silence filled the room. Finally, the Minister got to his feet. "Why, you insolent bastard!" he bellowed. "How dare you speak to me like that!" The Minister's face was bright red. "Get this person out of my office!" he shouted at Bate, practically spitting out the word "person."

Bate hurried Taylor out of the room. "Do you know how long it took me to set up this meeting?" he demanded angrily. "The job was all but guaranteed, and then you go and say a thing like that!"

Fortunately, Bate knew he still had an ally in the Deputy Minister. "Don't even open your mouth when you meet him," Bate ordered. He hustled Taylor along the corridor to the Deputy's office. By the time they reached the door, both men were calmer. "I'll do all the talking this time!"

The meeting with the Deputy Minister went smoothly. He was an avid hockey fan who knew all about Taylor's on-ice exploits. A clerk's position was arranged, at a salary of thirty-five dollars a month.

"Welcome to the Civil Service," the Deputy Minister said.

With his job in the Immigration Department now secure, Fred Taylor's thoughts turned back to hockey. The 1908 season was scheduled to start the first week in January. The Ottawa Senators opened training camp in early December. Considering the controversy his signing had set off, Taylor didn't know what kind of reception he would get when he reported for his first practice. It turned out to be even worse than he had anticipated. The coach, Petie Green, wasn't convinced that the front office had done the right thing in adding this newcomer to his veteran roster, and he did little to make Taylor feel welcome. The Ottawa players ignored him in the dressing room. On ice, Taylor was a marked man, and practices began to resemble his old battles with Newsy Lalonde, as his new teammates continually tested him. The situation came to the boiling point after the Senators opened the season with a humiliating 8–1 loss in Quebec City.

The Quebec game had been played under poor conditions on soft, rutted ice. Taylor had centred a line with Phillips on left wing, Smith on right, and Westwick at rover. Westwick and Smith had clearly been unable to skate with Taylor. Even the speedy Phillips couldn't keep up. Taylor was left trying to carry the bulk of the offence alone, and the game had been a disaster. The train ride back to Ottawa was almost as bad, with coach Green and the Ottawa veterans trying to drink the game away.

"Petie," said Alf Smith in a loud voice, as he waved in Taylor's direction, "this cocky new son of a bitch isn't going to do us any damn good. He just wants to play his own game out there."

"Don't go blaming that on me, Alf," Taylor retorted. "None of you guys were there tonight! Not that it would have made much of a difference, from what I've seen. We haven't even had one good practice yet. None of you old bastards ever gives me the puck. Hell, none of you will even give me the time of day! And any time I do get the puck, one of you is running up my ass, slashing the back of my legs. No wonder we didn't look like a team out there tonight. We aren't a team. A team is supposed to work together, not against one another!"

Taylor stormed off to his berth. Right away, he regretted his outburst. Not that it wasn't true. He just didn't like to lose control like that. As he sat alone, rethinking the wisdom of having signed with Ottawa, Petie Green walked in and sat down next to him.

"Fred," he said, "I've got to hand it to you. You've put up with a lot of crap here. I guess I'm as guilty as anyone for letting it happen. I'm not surprised you blew your top."

Taylor could see that it was hard for Green to say these things. As he spoke, the coach was fidgeting with a piece of paper.

"I should have put aside my personal feelings for the good of the team. Obviously you wouldn't have been brought here if the brass didn't think you could help us win. I should have made that clear to everyone from the outset. I didn't, and I'm sorry."

Taylor nodded his head. It was good to hear something encouraging at last.

"But listen, you can't let these guys bother you. Smith, Westwick, even Pulford, I think they're all just jealous, and maybe a little scared. They know they're nearing the end of the line and I think seeing you makes them know it even more. But don't worry, they'll come around. Hell, how can they help it? You're the best damn hockey player I've ever seen!"

Taylor smiled. He didn't want to, but he couldn't help himself.

"Now there's something else I want to discuss with you," Green continued, straightening out the piece of paper he had crumpled. "I'm going to move you from centre to cover point. I've been giving it a lot of thought and I think it's the best way for us to use your speed. You won't have to worry so much about blending in with the other forwards, so you'll be able to roam more freely with the puck. You'll also be more responsible for defence, but with your speed and skill you should have no trouble."

The Senators had a week to prepare for their next game, the home opener, and switching Taylor to cover point proved an immediate success. With Marty Walsh now centring Phillips, Smith, and Westwick, the forward line began to jell. Pulford, moved from cover point to point, was able to concentrate solely on the defensive aspects of his game, an area in which the hard-hitting player excelled. And Taylor, as Green had predicted, was roaming the ice pretty much at will, creating his own scoring chances or setting up plays for the offence, then blazing back to help Pulford defend Percy Lesueur in goal. By the time the new arena on Laurier Avenue opened its doors for business, the Ottawa Senators were ready.

The Laurier Avenue Arena was billed as the grandest in all the land. The large steel and cement structure had been built as a pentagon to fit in among the neighbouring buildings, but inside, the ice surface and surrounding seating area had been constructed in an almost-perfect oval. The main entrance off Laurier Avenue opened on to a small lobby, with the box office against the far wall, then expanded into a large rotunda that featured a smoking room in one of the building's few right-angled corners. Walkways and promenades lined the east and west sides of the building, leading the patrons to their seats. The arena had a seating capacity of 4500. Another 2500 could be squeezed into standing room sections. The arena also boasted private boxes from which government officials and visiting dignitaries could view the proceedings. The building was not insulated, because the ice area had to be kept cold, but the promenades, lobby and rotunda, as well as the players' dressing rooms, were heated by steam — a welcome innovation during the cold Ottawa winters.

The Senators' opposition on opening night was the Montreal Wanderers, who had been Stanley Cup Champions for each of the past two seasons. The arena was packed to overflowing with a crowd of 7140 jamming every available perch, willing to stand wedged close together for hours to watch the battle. None of them went home disappointed.

The natural ice surface was in excellent condition, glistening like a newly polished mirror, as the two teams took to the ice. When the referee called the teams to centre ice to line up for the opening face-off, Marty Walsh easily won the draw from Ernie Russell, and the Senators swarmed to the attack.

For eleven minutes of the first half, the Wanderers succeeded in keeping the puck out of their net, despite being constantly on the defensive. Finally, with Ottawa forwards peppering goalie Riley Hern with shots, Marty Walsh swiped at a waist-high rebound and batted the puck into the cage. A minute later, Walsh scored again, batting in yet another rebound, this time after a rink-long rush by Taylor had been thwarted by Hern.

The Wanderers were caught off guard by the injection of speed and stamina the new players had added to the Senators' lineup. For the rest of the first half, the Montreal players chased Ottawa all over the ice, as the forward line of Walsh, Westwick, Phillips, and Smith shot up the sheet, snapping the puck from one to another. Phillips finished off three rushes by hammering the puck into the back of the net. Taylor, meanwhile, dashed from end to end, helping to set up the offence and teaming with Harvey Pulford to shut down the Wanderers on the rare occasions that they ventured into the Ottawa end. He had not yet scored, but his speed and daring won him roar after roar of applause from the spectators.

With only about a minute left until intermission, Taylor took possession of the puck near his own goal after a save by Lesueur. He sped up ice with it, as the huge crowd began buzzing. The noise from the stands grew steadily louder as Taylor, making two clever zigzag shifts, eluded Montreal forwards Moose Johnson and Ernie Russell.

"Fred!" Marty Walsh called, shouting for a pass, as the speedy cover point raced towards centre.

Taylor heard the cry and spotted Walsh on his right. He looked over in that direction, setting himself to make the pass, but played the puck to the left instead, bouncing it off the boards and right past a surprised Pud Glass. Side-stepping the beaten Wanderers forward, Taylor picked up the puck again after it rebounded around Glass and started a straight run down the side. The crowd noise grew greater still. As he streaked in on the Wanderers defence, Taylor cut back towards centre, turned on an extra burst of speed to split through

Tom Hooper and Art Ross, shifted to his backhand and then, drawing back to his forehand, slipped the puck past Hern to score.

The audience exploded with a deafening roar, shouting, clapping, and stamping their feet in appreciation of Taylor's stunning goal. The cheering had not yet subsided when the bell rang one minute later to end the half, with the score standing 6–0 in favour of the Senators. Ottawa continued to dominate the Wanderers in the second half, and when the final bell rang, the defending Stanley Cup champions found themselves on the wrong end of a lopsided 12–2 score.

Inside their dressing room, the Senators whooped it up. A ten-goal victory seemed to be just the tonic needed to unite what had been, just one week before, a bitterly divided team. As the Senators celebrated, the large crowd spilled onto the streets buzzing about the contest. Those who had supported the influx of new talent felt vindicated. Those who had opposed it now admitted that the newcomers would certainly do. Marty Walsh had scored five goals. Tommy Phillips had added four. Taylor had netted a pair of goals, but it was his end-to-end dashes that had made him the idol of the crowd.

Among the most enthusiastic of Taylor's new supporters was the city's best known sports fanatic, the Governor General, Earl Grey. His Excellency had earned a reputation as an avid sports enthusiast, a football fan who often sneaked away to the Ottawa field during office hours at Government House. He also enjoyed hockey, and was impressed by the speed and skill Fred Taylor had displayed that evening.

"That new player, Taylor," the Governor General remarked on his way out of the arena, "he's a cyclone if ever I saw one."

The remark was overheard by Malcolm Brice, who reported it in his newspaper column the next day. "In Portage La Prairie they called him a tornado. In Houghton, Michigan, he was known as a whirlwind. From now on he'll be known as Cyclone Taylor."

The ten-game hockey season was nearing completion when the Senators travelled to Montreal in early March for a rematch with the Wanderers. The early season fiasco in the nation's capital had caused fans to wonder if the loss of Lester Patrick and the death of Hod Stuart were too much for the Wanderers to overcome. But with Bruce Stuart, who had joined the team shortly after the 12–2 drubbing, and Art Ross, the Montreal side had proved to be every bit as dangerous as in the past. Both the Senators and Wanderers sported league-leading

6-and-2 records heading into the eagerly awaited rematch and, with just one game to go after that, the winner would be virtually assured of the league title. More importantly, because the Wanderers still held the Stanley Cup, and because beating the Cup holders for their own league title was equal to beating them in a challenge series, hockey's most prized trophy was also at stake.

Cyclone Taylor had by this time firmly established himself as the brightest new hockey star in Eastern Canada, but Art Ross was not far behind. Ross, who also played cover point, had been embarrassed by Taylor in their early season match-up and was out for revenge this time. Ross was a big man, heavier than Taylor by at least twenty-five pounds, and he played a tough but clean game. He wasn't blessed with Cyclone's exceptional speed, but he was skilled and smart.

From the opening face-off of the second Senators-Wanderers game, Ross and Taylor dominated as they darted across the ice, checking hard on defence and looking for opportunities to carry the puck. Twice in the first half, Ross sent Taylor sprawling to the ice with solid body checks. Not to be outdone, Taylor belted Ross with a head-on thud that left blood streaming from the defenceman's nose, dappling the ice with red splotches as Ross refused to leave the game for treatment.

The battle between the rival cover points kept the Montreal Arena's packed house of 6500 enthralled all night long. Taylor appeared to be getting the better of his dogged Montreal counterpart though, as twice he managed to break free of Ross, setting up a goal by Tommy Phillips on one occasion and scoring one himself on the other. Shortly after his goal, Taylor was off on another dazzling rush, but this time he could not shake his shadow. Ross laid him out with a sidelong check that knocked him off balance and sent him crashing into the boards. Taylor's head hit the wood with a thud. He fell unconscious to the ice.

As their star player was carried off, the Senators protested to the referee that Ross's hit had not been legal, but the referee ruled correctly that Taylor had been hit cleanly in open ice, and had merely fallen into the boards. With the Ottawa cover point now stretched out on a bench in the dressing room, and the rest of the Senators scrambling to pick up the slack, the tide turned in the Wanderers' favour and the Montreal side rallied for a 4–2 victory. For Ottawa, the game, and the season, were over.

XII

THE OTTAWA SENATORS UNDERWENT MANY OFF-SEASON changes after the 1908 campaign. Left with only Taylor, Walsh, and goaltender Percy Lesueur from the previous season, the Senators looked elsewhere to restock their team. Billy Gilmour was lured out of retirement. He had first joined the club back in 1902, when it was still known as the Ottawa Silver Seven, and had stayed with the squad through its three-year Stanley Cup reign before retiring in 1906. Dubbie Kerr of the rival Ontario Professional Hockey League was persuaded to leave Toronto for Ottawa. Bruce Stuart, Taylor's teammate from the Portage Lake days, came over from the Wanderers, lured by the promise of becoming team captain. Fred Lake was brought east, after a season in the Manitoba League, to team with Taylor on Ottawa's defence.

Much was expected from the new Senators team, but the newly expanded twelve-game season got off to a disappointing start when they were beaten 7–6 in overtime by the Wanderers. The Senators, however, were quick to make amends, whipping Quebec City 13–5 in their next outing, beating the Montreal Shamrocks 11–3, then crushing Quebec again, this time 18–4. Goals were the only official statistics recorded by the Eastern Canada Hockey Association, so the fact that almost half of Ottawa's scores had resulted directly from plays made by Taylor did not show up in the summaries. But word spread. Taylor was fast becoming the most acclaimed hockey player in the country.

Casual fans and hockey experts alike kept the high-scoring totals rung up during the seven-man era in perspective. There was greater concern with, and appreciation for, the general skills necessary to play the game. No one possessed those in greater abundance than Cyclone Taylor. He could skate like no one else, rushing the puck with electrifying expertise, setting up plays for others or scoring himself when called upon, and doing it all without sacrificing the defensive aspect of his game. As a cover point, defence was truly his main responsibility, and he could break up a dangerous attack as well as any man.

Despite the Senators' early season success, however, Cyclone Taylor had more than hockey on his mind. A year ago, shortly after his arrival in Ottawa, he had fallen in love.

Thirza Cook was a slender blonde with a vivacious personality and a twinkle in her blue eyes. She was employed as a secretary in the Immigration Department, and the co-workers had met shortly after Taylor's dazzling performance on opening night at the Laurier Avenue Arena.

Their first encounter was brief, with time for little more than an introduction and a compliment from Thirza on Fred's performance in the game. Yet Taylor was smitten. Confident as always, he asked her out for that very evening.

For their first date, the young couple went to the Rideau Canal. "I'll teach you to skate," Taylor offered loftily.

Taylor finished lacing up his skates first and took a few strides out onto the frozen canal. He turned towards Thirza and held out his arms to her, like a father teaching his young child.

"Now you try," he said.

Thirza made a few tentative moves towards him. She stopped, shrugging her shoulders helplessly. Then, smiling impudently, she blazed past Taylor, did a pirouette, and came to a stop. She bowed like a figure skater.

"Why you . . . !" Taylor cried, his voice a mixture of surprise and delight. "You're a fancy skater!"

"I'm sorry, Fred," Thirza laughed. "But the way you said to me 'I'll teach you to skate' without even asking me if I knew how — well, I just decided I'd play along, and then I'd show you a thing or two!"

"Well, holy crow, you certainly did that," Taylor replied, feeling put in his place. "But where did you learn to skate so well?"

"I've been a member of the Minto Skating Club ever since I was a little girl," Thirza explained. "I even play for their women's hockey team."

"Really," said Taylor, suitably impressed. "I'd love to see you play sometime. Especially if you're as good at that as you are at the little display you just put on for me.

"You know," he went on, his cockiness returning, "there's going to be an exhibition of fancy skating at the Olympics in London later this year. Maybe they'll ask you to go along."

"Do you really think I'm that good?"

"You could be," Taylor said slowly, as if considering the matter, "— if you'd take a few pointers from me."

The smile, as he held out his arms for Thirza, let her know he wasn't really bragging. She took his hand and, together, they glided and twirled across the canal.

As usual, there were many other skaters on the Rideau Canal that evening. Some, bent forward in the position of a speedskater, sped along the ice quickly, swinging one arm. Others, like Taylor and Thirza, skated arm-in-arm at a more leisurely pace. Still others, mostly young boys, gathered in small groups to play hockey.

"I'm Marty Walsh!" shouted one youngster, as a group of four boys prepared to play shinny.

"I'm Tommy Phillips!"

"I'm Fred Taylor!"

"No," said Taylor, leaving Thirza for a moment to join in the boys' fun. "I'm Fred Taylor!"

"WOW!" shouted the three boys, their young voices rising in unison. "It's Cyclone Taylor!"

"How do we know he's the real Cyclone Taylor?" the fourth boy asked cynically. "None of us have ever seen him before."

"That's him, all right!" said the boy who had wanted to be Fred Taylor. "I saw his picture in the newspaper once."

"It's me, sure enough," Taylor told the boys. "And how would you like it," he said to the one who had doubted him, "if I gave you and your friends four free tickets to next week's game?"

"WOW!" the boys exclaimed again — all four of them this time — when Taylor pulled the ducats out of his pocket.

"Now let's see how well you boys play!"

Taylor watched them for a few minutes, giving both encouragement and the occasional tip. Only when one of the boys shot the puck too far, sending it whizzing past Thirza, who had been looking on patiently, did Taylor remember he was not alone. "I've got to go," he said with a wave, and skated back to his abandoned date.

"I'm sorry, Thirza. I guess I just got carried away. How about if I make it up to you by buying us some apple cider?"

Thirza and Taylor skated off to find one of the vendors who sold the heated cider from large tin drums.

"Two cups, please," Taylor said.

"That'll be five cen— Hey! Aren't you Cyclone Taylor?"

"That's me," the hockey star confirmed.

"I was at the arena on opening night," the vendor gushed. "You were great. Just great!"

"Well thank you," Taylor responded, pulling out a nickel to pay for the drinks.

"Nah," said the vendor. "This one's on me!"

"That was very nice of him," Thirza said, as Taylor handed her the hot apple cider.

"Stuff like that happens a lot," Taylor said, shrugging off his celebrity.

"You were wonderful with the boys back there."

"I love kids," Taylor explained, with just the hint of an embarrassed grin. "They're the future heroes of the Empire."

"You're so sweet," Thirza told him, as she leaned forward to give him a peck on the cheek.

For their second date, Taylor attended one of Thirza's hockey games. He had no idea what to expect from a women's hockey game. He knew there were lots of women's leagues around the country now, but he had never actually seen a woman play the game. He envisioned skirts and knee socks and giggling girls chasing the puck playfully across the ice. He had the uniforms just about right, but the rest of his vision couldn't have been more wrong. The women's game was played every bit as seriously as the men's. There was not as much contact — the women didn't wear much padding — but the action was fast and exciting. Taylor soon found himself cheering for Thirza almost as wildly as the fans who usually screamed for him.

"You girls were great!" Taylor told Thirza when they met outside the rink after the game for the walk home. "I never imagined it would be so exciting."

"You live here?" Taylor asked, staring in awe at an opulent Sandy Hill home.

"Yes," said Thirza. "Would you like to come in?"

"Are you rich?" he asked, much too impressed by the size of the house to realize how presumptuous his question was.

"Are we rich?" she laughed, amused by the usually self-confident man's wide-eyed innocence. "No."

The Cooks had come to their position in the Ottawa upper crust through Thirza's aunt, who had married into the Booth family of multimillionaire lumber tycoons.

"Some people think so, but we're not really."

Thirza led Taylor into a small, low-ceilinged sitting nook under the stairway off the main hall. The sitting nook, though tiny, was lined with heavily padded divans scattered with cushions and bolsters, with several small tables of painted wood and polished brass placed near them. Taylor could smell the almost-too-clean aroma of furniture wax, as he picked his way through the bric-a-brac and potted plants which gave the room the cluttered effect so much in fashion. During the day, the sitting nook would be lit by two small windows at the far end, but, as Taylor and Thirza sat upon the settee, the room was illuminated only by the flickering light of a crystal gas fixture. The only sound was the loud ticking of the clock on the shelf.

As they sat beside each other in the tiny room, Taylor felt he and Thirza were in a private world of their own. He put his arm around Thirza's slim waist and pulled her towards him. Their lips met. That was when the hockey star first met Amelia Cook.

"Mother!" Thirza gasped. Taylor drew back quickly. "What are you doing up?"

"I was about to ask you the same question," Mrs. Cook shot back sternly, no trace of humour in her dark eyes.

"We were just saying good night," Thirza explained. Gathering her wits about her, she realized an introduction was in order.

"Mother, I would like you to meet Fred Taylor. He plays for the Ottawa hockey team."

"Pleased to meet you, Mrs. Cook."

Thirza's mother ignored the polite remark. "I think it's time you went home, Mr. Taylor," she said frostily.

For a moment, Taylor just stared at Amelia Cook. Then, slowly, he stood up. "Good night, Thirza. I'll see you at work tomorrow."

Thirza's widowed mother led Taylor to the door, her disdainful expression making it clear to him that in her mind he was nothing more than a lowly hockey player, even if he was being hailed as a local hero.

"I don't want you to see him again," Amelia Cook told her daughter, after returning to the sitting nook. "He's not a suitable companion for you. The social gap is simply too great. You should know that, dear."

"Mother, I don't think you've given him much of a chance."

By the time the Ottawa Senators came to the end of their home-ice schedule in 1909, they had added six more victories to their early season winning streak and stood atop the league standings with a 9-and-1 record. Their final home game would be against their archrivals, the Montreal Wanderers, who were a close second with a mark of 9 and 2. A Wanderers victory would move them past the Senators and assure them of nothing worse than a tie for first place. An Ottawa victory would clinch the league title. The Stanley Cup would then return to the Capital, the Senators having beaten the defending Cup champions for their own league crown.

Four nights before the big game, the Ottawa club hosted the Montreal Shamrocks in a Saturday night game at the Laurier Avenue Arena. Cyclone Taylor, as usual, was at his dashing best, electrifying the crowd with his end-to-end rushes, one of which resulted in an Ottawa goal. Minutes later, Taylor was off again, picking up the puck in his own end and carrying it up ice. The large audience groaned as Taylor was stripped of the puck by Shamrocks defenceman Jack Laviolette, who knocked it behind the net. Taylor, seeing that Billy Gilmour had dropped back to cover his defensive position, chased Laviolette behind the goal and fell down. As he did, his right foot was caught by Laviolette's skate. A loud ripping sound could be heard as the leather boot of Taylor's skate gave way. In an instant, blood gushed from the tear.

Frightened fans watched in silence as Taylor limped off the ice, leaving a glistening red trail that quickly froze solid. In the dressing room, a clubhouse boy removed the torn, blood-soaked skate. Blood continued to pour from the wound, a three-inch jagged gash between Taylor's right ankle and heel that cut deep, almost to the bone. The team physician wrapped a towel around the foot and Taylor grimaced as pressure was applied in an attempt to stop the bleeding.

"I hope this won't keep me from playing on Wednesday," Taylor said between clenched teeth, trying to maintain an aura of calm.

The doctor sighed. Hockey players, he thought, shaking his head. "It's a pretty bad cut, Cyc. I'm going to put in some temporary stitches, then send you to the hospital for a more thorough examination. As for playing Wednesday, well . . . " The doctor just shrugged.

As the fallen hockey hero was being tended to, a light but insistent knocking was heard on the dressing room door.

"Go see who it is," the doctor told the clubhouse boy. "But if it isn't someone important, send them away."

The boy returned a moment later.

"It's Miss Cook, Cyclone."

"She's my girl," Taylor told the doctor. Despite her mother's disapproval, Thirza had continued to see him. "Is it all right if she comes in?"

"I wouldn't advise it," the doctor said. "But it's up to you."

"Bring her in, Henry," Taylor instructed the clubhouse boy.

Thirza was shocked when she saw him. He was so pale after losing all that blood. Reflexively, she lowered her gaze away from him, but the pile of bloodstained towels she saw on the floor was an even more sickening sight. She was forced to look up again. Her voice trembled.

"How do you feel, Fred?"

"The doc says I'll live." But the self-assured look on his face vanished quickly as the doctor began sewing up the deep cut. When he was done, there was a lot of excess skin left hanging from Taylor's foot, so the doctor grabbed a pair of scissors and trimmed it off.

That was too much for Thirza. She felt a strange dizziness come over her and feared she was about to faint. She sat down weakly on a bench and lowered her head. When she regained her strength, she informed her beau that she wouldn't be attending any more games.

The Senators went on to beat the Shamrocks 11–2 that night, but all the talk for the next few days was of whether Cyclone would be ready in time to face the Wanderers.

Despite the cold snap that gripped Ottawa in the days leading up to the pivotal game, fans began lining up at the Laurier Avenue and Slater Street entrances to the arena at half past five on game day. The early arrivals were mostly youths who could not afford the $1.25 price tag attached to the reserved seats and most certainly couldn't pay ticket scalpers three and four times that. They had paid fifty cents for rush seats or a quarter for standing room, and they had to be there well ahead of time to claim the best possible spots.

By seven o'clock, a full two hours before face-off, the crowd outside the Laurier Avenue entrance extended well into the road, while from Slater Street a long, winding column stretched almost two full city blocks up to Queen. A decision was made to open the doors. The people in line, who had been stamping their feet in an effort to stay warm, saw the opening of the doors as a signal to begin their wild rush, but after several minutes of heated tussling, everybody seemed to settle down and accept what would still be a long wait. Some thirty policemen no doubt helped the crowd make up its mind.

Once inside, fans of both teams went about the business of decorating the arena in a manner befitting a Stanley Cup game. Large white banners bearing the broad red band and red "W" of the Wanderers were held aloft by the Montreal faithful, but they were all but overwhelmed by the red, white, and black colours displayed by Senators fans. As the crowds continued to pour in, the reserved section was soon filled to overflowing. Even the beams extending over those seats were occupied, as some of the more daring fans crawled out to the ends. There, perched high above the multitudes, they enjoyed an unobstructed, if somewhat dangerous, view of the action.

At half past eight, team captain Bruce Stuart led the Ottawa Senators onto the ice. The crowd, buzzing in anticipation for over an hour, exploded in thunderous cheers. All eyes turned to the opening behind the Ottawa bench as the fans waited to see who would appear. Stuart was followed by Percy Lesueur, then by Walsh, Kerr, Lake, and Gilmour. The crowd was then quieted by the arrival of Edgar Dey. Did the appearance of the little-used substitute player mean what they thought it meant?

Suddenly, from behind the Ottawa bench, emerged the familiar redtoqued figure of Cyclone Taylor. With his injured right foot bound in cotton batting and lint, encased in a skate boot protected by a broad welt of stiff leather extending from the sole to the top, Taylor skated onto the ice. His first few strides showed he was still in pain, as he appeared to limp on his skates and tended to drag his right foot. Taylor tried to take it easy in the warm-up until his foot got used to the strain. The cold weather had left the ice very hard, which made skating easier, and soon Taylor was darting up and down the sheet, going through his limbering-up exercises. When he took off with his defence partner, Lake, on a brisk practice rush, the crowd roared its approval. Cyclone was all right!

The game got under way at a quarter past nine. Wanderers centre Steve Vair beat Walsh to the draw and carried the puck into the Ottawa end, only to be stopped by Taylor. The large throng rose in anticipation of a Cyclonic rush, but instead of carrying the puck back up ice, Taylor fed it across to Lake, who flipped it into the far end. But soon the crowd was on its feet again, as Taylor took a drop pass from Billy Gilmour. This time Cyclone streaked up ice on his first rush of the night, and set up Marty Walsh for the game's first goal. Taylor wasn't letting the big crowd down.

Within a few minutes, Ottawa's lead was upped to 2–0, but the Wanderers fought back when Steve Vair managed to slip the puck past Percy Lesueur to halve the Senators lead. A short time later, Vair collided with Lake and had to leave the game with a wide cut above his knee. Kerr was sent to the bench to even up the sides until Moose Johnson, who was sitting out the game as the Wanderers' substitute player, could suit up and get into action.

Lake was penalized for his hit on Vair, so the Wanderers went on the man advantage, six players to five. When Bruce Stuart was sent off for a tripping penalty, the Senators were left with only four men on the ice. The Wanderers were all around the Ottawa net, pressing for the equalizer, but their efforts backfired when Cyclone Taylor spotted an opening. Taking the puck behind his own goal, he noticed Art Ross had pinched in too far and was slow in returning to his defensive position. Taylor headed up ice. Outskating all who tried to stop him, he streaked down the open side of the ice and, from a sharp angle, fired the puck past Hern. The crowd leaped to its feet, chanting his name.

The Wanderers, proud champions that they were, fought back from the 3–1 deficit and tied the game before intermission. However, the flow of the game turned in Ottawa's favour during the second half, with the younger and better conditioned Senators taking the play to the more experienced but ageing Montrealers. When Marty Walsh scored, to put the Senators ahead 5–3 with just five minutes to play, the game was all but over. Dubbie Kerr rammed home a trio of goals in the final three minutes to bring the final score to 8–3. The Stanley Cup had returned to Ottawa.

With the ringing of the bell to mark the game's conclusion, nearly half of the 6500 fans swarmed out onto the ice. Lake, Walsh, Gilmour, and Taylor were swept off their feet by the adoring crowd, the Ottawa rooters robbing Taylor of his stick and gloves as souvenirs of the brilliant struggle. Cheer after cheer rang out as fans began to spill out of the arena, screaming the news to the outside world. Taylor was hailed as the star of the game, and for hours afterwards shouts of "Cyclone!" could be heard ringing through the streets. No one who saw him play that night would have believed that this was the last time Cyclone Taylor would ever appear in Ottawa dressed in the home team's red, white, and black.

Great changes were afoot in the hockey world as Cyclone Taylor prepared to report to training camp with the Senators for the 1910

season. He'd heard all about the meetings in Montreal the month before, where the Wanderers had been booted out of the newly created Canadian Hockey Association. It just didn't seem right, Taylor thought, not to be playing the Wanderers this season. He couldn't understand what the league directors had been thinking. How could they freeze the Wanderers out of the new league simply because they didn't approve of the team's move to the smaller Jubilee Rink? Hockey owners are so damn greedy, he decided.

Taylor had also heard about the rival league formed by the Wanderers and Ambrose O'Brien: the National Hockey Association. He remembered the O'Briens from his last days in the International League, when they had offered him great sums of money to join the team they backed in Cobalt. He'd heard they were offering big money again, this time to lure players to their team in Renfrew. He wasn't surprised when he was soon being followed to and from work by George Martel. The O'Briens had assigned Martel the job of getting Fred Taylor's signature on a contract.

The press soon got word of the negotiations, and sportswriters were having a field day. Stories appeared daily in the Ottawa newspapers reporting that Taylor had signed with Renfrew, or that he was about to sign. Others claimed he had agreed to stay with the Senators. Only one thing appeared certain — the stakes were high. Renfrew was reported to have offered $2000 each to Ottawa stars Taylor, Lake, Kerr, and Walsh. Soon the offer was reportedly up to $2500 a year for two years, plus off-ice jobs for anyone who wanted them. Kerr and Walsh, the papers said, had actually met with M.J. O'Brien himself to discuss finances.

The rival league was beginning to win admiration for the way it was conducting business. "The Renfrew club," reported the *Ottawa Citizen*, "has been playing it high but honestly, as they gave Ottawa to understand that it was to be war to the hilt, and have been carrying on all their negotiations in a straight businesslike manner." Martel, when accused of tampering by Malcolm Brice, told the *Free Press* reporter, "We are not stealing the Ottawa players. All our dickering has been done openly and above board. Before we talked business with any of them, we first asked each player to go to the Ottawa club and tell the officers that they had been approached by us, and not until the Ottawa club had made their terms to any player did we make our offer. We want the very best team that money can buy, the best team in the world, in fact, and we don't care where they come from.

We are after the Ottawa men because we think they are the best in the country."

Martel followed him around for about a week before Taylor finally agreed to talk terms. They met at the Windsor Hotel, a fashionable establishment on the corner of Metcalfe and Queen. It was the most desirable hotel in the city for businessmen, since it boasted what the hotel management modestly called the finest bar in Canada. Many a deal was finalized among its antique oak finishings. The Windsor Hotel was where M.J. O'Brien made his headquarters in the city.

Martel wasted little time. "Mr. Taylor," he began, "we in Renfrew have been looked down upon and laughed at by the hockey establishment for too long now. That is going to stop. We are going to ice the greatest hockey team anyone has ever seen, but we can't do it without you. There is no disputing your status as the biggest star in the game. What will it take to get you to sign with us?"

Taylor got out of his chair and began to walk around the room. He picked up several of the objects scattered about, turning them over in his hands, examining them and then putting them back down. He knew he held all the cards in these negotiations, and he had a figure in mind.

Amelia Cook had never warmed up to Cyclone Taylor. For two years, he and Thirza had continued seeing each other, despite Mrs. Cook's discouragement. By this time, Taylor very much wanted to marry Thirza, but he had not yet asked her. There was something he wanted to accomplish first.

Taylor had been poor as a child. He had first learned to play hockey wearing his older sister's skates, because his parents could not afford a pair for him. He'd been forced to leave school and take a job to supplement the family income. He had not always been able to get what he wanted then, but in the years since, he had found that, if he tried hard enough, he could usually get what he needed. What he needed now was Thirza: he loved her and was certain that she loved him.

Taylor was tired of constant rebuffs from Mrs. Cook. He could do nothing about his lack of a pedigree, but if Mrs. Cook wanted financial security for Thirza, then he was determined to show her he could provide that. He had embarked on a strict savings program, and though his combined salary from hockey and the civil service was now almost $3000 per year, he knew it would take a lot longer than he would like to build his savings to an amount large enough to impress Thirza's mother — unless something much more lucrative came along.

Taylor took a deep breath. "I want $10,000," he told Martel, and sat down to await his reaction.

To Taylor's surprise, the Renfrew hockey official took his enormous request in stride. "I think we could work out a three-year contract paying you $10,000," Martel replied smoothly.

Taylor, ever the shrewd negotiator, was not impressed. "I'm not looking for a three-year contract," he stated, though $3300 had been about what he had calculated would be the most he could get for a single season. Now he was going to see how much higher Martel was prepared to go.

"I'll settle for $5000 for this season," Taylor said firmly.

Martel sat for a moment thinking it over. "Yes, I think that could be arranged," he said. It was all Taylor could do to keep from leaping out of his chair in triumph, but there were a few more things he wanted to settle first.

"You'll have to arrange for a leave of absence for me from my job here. Five thousand dollars is a lot of money, but I'm not prepared to give up a promising future in Immigration."

"Fair enough, Mr. Taylor. Consider it done. You'll find the O'Briens have many friends in high places. Your job will be waiting for you when the season is through."

"I also want the money deposited in my Ottawa bank before I leave the city. I hear you offered to do that for Walsh and Kerr."

"We did indeed, Mr. Taylor. But they were only offered $2500. We'll deposit the sum in your bank as you wish, but with one condition. The money is not to be withdrawn until the end of the season."

"In that case, Mr. Martel, I shall require a ten percent bonus, payable upon my arrival in Renfrew. I'm going to need some kind of money there."

"True enough, Mr. Taylor, and if you're willing to settle for a five percent bonus, I can write you a cheque right now."

Taylor agreed. He and Martel shook hands on a $5250 deal that would pay Cyclone Taylor more money per game than any other athlete in all of North American team sports.

Ambrose O'Brien was at the family home in Renfrew when George

Martel phoned to tell him he had gotten Taylor to sign a contract. It was the best possible news. Ambrose knew Cyclone Taylor was the key to success. He was the top draw in hockey, and the fact that Ambrose had gotten him for the National Hockey Association gave the new league instant credibility, while at the same time seriously damaging the reputation of the Canadian Hockey Association. Not only that, but with Cyclone Taylor joining the Patrick brothers in Renfrew, the team was quickly shaping up as a powerhouse. Ambrose knew that, even if he could lure no other top talent, he already had a team capable of winning the trophy all the town coveted: the Stanley Cup. The pursuit of the elusive prize was proving expensive, but with victory within his grasp, no amount of money seemed too much.

XIII

The Western Hemisphere . . . has no cause for humiliation for the part it has performed in the march of civilization. It has not accomplished everything; far from it. It has simply done its best, and without vanity or boastfulness, and recognizing the manifold achievements of others, it invites the friendly rivalry of all the powers in the peaceful pursuit of trade and commerce. . . . Isolation is no longer possible or desirable. . . . No nation can longer be indifferent to any other. . . . The period of exclusiveness has passed.

William McKinley,
President of the United States.
September 5, 1901

OTHER PEOPLE IN OTHER PLACES HAD OTHER CONCERNS. Concerns that had nothing to do with how much money might be spent on a hockey player or a hockey team. Nothing to do with who won the Stanley Cup. These concerns — and how they were resolved — would affect not only the great Canadian game, but the country itself.

While Ambrose O'Brien sat at home in Renfrew considering his good fortune, a man named Sean Mitchell was huddled together with three other men in the dimly lit back room of an Ottawa tavern. Mitchell was a man with few distinguishing characteristics. He was of average height and average weight. His clothes were well tailored. His medium-length brown hair was neatly cropped, his moustache trimmed just below his upper lip. But Mitchell's appearance was deceiving. Below the calm facade was an intense man. A driven man. Still, he was a man well versed in all the social graces, and accustomed to moving in elite circles.

Mitchell and the others sat around a heavy wooden table. Racks of wine bottles lined the walls.

"Gentlemen," said Mitchell, as he poured drinks for the others, "I wish to refresh your memories of an event that took place some years ago." He then proceeded to tell his tale.

On Saturday, August 31, 1901, Leon Czolgosz walked into the barroom of J. Nowak's hotel and saloon on the east side of Buffalo, New York. Looking around, he saw the bar on the far side of the room and behind it a man who looked to be in charge. It was the innkeeper himself, John Nowak.

"A room for one, please," Czolgosz said quietly. He dabbed at his forehead with a handkerchief, wiping the sweat from his brow. It was evening now, but the afternoon's humidity still hung in the air. It had been a hot day. It had been a hot summer.

"Here for the Pan-American Exposition, are you?" the innkeeper asked, though it was more a statement than a question.

Nowak eyed the newcomer. He liked to get an idea of what type of man he was dealing with before renting out a room. Nowak was reassured by what he saw: Czolgosz was neatly dressed in a grey suit with a black shoestring tie. Nowak thought the man might be a bartender himself, in Buffalo on holiday to see the fair, though there was something about the faraway look in his eyes that suggested something else. It was almost a dreamy look that hinted at a more creative side. Perhaps the man was a writer or even an artist.

"It's two dollars a week," Nowak said, deciding Czolgosz would be an acceptable tenant. "Payable in advance."

Czolgosz pulled a large wad of money out of his billfold. He peeled off two crisp one-dollar bills and placed them on the bar.

"What name shall I write on the receipt?" Nowak asked. The answer surprised him.

"John Doe."

Czolgosz deviated little from the everyday routine he settled into after first making his appearance at Nowak's. For three straight mornings, he woke early, read his newspapers, then left his dark, dreary room for the ornately decorated grounds of the Exposition. He returned to the hotel every night, a roll of newspapers tucked under his arm. He might linger at the bar for a few minutes before heading to his room, ordering a drink or just watching a card game. He always ordered good whiskey, Nowak noticed with approval. None of that five-cents-a-shot rotgut most of his other patrons purchased.

In the Buffalo newspapers Czolgosz took to his room each night and studied each morning was ample information to help him plot strategy for the stunning deed he planned. President McKinley was coming to town for a three-day visit. Sometime during those three days, Leon Czolgosz was determined to murder the President of the United States.

The President's train, Czolgosz read on the morning of September 4, would arrive at the Amherst Street station on the Pan-American grounds at six o'clock that evening. At least 40,000 people were expected to turn out to greet the President. He would be closely guarded. Still, Czolgosz decided, he too would be at the station that day. He hoped to act as soon as possible. Before he lost his nerve.

Czolgosz made a slight alteration to his carefully followed daily routine that afternoon. He had brought a single-shot handgun to Buffalo, but had decided since then that he would need an automatic revolver, one that could fire several shots in succession if need be. He stopped at a hardware store on Main Street and purchased a nickel-plated .32 calibre Iver Johnson six-shot automatic. It was even easier to buy than he had imagined. He simply picked out the gun he wanted, paid for it, and went on his way.

By late afternoon, shortly before the scheduled arrival of the President's special train, Czolgosz made his way to the Amherst Street depot. He found a huge crowd of well-wishers already gathered there, perhaps even more than the estimated crowd of 40,000. He began pushing his way through the dense throng, using his elbows to fight his way along. His hands were pressed firmly in the outside pockets of his suit jacket. His right hand caressed the ivory butt of the pistol, his index finger twitching nervously around the trigger.

As he neared the inner area of the station, Czolgosz noticed several dapper Victorias drawn up in front of the railway gate, waiting to whisk away the presidential party. How inappropriate the decorative little four-wheeled carriages with their fancy folding tops will be, Czolgosz thought to himself, when I get done here. They'll wish they had thought to bring an ambulance. Or better yet, a hearse.

Throughout his brief moment of daydreaming, Czolgosz continued to push forward through the crowd, but, lost for that moment in his own thoughts, he pushed too far. He found himself moving through a gate into an area that had been cordoned off for the President's safety. A guard, one of many protecting the President — there were soldiers in colourful parade dress mounted on horses, plain-clothed detectives, and uniformed Exposition guards patrolling the area — was on top of him instantly, yelling first, then brandishing his club.

Czolgosz was terror-stricken. His brief moment of fantasy had left him in peril. His plan would have to be aborted for now, but that was the least of his worries. If he was caught with a gun in his pocket, he would surely be jailed. He turned and began to run. He had not taken more than a few steps when he felt the guard's big hand on his shoulder. In the next instant, a shove from the guard sent him sprawling in the dust. Czolgosz lay there for a moment, afraid to get up. Afraid even to look up. He expected to be seized and taken away. Instead, he heard an ear-splitting train whistle, and then another, and another, and another until it seemed every whistle in the city had joined in. Finally, Czolgosz looked up. The guard, along with all the other guards, soldiers, and policemen, had turned away and was moving towards the tracks to welcome the President.

Czolgosz picked himself up, and, without even bothering to brush off the dust, fled the station. It was not until he had lost himself in the great crowd of the Exposition that he realized no one was taking the slightest notice of him. A wave of relief washed over him.

September 5, 1901, had been designated President's Day at the Pan-American Exposition. The citizens and guests of Buffalo awoke to glorious sunshine streaming from a cloudless sky. The streets were awash in red, white, and blue as thousands of American and Exposition flags flew, it seemed, from every office building, street corner, and front porch in the city. It was a perfect day.

Leon Czolgosz was among the many who arose early that morning. More than 50,000 people were expected to jam the Esplanade in the centre of the Exposition grounds to catch a glimpse of the President and hear him speak. Czolgosz wanted to find the ideal spot from which to carry out his crime.

The grounds of the Pan-American Exposition were huge, one mile in length and almost the same distance in width. The dominating structure of the Exposition was the 389-foot Electric Tower. As it climbed skyward, the Electric Tower tapered into a three-stage crown of diminishing proportions, with each level slightly more ornate than the level below. On the very top of the building was a guilded statue of the Goddess of Light. At night, the entire Exposition glittered in the dazzling brilliance of over a half-million electric lights — each one powered by the turbines at nearby Niagara Falls — but no building shone more spectacularly than the Electric Tower.

Beyond the beauty of the Electric Tower lay a maze of colour and an amalgamation of architectural styles. The Spanish Renaissance style prevailed, in keeping with the Exposition's Pan-American theme, but scattered, seemingly at random, throughout the grounds were structures modelled after those in ancient Rome and Greece or Victorian England, and others that seemed inspired by the tales from the *Arabian Nights*. Fountains were everywhere and a number of lakes, canals, and bays had been created to add to the beauty of the surroundings.

Czolgosz arrived at the Esplanade at the centre of the Exposition grounds shortly before nine in the morning. Much to his dismay, the area was already teeming with people. Czolgosz again elbowed his way through the crowd, hands in his pockets. He hoped to find a spot where he could whip out his weapon and fire upon his victim from close range, but that, he soon realized, was not going to be easy. Although the police presence around the big, purple-draped rectangular stand on the Esplanade was much more modest than Czolgosz had expected, the crush of people would still make his task difficult.

Czolgosz was staring straight ahead, eyeing in the distance the spot where the President would soon appear. William McKinley was fifty-eight years old. Polite reports referred to him as "portly," but the President was, in fact, fat — not with the muscular bulk of a large man, since he was actually of less than medium height, but simply with the bloated belly of a man who had lived the good life. McKinley's less-than-perfect physique, however, did not detract from a handsome face that showed no wrinkles or any other signs of the strains of the Presidency. He possessed a calm, unruffled manner, and only the greying around the temples of his thinning hair hinted at the pressures of his high office. He looked, most people, thought, as a President should.

William McKinley was the most popular man in the White House since Abraham Lincoln. While in office, McKinley had seen the United States return to prosperity behind a policy of high tariffs, after the lean years under President Grover Cleveland. He could boast of the American victory over Spain in the Spanish-American War, and of overseas expansion with the annexation of Hawaii and the acquisition of the Philippines. All in all, under his leadership, the United States had emerged as a powerful force in world affairs.

Of course, McKinley was not without his detractors. There were those who charged that his protective tariffs did little to help the average American. In fact, far from protecting the masses, McKinley's opponents cried, the tariffs only served to subsidize the rich. Still, McKinley had had no trouble gaining re-election and now, six months into his second term, he felt he had the nation solidly behind him — though there were rumours that he was ready to back down from his long-standing tariff policy.

Czolgosz was still staring straight ahead, squeezed in on all sides so that he could hardly move. Hands still in his pockets, he studied the great canopy rising above the purple-draped stand. The canopy rose at least twenty feet above the dais from which the President would address the crowd. The poles supporting the canopy were striped red and white. A gold painting of an American Eagle had been placed at the very top of the canopy, and flags sprouted out from behind the eagle, as if they were an extension of its raised wings.

Suddenly, Czolgosz heard a deep boom over the murmuring of the crowd. His heart pounded madly. He first thought was that his twitching finger had inadvertently shot off the gun in his pocket. The second boom eased that fear. His heartbeat slowed to normal when he realized, as shot after shot rang out, that the President was being accorded a twenty-one-gun salute.

After the final shot had been fired, President McKinley appeared. Cheers drowned out the President's first words. He held up his left hand in a gesture asking for silence. When the crowd had quieted, McKinley went on.

Czolgosz burned inside as the President spoke. The twenty-one-gun salute would have been the perfect time to strike, but the large crowd had made it impossible to find an opening near the dais, and the jostling he had been receiving from the boisterous onlookers would have made it impossible to take dead aim. The cheers that rang in his ears added to the burning Czolgosz felt. It seemed to him as though the cheers mocked him. If he didn't get the President tomorrow, the opportunity would be lost.

Czolgosz knew from the newspapers he had read that President McKinley was scheduled to visit Niagara Falls on the final morning of his three-day visit. He would return to Buffalo later that afternoon to shake hands with the people at a public reception at the Temple of Music on the Exposition grounds. He considered following the President on his trip to the Falls, but decided against it. Better, he thought, to get to the fair early and secure a position in the reception line.

It was another hot, humid day as Leon Czolgosz stood in line outside the Temple of Music. The building was one of the most beautiful structures on the Exposition grounds. The top floor of the octagon-shaped Temple was slightly smaller than the base, like a two-tiered wedding cake. Intricately carved designs made from wood and stone framing the doors, windows, and ledges were complemented by stone sculptures in high relief on the walls. The glass bulbs for the electric lights that outlined the upper storey and its dome, though unlit during the day, reflected the brilliant sunlight, making the Temple of Music glitter.

Sweat poured off Czolgosz as he stood in the heat. It was just past noon, and President McKinley wasn't scheduled to arrive back at the Exposition until just before four, but Czolgosz hadn't wanted to take any chances. He'd seen the crowds the President had drawn and was determined to get close to McKinley this time. He dabbed at his fore-head with his handkerchief, mopping up the perspiration, when suddenly an idea came to him. What if he used his handkerchief as a bandage, wrapping it around his right hand as he held the gun tightly? He could carry the weapon right there in his hand without arousing any suspicion, and he would have it ready to fire the instant he needed it. It was a brilliant idea. Everything was ready now. All that remained was to stand in line and wait for his opportunity.

At three-thirty on the afternoon of September 6, the train that had taken President McKinley on his excursion to Niagara Falls chugged back into Buffalo. The President, as always, was immaculately dressed. The action of climbing down from his railcar caused the flaps of his frock coat to draw back, exposing a black bow tie and a Piccadilly collar atop his neat white shirt. The white cumberbund that wrapped around his thick waist was also visible. On his head was a black silk top hat. At five minutes to four, the President boarded his Victoria coach and, surrounded by a special army guard, proceeded to the Temple of Music.

The waiting crowd had swelled considerably since Czolgosz arrived. He ignored attempts by those in line around him to involve him in their idle chatter. He was lost in his own thoughts, but not so much so that he was oblivious to what was going on around him. He had noticed the increased security. Helmeted soldiers of not one but two National Guard regiments, rifles at the ready, marched before the entrance. Mounted policemen rode their horses up and down the Esplanade, maintaining a semblance of order among the growing crowd. Czolgosz estimated that he would pass before as many as eighty guards before reaching the President, not to mention the Secret Service agents who were sure to be at McKinley's side.

Just before four o'clock, Czolgosz heard a great cheer well up from behind him. Soon he saw the President's mounted escorts ride into view, the plumes of feathers atop their helmets bouncing in rhythm with their horses. The cheers grew louder as the President himself could be seen. Fluttering handkerchiefs waved in greeting. Some men tossed their hats in the air. Little do they know, Czolgosz thought, what they are about to witness. The President was escorted into the Temple of Music, and a moment later the heavy Temple doors swung open. The crowd filed in.

The President extended his right arm in a handshake, and used his left arm to move the well-wishers along. Czolgosz moved slowly. The soldiers and guards on either side of the line were so close he could reach out and touch them. But he just kept inching ahead, eyes glued on McKinley — unaware of anything else — until only one man stood between him and the President.

Czolgosz was then shaken from his trancelike state by the approach of one of the President's Secret Service agents. Panicked, Czolgosz looked around quickly. Had something given him away? He glanced down at his right hand. The handkerchief still concealed his weapon. No one could have known there was anything but his hand under there. What had gone wrong?

Czolgosz watched in amazement as the Secret Service man brought his hand down roughly on the shoulder of the man who stood in front of him in line. It was this man who had aroused the suspicion of the guards! He was short and heavy, with darkish skin, a thick black moustache, and shifty, dark eyes. After a moment's investigation, the suspicious-looking man was allowed to move on. No one suspected anything from the neatly dressed young man behind him.

President McKinley extended his right hand to Czolgosz, but hesitated for a moment when he saw the bandage. A handshake seemed an improper gesture under the circumstances, but he was unsure of what would be correct. He never got a chance to make up his mind. Two shots rang out in quick succession.

The first shot sounded muffled, like a small firecracker exploding. The President rose on his toes, clutching his chest. He started to pitch forward. A small cloud of smoke billowed forth from the handkerchiefed hand of the man in front of him. A second shot rang out, striking McKinley in his large stomach, driving him back with the force of the blow. He slumped to the ground, an expression of shock and pain on his face.

The explosion of gunpowder had caused the handkerchief to burst briefly into flames. Czolgosz flung the burnt rag to the ground. Other than that, he did not move. For one long second it seemed that no one moved. In the next instant, two of the President's security guards flung themselves at McKinley's assailant, driving him to the ground. Then Czolgosz was buried under a flurry of fists and feet. He was attacked not only by soldiers and policemen, but by many of the people who had been standing in line behind him. Czolgosz himself might have been murdered on the spot, but for the actions of the President. Though dazed by the two blows he had received, McKinley fixed his eyes upon the badly beaten and bloodied assassin.

"Go easy on him, boys," the President murmured before sliding into unconsciousness. It was a state from which he would never recover.

"Gentlemen," said Sean Mitchell, "I'd like you both to meet the man responsible for the death of William McKinley. The man who will help us solve our problems with Wilfrid Laurier."

XIV

Leon Czolgosz and other men of his type, far from being depraved creatures of low instincts, are in reality supersensitive beings unable to bear up under too great a social stress. They are driven to some violent expression, even at the sacrifice of their own lives, because they cannot supinely witness the misery and suffering of their fellows. The blame for such acts must be laid at the doors of those who are responsible for such injustices and inhumanity which dominate the world. As I write, my thoughts wander to the young man with the girlish face about to be put to death. . . . My heart goes out to him in deep sympathy, as it goes out to all the victims of oppression and misery, to the martyrs past and future that die, the forerunners of a better and nobler life.

Emma Goldman,
Anarchist.
October 6, 1901

"I DON'T UNDERSTAND," SAID ONE OF THE TWO MEN WHO had been listening to Sean Mitchell tell the story of McKinley's assassination. "How can this be the man responsible for the death of the President? As I remember it, the guy who shot McKinley got the electric chair."

"Quite true," Mitchell agreed. "Quite true. But I did not say this was the man who shot McKinley. I said this is the man responsible for his death."

"There's a difference?"

"Oh, there's a big difference. Perhaps I should let Mr. Roberts take over at this point." He turned to look at the man he had just introduced. "David."

David Roberts was a little man, barely more than five feet tall, with tiny hands and tiny feet. He had jet-black hair, parted in the middle and slicked down to either side. He had a long, pointed nose and a little slit of a mouth with lips so thin and pale they could barely be discerned. His brown eyes seemed to look right through whatever he focused on. The only thing about Roberts that wasn't tiny was his ears. Big and round, his ears made him look like a mouse.

As a child, the scrawny Roberts had been beaten up almost daily until he learned how to use his brains to outwit the brawn of the stronger children. It was a lesson he never forgot. His ability to manipulate people, to use them for his own purposes, had served him well over the years.

"Gentlemen," David Roberts began, "I am the sort of person people come to when they have a situation they cannot handle themselves. I eliminate problems." He paused for a moment, letting his words sink in. Noticing the confused look on the faces of his small audience, he continued.

"About ten years ago, I was approached by a man who represented several important business people. They were concerned about reports (which, through their contacts in Washington, they knew to be true), that President McKinley was going to relax his tight restrictions on foreign goods entering the U.S. marketplace. Such a move, you must understand, would have cost these people a great deal of money. They asked me to take care of the problem for them. I took care of it."

"I still don't understand," said the man who had been confused from the start. "You killed McKinley, but this guy, Czolgosz —" "Sol-guz" he said, pronouncing the difficult name incorrectly, as most people did, "he got the chair for it?"

"No," Roberts said with a patience that masked his disbelief at the man's difficulty in putting the pieces together. "Leon Czolgosz,"

("Cholgosh" he said correctly) "shot the President. He just had a little help in deciding to carry out the deed. That's all."

"Perhaps you should explain from the beginning," said Sean Mitchell.

"I think you're right," Roberts agreed, but he didn't start from the beginning. He picked up where Mitchell had left off.

"Go easy on him, boys," the President had murmured. The presidential directive came in a halting, staccato gasp, but it was sufficient to stop the beating. Czolgosz, blood spilling from his eyes and nose, his clothes torn, was hauled to his feet and dragged off to a room where he would be held until it was safe to transport him to police headquarters.

"I done my duty," Czolgosz answered when asked to explain his act. But slowly, under a barrage of questions that came at him with almost the same ferocity as the punches and kicks he had endured just a short time before, a confession began to emerge.

Eight days before, while in Chicago, Czolgosz told police, he had picked up a newspaper. He saw that President McKinley was to visit the Pan-American Exposition. It was at that point, he said, that he decided to go to Buffalo, "but not till Tuesday," Czolgosz lied, "did the thought of shooting the President take hold of me. It was all I thought about — nothing else. I couldn't have turned back if my life was at stake."

Czolgosz went on to outline his failed attempts on the life of the President, which, he further explained, was why he had been among the first to arrive at the Temple of Music.

"Then I saw him, the President — the ruler — and I trembled as I stood in line until I got right up to him. I shot twice through my handkerchief. I would have fired more, but a punch in the face knocked me down. Then everybody jumped on me. I thought I would be killed. I was surprised how they treated me."

Under further interrogation, Czolgosz denied he had any accomplices. "I had no one to help me," he stated. "I was alone. Absolutely."

Czolgosz kept his blue eyes fixed upon some faraway point it seemed only he could see. He showed no remorse for the violent and terrible crime he had committed. He showed little emotion of any kind.

"Did you really intend to kill the President?" Czolgosz was asked again.

"Yes, I did."

"What was your motive?"

"I am an anarchist," Czolgosz explained. "A disciple of Emma Goldman. Her words set me on fire."

"Well, you can imagine the furor that revelation set off," David Roberts said dryly. "Emma Goldman, the High Priestess of Anarchism."

Anarchism was an international radical movement that had emerged in the mid-nineteenth century. Anarchists were socialists, but of a particular kind. Not content simply to challenge the capitalist system, anarchists were violently opposed to the state and all forms of centralized authority. Rather than capturing state power, the anarchists sought to destroy it. They did not wish to build mass political parties and elect socialist governments; instead they formed small militant groups to spread the anarchist ideology by means of newspapers, lectures, and demonstrations.

Emma Goldman had come to America in 1885, a sixteen-year-old immigrant from Russia seeking to live out the American dream. Settling in Rochester, New York, with her family, she did not find the streets paved with gold. Instead she found want and misery, the poor exploited by the rich, forced to work long hours in the sweatshops for meagre wages. At the age of twenty, she moved to New York City, where she sought out the leaders of the radical movement she had read about. Almost from the moment she entered the anarchist movement in 1889, Emma Goldman earned a notoriety unequalled by any other woman in American public life. Admired by some, she was feared and hated by most for her outspoken attacks on conventional values, speaking out against the church and organized religion in general, calling for equality between the sexes, and supporting the theory of free love. While she was not a proponent of violence for its own sake, preferring literature and drama as vehicles for changing social attitudes, her public defence of political terrorists only fuelled the hatred of her opponents.

"Emma Goldman is considered a monster," Roberts said in obvious delight. "Something less than human. Why the very mention of her name is enough to produce a shudder."

Roberts fell silent for a moment, eyeing each of the three other men who sat around the table with him. He wanted to be sure they understood the terror the woman's name carried.

"I had decided almost from the start," Roberts continued, "that I would find an anarchist to assassinate the President."

He had remembered the newspaper articles from the summer before, when a government operative had managed to infiltrate an anarchist lair. The agent's report had contained a list of crowned heads who were to be eliminated. The first two, the Empress Elizabeth of Austria and King Humbert of Italy, had already been killed. Others on the list were the Czar of Russia, Queen Victoria, the Kaiser of Germany, and the President of the United States.

"I knew if I found an anarchist to perform the deed," Roberts continued, "the police would feel there was no need to look any further to uncover a plot. The men I represented would be safe.

"I also assumed," Roberts added, "that it wouldn't be difficult to find an anarchist willing to exchange his life for that of the President. Czolgosz was even easier to convince than I expected. Instantly, it was as if the idea were his own."

Leon Czolgosz had led a miserable life. Born in Detroit in 1873, the son of a Polish immigrant, he was the third of eight children. His mother died after giving birth to her eighth child and his father remarried. Czolgosz was distrustful of his stepmother from the very beginning. She thought him crazy. Over the years, their hatred of each other deepened.

The Czolgosz family moved often during Leon's childhood, drifting across Michigan. When he was sixteen, Leon's family moved to Natrona, Pennsylvania, where he found his first job, working in a bottling plant. Two years later, the family was on the move again, this time to Cleveland, where they finally settled down. Czolgosz got a job in a wire mill.

Miserable at home, he was equally unhappy in his work. For seven years he put in long hours for little pay, and while his bosses got rich he had virtually nothing. He brooded over the injustices and inequalities that surrounded him. Thousands were going to bed homeless and hungry every night while the rich feasted on ten-course dinners served up on gold plates, then washed down their food with champagne and cognac. When he got sick, Czolgosz scoffed at suggestions he enter a hospital.

"If you have lots of money," Czolgosz grumbled bitterly, "you get well taken care of."

Reading was the only thing within his bleak existence that gave Czolgosz pleasure. He was regarded as the intellectual of the family because of his love of books, though he had only received five-and-a-half years of formal schooling. Czolgosz read anything he could get his hands on: pamphlets, newspapers, anything. He particularly enjoyed the papers that came out against the President, since he agreed with their criticism of McKinley as a hypocritical friend of big business.

Soon Czolgosz was attending political meetings. He was a socialist, but quickly tired of the local socialist movement. When he read that Emma Goldman, the famous woman radical, would be addressing the Franklin Liberal Club in Cleveland, he decided to attend her lecture.

The notorious woman was already speaking when Czolgosz entered the hall. He was instantly mesmerized by her. The power and conviction of the words the little woman spoke swept him away. He was lost in her magnetic energy.

In her speech that night, Emma Goldman laid down the principles by which she expected universal anarchy to prevail. She denounced the rule of government and cited anarchism as the only path leading towards freedom. She stressed that education was the key to social betterment. She did not, in her speech, condone violent measures, but did review the recent acts of violence undertaken by fellow anarchists and praised those who had taken part for their refusal to stand aside while workers suffered. Their motives were high and noble, she said.

"Men under the present society are products of circumstance," Emma Goldman stated in summation that night. "Under the galling yoke of government and ecclesiasticism, it is impossible for the individual to work out his career as he could wish. Anarchism aims at a new and complete freedom."

The words Emma Goldman spoke that night echoed for days in Czolgosz's head. He decided he must see her again, and caught up with her in Chicago a few weeks later. Soon after that, he shot the President.

"I am an anarchist," Czolgosz explained. "A disciple of Emma Gold-man. Her words set me on fire."

"I learned of Czolgosz," David Roberts said, "through a man I know in Cleveland. From this man I found out that Czolgosz had begun making regular visits to Emil Schilling, the treasurer of a Cleveland anarchist group known as the Liberty Club. I also learned that Schilling was suspicious of Czolgosz, since he appeared to know next to nothing about anarchism and had a habit of posing questions, asked in a quick way as if in an attempt to catch him off guard, about secret societies. Czolgosz also repeatedly referred to acts of violence, such as the assassination of the King of Italy. I knew I had found my man."

Roberts paused again, chuckling softly at the memory. It seemed an odd reaction to the other men, but then what else was to be expected of a man who arranged murders for a living?

"When the cops heard what Czolgosz had to say, they were all over him looking for evidence of an anarchist plot. Hoping for any solid proof to connect Emma Goldman to the crime. As I had suspected, they gave not a moment's consideration to any other conspiracy, even though Czolgosz continually denied that his plot had been precon-ceived by any branch of anarchist society."

"Have you ever taken any obligation or sworn any oath to kill any-body?" Czolgosz was asked. The question was posed by Chief William S. Bull, Superintendent of Police in Buffalo.

"You have, haven't you? Look up and speak!" the police chief shouted, grabbing Czolgosz roughly, yanking on his hair to pull his head up. "Haven't you done that?"

Czolgosz stared straight ahead, blinking under the bright electric light. The room was dark except for one bulb hanging directly over-head. He sat on a hard wooden chair, his feet tied to the legs, his arms bound behind his back.

"No sir," he answered quietly.

"Who was the last one you heard talk against rulers?" Bull demanded.

"Emma Goldman," came the almost inaudible reply.

"You heard her say it would be a good thing," Bull went on, trying to put words in the assassin's mouth, "if all these rulers were wiped off the face of the earth?"

"She didn't say that."

"What did she say? What did she say about the President?"

Czolgosz sighed before giving his answer. "She says . . ." He paused for a moment, then began again. "She didn't mention no presidents at all. She mentioned the government."

"What did she say about it?"

"She said she didn't believe in it."

"And that all those who supported the government ought to be destroyed. Did she say that?"

"She didn't say they ought to be destroyed."

Bull was losing his patience. The prisoner had said nothing that would implicate Emma Goldman. Bull switched tactics.

"You wanted to help her in her work," the police chief said, in a friendlier, more agreeable tone, "and you thought this was the best way to do it. Was that your idea or was it hers? Tell us which it was."

"She didn't tell me to do it."

Later that night, Leon Czolgosz signed a confession in which he stated that he was an anarchist, and that he had become an enthusiastic supporter through the influence of Emma Goldman, whose writings he had read and whose lectures he had heard. He said in his confession that he had been induced by her writings to decide that the present form of government in the United States was all wrong and that he thought the best way to end it was by killing the President.

Czolgosz admitted that the words of Emma Goldman had inspired him, but he continually denied that she had instructed him directly or that he was part of a deeper plot. The police doubted his story.

"It's plain to anyone," Chief Bull admitted to reporters, off the record, "that the assassin is in love with Emma Goldman. I have no doubt he would do anything she asked him."

Bull dispatched a detective to Cleveland to question the Czolgosz family and look into the prisoner's background. He had his local force round up anyone who had come into contact with Czolgosz during his stay in Buffalo. They picked up innkeeper John Nowak, his clerk, and one of the other boarders. No one was able to provide any insight. Meanwhile, the most wanted woman in the world was Emma Goldman.

Goldman was in St. Louis when she learned of the death of President McKinley. To her absolute astonishment, she read of the shooting beneath a headline that shouted:

ASSASSIN OF PRESIDENT McKINLEY AN ANARCHIST
Confesses to Having Been Incited by Emma Goldman
Woman Anarchist Wanted

When she read that nine of her associates back in Chicago were being held in jail without bail until she was found, she decided to return there immediately. She made her way to the Wabash train station, where she boarded a Pullman car on a train bound for the Windy City.

Arriving in Chicago the next morning, Emma Goldman awakened to a stream of profanities directed at both her and Czolgosz.

"I can't believe that wild woman has not been locked up," shouted one man.

"Locked up, nothing," retorted another, "she should have been strung up to the first lamp-post!"

Goldman had heard such venomous words many times before, but in view of her supposed involvement in the death of the President and the fact that she was travelling unescorted, she was truly afraid, for a moment at least, until she realized the verbal assault was not being directed at her person — merely at her name. The indignant speakers had no idea she was on the train.

Relieved by this understanding, she sat in her berth unconcerned. She even chuckled to herself at the thought of how those people outside might look if she were to step out and announce her presence. "Here, ladies and gentlemen, true followers of the gentle Jesus," she imagined herself saying, "here is Emma Goldman!" She decided she did not have the heart to cause them such shock and remained on board a little longer, hidden behind her curtain.

Goldman was prevailed upon by her friends in Chicago to go into hiding, at least until she could collect the $5000 reward the *Chicago*

Tribune was offering for an exclusive interview. The money, her friends convinced her, might become necessary in the legal ordeal she would no doubt face. She was tucked away in the home of a prosperous friend who lived in a fashionable neighbourhood. Since the friend was the son of a well-to-do minister, his home was chosen as the least likely to attract suspicion.

On the morning of September 10, four days after the assassination of the President, Emma Goldman was in her bath when she heard the sound of broken glass coming from the floor below. She pulled on a robe and rushed into an adjoining room just ahead of the police, who were now storming the house and demanding to see the anarchist menace. She easily slipped into the role of a Swedish maid unable to speak English and, stating that her name was Lena Larson, communicated in halting speech that she did not know Emma Goldman.

The police continued to search the home, until the captain in charge walked over to the bookshelf.

"Hell, this is a regular preacher's house," the captain remarked. "Look at them books. I don't think Emma Goldman would be caught dead in a place like this."

The captain was about to call off the search, when one of his detectives rushed over to him, waving a small, shiny object in his hand.

"Look at this," the detective exclaimed. It was a gold fountain pen with Emma Goldman's name inscribed on it.

"Well now, that's a find," the captain said excitedly. "She must have been here and she may come back!"

The captain ordered two of his men to remain behind, and Emma Goldman, realizing that the game was up, admitted her identity.

The captain and his men stood there for a moment, as if petrified to be in the presence of the infamous woman.

"Well, I'll be damned," the captain finally said. "You're the shrewdest crook I ever met!" Then turning to his men he instructed, "Take her, quick!"

Emma Goldman was taken to police headquarters, where she was held for over eight hours in a stifling little room while at least fifty detectives passed before her, grilling her over the alleged connection to the President's assassination. Attempting to extract a confession, the detectives shook their fists in her face.

"You was with Czolgosz in Buffalo! I saw you myself," one detective shouted. "You'd better confess, do you hear?"

"Look here, Goldman," another officer said, "I seen you with that son of a bitch at the fair! Don't you lie, now — I seen you, I tell you!"

"You've faked enough," added a third man. "You keep this up and sure as you're born you'll get the chair. Your lover has confessed. He said it was your speech what made him shoot the President."

Emma Goldman had been arrested many times in her life — it was an occupational hazard for a noted anarchist — but she'd never been subjected to the verbal abuse and physical bullying she endured that day. After hours of torturous treatment, lips parched and head throbbing, she was led off to jail, where she was locked up in a tiny, cage-like cell that left her exposed to view from every side. And here she was grilled again, this time by Chicago Chief of Police O'Neill, who, like those before him, failed in his attempts to make the anarchist implicate herself in the crime.

Meanwhile, officials in Buffalo were trying to arrange to have her brought to that city. Although no one had been able to connect her to the crime, there were those who felt sure that if Goldman were brought to Buffalo a case could be made against her. Chief O'Neill didn't agree. After becoming convinced of her innocence, O'Neill worked to have the charges against her dropped. After fifteen days in jail, Emma Goldman was free to go.

Leon Czolgosz was brought to court on September 23, 1901, to face a charge of murder in the first degree in the assassination of President William McKinley. The entire trial lasted just five and a half hours. The jury deliberated for only thirty-four minutes before returning a guilty verdict. The convicted killer was sentenced to death by electric chair.

Two days after his trial concluded, Czolgosz was loaded aboard a train headed for Auburn, New York, site of the state penitentiary, where he would be held for another month before the death sentence would be carried out. It was just after ten o'clock at night when the train carrying him, two police officials, and several guards, as well as a smattering of reporters, pulled out of the station. The "journey to the tombs," as one of the newspapermen had referred to it, had begun.

Czolgosz, handcuffed to one of the police officials, stared silently out the window, just able to make out the shapes of farmhouses against the moonlit sky as the train rolled on. He shuddered as he noticed a graveyard.

It was 3:05 AM when the train arrived in Auburn. It had been scheduled for this early hour in hopes of avoiding a mob scene, but, much to the horror of the doomed assassin, an ugly crowd of some 1500 people awaited him.

Cries of "Kill him! Kill him!" rang in his ears as Czolgosz, surrounded by guards, was led off the train. Only the lights of the prison gate in the distance broke through the blackness. Still, it wasn't hard for Czolgosz to see the mob as it rushed towards him, hands raised like claws in hopes of getting a piece of him.

"Keep close to me," instructed the police official to whom Czolgosz was handcuffed. "And for God's sake, keep your head down!"

As he heard the cries and screaming threats of the mob, the prisoner trembled, stumbling to his knees.

"Get up, man!" the officer yelled, but it was no use. Another guard grabbed hold of Czolgosz and the two men dragged him through the gates of the prison. Czolgosz, only half-conscious and moaning with terror, was carried up the stairs to the prisoners' entrance. He was led to the chamber of the condemned, where a tiny cell would be his home for the thirty-one remaining days of his life.

Just before 7:00 AM on October 29, Leon Czolgosz was awakened to face his final moments on earth. As the prisoner was led to the electric chair, the prison superintendent tried for one last time to get Czolgosz to implicate Goldman in his crime.

"You know Emma Goldman says you are an idiot," the Superintendent stated. "She says you're no good and that you once begged a quarter of her."

"I don't care what she says," replied the prisoner wearily. "She didn't tell me to do this."

When Czolgosz stumbled twice, the guards carried him forward to the rubber-covered platform upon which rested the chair of death. The large wooden chair rose from the platform on four sturdy legs. Attached to the two front legs were a pair of metal shackles which would be fastened around the prisoner's ankles. An electric cord snaked along the floor, leading away from each of the shackles. The hind legs rose higher and, with three slats of wood between them, formed the back of the chair. Two more slats of wood extended from the back legs at ninety-degree angles, forming the arms of the chair. Stiff leather straps were attached to the arms. They would wrap around the prisoner's wrists. There were other straps that would go around his thighs, waist, and chest. Rising above the back of the chair was a tall metal pole that curved forward at the top with a metal skullcap hanging from it.

Czolgosz was placed in the chair. There was no give at all to the heavy wooden seat. As the straps and electrodes were adjusted, the condemned man spoke his final words.

"I am not sorry," he said. "I did this for the working people. I did it alone. I did it for the American people."

At 7:12 AM the warden gave the signal to throw the switch. A surge of 1700 volts hurled the body of Leon Czolgosz against the electric chair straps so violently that they cracked. His hands clenched, his body stiffened. The full current was maintained for forty-five seconds, then reduced slowly. As the current lessened, the body collapsed. The attending physician stepped forward and felt the assassin's heart. He could detect no beat. Czolgosz was pronounced dead.

David Roberts was done with his story.

"Do you understand now?" asked Mitchell, as he stared at the man who had been asking all the questions.

The man nodded.

"And so, Mr. Roberts," Mitchell continued, "will you find a man to help us with our problem?"

"Yes," said Roberts, though he knew it wouldn't be easy. It would be difficult to find another anarchist to carry out the deed, since the anarchist movement wasn't nearly so well established in Canada as it was in the United States. "I believe I can find someone for you."

"Excellent," said Mitchell, nodding his approval.

"Wait a minute," said the man with all the questions, as a look of disbelief came over his face. "Sean, are you telling me we're going to kill the Prime Minister? That goes way beyond anything we've talked about!"

Mitchell had anticipated this reaction. "Well, if you don't want in on it, I want you to leave this room right now and never breathe a word of this conversation to anyone. Ever. If you stay, you're in this all the way. There will be no backing out."

"I can't go along with something like this, Sean."

"Well then, there's the door. Mr. Lawrence will see you out." He looked over at the fourth man at the table, who who had remained silent throughout the proceedings. "Won't you, Richard?"

The two men got up from the table. The man with all the questions headed directly for the door. Richard Lawrence followed, hands in his pockets, his six-foot, three-inch frame towering over the other man. Suddenly, his hands appeared, and a steely glint of something was visible in his right hand. It was a length of piano wire. All in one motion, Lawrence stretched out the wire and wrapped it tightly around the man's neck. He grabbed at his throat, trying desperately to pull at the wire. But Lawrence was too strong for him. The man's hands were quickly covered in blood as he choked and struggled. Lawrence pulled the wire tighter still, holding on until the man's lifeless body slumped to the floor. Then Lawrence leaned over, wrapped his arms around the man's body, and dragged him out the back door.

Sean Mitchell turned away, his face pale. It was he who had told Lawrence he would likely have to kill the man, but he had not expected it to be done right in front of him. To plan a murder in the abstract was a far cry from actually watching a man die.

Mitchell took a moment to compose himself, running the thumb and index finger of his right hand back and forth along the braided gold chain of his pocket watch. "There can be no loose ends," Mitchell offered weakly, by way of explanation for the gruesome killing.

David Roberts simply nodded his approval — murder did not bother him. Raising his glass, he offered a toast to the success of their plot.

Part III
The Game

FIRST HALF
_____

XV

RENFREW, NESTLED IN THE FERTILE VALLEY OF THE
Bonnechere River, fifty miles from Ottawa, was named by its founders
for a region of Scotland — an ancestral home of the royal family. In
1848, ten years before Renfrew was incorporated as a village, the land
was surveyed and laid out in streets and lots. Within a decade, it was
home to some 450 residents.

With the Bonnechere River flowing into the Ottawa River just nine
miles away, the area was provided with easy access for settlers. Renfrew
grew quickly. The hamlet produced and supplied all things necessary
for its own needs. Local farmers grew grain for the bakers, supplied
meat for the village butchers, and provided cowhides for local tanners,
who then turned the leather over to cobblers or harnessmakers, who
in turn made sure the local farmers had the necessary equipment for
the horses that worked the fields. The lumber industry, prevalent
throughout the Ottawa Valley, supplied Renfrew's woodworkers with
abundant material to fashion into chairs, tables, cupboards, and shelves.
The village soon prospered. Bank accounts soared.

By the fall of 1909, Renfrew was a town of close to 4000 people.
Still, it was virtually unknown to all but the residents of neighbouring
Ottawa Valley towns when Ambrose O'Brien established the upstart
National Hockey Association and began his quest to bring the Stanley
Cup to his home town.

Ambrose and his associates, George Martel and Jim Barnet, had not
been forced to start from scratch in building their hockey team. Only
a year before, they'd helped establish professional hockey in Renfrew,
serving on the board of the town's Federal League team. The Renfrew
Federals, as the team was called, disbanded after their championship
season culminated in yet another snub from the Stanley Cup trustees,
but four players from that team — goaltender Bert Lindsay and forwards Larry Gilmour, Bobby Rowe, and Ernie Liffiton — were retained
for the new venture. All four were considered first-rate players.

Jack Fraser, an Ottawa Valley boy from nearby Arnprior, who had
played professionally in both Ontario and Manitoba, was the club's
first outside acquisition. Ambrose then signed Frank and Lester Patrick,
amid much fanfare, as the first high-profile members of his new hockey

club. Cyclone Taylor and Marty Walsh were next on Ambrose O'Brien's wish list. Taylor signed a landmark contract, but when Walsh, the Ottawa centre who had been the top scorer in Eastern Canada for each of the past two seasons, turned down a lucrative offer from George Martel, the Renfrew club looked to another high-scoring centre: Herb Jordan.

Herb Jordan had played in Quebec City since 1903. He had scored in each of his team's twelve games the season before, and his twenty-nine goals overall were second only to Walsh's thirty-eight, but, lacking any solid supporting players for almost all of his seven seasons in Quebec, he had toiled in relative obscurity. The prospect of finally playing for a winner, as well as an off-ice job connected with M.J. O'Brien's business affairs, convinced Jordan that he should jump to Renfrew.

Two more signings completed the roster for Renfrew's entry into the National Hockey Association. Fred Whitcroft and Hay Millar of Edmonton agreed to join Renfrew for $2000 apiece. They were coming east before the 1910 campaign for an early season Stanley Cup challenge against the Senators and would join their new club a few games into the new year.

Ambrose now had his team: the greatest hockey team money could buy. Renfrew, always proud of its agricultural heritage, was known as the Creamery Town for the fine quality of butter and dairy products it produced. As a result, its new hockey team was dubbed the Renfrew Creamery Kings, but the name was never adopted by the fans. Because of the club's prominent backing and huge salaries, the team became known as the Renfrew Millionaires.

Within weeks, the name of a town almost no one had ever heard of was on everybody's lips. Sports fans from Halifax to Vancouver were reading about the star-studded hockey team that had been assembled in Renfrew. The upstart National Hockey Association, a league that had not even existed just a few weeks before, was now, largely thanks to the headlines garnered by Ambrose and his team in Renfrew, considered by most fans and hockey experts to be on a par with, if not already superior to, the Canadian Hockey Association. The Renfrew Millionaires were being tabbed as the top team heading into the upcoming season. Newspapers all over Quebec and Ontario planned to send reporters to cover games. Ottawa newspapers even decided to send writers to report on every practice at the Renfrew Rink.

Cyclone Taylor came to the Creamery Town a few days after Christmas. He arrived quietly on an evening train, informing Ambrose of his imminent approach only hours before, via telegram from the train station in Listowel, where he had returned to spend the holidays.

Ambrose was waiting at the station as Taylor's train neared town. Before he could see or hear the train, he could make out, in the distance, the thick black clouds puffing from the smoke stack. A moment later, Ambrose heard the shrill blast of the train's whistle. Soon the ground shook and the air was filled with a loud rumbling as the locomotive approached. Slowing down as it reached the station, the train screeched to a stop and Cyclone Taylor stepped down.

Taylor wore a heavy overcoat and a dark suit. He had on new leather boots, bought with the advance money on his Renfrew contract, and held a new hat in his hands. His dark hair was combed back, trying unsuccessfully to hide a growing bald spot. Hair loss was a sore point with Taylor. During the past season with Ottawa, he had taken to wearing a red toque during games to hide his thinning hair.

Taylor was the only person who got off the train in Renfrew. He found just one man waiting on the platform. The man was a few inches taller than he was, probably about five-feet-nine, and somewhat stockier. He had dark hair, dark eyes, and a round face with a wide nose. He sported a fur-collared coat and was chewing on a cigar. The man stood with his hands in his back pockets, looking Taylor over and nodding ever so slightly. Then, moving with short, quick strides, he began walking towards the hockey star, his head held high, his jaw jutting out in front of him.

"Fred Taylor?" he asked.

Taylor nodded.

"I'm Ambrose O'Brien. It's nice to finally meet you. Welcome to Renfrew."

Ambrose stuck out his right hand, and Taylor shook it. A firm grip, he noticed approvingly. Ambrose handed a half-dollar tip to the porter who had unloaded Taylor's suitcase, duffel bag, and trunk. Cyclone noted the young man's largess. It must be nice to have that kind of money, he thought, Thirza and her mother coming to mind.

"How was your trip?" Ambrose inquired. "You know," he added

before Taylor had time to respond, "if you'd told me ahead of time that you were planning to come today, I could have arranged for father's private train to bring you here." Ambrose wasn't being boastful when he said it; he was merely stating it as a matter of fact.

"The train ride was fine," Taylor answered. "Thank you for asking."

Ambrose was two years his junior, but Taylor found himself trying to impress the young man, and yet not sure of what to say. He'd never met a man of such wealth, and he felt somewhat intimidated by him. But Ambrose was not a man enslaved by the trappings of wealth — his father had made sure of that as he grew up. He was equally at home in big-city society or at small-town gatherings, in the board room sweating out corporate decisions, or around a table in a tavern swapping stories with the labourers working on his railroad contracts. He sensed Taylor's discomfort, and was quickly able to make him feel at ease. Within a few minutes they were chatting like old friends.

Most of Taylor's new teammates had arrived in Renfrew before the holidays and had already started training. "I imagine you'll be wanting to get down to the hockey rink and meet the boys," Ambrose said. "I informed them that you'd be arriving this evening. They're holding a workout now and they're expecting you."

"Yes, I'd like that," Taylor said. He hadn't been on the ice since March, and he looked forward to meeting his new teammates and getting back into action.

Taylor bent down to pick up his belongings, but Ambrose waved him off. "Don't bother with that. I'll have my driver load your things on the carriage. I thought I'd walk you over to the rink. It's only a few minutes from here. Your gear will be waiting for you when we get there."

There was no tour for Taylor upon his arrival in Renfrew, as there had been two years ago when he first came to Ottawa. He hadn't expected there would be, and the idea never even occurred to Ambrose. There were no special attractions. No Prime Minister's residence. No Parliament Buildings. Certainly there were some beautiful buildings along Raglan, the town's main street, but anything there was to see, Taylor would discover on his own as he settled back into small-town life.

Taylor's next reminder that he was no longer in Ottawa came when he and Ambrose arrived at the Renfrew Rink. For the past two seasons, Taylor had played in the greatest hockey facility in the country. The hockey arena he stared at now might easily be mistaken for a barn.

There were large double doors in front, through which Ambrose led Taylor. A small lobby welcomed them with a ticket booth on one side and a doorway leading to a large room on the other. This room served a variety of purposes. It had a wood stove inside to warm up season-ticket holders as they filed in at half-time. It also contained hinged benches with wooden boxes underneath. Those who paid $2.50 for a winter-long public skating pass could store their skates in the boxes throughout the season. In the far corner was a small telegraph office used by newspapermen to wire game reports.

After they passed through another set of double doors at the back of the lobby, Taylor could see the playing surface. The large oval expanse of ice stretched out in front of him, ringed by wooden boards about four feet high. As Ambrose led him around the playing area, he saw a row of numbered seats behind the boards, running all the way around the ice. There was a second tier of seats on a raised platform behind them. Reserved tickets in the front row sold for a dollar apiece, the back row for seventy-five cents. A narrow walkway circled the building behind the two rows of reserved seats, with a number of stairways leading up to the general admission seats, which cost fifty cents.

A crew of workmen was installing new seats just above where Taylor was standing. The Renfrew Rink had undergone a lot of renovation in the past few weeks, to try to bring it up to big-league standards. No one was really sure now how many people the place would now hold. Some estimated the entire town could be crammed in. Right now, there were dozens of fans scattered through the seats. Training camp was open to the public, with practices taking place in the early evening so that people could stop by after work. With the kids off school for Christmas vacation, crowds at the workouts were quite large.

Well O.K., Taylor thought, the Renfrew Rink most certainly isn't the Laurier Avenue Arena, but "I like it," he said aloud. It reminded him of the arena back in Listowel, where he had starred as a youngster almost a decade before. If the fans in Renfrew were anything like the fans he remembered from his home town, and the large turnout for the practice led him to believe they would be, he was going to enjoy playing here.

"Fred . . . Fred," Ambrose was calling, but it took a moment for Taylor to notice. He was soaking up the atmosphere. "This way, Fred," Ambrose said, after gaining Taylor's attention. He was pointing to a short tunnel under the stands and a flight of wooden stairs. Ambrose led Taylor up the stairway, which rose from behind the players' bench and up to the dressing room. There they were greeted by a familiar face.

"Mr. Taylor," said Ambrose formally, "I believe you know Alf Smith. We've brought him in to serve as our coach. He guided the Ottawa Cliffsides to the Allan Cup last season — amateur champions of the nation.

"I'll leave you two to get reacquainted," Ambrose added. "See you both later."

"It's good to see you again, Cyc," Alf Smith said with a smile, thrusting out his right hand in friendship.

Taylor took it. "Alf," he mumbled quietly. He was not happy. Had he known Alf Smith was going to be brought in as coach, he might not have signed with Renfrew. He felt betrayed.

Taylor hadn't seen his former teammate in over a year. He realized now that he had not gotten over the resentment he felt when Smith and the other Senators veterans had made him feel so unwelcome upon his arrival in Ottawa. He remembered Smith's remark on the train after that first game in Quebec City. "This cocky new son of a bitch isn't going to do us any damn good. He just wants to play his own game out there."

Smith knew what Taylor was thinking. He could see it in his face, and in the way his shoulders drooped when they first saw each other. "Look, Cyclone," he began, "there's no point in dwelling on our past relationship. What's past is past, I like to say. I just want to tell you this. I never had a fraction of the talent you have. I had to work hard for every break I got in the game, fight every inch of the way, and I guess that's why I was always looking for trouble. I used to think that the way we played hockey in Ottawa in the old days was the only way to play. I suppose that's because it was the only way I could play. But you're the greatest hockey player I've ever seen. I guess I really knew that two years ago, but I never would have admitted it then. I could never play the wide open game you do. But that's the way the game is played these days and hell, we've got a team full of all-stars so that's how we're going to play it here. Now suit up, and get out on the ice. We've got a Stanley Cup to win this year!"

With that, Smith left the room.

Taylor felt foolish. Why had he bothered to carry a grudge for so long? Well, if Alf Smith could accept him now, he could accept Alf Smith. He would put aside the resentment he'd felt just moments before and go on about his business. "We do have a Stanley Cup to win this year," he told himself as he quickly dressed.

The walk down the stairs from the dressing room to the ice reminded Taylor of the trek to the Piggery as a youngster in Listowel. Each step closer brought a rise in anticipation. The sounds of the on-ice struggle got louder and louder until suddenly he emerged from the tunnel under the stands and the game was upon him.

With only eleven men on the team, and Taylor and the players from Edmonton still to arrive, the Renfrew Millionaires had been working out with the local amateur team, the Renfrew Rivers. Practice consisted of scrimmage games between the two teams, with breaks taken about every ten minutes so that the coaches could instruct the players on what they wanted them to work on. A scrimmage game was already under way when Taylor found himself at rinkside. He was preparing to settle in on the bench and wait for a break in the play, when suddenly an idea popped into his head. With a slow smile spreading across his face, he pushed open the door to the ice and, in his mind, was transported back in time.

Taylor hit the ice with the game already in progress and made a couple of lightning-fast circles around the edge of the frozen surface. The cold rush of air against his cheeks took him back to his days on the Piggery. The "swish, swish, swish" from his blades filled his ears, further fuelling his imagination. When he looked up, he didn't see seats ringing an arena, he saw tall, snow-covered trees.

Taylor's unexpected appearance silenced the spectators at first, but slowly the confusion ended and a murmur of excitement swept the crowd. Cries of "It's Cyclone Taylor" swept through the stands, as fans began to recognize the red-toqued stranger. The players were also surprised and the game came to a halt as he circled the rink. Cyclone spotted the puck behind the Rivers net and he scooped it up on his final swoop around the arena. The players, unaware of their roles in Taylor's little fantasy, did not chase him as his boyhood pals on the Piggery used to, so he merely weaved his way in and out between them until he reached the far end of the ice. Once there, he brought the puck in close to his feet and with a snap of his wrists flipped it about waist high into the air. As the puck began its descent, he lifted his stick and, turning the blade flat side up, knocked the disk higher. Next, he drew his stick back and swung it like a baseball bat, sending the puck flying into the far reaches of the general admission seats. A group of youngsters scrambled to retrieve it, while the rest of the fans roared a welcoming ovation. The great hockey star waved to the crowd, then bowed graciously.

Taylor remained bent over at the waist for an extra few seconds as he tried to catch his breath. He'd not been on skates since the end of the previous hockey season, and his thighs were burning and his calves already beginning to tighten up. Five hours on a train had not been the proper warm-up for his now aching muscles.

Slowly, the rest of his Renfrew teammates made their way over to him. They were all smiles now, after staring blankly as Taylor had bobbed and weaved his way among them. "That was quite an entrance," said the tall, handsome fellow who appeared to be their leader. "I'm Lester Patrick," he added. "Glad to have you on board."

XVI

LESTER SLAPPED A GLOVED HAND DOWN ON TAYLOR'S shoulder after introducing himself, then led the much-celebrated newcomer around to meet the rest of the Renfrew squad. Lester was, as Taylor had suspected, the team captain. The honour had been bestowed upon him before any of the players had even taken their first skate together. It was an acknowledgement of the leadership qualities he had shown with the Montreal Wanderers in leading them to two Stanley Cups just a few seasons back. As captain, he was responsible for his teammates both on and off the ice. "Why don't you take a few minutes to get properly warmed up," Lester told Taylor. "We'll take a break. Let me know when you're ready to go."

Taylor went through a few brief stretching exercises. Deep knee bends first to get the juices flowing in his legs, then, laying his stick across the back of his shoulders like a farm hand carrying milk buckets on a yoke, he stretched down from side to side, then over at the waist, loosening up his back as he skated up and down the ice. Even these routine warm-up exercises brought cheers from the crowd. And from one person especially.

"Come on Cyclone! Bend that waist! Touch those toes! Stretch those legs! Let's go! Let's go!"

It was a young girl doing the shouting. She was easy to pick out among the many young people on hand. Taylor thought she looked to be about thirteen years old. She was short and plump, but stood as tall as she could in a rail seat next to the team bench. Her hands pressed against her chubby cheeks, she cupped her mouth and shouted out encouragement in a hoarse voice.

With the cheers of the girl, and the others in the crowd, ringing in his ears, Taylor was soon tearing up and down the sheet again, first doing some stops and starts, then racing around the rink at speeds that had everyone hollering.

"CYY-*CLONE!*" shouted the fans, in the same sing-song way the Ottawa faithful had chanted it. Though all the voices tended to blend together as he raced around the rink, Taylor could still make out the sound of the one girl's raspy voice. He waved to her as he sped by, and smiled as she shrieked with glee.

A short time later, Taylor informed Lester that he was ready to play. Herb Jordan went out to centre, as the team lined up for the rest of the scrimmage. Lester set himself for the face-off about twenty feet behind Jordan, manning the rover position. Bobby Rowe flanked Jordan on the right wing, Jack Fraser on the left. Larry Gilmour and Ernie Liffiton sat on the bench. They would substitute on the wings. Bert Lindsay stood in goal; white leather pads about an inch or two thick and stuffed with strips of felt were strapped to his legs. Lester's brother Frank, playing point, stationed himself directly in line with the goaltender, about fifteen feet in front of the net. Taylor, at cover point, settled into a position between the two Patricks, though closer to Frank and directly in front of him. But before they started playing, Taylor had a question.

"Who's the girl with the leather lungs?"

Frank laughed. "That's Charlotte Whitton. She collects those hockey cards the Imperial Tobacco Company gives out," he explained. "I guess her father smokes them," he added with a shrug. "Anyway, because she has all those cards, she knew each one of us by name the first time she saw us. She's been here every night, sitting at rinkside and shouting to us in that scratchy voice."

Charlotte Whitton's cheering might have become irritating if she weren't so sincere in her devotion to the team. Instead, she was becoming a favourite of the players, almost like a mascot or a good-luck charm.

The two Renfrew teams — the Rivers and the Millionaires — scrimmaged for about half an hour before calling it quits, having already played that long before Taylor had joined them. Cyclone held himself back during the game, not wanting to exert any more energy than necessary in his first workout, but all in attendance could see the polished work that gave him claim to being the greatest hockey player in the world. Fans went home discussing the fine points of his play, and looking forward to seeing him really open up his game.

As they left the ice and headed for the stairs to the dressing room, the players stopped to speak with the many young fans who had lined up under the stands to greet them. Naturally, Taylor, as the greatest star and the newest attraction, drew the largest group of admirers.

"What your name?" Taylor asked one young boy, as he signed his autograph book.

"Henry," the boy whispered shyly.

"How old are you, Henry?"

"Eleven."

"Do you play hockey?"

"Yes, Mr. Taylor," the boy answered. His voice was gaining confidence as he perceived that the hockey star was taking a genuine interest in him. "I play with my friends on the river on Saturdays."

"Then maybe you'd like this," Taylor said. He tossed Henry his red toque. "It'll keep you warm."

"Really?" the boy gasped. "I can have it? Really?" Henry held the toque in his hands the way he would hold something that might break if he dropped it.

"Of course I may want to borrow it sometime, when I come down to the river to watch you play."

"WOW!"

For the next few minutes, Frank, Lester, Taylor, and the other players were kept busy signing autographs. Every request was met with a smile. Every "thank you" from a child got a "you're welcome" from a player. The hockey stars did it, not because it was expected of them, but because they truly enjoyed it. But even the most obliging of players could not go on giving autographs forever.

"Sorry, kids," Lester announced, after about ten minutes of signing and making small talk, "but we've got to go now."

"Awwh! No!"

"Hey," Frank said, "we've got to get changed out of these sweaty clothes." He shrugged apologetically. "Some of you are hockey players. You know what I mean."

"Besides," Taylor added, "you all know where to find us. We'll see you again tomorrow."

"They're right," a girl's voice said. It was Charlotte Whitton. "Come on," she urged the other children. "It's time to go home.

"It was an exciting practice, Lester," Charlotte called out to the captain before leaving. Already outspoken at the age of thirteen, she was the only child who called the hockey players by their first names.

"Oh, so you enjoyed it," Taylor shot back before Lester could say anything. "You'd never know it by the way you acted back there."

Charlotte smiled. She wasn't offended by the sarcastic remark. "I think the new recruit will do," she said to Lester, acting as if Taylor weren't there. "With a little bit of work, he might even make a name for himself someday."

As Charlotte led the children out of the Renfrew Rink, the hockey players climbed the stairs to their dressing room where Cyclone Taylor held court, swapping stories with Bert Lindsay about their days in the International League, and comparing notes with Lester on the two sides of the old Wanderers-Senators rivalry. Soon, talk turned to other sports, with the players trying to outdo one another in narrating their thrilling experiences on the baseball diamond. Taylor listened to all the stories, grimacing with mock disgust, before proceeding to tell the tale of one of his own speedy stunts.

"I was on the diamond one afternoon," Taylor began, putting on an arrogant air that indicated his story was going to top them all, "and we had men on second and third. Our team was down by three when I came to bat, and, taking a mighty wallop, I knocked the ball far out in deep centre. Seeing that it was a long drive, I put my head down and just kept on running. And, would you believe it?" He paused for effect, before continuing. "I beat both men to the plate!"

Taylor smiled triumphantly at his yarn, then ducked as Jordan, Rowe, and Fraser pelted him with their rolled-up hockey socks.

The players continued to strip off their gear and get changed into their street clothes. The Renfrew Rink had no running water for showers, so they all had to return to their hotel rooms or boarding houses to get cleaned up.

"Where are you staying, Cyc?" Lester asked.

"Ambrose had my bags sent over to the Dominion House Hotel. He's arranged a room for me there tonight. I guess I'll have to look for something a little more permanent tomorrow."

"There's a room available in our boarding house," Frank chimed in. "I'm sure we can convince Miss Stack to take in another hockey player," he said with a smile. The people of the town had opened their homes, as well as their hearts, to the new hockey warriors who promised to bring them the Stanley Cup.

"Oh, there's one more thing," Lester announced for the benefit of all in the room. "Tomorrow's practice starts at four o'clock, not seven. We're to be the guests of honour at a performance at the Opera House, beginning at eight."

The hockey players were already becoming well known to the rail-birds who had been attending practice at the rink, but for many other citizens of Renfrew, the visit to the Opera House would provide their first glimpse of the team.

Even from the outside, Renfrew's Opera House was striking. It was a four-storey red brick building. White stone piers decorated the main supports on the ground floor, while white stone arches traced the tops of the windows on the three upper floors. The top floor featured six Greek-style columns rising from a small balcony below the centre and topped by a white pediment and cornice on the roof. The front entrance to the building extended all the way out to the road, its white marble flooring inlaid with green tiles forming the Arabic numerals 1909, to commemorate the year the Opera House had opened.

"This place is beautiful," remarked one of the players as the team was led inside. Though the statement was made quietly, it was met with many nods of agreement. The players were taken to an upstairs office where M.J. O'Brien held court. The office was on the second floor of the Opera House he had constructed, behind the first balcony, in a big room overlooking the main street. Cyclone Taylor, Frank and Lester Patrick, and the rest of Renfrew's new hockey heroes were ushered into the office's waiting room. It would be the first time any of them except Herb Jordan had met the maverick multimillionaire.

The players had pestered Jordan in the dressing room after practice for any information about the man they were soon to meet, but Jordan, who had met O'Brien only once, could provide little more than a physical description. Questioning the townsfolk about the man they had come to consider their benefactor only increased the mystery surrounding O'Brien. He had become a legendary figure in Renfrew, too rich and powerful for people to feel at ease with. Even people he knew would think twice before hailing him on the street.

The hockey players sat in the small waiting room anticipating their meeting, which had been delayed slightly while O'Brien took a long distance telephone call about his silver mines in Cobalt. The players were tense, some crossing and uncrossing their legs as they sat, others fidgeting with their hands, and still others tugging in agitation at their collars or ties.

Finally, the team was ushered into O'Brien's office. The great man stood behind his desk, suit jacket draped over the chair behind him. He wore a silk vest, which was unbuttoned, and a neatly pressed white dress shirt with the sleeves rolled up to the elbow. His tie had been loosened, but a diamond-studded stick pin was still clearly visible below the knot. O'Brien's mouth was all but invisible behind a thick moustache and beard that contained almost as many white hairs as black ones. His intense blue eyes darted around the room, for just as it was the players' first glimpse of him, it was his first look at most of them. At six feet, two inches tall, O'Brien towered over most of his athletes, even standing an inch or two taller than Lester, who was easily the tallest man on the team.

"Welcome, gentlemen," O'Brien stated, in a deep voice accustomed to commanding respect. "Please sit down."

Ten chairs had been placed in the office, one for each of the nine players and their coach, and the men took their seats like a class of oversized schoolboys, shifting and scraping their chairs on the floor.

"First of all, gentlemen," O'Brien continued, after his audience had settled in, "I'd like to tell each of you how proud we are that a fine collection of men such as yourselves will be representing our town in the hockey wars this winter. We feel confident that you gentlemen, plus Messers Whitcroft and Millar, who unfortunately are unable to be with us tonight, are the greatest collection of hockey players ever assembled on one team." He paused for a moment, then added with a smile, "And you are certainly being paid accordingly."

The players chuckled agreeably.

"Yes," O'Brien continued, "we have spared no expense in bringing you here and will continue to provide you with the best available services during your stay in Renfrew. You will travel from town to town in my own private railcar, and you will be boarded in the best hotels." He paused again, letting his words sink in.

"Gentlemen," O'Brien went on, striking a more serious tone, "you've been welcomed with open arms in our town and I will not have anyone abusing the privileges they will be accorded here. I am paying you all a great deal of money, and while you are here you will play by my rules. First and foremost among them is this: I will not tolerate even a single display of public drunkenness. Now even I enjoy a shot of brandy before turning in at night, and I'm not asking any of you to abstain completely from whatever it is you take pleasure in; I'm simply asking that you be sensible and circumspect in whatever you do. I know hockey players have a reputation for roughness, but you will all behave as gentlemen while you are here."

O'Brien smiled. He was finished with the speechmaking, and, reaching behind his desk, he pulled out a silver tray bearing eleven crystal champagne glasses and a bottle. O'Brien opened the bottle with a pop, champagne flowing from its long neck. He poured out a drink for each of the men in the room, and motioned them forward. "To the Renfrew Millionaires," he toasted. "May we enjoy a long and rewarding run." The room was filled with the sound of clinking crystal as O'Brien and his players drank to their future.

"Now gentlemen, we've got a show to see." With that, O'Brien led the players out of his office and downstairs to the opera hall.

M.J. O'Brien had announced plans to build what he modestly referred to as a "hall" in the early summer of 1908. "It is, according to the plans, practically an opera house," enthused the *Mercury*, Renfrew's local newspaper. From that point on, the structure was known to one and all as the O'Brien Opera House.

O'Brien, always trying to provide the best of everything for his adopted home town, had built the Opera House because he believed the people of Renfrew deserved to be entertained in luxurious surroundings. Before the opening of the Opera House, the Temperance Hall had been Renfrew's main public hall, also serving as a theatre. The Temperance Hall was fine for moving pictures, which had been shown there as early as 1897, but not for live theatre. Whenever visiting shows had come to town they had worked under canvas, not unlike a circus big top. M.J. O'Brien wished to change that.

The O'Brien Opera House gave the town of Renfrew, small as it was, one of the finest performance halls in Ontario. Touring companies who had been seen on the stages of London and New York now included stops in Renfrew as they toured between Montreal, Ottawa, Kingston, and Toronto. The "hall" O'Brien had built could hold almost 1000 people. The lower level, including four ornate boxes, held 350 patrons in the comfort of plush, cushioned seats. Five hundred more could be seated in the first and second balconies. But the O'Brien Opera House wasn't simply large. It was also beautiful.

The audience for the evening had only just begun to file in as the hockey players entered the hall, so there was still ample time to take in the building's many adornments — once their eyes adjusted to the limited light. Though it was equipped with electric lights, the inside of the Opera House was bathed in candlelight on the night of any performance. On this night, the soft flickering glow from the candles not only added to the elegance of an evening at the theatre but to the festive atmosphere surrounding the public unveiling of the town's new hockey team.

"Very impressive!" Frank remarked, as he ran his hand along one of the finely polished railings that lined the walkway. Handsome wood-work highlighted the hallways and stairways throughout the Opera House, but some were more impressed by the luxurious draperies covering the walls.

"Feel this material," Lester said to Taylor, as he lightly rubbed the smooth velvet between his fingers.

Cyclone waved off Lester's offer with a scowl. Thirza's mother had soured his attitude towards other people's riches, and he was trying hard not to be overwhelmed by the sights of the Opera House. Still, he couldn't help but gaze upwards at the theatre's metal ceiling. Painted white, it was decorated with a design of angels. Looking down again, Taylor could not suppress a smile as he watched the men and women of Renfrew, dressed in their finest evening clothes, continuing to make their way into the hall.

The hockey players watched the musical staged in their honour from the lower box seats on the east side of the building. Before the show, a spotlight was turned on the players' box. Each man stood as his name was called, until all nine men were standing and waving to the exultant crowd. M.J. O'Brien rose next, and addressed the audience.

"Ladies and gentlemen," O'Brien's voice boomed, "I give you the Renfrew Millionaires. The finest hockey team ever assembled — right here in our home town! And, I'm sure you will agree," O'Brien continued, when the applause died down, "as fine looking a lot of men as we could ever have hoped for."

The crowd stood and cheered O'Brien's pronouncement. Dressed in their best suits and not yet cut or bruised by the hockey struggles that would soon begin in earnest, the players were indeed a fine-looking lot.

A throng of reporters was waiting outside the Opera House after the night's entertainment, hoping to get a comment from M.J. O'Brien or any of the players. Lester Patrick, as team captain, took on the job of team spokesman as well and addressed the assembled mob.

"Lester! Lester!" shouted an Ottawa reporter. "Do you think your new league will be able to compete at the box office with the more established teams in the Canadian Hockey Association?"

"Let me tell you something," Lester answered. "I believe that Ottawa and those other hockey clubs have cut their own throats by freezing out Renfrew and the Wanderers."

"You do?" called out another newspaperman. "Why?"

"We've already got the best player in hockey in our league," Lester responded, nodding in the direction of Taylor, "and I have no doubt that the National Hockey Association will not only survive, but will prosper."

Just then, M.J. O'Brien emerged from the Opera House and the scrum of scribbling scribes descended upon him, leaving Lester by himself.

"Mr. O'Brien," a reporter inquired. "You're backing four franchises in this five-team circuit. Your son has spent great sums of money building up this team in Renfrew. Why?"

"The answer is simple," O'Brien responded. "I enjoy the game. In fact, I like nothing better than watching hockey."

"That's a laugh," Ambrose whispered. He'd made his way over to Lester and was standing next to him. "We're backing four hockey teams now and I don't believe he's even seen the inside of an arena. I think he just wants to rub Ottawa's nose in it for denying Renfrew's application to the other league in the first place."

XVII

The Bill which will be laid upon the table is entitled An Act Respecting the Naval Service of Canada. It provides for the creation of a naval force and a volunteer force. . . . There is also an important provision to which I at once call the attention of the House, that while the naval force is to be under the control of the Canadian Government . . . in case of emergency, the Governor in Council may place at the disposal of His Majesty for general service in the Royal Navy the naval service or any part thereof.

Sir Wilfrid Laurier,
Prime Minister.
Naval Debate, 1910

THE JANUARY 15, 1910, OPENING OF THE NATIONAL Hockey Association was little more than two weeks away, and as much action was taking place in the boardroom as on the ice. The Canadian Hockey Association had opened its season on December 30, hoping that an early start would give it a leg up on the rival league in the anticipated box office battle. Instead, it had become painfully obvious that public interest could not be maintained under the current two-league setup, particularly with five teams in Montreal. An early match-up between the Montreal Nationals and Montreal Shamrocks attracted only 800 fans. Only a few more turned out two nights later when the defending Stanley Cup champion Ottawa Senators took on All-Montreal.

The Canadian league, by arrogantly dismissing Renfrew and the Wanderers, had created much more trouble for themselves than they had ever bargained for. They had inadvertently spawned a rival hockey league with which they could not compete. There were reports that the older teams would ask for a complete amalgamation of the two leagues.

"I don't want anything to do with those bastards," wailed the Wanderers' Jimmy Gardner, when talk of possibly joining forces came up at an NHA meeting.

"I'm inclined to agree with you," Ambrose replied mildly. He didn't want a merger either. "But consider this for a moment, Jimmy. If you really want to get back at the league for freezing out the Wanderers, let's offer to take in some of their hockey clubs, but not all of them. That's the surest way I know to make the other league close up shop."

"Jeez, Ambrose," Gardner whistled, "you've got balls. It's a gutsy idea, but I still say fuck 'em. Let 'em twist in the wind."

Ambrose took a long puff on his cigar. He could see that this was going to take some time. Ambrose had given his proposal a lot of thought. He was not a hockey man the way Gardner was, but he was an astute businessman, and it made no sense from a business standpoint to remain angry with Ottawa. The capital city was the centre of the hockey universe. Its proximity to Renfrew, and the feelings of resentment Ottawa had created among the citizens of his home town for originally quashing their hockey dreams, would make the Senators a natural rival — and a solid rivalry was good for ticket sales.

"And the Montreal Shamrocks," Ambrose reminded Gardner, "are the only club in your city that can match the Wanderers in terms of fan support. Why have them, and those fans, working against us when we can have them working for us?"

The rest of the NHA club managers agreed with Ambrose, not only because, technically, they were O'Brien employees, but because they could see that the plan made solid business sense. Gardner, too, was finally convinced, and Ottawa and the Shamrocks were asked to join the league. The two clubs jumped at the opportunity, promptly abandoning the CHA, which, as Ambrose had predicted, then quickly ceased operation. The National Hockey Association had won the power struggle, and the newly expanded seven-team circuit was unanimously hailed as the top league in the country. With the defending Stanley Cup champion Senators in the NHA, a Cup challenge would not even be necessary now, since the league champion would simply claim the nation's top hockey prize. It was being freely predicted that the talent-laden Renfrew Millionaires would be the team to beat.

Because the Renfrew Millionaires had been assembled at such a late date, it had been decided shortly after New Year's to hold practice six days a week. Sunday would be the lone day off. The Millionaires continued to practice against Renfrew's amateur club. "The Rivers," the *Renfrew Mercury* reported, "have been putting up a fast and clever exhibition of hockey in their workouts with the Millionaires." The players seemed pleased with the workout they were getting. "They are quite enthusiastic," the *Mercury* said, "over the way the Rivers make them extend themselves."

Not everyone agreed with the *Mercury's* assessment. Frank Patrick, a hockey player who relied on his brains more than his talent to excel in the game, wasn't happy with what he was seeing. If the shouts from Charlotte Whitton and the other youngsters were any indication, the scrimmage games were exciting for the fans, but Frank wondered if they were beneficial to Renfrew's aggregation of all-stars. The Millionaires, he thought, weren't playing as a team; they were relying solely on their own natural abilities. Taylor, Jordan, Rowe, and even Lester would take off on spectacular individual rushes, almost as if they were taking turns showing off, and not paying much attention to other aspects of their game, such as combination play, checking, and defence. Such individualist tactics might work against the tough, but obviously overmatched, Renfrew Rivers, but how well would it serve the Millionaires in their upcoming struggles with first-rate teams like the Ottawa Senators, the Montreal Shamrocks, and the Montreal Wanderers?

Compounding Frank's concerns was the fact that coach Alf Smith didn't appear capable of handling the team. He seemed in awe of the many great stars and did nothing to discourage their solitary style of play. Worried though he was, Frank kept his thoughts to himself. There was no way of knowing if he was right. At least not yet. Maybe natural talent would be enough. The team certainly had that in abundance, and besides, life in Renfrew was proving so pleasant, he had no desire to become a disruptive force. Meanwhile, he worked hard in practice. "I'll be ready when the season starts," Frank told himself, "even if no one else is."

Hockey was not all that occupied the new Renfrew players during their six-day work week. Taylor, Frank, Lester and their teammates were much in demand at O'Brien social functions as well. During the two-week period leading up to the start of the season, every other night was spent at the O'Brien's large home on Barr Street.

M.J. O'Brien had renovated and expanded the house, which had originally been built for a priest almost twenty years before, to almost twice its original size. A newly created third floor had three large rooms, one of which was used as a ballroom. A gallery had been added to a second floor that already featured six bedrooms. On the evening of his first party for the hockey players, O'Brien walked the halls of the second floor, not nervously but with an attentive eye, nonetheless.

Before leaving the master bedroom, O'Brien leaned against one of the posts of the big brass bed and watched his wife finish dressing. Jennie looked as beautiful to him now as she had that day almost thirty years ago when he had first seen her washing the day's dirt off her legs and feet on the porch of her father's farmhouse. Her hair was still thick and dark, and tonight she wore it up, exposing the pale skin on the back of her neck. As Jennie fumbled with the clasp on her string of pearls, O'Brien leaned forward and kissed the soft nape of her neck.

Although Jennie had seen him in her mirror as he approached her, she still managed to express surprise.

"Why Michael John O'Brien," she said, playfully, "whatever has come over you?"

He said nothing. Only smiled.

"Run along now," said Jennie, in a voice she might use when scolding a child, "and let me finish dressing."

But, when O'Brien didn't leave, she kissed him back.

O'Brien left the master bedroom a short time later, smiling to himself as he turned the large crystal doorknob. All doorknobs were crystal in the Barr Street home. All the bathrooms had marble wash basins. O'Brien would settle for nothing but the best. He took obvious pleasure in his beautiful house as he walked down the second-floor hallway to the bedroom of his oldest daughter, where he knocked firmly on the heavy wooden door.

"Come in, father," Stella O'Brien said. It was not hard to recognize his forceful knock. Besides, she had been expecting him.

Stella was a pretty young woman, twenty-two years old, with a pleasing smile and bright blue eyes. She was sitting in front of her oak dressing table, next to the matching oak bureau, while a maid put up her long, dark hair.

"I have a favour to ask of you," O'Brien said, as he entered the room.

Stella knew what the favour would be. It was the same thing her father always asked of her before every social function. "You want me to make things pleasant for the new hockey players," Stella said, flashing a smile for her father.

O'Brien smiled back. It struck him then how much Stella resembled her mother at that age.

"I just want you to talk with them, Stella. Some of them are bound to feel uneasy. You know they're mostly small-town boys. They won't be used to surroundings like this, or to mixing in society. Help them to feel comfortable. Would you please?"

The hockey players were invited to the house on Barr Street to impress M.J. and Ambrose O'Brien's society friends and business associates. Of course, that didn't mean the players weren't capable of being impressed themselves. Even Cyclone Taylor, who would have liked to remain aloof, marvelled at the grandeur of the large entrance hall, from which a drawing room opened on the left and an oak-panelled dining room on the right. Even the food in the dining room was impressive. A lavish dinner was served, with course after course of beautifully prepared food: fruit, followed by soup, salad, then a choice of turkey, roast beef or ham smothered under rich sauces and accompanied by a dizzying array of vegetables; then, for dessert, pies, cakes and an assortment of other sweets.

Taylor forgot all about his self-imposed exile from the class struggle as he surveyed his luxurious surroundings. "You know, Miss O'Brien," he remarked to Stella, who had been seated next to him, "when I was a boy we were so poor we had nothing on the table but our elbows!"

Stella laughed at Taylor's witticism — not the haughty laugh of a rich girl, but the appreciative laugh of a friend. Lester, sitting across the table with his brother Frank, smiled at Stella's response.

The players ate that night until they could eat no more, then retired to the drawing room and mingled with the rest of the guests. With Frank building him up as a storyteller of great renown, Lester was soon prevailed upon to entertain the gathering.

"Why don't you tell us about your first trip to Slocan City," Frank said.

Lester produced a wry half-smile at the memory Frank had just conjured up for him. Then he proceeded to tell the tale.

"I'd only been in Nelson two or three days," Lester began, "but my

father put me to work right away. He needed help staking out the
limits of his lumber claim, so he took me up north with him to survey
our land.

"Because we were both new to the area, Joe — he's my father —
hired a guide to lead us. The three of us rode into the dense forest
country on horseback, marking logging campsites along the way. We
figured it would probably take us a week, but we had brought enough
dried meats, bacon, beans, and biscuits to last ten days. Just to be on
the safe side. But the rations only lasted two days. Seems we got a
visit from a bear . . ."

"A bear!" gasped Stella O'Brien. "Weren't you scared?"

Stella was doing more than playing the role her father had requested.
She was truly caught up in Lester's story.

"Was I scared?" Lester said. "No. Not really."

Seeing doubting faces on many in his audience, Lester laughed and
explained.

"You see," he said sheepishly, "we were asleep when it happened.
None of us was scared because none of us actually saw the bear!"

"But you had no more food," said Stella, interrupting again. "What
did you do?"

Lester didn't mind the interruptions. It was much more fun to tell
a story when there was a good response from the audience — especially
from such a pretty member of the audience.

"We all had rifles," Lester explained, "so we just fanned out on a
little hunting expedition. Of course, I had no idea that I would almost
become one of the hunted!"

"What happened?"

"When I came across a cabin at the edge of a clearing, I found the
proprietor with his gun trained on me!" Lester chuckled now at the
memory. He hadn't found the incident quite so funny then. "Seems
we weren't the only ones that bear had visited. The man heard me
rustling around outside and thought I was the bear coming back again
to do some more damage.

"He put the gun away when he saw I was a man instead of a bear.
I introduced myself and explained our predicament, and I noticed a
look of disbelief on his face. But I couldn't understand why until he
spoke.

"'You're not Lester Patrick the hockey player, are you?'

"'Yes I am,' I said, amazed that anyone would have heard of me
way out there in the backwoods of British Columbia.

" 'I saw you play at the Montreal Arena two years ago!' the man told me. 'It was a game against Quebec. You scored two goals!'

"As I remembered it, I scored three times," Lester told his listeners, "but I wasn't about to argue with this gentleman!"

Lester's last statement was met with much laughter and even some applause, but there were some skeptics as well.

"Did that really happen?" Stella asked, fearing that she'd been duped.

"It's all true, Miss O'Brien," Lester promised. "Cross my heart. The man even invited us in for dinner and gave us enough extra rations to make it back home safely."

Parties at the O'Brien house often stretched into the wee hours of the morning. Some of the players, including Lindsay, Gilmour, and Rowe, who'd played in town the season before and were better acquainted with the Renfrew girls, would bring a date to the gathering and there would be dancing in the upstairs ballroom. Lester, with his girlfriend Grace back home, hadn't sought any female companionship, but he couldn't help taking notice of Stella. She was full of life, and so easy to get along with. Just the type of woman Lester liked.

"What do you think of Stella?" Lester asked Frank after one of the O'Brien get-togethers. "She reminds me a lot of Grace. I even think she looks a bit like her, don't you?"

"She's a lovely girl, Lester," Frank replied cautiously. "But just don't forget she's not Grace."

"What do you mean by that?"

"I mean just what I said. She's not Grace. Grace is waiting for you back in British Columbia. You two are practically engaged, and it wouldn't do to have any stories getting back to her about you running around with somebody else."

"I'm not running around with somebody else. I just said I like her, that's all. And just how would any stories get back to Grace, anyway?"

"I might tell her," Frank said with a straight face. Then he started to laugh. He didn't do it often, but he did like to get his older brother flustered. "Besides, Stella's out of your league. She's a millionaire's daughter. What would she want with you?"

Both brothers were laughing now.

Talk at the great O'Brien social soirees usually centred on hockey. But not always. Not when the men got together in M.J. O'Brien's den, away from the women. Befitting his railway background, O'Brien's den was the closest part of the house to the Canadian Pacific Railway tracks that ran along the north side of the large, wedge-shaped lot, though the whistles and rumblings of passing trains could easily be heard from anywhere in the large house. Whenever O'Brien heard a train approaching, he pulled out his pocket watch, which hung from his vest on a thick gold chain, to see if the train was on time. When the men retired to O'Brien's den, to smoke cigars or drink brandy, the conversation often got around to politics.

"How about that Liberal Prime Minister of ours," Taylor griped on one such occasion. "After twelve years of hemming and hawing on what to do about England's requests for contributions to the British Navy, he's finally decided to take a stand." Taylor was shaking his head, obviously dismayed at the Prime Minister's decision.

"He wants to build a Canadian Navy," Taylor went on. "I don't understand it. We're subjects of the British Empire. That means the British Navy is our navy. Why don't we support it, then? It's the mightiest fleet in the world."

"I don't know how much longer that's going to be true, Cyc," Frank rebutted. "I've read where Germany is building those new Dreadnought battleships in such quick order that it may soon pass Britain in naval strength."

"Well then, that's all the more reason to support the British Navy," Taylor shot back, his face flushed. "What good will Laurier's tin-pot navy be if Germany goes to war with England?

"Damn French Canadians," Taylor continued. "They don't want to do anything that supports the Empire! I think Laurier's afraid to stand up to them. That's the problem. It's going to tear this country apart — you wait and see."

Taylor's last comment caused a dull pain to well up in Lester's stomach. For an instant he was overcome with the unsettling sensation. "Well, Cyc," he said, trying to lighten the mood, "I wouldn't dwell on it. We've got more immediate concerns, like the Montreal Wanderers on Saturday night."

XVIII

The proposals of the government are weak and ineffective. . . .
They afford no immediate aid and assistance. . . . I say it would
be the proper course . . . to do that which, after all, is the most
important thing: stand side by side with the mother country
under the conditions which confront her at the present time.
The needs of the Empire are before our very eyes today. We
have the splendid example of the other great dependencies of
the Empire. Are we of less faith and of less courage than they?
Shall an Australian fleet and a New Zealand Dreadnought
defend the flag which floats above us while our little cruisers
are fleeing helpless before an enemy?

Robert Borden,
Opposition Leader.
Naval Debate, 1910

"I THINK MY SISTER IS SWEET ON YOU," AMBROSE TOLD
Lester, as the train carrying the Renfrew Millionaires rolled eastward
to Montreal. "She was asking about you at the station."

Stella had been among the large delegation that had turned out to
see the team off on its first journey in the quest for the Stanley Cup.
It had been quite a send-off: the station swarming with people, the
local high school band playing marching tunes, children waving flags,
and O'Brien's private railcar, which would carry the team to Montreal,
decked out in red-and-white striped bunting draped from gold-plated
studs. Lester had easily picked out Stella among the large crowd, since
she was wearing an eye-catching floppy white hat with a huge red
feather in it. Her father had not been present. Away on business in
Ottawa, O'Brien had wired his best wishes, instead. Ambrose had read
the telegram aloud for all present to hear. "Do us proud, gentlemen,"
it had concluded. The message had been met with loud cheers.

"I told her you had a girl back home," Ambrose went on. "She said she knew that, but she hoped it wouldn't stop you from asking her to dance the next time we have a party." Ambrose laughed. "She'd probably kill me if she knew I was telling you this."

Lester laughed too, somewhat nervously. He liked Stella, and now he knew that she liked him. Frank elbowed him in the ribs.

"My brother, the lady's man!"

The players proved an interesting study in contrasts as they rode the train to Montreal. Goalie Bert Lindsay sat by himself, staring out the window, pondering Wanderers sharpshooters like Pud Glass, Ernie Russell, and the hot newcomer, Harry Hyland. Larry Gilmour also sat alone, but he was reading a book. Some of the players had teased him a bit about that. Most of the others passed the time playing cards. Bobby Rowe and Jack Fraser played gin. Ambrose dealt blackjack for Taylor, Herb Jordan, and Ernie Liffiton, but they played for poker chips, not real stakes. Ambrose was a gambler, but didn't wish to take his players' money. Instead, he'd bet on them. "I've got $2000 riding on you boys tonight," Ambrose told them. "Don't let me down."

Frank was playing cards, too. He liked to be by himself on game day, and playing solitaire seemed like the best way to accomplish that on a crowded train. Lester, on the other hand, liked to keep busy. He walked among the players, giving tips to Lindsay — after all, he had played two seasons with Glass and Russell — giving the needle to Gilmour about his book, and keeping tabs on the card games.

"You can move that row under the black ten onto the red jack, Frank," he said, sitting down next to his brother. "Look at that!" he said excitedly, as the removal of the ten turned up a black queen. "Now you can shift the whole thing back over on the queen, and then move up that red king you've got and slide the pile over there."

"I know how to the play game, Lester," Frank said testily. "You know, they call it solitaire for a reason."

Frank was in a bad mood. His nose had been broken in an on-ice mishap three days before. It wasn't a bad break; still he wasn't likely to see any action in the opening game, though he might dress as a substitute.

"Sorry Frank." Lester shrugged his shoulders and arched his eyebrows in an a exaggerated "excuse me" expression. He left his brother alone for the rest of the trip.

The team's train arrived in Montreal at two-thirty in the afternoon, six hours before game time. Two horse-drawn carriages, which Ambrose had hired in advance, were waiting at the station. The hacks transported the players, their coach, and Ambrose to the nearby Queen's Hotel. Once there, the team was escorted to the hotel dining room, where they shared a pregame meal of steak and eggs before retiring to their rooms for a nap.

Cyclone Taylor, as was his custom, was the first player to arrive at the arena. He liked to get to the rink early. He would sit in the stands by himself for a while and stare out at the ice surface, thinking about the game at hand: what to expect from the opposition, and what he hoped to accomplish himself. Sometimes the arena would be empty. At other times, the rink manager might be present, filling in cracks in the natural surface with snow, or pouring buckets of water on the ice and spreading it around with what appeared to be a push broom lacking bristles, to ensure a flat, even playing surface.

This day, the rink was empty. Taylor liked it better that way. After sitting in the empty arena for about half an hour, Taylor made his way to the Renfrew dressing room, where, sitting on a small, three-legged stool in front of his cubicle, he read the newspaper. Flipping to the sports page first, he read about the evening's hockey game. The Montreal reporters were hoping for a return to championship form by the Wanderers, after the team's three-year Stanley Cup reign had been ended by Ottawa the previous season. Taylor smiled at the memory of that triumph. After a moment, he turned back to the front page and read about the Naval Debate in the House of Commons. No smiles came from that story.

When Taylor was finished with the newspaper, he turned his attention to the new hockey stick he had selected for the season. With any luck, it would last him through all twelve games. It was a sturdy, heavy piece of lumber. The long shaft of Taylor's stick was nearly three inches thick, and the blade angled off at almost ninety degrees. Taylor liked his stick that way. It forced him to keep the puck close to his body as he carried it, which made it easier for him to control, while at the same time making it tougher for his opponents to take it away.

Taylor inspected his new stick, holding the butt end up in front of his eye with his right hand, thumb along the bottom edge, his left arm outstretched supporting the rest of the stick, as he held it up to the light searching for any nicks or other damage that might have been inflicted on the journey from Renfrew. With no damage found, Taylor began to apply the tape. He started from the front of the blade and worked towards the heel. With the tape in his left hand and stick in his right, Taylor worked fast, his wrists snapping in a quick up-and-down motion, until he had covered all but the very tip of the blade in a double layer of black tape.

Frank's injury was going to cause some changes to the Renfrew lineup. The team had tried a variety of combinations in their last practice session, and now it was time to make a decision. Lester was sitting with Alf Smith in the small coach's office off the visitor's dressing room in the Jubilee Rink, pitching what he felt was the best possible roster under the circumstances.

Outside the office, the rest of the Renfew players were beginning to file into the dressing room. They found their hockey gear already laid out for them in front of an assigned cubicle. Each player's name was written in chalk on a slate board mounted above his cubicle. Suspended from a wooden hanger on a metal rod running the two-foot width of each cubicle was the player's new uniform. The body of the thick woollen sweater was white, but the top, from the chest and shoulders right up to the high turtle neck, was bright red. Bright red trim also circled the cuffs of both sleeves and ran along the lower edge of the sweater. A red, stylized "R" was emblazoned on the chest of each sweater. The hockey socks were white, with red bands around the knees.

When all the the players were present, about an hour before game time, Lester emerged from Alf Smith's office to inform them exactly what the lineup would be for their opening game with the Wanderers.

"Here's how we're going to set it up, fellows," Lester began. "Bert is in goal."

"Nice call, Lester," heckled Bobby Rowe. Bert Lindsay was, of course, the team's lone goaltender.

The other players laughed. Lester smiled and went on.

"Fred," he said, nodding his head in Taylor's direction, "will be at cover point. I'll be dropping back as his defence partner to take Frank's place on the point."

"Oh, another clever call," joked Bobby Rowe again. "At least with Cyclone back there we know we've got one sound defensive player." This brought another round of chuckles from the players, though they all knew Lester was a more than capable defensive replacement.

Lester turned in the direction of his heckler and, in jest, shot him an icy stare. "Mr. Rowe," he said slowly. "You'll be taking over my position at rover. Think you're up to it?"

The rest of the Renfrew lineup that night placed Herb Jordan at centre, Jack Fraser at left wing, and Ernie Liffiton on right. Frank and Larry Gilmour would ride the bench as substitutes in case of injury.

With game time still about an hour off, the players settled into their individual routines of preparation. Bert Lindsay sat by himself, slowly lacing his skates and strapping on his pads. Frank, sitting alone in his long johns, laid out all his equipment on the floor in front of him so that it looked as though a flattened, invisible hockey player had fallen at his feet. There wasn't much equipment there. He had a pair of cane knee pads, which buckled on his legs outside of his hockey socks. Most defencemen wore this type of protection. Forwards had smaller pads they wore under their socks. Protecting the shins was pretty much a personal matter. A leather pad might be employed, but many players still used layers of newspaper or, better yet, a couple of magazines. Thick department store catalogues were a favourite.

Frank had a triangular-shaped tin cup with rounded edges he wore to protect his private parts. It fit into a pocket that had been sewn into the front of his hockey pants. The canvas pants offered little further protection: some stiff strips of leather or small slats of wood stitched into the thighs, some extra padding in the seat to protect the tailbone. Stretchy suspenders that crossed in the back held up the pants. There was no equipment to protect his shoulders and elbows, only the extra layers of cloth and felt stitched into his long johns and hockey sweater. Padded leather gloves shielded his hands. His fingers and the backs of his hands were guarded by pudgy strips of leather that looked like sausages. The joints on the fingers of the gloves were white and made of more flexible material that allowed for better manual dexterity. The gloves extended high above the wrists with much narrower bands of leather there. Frank's feet (and those of his teammates) were given little protection other than the stiff leather used around the toe and heel of the skate boot. Double rows of tiny metal eyelets ran up the front of the skates, to anchor the long laces that criss-crossed up the foot and above the ankle.

Frank dressed slowly, inspecting each piece of equipment before putting it on. He began with the small pads he wore on his shins, strapping them in place with two thick elastics. Next, he pulled up his hockey socks and attached them to the sharp clasps at the ends of the straps hanging from a belt he wore around his waist. His hockey pants came next. After sliding them on, he left the suspenders hanging to either side so that his arms were free to move as he laced his skates. Once the skates were sufficiently tightened, he attached his knee pads, buckling them in front where they were easier to see and then turning them around the proper way. Lifting his suspenders over his shoulders, he then slipped his hockey jersey over his head and was ready to go.

The starting forwards — Jordan, Rowe, Fraser, and Liffiton — all sat together as they dressed. They chattered among themselves, mostly talking strategy. They paid special attention to the Wanderers' great centre, Ernie Russell. Russell had joined the Montreal team back in 1906, the same year Lester had come aboard. In 1907, he had scored the astounding total of forty-two goals in just nine games. He had not come close to matching that record total since, but was still a very dangerous scorer and the central figure in the Wanderers' offensive attack. As the opposing centre, Herb Jordan wondered how to shut down his Montreal counterpart.

"What do you think is the best way to deal with Russell?" Jordan asked Lester. "Do you think that Bobby or I should shadow him everywhere he goes? Or maybe we shouldn't assign one person to him? Maybe all the forwards should converge on him when the Wanderers go on the attack. You guys on the defence can pick up his linemates."

Lester was about to answer when the conversation took a twist.

"You know," Cyclone Taylor offered to no one in particular, "at least one good thing has come out of this Naval Debate so far. After Borden pushed him on that clause about Canada having the authority to place our navy at England's disposal, Laurier agreed with him that he would consider Canada to be at war when Britain is at war."

Taylor's outburst got Frank's attention. "Come on, Cyc! This isn't the time or the place for that kind of discussion."

"I can't believe Laurier would say something as bold as that," Herb Jordan chimed in, not yet allowing the conversation to drop. "It's not like the old man to take such a divisive stand. The French will be all over him for that one. You watch. He's gonna have to figure out some way to back down without angering Ontario."

"C'mon, guys!" Frank pleaded.

"What do you think, Lester?" Jordan asked.

Lester didn't respond at first. He had slipped back to that stormy day in 1900, the day of the Boer War riot when he had learned first hand about "the French problem." In his mind he could see himself standing in front of the French university, cold, wet and scared after the students there had turned the hose on the mob. People were running in all directions, but Lester was too scared to move, unable to duck as an elbow struck his cheekbone, sending waves of pain pounding throughout his head. As Lester imagined the elbow coming at him, he jerked his head back in an attempt to dodge it, and slammed into the wall behind him. The pain snapped him back to reality. Fortunately he had not hurt himself.

"Lester? What is it? Are you all right?"

Lester nodded. "I think," he said slowly, "that as the rover, Bobby Rowe should stick with Russell wherever he goes." The other conversation was not one in which he cared to take part.

With the start of the game now only minutes away, Lester slapped his stick on the floor, signifying to his teammates that it was time to leave the dressing room. As captain, he led the procession of players onto the ice. The tall, handsome man was instantly recognized by the capacity crowd of 3000 that had jammed into the tiny Jubilee Rink and was accorded a warm welcome. The Wanderers faithful had not forgotten that just a few years ago this same man had given them their first taste of Stanley Cup glory. Lester held up his right hand as he skated across the ice, not quite in a wave but nonetheless in a gesture of acknowledgement for the ovation.

With gametime fast approaching, the Renfrew players gathered around their goalie to give Bert Lindsay a last-minute whack on the pads for encouragement and to await any final instructions from their captain.

"Gentlemen," Lester said, "this is why we've all been brought here. To play hockey. A lot of people are counting on us. Let's not let them down."

Herb Jordan was already lined up at centre awaiting the face-off when Ernie Russell glided into the area and put his stick down. The referee placed the puck on the ice between them and shouted "Play!" Russell and Jordan both took a swipe at the puck without making contact, their momentum carrying them forward. Jordan pushed Russell back with a jolt of his shoulder, scooped up the puck, and fed it back to Bobby Rowe.

Taylor, seeing Rowe clearly in possession of the disk, rushed forward from his cover point position. "Bobby, Bobby," he shouted, calling for a pass. Rowe slid the puck back to him. Taylor cut towards the centre of the ice, then faking back to the left with a deft nod of his head, he shook off Wanderers rover Pud Glass. Montreal forwards Harry Hyland and Jimmy Gardner — the same Jimmy Gardner who as spokesman for team owner P.J. Doran had inspired Ambrose O'Brien to create the National Hockey Association — closed in from their positions at left and right wing to try and snuff out Taylor's rush before he could gain a full head of steam. But Taylor roared right through them.

"Fuck," cursed Gardner, as he turned in pursuit of Cyclone.

In full flight now, Taylor bore down on Moose Johnson, his Wanderers counterpart at cover point. Johnson had been a winger in Lester's days with the Montreal team, but the remarkable agility of his six-foot frame, combined with his courage and toughness, convinced the Wanderers brass that they should convert him to a defensive position. Johnson had long arms and played with an exceptionally long stick, giving him a tremendous reach. He handled his stick very effectively and had developed an outstanding poke check.

Johnson was a difficult man to get around, and, realizing this, Taylor looked for someone to drop the puck to. But no one was there. The other Renfrew players had been too slow to get up ice with him. They had seen him start and complete similar rushes all by himself, almost at will, for the last two weeks in practice. Not this time. With no other option open to him, Taylor flipped a long shot on goal.

The play had only taken a few seconds to develop and fizzle out, but it had been long enough for Frank, watching from the Renfrew bench, to notice. "Dammit," he muttered, as Wanderers netminder Riley Hern easily turned Taylor's shot aside. It was exactly the disorganized play Frank had feared.

Wanderers point man Jack Marshall picked up the loose puck and lofted it the length of the ice. Lester positioned himself under the puck, but it landed on its edge and scooted past him into the corner. The Wanderers forwards, seeing an opportunity, bore down on the puck. Lester retrieved the rubber after it bounced off the boards, but found Jimmy Gardner right on top of him. Gardner, who was closer in on Lester than the Renfrew captain had anticipated, stripped him of the puck, and fed it back to Hyland. Harry whipped a hard shot on goal before Bert Lindsay had a chance to set himself. The puck found net. The Wanderers had taken a quick 1–0 lead.

"Look how slow everybody was coming back into our zone," Frank moaned.

"Hyland was wide open," Larry Gilmour agreed.

The first minute of the game set the tone for the next twenty minutes. Renfrew's faster skaters couldn't penetrate the Wanderers defence. Taylor, Jordan, Lester, and Rowe continually had their rushes thwarted by the tight checking of the Montreal team, and the slowness of the Millionaires to get back into position after each rush created numerous scoring chances for the Wanderers. Lindsay was kept busy, darting from post to post, kicking out the rubber or blocking shots with a gloved hand, but three more times he was beaten, as the score climbed to 4–0.

Following the fourth Montreal goal, right winger Ernie Liffiton collided with Pud Glass. He fell to the ice, landing awkwardly on his right elbow and injuring his arm. Liffiton retired to the bench, and Frank entered the game as his replacement.

With Frank now in the lineup, Renfrew reverted to its standard roster. Lester moved up to rover, leaving his brother in the point position, and Rowe moved from rover to right wing. The move paid dividends just seconds before half-time, when the Millionaires got on the scoreboard. Lester picked up a loose puck at centre, carried it to the Montreal end and flipped it to Taylor, who pulled Riley Hern out of position before flicking a quick pass across to Bobby Rowe. Rowe jammed the puck into the yawning cage.

The Renfrew players trudged off to the dressing room, trailing 4–1. Their improved play in the last ten minutes, and the goal in the final seconds, had some players feeling better about the first half than they actually had a right to.

The players slumped into their seats, thoroughly exhausted by the pace the Wanderers had set. Clearly the Montrealers, though older on average than the Renfrew squad, were the better conditioned of the two teams. Undoubtedly their training camp had included a lot fewer full-course dinners in the house of a millionaire.

Taylor sat on his stool, bent over at the waist. He had done the best work for Renfrew in the first half, but was breathing heavily as he loosened his skates. He exhaled contentedly as he pulled them off and began circling his feet around to loosen them up, flexing and relaxing his toes to work out any cramps. Jack Fraser sat on the floor, where only his shoulder blades and the back of his head resting against the wall kept him from sprawling out completely. His arms hung limp at his sides. Too many late nights at the O'Brien house. The same could be said for his teammates.

"Good work out there, fellas," Alf Smith enthused, apparently sincerely, as he entered the dressing room. "I thought we looked pretty good."

"Dammit, Alf," Frank snapped back, "what game were you watching? We were terrible. No one was thinking like a team player. We were all just standing around waiting to see what everybody else was going to do."

"I don't think it was as bad as all that, Frank," Taylor piped up.

"No Cyc, maybe it wasn't as bad as I say. We've got a lot of talent here and that kept us competitive. Sort of. But if we don't start to work together, things aren't going to get better."

"Well, Frank," reasoned Bobby Rowe, "you've got to remember that we've only been together for two weeks. Most of those guys have been playing together for four or five years."

"So what? Are you making excuses for us already? That's a fact we were all aware of heading into this season. Are we going to trot it out all year long? I don't think there are too many people in Renfrew who'll put up with that. I certainly know two wealthy businessmen who won't."

"Frank's right," Herb Jordan agreed. "We've got to pull together in the second half. Do a better job. If we can just get the first goal . . ." His voice trailed off.

The dressing room remained silent. The players knew that the problem they had couldn't be solved by brave talk. It was going to require patience and hard work, harder work than they had done in preparing for this game, if they were to improve as a team. Still, they were only down by three goals with thirty minutes yet to be played, so there was no point in getting too far down on themselves.

When the intermission was over, Lester again slapped his stick on the floor, and the players made their way back out to the ice.

The Renfrew players came out strong in the second half, and within five minutes they scored the goal Herb Jordan had hoped for, but 4–2 was as close as Renfrew would get.

The five-minute burst of energy that resulted in Renfrew's second goal took its toll on what had already been a tired group of Millionaires. Occasionally, Taylor or one of the two Patricks would take off on a rush, but if the Renfrew forwards raced up ice with them, they were too slow in getting back. If they exerted too much energy helping out on defence, they were unable to take part in the rush. Too often, the Renfrew players were forced to flip the puck into the stands to catch a quick breather. It wasn't enough to help the poorly prepared team. The Wanderers poured in three late goals and registered a relatively easy 7–2 victory. The best team money could buy had been soundly defeated.

"Dammit!" Frank growled, swinging his stick at the metal garbage can that sat in the middle of the Renfrew dressing room, then plopping himself down on his stool. He peeled off his sweaty jersey and flung it to the floor. Similar sentiments were expressed by the rest of the players as they made their way towards their cubicles.

The Millionaires sat in dejected silence, with only the occasional profanity uttered. Meanwhile, they could hear howls of delight from the Wanderers' dressing room across the hall, making the painful defeat sting that much more. A short time later, Ambrose entered the room. The heads of all nine players dropped immediately. No one wished to look their benevolent owner in the eye.

"Buck up, fellows," Ambrose advised. "It seems to me, and I think Mr. Taylor will back me up on this, that Ottawa dropped its opening game to the Wanderers last season and still managed to do all right, didn't you, Cyc?" Taylor nodded, a wistful look crossing his face as he remembered the taste of the champagne he had sipped from the Stanley Cup.

"Don't worry about this one. We've got eleven more games to play. I still think we're gonna win this thing," Ambrose added reassuringly. "Oh, one more thing," he said with a smile. "You guys owe me $2000!"

The fact that Ambrose could so easily laugh off the large bet he had lost did more than anything else he had said to help put the players' minds at ease.

"Ambrose? May I speak with you a moment?" Lester asked. "Alone?"

"Certainly, Lester." Ambrose held the door open to the small coach's office. "Let's go in here."

Once inside, Ambrose could see something was bothering Lester. "What's on your mind, Cap'n?" he asked.

Lester paused for a moment. He knew that what he was about to say might have serious repercussions. His brow furrowed with concentration as he searched for the right words.

"Ambrose," he said slowly. "I don't think there should be another party for the players for a while."

When Ambrose said nothing, Lester went on, almost apologetically. "It's not that we don't appreciate everything you and your father have done for us, but . . . Well, you saw the game tonight. We were terrible."

"I don't know . . . " Ambrose said, his voice fading into silence.

Lester wasn't sure if Ambrose meant that he didn't think the game was so terrible or that he didn't know about calling a halt to the parties. It was the latter. Ambrose was reluctant to give up the partying. Like his father, he enjoyed his power to impress. Unlike his father, Ambrose knew that he could never command the same kind of respect as a man who had worked himself up from nothing. As able a businessman as he had already become in his own right, he still felt lost in his famous father's shadow. Putting together the world's greatest hockey team would be his way of making his own mark, and he wanted to bask in the reflected glory.

"We're no good to you if we don't win," Lester said.

It was almost as if he had read Ambrose's mind. Ambrose could see Lester's point. "I'll bring it up with my father," he said. "Hopefully, he'll agree to it."

Ambrose and Lester exited the office a few moments later. "It seems as though the opening of the hockey season has interfered with our Renfrew social season," Lester said to his teammates. "We can't please the O'Briens in the drawing room and in the arena as well."

The other players realized what Lester was driving at. They had all enjoyed the parties at the house on Barr Street, but they also knew the soirees had had a detrimental effect on their preparation for the game.

"From now on," Lester concluded, "there will be less emphasis on fun and games and more on hockey."

The Millionaires arrived back at the train station in Renfrew on Sunday evening, after spending Saturday night in Montreal. The reception they got upon their return put no one in the mind of the send-off they had been given just the morning before. Stella O'Brien was among the small group that turned out. She smiled at Lester as he climbed off the train. He smiled back, a little wanly.

"Good evening," Lester said graciously, bowing ever so slightly.

"Hello," Stella said cheerfully. Then she added in a more serious tone, "I was sorry to hear about the results of last night's game."

"No more so than I, Miss O'Brien. No more so than I."

XIX

I stated the other day that the Parliament of Canada would have control of the Navy, and would declare when it should or shouldn't go to war. Upon this point we have been assailed right and left. . . . We have been assailed in Quebec because it is said there that under no circumstances should Canada ever take part in any war of England. Assailed in Ontario because there it is said that under all circumstances Canada should take part in all wars of England. . . . The other day when introducing this measure, I stated that when England is at war we are at war. . . . The truth is that in making the statement that when England is at war we are at war, I was simply stating a principle of international law. . . . It does not follow, however, that because England is at war we should necessarily take part in that war.

Sir Wilfrid Laurier,
Prime Minister.
Naval Debate, 1910

SLEEP DID NOT COME EASILY FOR LESTER THAT SUNDAY night. He lay in his bed at the boarding house in Renfrew, tossing and turning and tugging at the sheets. Frank had been right when he said during the half-time break that the Renfrew players were not thinking like a team. He'd also been right when he said that the fact that the team had been together only a couple of weeks wasn't going to hold up as a valid excuse for their poor performance. If they had worked harder during those two weeks, it probably wouldn't even be an issue now.

"We've only got three days until our next game," Lester mumbled as he lay awake in bed. "How are we going to turn this around in that time?"

Les Canadiens were next on the Renfrew schedule, coming to town for a game on Wednesday night. That should make the task a little easier, Lester thought. The new Montreal club would be playing its first official league game and might well be experiencing some of the same growing pains that the Millionaires were going through. Still, Lester knew, that did not solve the problem. How was he going to get a collection of all-stars to start playing like a team? A number of ideas went through his head, but he had not reached any conclusions when sleep finally came to him.

That night, Lester dreamed he was back home in Nelson. He was in a small boat with Grace, rowing a few dozen yards off the shore of Lakeside Park on Kootenay Lake. Grace looked beautiful, wearing a wide-brimmed white sun hat that was tied beneath her chin with a thick red ribbon, and her white lawn dress with the lacy collar and cuffs. The act of sitting in the boat caused the dress to bunch up at the waist before rounding out again over her hips. Though the dress Grace wore in Lester's dream modestly covered her, it could not obscure her lush figure. He could easily imagine the sight of her shapely legs beneath all that white material. Looking up, he could see her round breasts straining against the delicate lace of her bodice. Lester reached out, touching her blushing cheek, stroking it gently. He leaned closer, drawing her lips towards his. Suddenly, just as their lips were about to meet, he saw that the woman was Stella O'Brien.

Lester's eyes sprang open as he awoke with a start, not sure of where he was. He stared at the ceiling for a while, trying to blank all thoughts from his mind. It was a long time before he fell back to sleep.

Lester awoke to sunlight streaming in the window. Since his room faced south, he realized it must already be quite late in the morning. Getting out of bed, he put on his robe over his flannel pajamas, pulled on his slippers, and shuffled off to the bathroom. He filled the wash basin with cold water and splashed some on his face. Checking the mirror, he grabbed a comb and did some quick work on his hair, attempting to groom the just-awakened look from his tangled shock.

Heading towards the kitchen of the boarding house, Lester found his brother cooking breakfast. Taylor sat drinking coffee while looking over several newspapers. Lester poured himself a cup of plain hot water, grabbed one of the papers and sat down. He always drank one cup of hot water a day during the hockey season. "Good for your constitution," he would explain, if asked.

"Look at this," Taylor moaned while pointing at a headline in a newspaper from a nearby town. " 'The Renfrew Gold Bricks' they're calling us. And look at this in the *Mercury*: 'Alas! Poor Renfrew!' " He shook his head. "Two days ago we were the toast of the town. One loss and we're bums."

"You take it all too personally, Cyc," Frank said, looking over his shoulder as he stood at the stove. "What do you care what those reporters say? None of them ever even played the game. Hell, if we weren't giving them something to write about, they'd have to make things up."

"Seems to me this piece in the *Mercury* is pretty accurate," Lester stated flatly, reading the article over Taylor's shoulder. "Listen. 'Taylor was good but his rushes, while very spectacular, lacked results because of the failure of the forwards' combination. Another thing that hurt badly was the time it took the team to get back into position after a rush.' "

"Can't argue with that," Frank said with a shrug. "Now what are we going to do about it? We've only got practice tonight and tomorrow to get something worked out before Wednesday's game."

Frank carried three plates to the table. Each one was loaded down with two eggs, four strips of bacon, and a mound of fried potatoes. A basket of freshly baked muffins already sat in the middle of the table, courtesy of their landlady, Miss Stack.

The players talked strategy as they gobbled down breakfast. Actually, it was Frank and Lester who did most of the talking; Taylor's head just swivelled back and forth as he tried to follow the flow of the conversation. Talking helped both Frank and Lester put Saturday's loss in perspective. Both men simply resigned themselves to the fact that it was going to take some hard work for the team to click. By the end of the meal, they had also arrived at what they believed to be an effective way to get their teammates accustomed to playing with one another as a unit.

"So it's decided, then," Frank stated. "At practice with the Rivers tonight and tomorrow we won't allow anyone to score a goal unless at least two passes have been made to set up the play. No individual rushes."

"I'll talk your idea over with Alf," Lester said. "I'm sure he'll be agreeable. Of course, nothing is going to take the place of some good old-fashioned hard work, but maybe this can speed things up."

Practices were still being held in the evening. The Rivers players were all amateurs and had to work during the day. Most of the Millionaires were receiving high enough salaries to play hockey that they had taken leaves of absence from their regular jobs to come to Renfrew for the three-month hockey season. Herb Jordan was the most notable exception. He had come to Renfrew only because he had been offered a job handling business matters connected with O'Brien interests in town. It was a position Jordan took very seriously; so much so, in fact, that work, and not hockey, soon became his top priority.

Evening practice left plenty of free time during the day for roommates Taylor and the Patricks. For the past two weeks, on bright sunny mornings, many of the players had spent their time soaking up the sun on benches in front of the *Mercury* building. Such leisure activity didn't seem appropriate after the defeat in Montreal. Instead, the three players simply walked the main street of the town, visiting with shopkeepers. The hockey players had quickly become familiar figures on the streets, readily befriended by the locals.

Raglan Street, Renfrew's main thoroughfare, was not unlike those in most other small Ontario communities. It had grown up considerably since 1895 when Renfrew had been incorporated as a town. Before then, the street had still been unpaved and in times of wet weather, particularly in the spring and fall, the mud had risen almost to the hub of the wheels on the horse-drawn carriages. Conversely, during summer's dry spells, water had to be sprinkled on the street to keep the dust down.

The sidewalks in those days had been built from planks of wood placed high above the roadway, as a convenience for those getting in or out of their buggies, and also as protection from the messy street. Wooden ramps at regular intervals helped people to get across the muddy gutter should they have to cross the street on foot. Many of the shopkeepers along Raglan Street had had a stone block in front of their stores, fitted with a ring for tethering horses, but for many drivers a telephone pole or electric light standard had served the same purpose. Some of the poles had been wrapped with steel strapping as protection against the chewing teeth of impatient horses.

Much of this was still visible to the Patricks and Taylor, since only the Barnet family and the O'Briens owned a car in Renfrew. All others still relied on the horse and wagon, if not on their own two feet. However, little else on Raglan Street remained as it had been, and as they strolled along Renfrew's main street, Frank, Lester and Taylor could only imagine how different the town had once looked. Now there were brick buildings where log and stone structures had stood. Plank sidewalks had given way to concrete, and dirt and clay streets were paved with a closely packed, broken stone called macadam. The transformation of Renfrew was due in part to community spirit but could be attributed more directly to several far-seeing industrialists, most notably M.J. O'Brien and Alexander Barnet.

Taylor and the Patricks had already experienced some of the ways M.J. O'Brien had added to the beauty and sophistication of his town. But nothing more than a walk down main street was needed to see the civic contributions of Alexander Barnet. Towering over the smaller buildings on Raglan Street, the Barnet Block was easily the business district's most striking structure.

"Look at all those windows!" Frank marvelled. The twelve giant plate-glass windows that ran the length of the Barnet building's face on the second and third storeys always impressed him. Elegant fanlights rose above these large windows, adding to the building's beauty.

"It's a nice building, I guess," said Taylor. The old brick structure really wasn't to his taste. Construction like that rarely impressed him any more. None would ever measure up to the Parliament Buildings. "But I like the post office."

Built just two years before, Renfrew's new post office was made of limestone from a quarry on the edge of town. The stone had been chipped into shape by local masons.

"I like the way they used rough-looking stones on most of it," Taylor said, "but put those smooth limestone blocks around the front doors."

He also liked the mansard roof, with its steep sides and flat top, even though the copper had not yet had time to turn the pale green he had become familiar with in Ottawa.

Just down the road from the post office, at the corner of Raglan and Renfrew streets, was the Handford Photography Studio, the destination of the three hockey players.

"Hello, Gus," Taylor called out, sticking his head in through the door to the studio.

"Cyclone, Frank, Lester! Come in, come in," Augustus Handford beckoned. "So when are you fellows going to let me take your picture?"

"You can come down to the rink any time, Gus," Lester teased. He knew that the photographer, who specialized in portraits, preferred to work in his studio rather than go on location. That way, Gus explained, he had complete control of the situation. He determined how much light was needed, how to pose his subject, what angles were best — that sort of thing. Furthermore, the camera he used for his portraits was very large and hard to move, not to mention expensive and difficult to replace. He didn't want to risk an accident by lugging it around unless it was absolutely necessary.

"Yeah," Gus shot back, "I'll bring my camera down to the rink just as soon as you guys win a game."

"Ouch!" Frank winced in mock pain. "That was a cheap shot."

"You better be careful, Gus," Taylor scolded sarcastically, "or we'll get someone else to take the official team photo when we win the Stanley Cup."

They all laughed.

"So what brings you gents to my humble establishment? As if I didn't know."

Gus Handford's photo studio had become a favourite hangout for Taylor and the Patricks because Gus let them listen to records on his gramophone. Gus had a large collection of Victor records, the ones whose labels showed a little white dog, with brown eyes and ears and a spot on his back, staring down the horn on a gramophone. "He Hears His Master's Voice," the advertisements read.

Gramophones like the one Gus owned were a big improvement over earlier models. The new talking machines, as they were still sometimes called, played double-sided disc recordings instead of the large cylinders used on older gramophones. Even the bulky conical horns that the early machines had needed to amplify the sound were slowly becoming a thing of the past. But gramophones still had to be cranked up by hand.

"What are we going to listen to today, fellows?" Gus asked as he wound the handle, spinning the gears that put the machine in motion.

"How 'bout one of the English masters?" Taylor requested.

"Yeah," said Frank, seconding the motion. "Let's hear something by Harry Lauder."

Gus opened the box where he kept his records and pulled one out. Holding the brittle disc gingerly around its edges, the photographer placed it gently on the music machine. The players recognized the selection instantly as the bouncy tune floated through the air.

"She Is Ma Daisy," said Taylor, waving his arms as if he were conducting the music. "Come on, Lester. Sing it for us!"

Lester was glad to comply.

> For she's ma Daisy
> Ma bonny Daisy
> She's as sweet as sugar candy
> and she's very fond 'a Sandy
> And I'm weary
> Aboot me deary
> I would rather lose me whip
> then lose ma Dai-ai-ai-sy

Lester, with his strong tenor voice, always sang lead. He had to employ a Scottish burr for this selection. Frank whistled and hummed along, while Taylor conducted. But they all joined in on the finale. Gus chuckled as the players leaned together, barbershop style, with their hands over their hearts, for the corny conclusion to their song. "Old Harry's got nothing to worry about from you fellows. It's sure a good thing you can play hockey!"

It was the players who were laughing now.

Neither Taylor, Frank, nor Lester had been aware of how much time they'd spent in the studio that afternoon, until Gus's daughter, Lily, came home from school. The Handfords lived in a house behind the studio. There was a side door to the studio that led directly into the house, which Lily was supposed to use when she came home, but whenever she saw one of the hockey players inside she conveniently forgot the family rule and entered through the front door.

"Hello, Lillian," her father greeted her. The smile on Gus's face and the tone of his voice assured Lily she was in no trouble. Gus was a hockey fan. He had laid out twelve dollars for two reserved season's tickets for all six Millionaires home games, and he knew how much the occasional meeting with the town's hockey stars thrilled his daughter.

"Why hello, Miss Handford," Lester said with a grin. "How are you?"

"Fine, thank you, Mr. Patrick," she replied formally, with only a hint of the nervous smile of a twelve-year-old meeting one of her town's heroes.

"Just getting home from school, are you?" Frank inquired. "What was today's lesson?"

"We talked about the Naval Bill they're debating in Parliament," Lily answered. She liked talking to the hockey players. They spoke to her as if she were a grown-up. "We're going to follow it in our oral composition. We've even set up a mock Parliament in school. Wilfred Wilson is going to be the Prime Minister. Charlotte Whitton is the Leader of the Opposition."

"So Miss Whitton will be Robert Borden, eh?" Taylor said. "I knew I liked that young lady."

"Oh-oh, Lily, don't let Mr. Taylor get going on politics," Frank cautioned playfully. Lester laughed. Taylor just grunted.

"Well, Gus," Lester said, after the three players had chatted with Lily for a few minutes, "I guess we've taken up enough of your time. Thanks for the use of the gramophone."

"Any time, Lester. You know that." Gus shook hands with each man. "Hey fellas!" he called out as they left the studio. "How about those portraits? When are you going to let me take your picture?"

"We've got a workout at the rink tonight, Gus. Why don't you drop by?"

"Win a game first, Frank. Then we'll talk!"

XX

The Admiralty experts recommended the establishment of a fleet unit by such of the great dominions as were able so to contribute.... Australia, with two million less population than Canada, and presumably with resources in proportion to its population, unhesitatingly accepted the recommendation of the admiralty. New Zealand undertakes to furnish one Dreadnought.... We have no Dreadnought ready; we have no fleet unit at hand. But we have the resources and, I trust, the patriotism, to provide a fleet unit or at least a Dreadnought without one moment's unnecessary delay. Or, and in my opinion this would be the better course, we can place the equivalent in cash at the disposal of the Admiralty.

Robert Borden,
Opposition Leader.
Naval Debate, 1910

WE'RE GOING TO BE TRYING SOMETHING DIFFERENT IN practice the next two days," Lester told his teammates as they dressed for their Monday evening workout with the Rivers. "Frank has come up with something that might help us hone our combination skills a little more quickly. He's going to tell us about it."

Frank explained his idea that the players should be required to make at least two passes before firing a shot on goal. "The Rivers know nothing about this," he said in conclusion, "so it should be a pretty fair test."

"I don't get it, Frank," Bobby Rowe protested. "We've all played hockey all of our lives. We all know how to pass the puck —"

Frank cut him off. "The reason for this set-up isn't to teach anybody the skills necessary to play the game. Of course we all know how to pass the puck, but you've got to admit we did a pretty poor job of it on Saturday night." There were resigned nods all around on that point. "What I'm hoping this is going to accomplish is to give us each a better feel for what everyone else is doing on the ice."

"You lost me with that last bit," interrupted Jack Fraser.

Frank began again, trying to express his thoughts in terms everyone would understand.

"OK. Here's what I mean. We were weakest against the Wanderers just where they were strongest, namely in the teamwork that comes from players who are familiar with each other's style. Hard work over time is the only sure way of accomplishing that goal, but we haven't got much time. We frittered away most of the last two weeks with our fancy display of individual skills against a team we obviously over-match. We learned the hard way on Saturday night that that won't work. We've only got two days until our next game, and I think forcing us to pass the puck in practice is the best way for us to get used to playing together as a team."

The Millionaires were slow to adapt to the new system in Monday's workout. The players looked confused, never sure, when they got the puck, of exactly what they should be doing with it. Frustration was clearly beginning to show when coach Alf Smith whistled a stop to the play for the first instructional break.

"Jeez," Frank scoffed indignantly, "you guys just aren't getting it."

"What we're getting is fed up," Herb Jordan spat out bitterly, slapping the puck into the boards.

"Shut up, Herb!" Taylor shot back. The two players glared at each other.

"Relax guys," Bert Lindsay interjected in a calming tone. "I know what Frank's getting at." From his vantage point behind the play, the Millionaires goaltender had been able to see what was going wrong. "You guys are just firing the puck around haphazardly, trying to force passes that aren't there. That's not the point of this workout. You're supposed to be thinking. Looking for the open man. Creating openings yourself."

"Exactly!" Frank shouted excitedly. "That's exactly it!"

The scrimmage went better from that point on, and Tuesday's workout was even more encouraging. The players were charging up and down the ice, making crisp passes in smart combinations. The team appeared much improved from Saturday night's fiasco, but Wednesday's game against Les Canadiens would be the real test. The team wouldn't have a formal practice on game day, but Lester wanted the players to get together just the same.

"I think it would be a good idea," Lester said as the players prepared to leave the dressing room, "if we get together for a skate tomorrow morning. Just a light workout. Get the juices flowing. Fire some rubber at Bert. That sort of thing."

"Thanks a lot, Lester," the goalie joked.

"I can't make it," Herb Jordan said. "I've got to work tomorrow."

"What do you mean, you've got to work?" Lester asked. "You work for the man who owns this team. I'm sure he won't mind if you take the day off to prepare for a game."

"Well, I guess what I should have said is that I won't be here, not that I can't make it. Sure, I could probably get the day off if I wanted to, but I don't want the whole day. I'll knock off around lunchtime, so I'll be well rested for the game. Mr. O'Brien's concluding a business deal in Ottawa tomorrow and he needs someone in the office until noon. I intend to be that someone."

"Well all right, then," Lester shrugged. "How about if we hold the workout at one o'clock?"

"That'll be fine."

The town of Renfrew officially entered the world of big-time hockey on Wednesday night, January 19, 1910, when the Renfrew Rink played host to its first-ever top level game. Starting time for a midweek contest was 7:30 PM, but the ticket booth had opened at 10:00 AM and did a brisk business throughout the day. It appeared, too, that there would be more than enough fans to support the new all-French team. Lester had been among the skeptics. He knew, from his playing days in Montreal, that there were rarely more than a handful of French Canadians attending Wanderers games. The team appealed only to the city's English population. And the Shamrocks attracted supporters from Montrealers of Irish descent. Lester recalled that he had not even heard of hockey while growing up among the French Canadians of rural Quebec. Did the French care for the game at all, he had wondered? His question was answered with an emphatic yes when a trainload of hockey fans from Montreal arrived in Renfrew just after noon, followed by an influx of more out-of-towners from Shawville and Campbell's Bay across the nearby Quebec-Ontario border.

The carnival atmosphere surrounding Renfrew's first home game in the mighty new National Hockey Association was reminiscent of the mood when the circus came to town. Red and white ribbons were hung from the light poles on Raglan Street. The entrance to the rink was also decked out with red and white ribbons. Shopkeepers hung signs in their windows wishing the players well. There was electricity in the air.

Taylor, as always, was the first player to arrive at the rink. It was more than an hour before the doors to the arena were even scheduled to open, but already there was a crowd outside. Taylor stopped to talk with some of the fans, accepting their good wishes and signing a few autographs. When the doors to the arena finally opened, the fans were greeted on the inside by a small brass band playing ragtime music. Some men and women danced with each other as they made their way to their seats.

As game time approached, the visiting Canadiens took the ice, led by their captain, Newsy Lalonde. Newsy was still unknown to many hockey fans. Although he had begun playing professionally in his home town of Cornwall five years back when he was only seventeen, he had not yet played in any of the established major Canadian circuits. Newsy had spent two years in the International League and two years in the new Ontario Professional Hockey League before being recruited for Les Canadiens. Now that he was in the NHA, his fame was growing, although there were nearly as many fans who hated him as loved him, because he was as nasty on the ice as he was talented. His supporters turned out to cheer him, while others paid their way in to taunt him with shouts of "get Lalonde!"

The French Canadian team sported deep-blue sweaters with white edging and a large white "C" in the centre. A white trim cut down from the shoulders and across the chest, through the "C" just below its middle, making the top of the jersey resemble a sailor's bib. Les Canadiens were cheered by the small group of out-of-town fans who had managed to obtain tickets, but were booed lustily by the larger Renfrew majority. There was no underlying feeling of prejudice beneath the loud booing directed at the French team. Violent partisanship was the standard of the day.

The Renfrew fans displayed their loyal support for their home team just a few minutes later, when Lester led the Millionaires down the stairs from their dressing room and onto the ice. The home town faithful rose to their feet in a great ovation. Many of the children present were waving the same flags they had held days before at the train station. The women fluttered handkerchiefs while the men clapped vigorously or cupped their hands to their mouths, shouting encouragement. All were dressed in furs or heavy woollen garments with warm hats and gloves. Many huddled under blankets for extra protection against the cold. Some had even brought bricks, heated all day in their stoves at home, which they used to keep their feet warm.

As the ovation died down, a short red carpet was rolled out on the ice in front of the Renfrew club's bench and a lone trumpeter emerged. The boisterous crowd quieted down. Men removed their hats and bowed their heads as the trumpeter prepared to play "God Save the King." For a moment, only the notes of the instrument could be heard, but suddenly, from within the pocket of French Canadian fans, the sound of singing emerged.

"*O Canada. Terre de nos aïeux. Ton front est ceint, de fleurons glorieux . . .*"

On and on the singing went. It had begun quietly, but, as the song continued, it got louder and louder as more and more French voices rang out. There was no immediate reaction from the Renfrew crowd; most were simply stunned that their respectful silence for the anthem of the Empire had been disrupted. Soon though, there were some who began to sing out the words to "God Save the King," hoping to drown out the unexpected and unwelcome interruption. Others shot icy stares in the direction of the French Canadian singers, some calling out for them to be quiet, others shouting obscenities. Most of the fans simply shifted uneasily from one foot to the other, upset by what was going on around them and unsure of what to make of it.

The players on the ice were equally unsettled. "What the hell are they singing?" Taylor wondered aloud, though not expecting anyone to have the answer.

"It's the 'Chant Nationale,' " Herb Jordan replied quietly. He had spent seven years living and playing hockey in Quebec City and had become familiar with the song. "It's sort of the anthem of the French Canadian Nationalists, I guess you might say." The song had been widely sung in Quebec since the 1880s, but had not been heard in English Canada until after the turn of the century, and still rather infrequently at that.

When the singing subsided, a banner was unfurled:

PAS D'ARGENT POUR LES GUERRES BRITANNIQUES

"I wonder what that means?" Taylor asked.

"No money for British wars," Lester said.

Taylor had thought Herb Jordan might know the answer, but hadn't expected a translation from Lester. There was a suspicious look of surprise on Taylor's face as he glanced towards his teammate.

Les Canadiens had been forced to juggle their lineup for their first official National Hockey Association encounter. Jack Laviolette, the man hired by Ambrose O'Brien to manage the French squad, as well as a star cover point, was sick with influenza. He had accompanied the team on its trip to Renfrew, but had not been well enough to dress for the game. It was a severe blow to the Montreal side. Laviolette was one of the fastest skaters in the game. Nicknamed "Speed Merchant," Laviolette's end-to-end rushes with his long black hair flying behind him had become his trademark. His absence meant Newsy Lalonde would have to drop back from centre to play cover point. That in itself was not much of a setback, as the talented French star was capable of playing any position on the ice, but his replacement at centre, Edouard Millaire, was not of the same calibre.

Joining Newsy on the Canadiens defence would be Laviolette's usual partner, Didier Pitre. Pitre was the first player Laviolette had signed for the new French Canadian team. The two had played together for a couple of years in the International League and had also teamed up for a season on defence with the Montreal Shamrocks. A big man, weighing close to 200 pounds, Pitre was one of the strongest players in the game and possessed perhaps the hardest and most accurate shot in hockey, earning him the nickname "Cannonball." Pitre was big, but by no means slow. In fact, Pitre's speed from his point position, combined with that of his defence partner Laviolette, soon had the sportswriters referring to the two as "The Flying Frenchmen."

The game began sharply at 7:30 PM with the referee placing the puck between Herb Jordan and Millaire. Jordan won the draw easily and fed the puck across to Larry Gilmour, who was starting at left wing in place of Jack Fraser. Gilmour dropped the puck back to Lester, and the Renfrew captain carried it up ice, with Bobby Rowe on his right side and Taylor joining the rush from behind. Millaire turned from his position at centre and raced back to cover Lester, who, seeing the Montreal player approaching, snapped a short pass across ice to Rowe. Rowe slipped the puck back to Taylor and Cyclone was off.

The crowd roared as Taylor sped toward the Canadiens' end and a meeting with his old International League nemesis, Newsy Lalonde. It had been more than two years since the two great players had clashed on the cold rinks of northern Michigan's copper country, but Taylor had not forgotten the violent attacks he had been forced to endure. He had hoped to get a chance to beat Lalonde on the ice early, and here it was.

Taylor raced towards Newsy, his skate blades cutting sharply into the hard ice and propelling him forward at breakneck speed. Lalonde backed up slowly, his eyes darting quickly from side to side taking in the entire situation, and a snarl clearly visible on his face. Taylor had Gilmour on his left side and Herb Jordan to his right. Faking a pass to Gilmour, Taylor forced Newsy to take one fateful step to that side. This was all the opening Cyclone needed. He dashed to his right as Newsy spun almost a complete 360 degrees to get back into the play, swinging his stick wildly to try to strip Taylor of the puck. The great Renfrew star merely pushed the piece of rubber forward and hurdled over Lalonde's stick, picking up the puck again on the other side.

"Ha!" Taylor barked sarcastically.

"I'll get you," Newsy growled under his breath.

Taylor now had only Pitre to beat and still had Jordan and Gilmour with him. The big defenceman had moved directly in front of Taylor, but was shading slightly towards Jordan, the more dangerous goal scorer. Taylor darted over to Jordan's side of the ice, pulling Pitre further that way, then slid a pass back in the direction he had come from, right on Gilmour's stick. The Renfrew winger snapped a quick shot at Les Canadiens' goal. It seemed destined for the twine on the goalie's short side, but the netminder was able to get just enough of his stick on the puck to deflect it wide and over the boards.

"Ooh," the fans gasped at the near-miss, all except the ones behind the net — they were too busy ducking the flying rubber. With the puck now out of play, the referee signalled a stoppage and waited for it to be returned to the ice. Then the referee paced off five yards at a right angle to where the goal line would be, if there were such a thing, and in line with the spot where Gilmour had stood when he made his shot. Jordan and Millaire faced off there.

Jordan again beat the French team's back-up centre, and swatted the puck back to Lester, who circled in Les Canadiens' end, looking for an opening before dropping a pass back to Taylor. Cyclone quickly fed the puck across to Frank, who moved forward a few strides and fired a hard shot on goal. Again a tough blast was turned aside by the netminder. Jordan, who was now in front of the goal, swiped at the rebound but before making contact was knocked to the ground by Didier Pitre. Newsy Lalonde scooped up the loose puck and brought it out of danger behind his net — or so he thought. As he turned to head up ice, Newsy was pushed off the puck from behind by Bobby Rowe, who then fed the disk back out front to Larry Gilmour. Gilmour unleashed another quick drive, but again the netminder proved equal to the task.

The Millionaires dominated play in the first few minutes, swarming around the opposing goal, snapping off sharp passes and firing dangerous shots. The Renfrew crowd roared its approval again and again, but although Renfrew had shown a definite edge in play, they had not been able to score. Newsy Lalonde was the first to accomplish that feat. He beat Bert Lindsay on a long shot that should not have eluded the Renfrew goaltender. Les Canadiens led 1–0 and the partisan Renfrew crowd was quieted.

"Don't worry about it, Bert," Frank consoled, as the goaltender fished the puck out of the net. "We'll get it back for you."

"I don't know what happened," the goalie muttered. "It just dipped or something." He shook his head in dismay.

True to his word, Frank was instrumental in a goal six minutes later that drew the Millionaires even. Taking a feed from Lindsay after the goaltender blocked another of Lalonde's long shots, Frank darted up the sheet, bobbing and weaving his way in and around the French players before sliding a pass over to Lester, who found the net with a high, hard shot from close range.

As the first half wore on, the Renfrew players, without realizing it, slowly began to revert to the poor form they had demonstrated in their opening game loss to the Wanderers. Taking off on more and more individual rushes, the Renfrew forwards were once again getting caught up ice too often, while Les Canadiens proved to be a faster team overall than the Millionaires had expected. It was the Frenchmen who now dominated play as they surrounded the Renfrew goal. Bert Lindsay, after allowing the initial weak tally, kept his team in the game, making save after save, until he was finally beaten by the blistering shot of Didier Pitre.

The thirty-minute first half was now a little more than two-thirds over, and the Millionaires found themselves trailing 2–1. Les Canadiens' defence pairing of Lalonde and Pitre was proving very tough to crack, but the Renfrew players tried stubbornly again and again to beat the two Frenchmen with individual rushes. Frank, Taylor, and Bert Lindsay were kept hopping as Lalonde and Pitre shut down the Renfrew offence and led their forwards on the attack. When Lindsay made a difficult glove save on a Lalonde shot that appeared labelled for the top corner, he earned an appreciative roar from the crowd. Corralling the rebound, he fed the puck back to Taylor.

"Nice stop, Bert," he called out as he circled around behind the net. Lindsay just nodded as Taylor started up ice. The Canadiens forwards had turned to rush back and help out on defence, so Taylor was left with a lot of room as he began his rush. A quick head fake beat Millaire at centre ice.

"You've got Lester with you," Frank shouted from behind the play as Cyclone continued to streak up ice.

Looking around quickly, Taylor spotted Lester on his left as the two Canadiens wingers closed in on him. A fake backhand pass across to his teammate momentarily froze the French forwards, and Taylor, with an extra burst of speed, squeezed between them.

"I'm with you, Cyc," Bobby Rowe called out from his right side as Taylor cut over to his left. Cyclone shot a quick glance in the winger's direction but held on to the puck himself and continued over to the left side. Moving down the boards, Taylor outskated Les Canadiens' rover and turned back towards the centre of the ice, where only Didier Pitre now stood between him and the goal. Pitre's positioning forced Taylor to slide all the way back across the ice to the right side, where Newsy Lalonde, unknown to Cyclone, was closing in on him.

"Look out, Cyc!" Taylor heard Lester call out, as he tried to go around the big French defenceman. The warning came just an instant too late. Newsy had caught up to Taylor, and pushed him over Pitre's hip from behind with a vicious cross-check that sent Cyclone cartwheeling to the ice. The spectators let out a loud, painful groan as if each of them had been hit, too. The referee's right hand shot into the air as he called Lalonde for a three-minute penalty.

The Millionaires capitalized on the man advantage immediately. Herb Jordan once again beat Millaire on the face-off and, stepping around the outclassed opposition centre, fired a shot on goal. The quick drive surprised the French netminder, who swiped at the puck with a gloved hand, but missed. The score was now 2–2.

The deadlock lasted only a few minutes before Lalonde, now back on the ice with the expiration of his penalty, pounced on a loose puck at centre. "Stop him! Stop him!" the Renfrew faithful shouted frantically as the fiery Frenchman led yet another foray into the Millionaires' end. Taylor was gaining from the rear, eager to lay a hit on the man who had levelled him, but Newsy snapped off a swift shot before Cyclone could overtake him. The hard drive got by the padded leg of Bert Lindsay as he stretched in vain to his right. It was 3–2, Les Canadiens.

The Millionaires got even just before half-time. Jack Fraser picked up a loose puck deep in Les Canadiens territory and, moving across the front of the net, held on to it until the last possible second before flicking a beautiful side shot over the shoulder of the French squad's netminder.

Fraser had not started the game, but had come on amid much controversy when Larry Gilmour was hurt. Gilmour had taken an elbow in the pit of his stomach, but Les Canadiens Captain Newsy Lalonde wasn't convinced the injury warranted the addition of a substitute.

"I barely hit the guy!" Newsy protested as Lester asked permission of the referee to replace the injured man. "He isn't hurt so bad. They just want to get a fresh body out there!" Nonetheless, the referee agreed to the switch. A few minutes later, Newsy instructed Millaire to go down with an injury so that Les Canadiens, too, could get a fresh man on the ice. The injury had obviously been faked, but Lester decided not to push the issue. The two teams finished up the half without further incident.

As the Renfrew players climbed the steps to their dressing room, many of their fans filed out of the seating area and into the warmth of the heated room off the lobby. Neither group was sure what to make of the first half. Talk among the fans tended to accentuate the positive. Lindsay's brilliant work in goal ... Taylor's scintillating rushes ... Frank's heady play, but there was an undercurrent of disappointment in the conversation. The Renfrew players were obviously more talented — only Lalonde and Pitre on Les Canadiens' side were on a par with their own great stars — so why were they not winning? Why weren't the Millionaires working as a team?

The same questions were being asked inside the Renfrew dressing room as the players discussed the first half, when suddenly there was a knock on the door and a man stepped inside.

"Hello!" Lester exclaimed, instantly recognizing the man who had entered the room. "I didn't expect to see you for a couple of days yet."

The man was Fred Whitcroft, the Edmonton forward who was to join the Millionaires, along with teammate Hay Millar, after the western city's Stanley Cup challenge. Lester recognized him from two years before, when he had been among the many ringers added to the Edmonton team for that season's Cup bid.

"Well, we've got tonight off in our series with Ottawa," Whitcroft explained, "so I hopped a train and here I am."

The first game of the Stanley Cup challenge had been played the night before. The Senators had beaten the Edmonton Eskimos 8–4. "The ice was too soft for our liking," Whitcroft explained, when asked about the defeat. The Edmonton club had hoped to rely on its superior speed to beat the Stanley Cup champs, but the slushy surface had slowed them down. Not many gave the Eskimos much of a chance of rallying in the second game of the total-goal series, to be played the following night, "but we're going to give them a battle," Whitcroft promised.

"That's enough about me, though. What about you guys? You should be toying with that French team out there."

Silence greeted Whitcroft's assertion.

"Look at the talent in here," Whitcroft went on. "Frank, Bert, Lester, Herb . . ." He shook his head. "And Cyclone," he said with obvious admiration, "is without a doubt the greatest hockey player I've ever seen.

"But Cyc," Whitcroft continued, "you're trying to do it all by yourself. I think all you guys are guilty of that. Look at how well you were doing at the beginning of the game. You were passing the puck all over the place, working beautiful combinations. You were all over them. But then it stopped. Why?"

Though it tallied with what the players had been discussing among themselves, hearing the words from someone looking at the situation from the outside had a fresh impact on the team. When Lester slapped his stick on the floor, they filed out of the dressing room fired up with determination to play a solid combination game for the final thirty minutes.

Herb Jordan lined up at centre, awaiting the opening face-off for the second half. Millaire set up opposite him, apparently recovered from his "injury."

"I see you're feeling better," Jordan said dryly.

Millaire did not answer, but the way he lowered his eyes showed that he had not been comfortable with the charade. Perhaps the rest had done him some good, though. For the first time in the game, he beat Jordan to the draw. Millaire fed the puck all the way back to Didier Pitre, who fired a long shot into the Millionaires' end. As Les Canadiens' forwards took off in pursuit, Taylor turned to retrieve the puck.

"Man on you!" Frank yelled from his point position.

Taylor took two quick looks back, glancing rapidly over each shoulder, and spotted Millaire closing in on his left side. As he scooped up the puck, Taylor immediately pushed his sharp blades hard into the ice surface, so that a spray of snow shot up from them. The quick stop surprised the French centre, and his momentum took him a few feet past Taylor before he was able stop. The clever manoeuvre gave Taylor the small opening he needed, and the great cover point headed up ice.

The crowd roared as Taylor carried the puck to Les Canadiens' end, but his intense concentration on the task at hand left him oblivious to the noise from the stands. He was staring at Lalonde, who loomed ahead.

Taylor had his teammates with him as he bore down on Les Canadiens' defence. Except for a quick check to see how they were aligned behind him, he kept his eyes on Lalonde. He made a beeline for his adversary. Newsy, who was now directly ahead, moved forward in anticipation of the clash. Taylor, still heading directly for him, braced for the inevitable collision. Just before they crashed, Taylor slid a pass back to Lester. He then loosened the grip of his right hand on the top of his stick, and thrusting his left hand back and forth quickly, drove a carefully hidden butt end into Lalonde's ribs. It was a not-too-subtle rejoinder to the bruising cross-check he'd received before intermission.

Taylor's tactics had effectively taken Newsy out of the play, which left Lester, who now carried the puck, with only Pitre to beat and four other teammates to work with.

"You've got Fraser on your left," Frank called out. Lester flipped a pass across to him. The left winger quickly fed the puck to Jordan who fired a shot on goal, but the French netminder knocked the puck away with a quick kick of his right leg.

The close call produced an excited buzz among the spectators, who remained hopeful as Bobby Rowe chased the rebound into the corner and beat Lalonde to the loose puck. Rowe circled behind the net, looking out front for someone to pass to, but Les Canadiens' forwards had scrambled back to the zone by this time, and the area in front of the net was congested with players. Rowe held onto the puck as Newsy chased him.

Taylor, seeing Rowe had nowhere to go, broke away from the pack in front of the net and dropped back a few strides. "Bobby!" he shouted as he moved into the clear. Rowe spotted him and snapped the puck back in his direction. Taylor played it cleanly and immediately whipped a low shot towards the goal, but it struck a leg among the maze of players and bounced harmlessly into the far corner, where Pitre picked it up. Jack Fraser was on him in an instant, but the big French defenceman merely shrugged off the check.

"Oomph," groaned Fraser, as Pitre's strong shoulder knocked him off his feet.

Pitre carried the puck up ice, only one hand on the stick as he looked around for someone else to join him on the rush, but he saw only Millionaires as they hustled back to break up the play. Taylor, who had come from clear across the other side of the ice, was the first player to catch up with Pitre. Gaining on him from behind, Taylor reached in with his stick and hooked the puck away.

"Great play, Cyc!" Lester yelled from up ice.

"*Merde!*" cursed Pitre. The French word for excrement was one of the few Taylor was familiar with. He smiled as Frank picked up the loose puck and took it back towards Les Canadiens' end.

Frank carried the puck along the boards, his stick slapping the ice lightly on either side of the rubber with rhythmic regularity as he stickhandled into Canadiens territory. Sidestepping one player and then cutting towards the middle of the ice, Frank dashed towards Les Canadiens' goal before tossing the puck over to Lester. Lester received the pass on his backhand, then pushed the puck across his body onto his forehand and snapped a hard shot on goal. It found net and, at 4–3, Renfrew had its first lead of the evening.

Clearly, the players on the Creamery Town team had shaken off their listlessness. Ten or twelve times the entire Renfrew team swept down on the opposing goal. The French goaler turned back many assaults, stopping numerous tough shots in sensational fashion, but it was impossible to get them all. As a result of their great work, the Millionaires added no less than five more goals in succession. Only when they had built up a six-goal lead did the Renfrew men ease up in their spirited aggressiveness.

As the game turned more and more in Renfrew's favour, Les Canadiens tried to play it rough, with Newsy Lalonde leading the assault. He and Lester tangled several times, both being banished to the penalty box on three occasions. Late in the game, Lester accidentally opened a cut on Newsy's forehead. The Renfrew captain's stick came up high as he wheeled around quickly after having the puck taken away. As soon as Lester got back in the play, Newsy got to him with a wicked cross-check. The violent shove knocked Lester off his feet and sent him crashing to the ice.

"That was a cheap shot, Lalonde," Frank screamed out, rushing to the defence of his older brother.

As Frank skated closer to confront the fierce Frenchman face to face, Newsy lashed out at him with a back-handed swing of his left arm. Frank managed to duck the elbow, but as Lalonde's arm continued to arc in his direction, Frank took a gloved hand in the side of the head. The butt end of Lalonde's stick, which he still gripped in his left hand, opened a gash behind Frank's ear. Off balance from eluding the initial punch, Frank was staggered by the force of the blow. As he went down, he swung his stick wildly at his antagonist and managed to hit Lalonde with his blade, slicing open an almost identical cut on the side of Lalonde's head. Newsy, too, was floored. The players were carted off the ice together and led to their respective dressing rooms for repairs. Both men returned to the ice a short time later.

Having built up a six-goal lead through twenty minutes of solid offensive hockey, the Millionaires were content to play defence for the remainder of the second half. Led by Taylor, whose speed and skill allowed him to break up several Canadiens scoring chances almost

single-handedly, the Renfrew players simply smothered the visiting forwards. Only Lalonde, who scored the game's final goal on a picturesque
rush from his cover point position, zigzagging through the Renfrew
players, was able to penetrate the defensive shell. When the bell sounded
to signal the end of the game, the Renfrew Millionaires were winners
for the first time. The final tally stood 9–4 in their favour. The cheers
and whistles of their excited fans were still ringing out as the players
climbed the stairs to their dressing room.

"Whoo!" whooped Taylor as he burst into the dressing room.

"Great game! Great game!" Bobby Rowe said over and over, punching the air with his fist occasionally to add emphasis to his pronouncement.

"Hell of an effort, boys!" Herb Jordan enthused as he plopped
himself down on his stool contentedly.

The self-congratulatory hooting and hollering went on for a while
before giving way to quieter reflection on the game.

"You see what happens when we play together like a team?" Frank
said. "The first and second halves were like two different games. Hell,
it was almost as if we were playing two different sports!"

"And we should only get better," Jack Fraser reasoned.

Bert Lindsay had sat quietly until this time, stripping off his pads,
which were now heavy with perspiration, pulling off his sweat-soaked
jersey, and removing the protective leather pads he wore on his shoulders and arms. "That Lalonde's a bugger," he finally offered to the
conversation.

"I'll say," agreed Taylor grimly. He was still fully dressed, except
for his skates.

"Yeah, but what a player!" Frank enthused as he slipped his jersey
over his head. Frank held no ill feelings for the man who had cut him
just a short time ago. He did not hold others accountable for rash
actions taken in the heat of the struggle. "I wouldn't mind having him
on my side in a tough battle."

There were nods all around, but not from Taylor.

The players didn't loiter in the dressing room any longer than they
had to. Some had girlfriends to meet. Others wanted to grab a late-
night snack. But all wanted to get cleaned up. All they had at the rink
to wipe off the grime — and often the blood — were dampened towels,
warmed in a storeroom heated by a stove. These helped cut through

the sweat and made putting street clothes back on a little easier, but they didn't do much to clean or refresh a player after a tough night's work.

Taylor, Frank, and Lester left the rink together, exiting the main door to Argyle Street. Taylor and Lester turned to head off towards their nearby boarding house, but Frank hesitated.

"You guys go on ahead," he told them when they turned around to see what was up. "I'll meet you at the house a little later."

With that, Frank took off in the other direction.

"Where would he be going at this time of night?" Lester asked.

"Beats me," said Taylor, picking up the pace. "First one back gets the hot water!" he called.

Lester laughed.

XXI

It is suggested that in the case of the Navy we are arming for our own protection. The responsibilities, however, are precisely the same, as far as political consequences are concerned, as if we are contributing in money or ships, to the British Navy. In the first case, we are arming for our own protection; in the second, we are making common cause with the Imperial fleet for Imperial defence. . . . But, in either case, the consequences are the same. The only variation lies in the mode of assistance.

Frederick Monk,
Conservative Member of Parliament.
Naval Debate, 1910

FRANK WALKED ALONE ALONG THE STREETS OF RENFREW. It was a crisp January night. Many stars and a nearly full moon were visible, though every so often a wispy cloud would obscure the view. Occasionally, a gust of wind would snatch some loose snow off the top of a drift at the side of the street. The snow would dance down the road, swirling like a tiny tornado, then disappear. As he turned the corner off Argyle Street, a sudden icy blast caused Frank to shiver. He readjusted his scarf and turned up the collar on his raccoon coat.

Frank was headed for the Dominion House Hotel, where Newsy Lalonde and the rest of Les Canadiens were being billeted for the night. Frank had been so impressed by Newsy's play that he wanted to introduce himself to the French Canadian star.

Frank entered the hotel and approached the front desk. It came up to the middle of his chest, with protective brass bars extending up to the ceiling. No one was there at this hour, but he could see the night auditor working in a room behind the desk and called out to him. The man recognized Frank immediately.

"Mr. Patrick. What brings you in?"

"I'm looking for Newsy Lalonde. Can you tell me what room he's in?"

Before the hotel man could answer, Frank heard a voice coming from the other end of the lobby.

"Who wants to know?" the voice asked.

Frank recognized the voice as Lalonde's, but he wasn't as sure of the tone. He couldn't tell if it was surprise he heard, or anger. The voice came from a couch in front of the fireplace, where Newsy sat facing away from the front desk, his eyes fixed on the flames that danced hypnotically over and around the logs.

Frank walked across the sparsely decorated lobby. "Newsy?" said Frank, as he neared Lalonde. "It's Frank Patrick."

Lalonde looked back over his shoulder and eyed Frank up and down. "What do you want?" he said, glaring at the intruder.

It was not uncommon for people to come looking for Newsy after a game in an opposing city. Sometimes it was a player who felt he still had a score to settle. Other times it was a fan of the home team, usually drunk, who had taken exception to Lalonde's rough play. Rarely were the visits simple social calls, so Newsy was on edge.

"*Calme toi*, Newsy," Frank said. "*Je voulais juste te dire allô.* We didn't exactly get a proper introduction earlier."

Lalonde was surprised that Frank spoke French. He hadn't met many English hockey players who could speak to him in his native tongue. "*Vous parlez très bien le français*, Monsieur Patrick," Newsy said. "Where did you learn to speak so well?"

"I grew up in several small towns in Quebec," Frank explained, still speaking French. "I got my first three years of schooling in French. Until we moved to Montreal, we never lived anyplace with a large enough English population to have its own schools."

Frank spoke some more about his boyhood in Quebec, and was surprised when Newsy told him that he had grown up in Ontario. The two men hit it off quickly, and Frank invited him back to the boarding house.

"We can grab a late snack and talk some more over a cup of coffee," Frank said.

"And compare stitches!" Newsy laughed.

"What's he doing here?" Taylor demanded, upon walking into the kitchen and finding Newsy Lalonde there with Frank and Lester.

Taylor had heard sounds from the kitchen and he'd come to investigate. What he found had truly surprised him. Lester, Frank, and Newsy were seated around the table, engaged in the strangest conversation he had ever heard. One of them might say something in French, while another would respond in English. Sometimes it was the other way around. There were even times when someone started out speaking in one language, then slid into the other in mid-sentence, apparently unaware that he had done so. It never seemed to confuse the other listeners. Taylor listened with growing annoyance, never quite picking up the thread of the conversation. After a couple of minutes in the doorway, unnoticed by the others, he blurted out his question about Lalonde's presence.

"I invited him over," Frank said matter-of-factly. "That's what he's doing here."

"Well, I don't want him in my house," Taylor shot back.

"It's not your house," Lester retorted, annoyed that Taylor was treating his brother's guest so rudely.

Newsy was surprised by Taylor's hostility. He preferred to vent his anger on the ice, and leave any personal conflicts behind when the game ended. He had assumed Taylor would be the same way. After all, Taylor had won Newsy's respect on the ice during their two seasons in the International League with the way he refused to back down from a challenge and with his ability to take punishment and dish it out. Those feelings had been reaffirmed in the game that night. To Newsy, that was all that mattered.

"I see," Newsy said to Taylor politely, "that unlike myself, you are not able to leave our rivalry at the arena." He pronounced the English words carefully, having trouble only with his th's and h's.

Such a statement was a clever tactic on Newsy's part. He had all but dared Taylor to behave in as gentlemanly a manner as he — a challenge from which he believed his adversary was not likely to back down.

Newsy was partly right. Taylor took a seat next to him and smiled congenially. He would not let Newsy get the better of him in a social setting, just as he would not allow it on the ice. But striking up a new friendship was not foremost in his mind.

"That was quite a performance your fans put on before the game tonight," Taylor said.

"You mean the singing?" Newsy asked. "As I am sure you know, there are many French Canadians who do not share English Canada's strong ties to Britain. To them, the attachment of the English to England is like saying that Canada will never be more than a colony, and shows their failure to develop a true loyalty to Canada."

Lester groaned. Frank lowered his head into his hands. They knew that to Taylor these were fighting words. To his credit, Cyclone kept his composure. "And so I suppose you are in favour of Laurier's Naval Services Act," was all he said.

"Actually, I am not."

Taylor was pleasantly surprised. "Well, I guess we have something in common," he said. "I imagine you're in favour of direct payments to the British Admiralty, then?"

"Oh, no!" Lalonde answered. "I like the idea of our own Canadian Navy. Just not under the terms Laurier has proposed. He says Parliament will decide in the event of war whether to place the Canadian Navy in the hands of the British Admiralty. But the English would never allow him to say no. The Canadian Navy might be Canadian in times of peace, but I fear English Canada will see to it that the Navy is British in times of war."

"And what would be wrong with that?" Taylor demanded.

"Canada will never become its own country that way." Newsy explained.

"But Laurier is a staunch defender of Canadian self-government," Lester reasoned, choosing to speak out on the issue for the first time, and taking the middle ground in the conflict. "It's just that, to him, it doesn't have to mean separation from the Empire. I think he's found a fair compromise by creating a Canadian Navy that the government can turn over to the British, if it so chooses."

Lalonde only shook his head, but Taylor went on the offensive.

"But Canada can never refuse to participate in British wars! Refusing to come to the aid of the Empire is a declaration of independence! It would be like burning the flag! And as for Laurier's tin-pot navy — it's a joke! A pipe-dream!"

Taylor was almost shouting. Realizing that he might be losing control, he paused for a moment to gather his thoughts.

"The Royal Navy," he continued more calmly, "has always been the first line of Imperial defence. If the British government says the the new German Navy is threatening the Empire, then we have to help keep the Royal Navy strong. Canada has to put up the money, like the British Admiralty has been saying all these years, or the Germans will sink them — and then where will we be?"

"But what about that sign at the game tonight?" Frank asked. "You remember. 'No money for British wars.' Obviously the French are against such payments."

"Fuck the French!" Taylor jumped up and stormed out of the kitchen so abruptly that his chair crashed to the floor.

"I'm sorry, Newsy," Frank said, once Taylor was safely out of earshot.

"Why should you be sorry?" Newsy shrugged. "He doesn't like me. There's nothing you can do about that."

The room was quiet for a time. Neither Frank nor Lester knew what to say. Finally, Newsy broke the silence.

"Taylor thinks I hate him," he said, "but I don't really. It's just that he's always been the best player on his team, so I must go after him."

But there was more to their rivalry than that, although Newsy could not put it into words. He had never forgotten the English boy who had taunted him in Cornwall so many years ago, on the night he had learned about the death of his childhood hero, Bernie Savard. Although he wasn't conscious of it, he had been taking out his anger on many an English hockey enemy since then. Taylor, as the greatest among them, had become Newsy's biggest target. As for his politics, Newsy also had not forgotten that Bernie had died 3000 miles from home in an English war.

"A long time ago," said Newsy, speaking French now, "somebody told me a hockey player shouldn't have any friends on the ice. I found out later that he was right."

XXII

Why do we ask Parliament to vote for this naval service? It is simply because it is a necessity of our condition and the status we have reached as a nation. Do these gentlemen forget that . . . the revenue of Canada is today $100 million and the population over seven million? Do they forget that our country extends from one ocean to the other, and from the American boundary to the Arctic Ocean, not on the map only but in actual and ever-increasing settlements . . . ? Do they forget we are going to build a railway from the interior to Hudson Bay? Do they forget we have gold mines under the Arctic Circle? Do they forget that Canada is expanding like a young giant, simply from the pressure of the blood in its young veins? Are we to be told under such circumstances that we do not require a naval service? Why, Sir, you might just as well tell the people of Montreal, with their half-million population, that they do not need police protection.

Sir Wilfrid Laurier,
Prime Minister.
Naval Debate, 1910

FRANK AWAKENED ON THE MORNING OF JANUARY 20 TO find blood dripping from the hastily stitched cut behind his left ear. This was the gash he had suffered in his stick-swinging encounter with Newsy Lalonde. There was a circular spot on his pillow, the outer edges dried to an ugly brownish colour, but the centre bright red. Frank reached up with his left hand and felt a mat of hair clumped together by the dried blood behind his ear. Since the cut did not seem to be bleeding too heavily, he decided to go to the drug store and attend to the wound himself.

Taylor and Lester accompanied Frank on his trip to the pharmacy. Cyclone had gotten over his anger of the night before. He was passionate about his politics, but not obsessive. He might lose himself in the excitement of a heated discussion, but, once the debate subsided, he tended not to dwell on it. There was, however, something that still intrigued him.

"Where did you fellows learn to speak French like that?"

Lester answered, giving Taylor the same explanation that Frank had given Lalonde the night before. Taylor was surprised to learn that the Patricks were from Quebec.

"I just assumed you two were from the West," he said.

It was a common misconception. Because he had come to Renfrew from British Columbia, some of the newspapermen had been referring to Lester as "the Great Westerner" in their reports. The fact that he had first come to prominence in Brandon, Manitoba supported the myth.

"But you're English, aren't you?" Cyclone persisted. He would hate to have his mistrust of the French undermined by learning that his two closest friends were in fact French Canadians.

"Irish, actually," Frank answered. "If you want to get technical."

"Would it make a difference to you if we weren't?" Lester inquired.

"No," Taylor answered, though his voice contained more certainty than he actually felt. Now that he had gotten to know them, would he really feel less friendly towards them, trust them less, if they were French? He shook his head, trying to remove the doubts he had.

"Hello, Dom," Frank called out over the tinkling of the bells behind the door, as he led Taylor and his brother into the Central Drug Store. Dominic Ritza, the pharmacist who stood behind the counter talking to a customer as the players came in, looked up briefly. He smiled at Frank and the others and held up his hand to indicate he would be with them shortly. Dom was a keen sportsman who had played hockey for his college team and was delighted by the chance to hobnob with some of the game's best players.

"I've got just what you need," the pharmacist exclaimed, after Frank showed him his problem. He produced a glass jar containing a milky pinkish-white ointment, and also gave Frank some gauze and bandages for his cut. "And keep it covered," Dom advised, "at least until Saturday." The Millionaires, he knew, would be travelling back to Montreal on Saturday for a game against the Shamrocks.

The players headed back to the boarding house, where they were surprised to find Ambrose O'Brien waiting for them.

"You fellows no longer owe me $2000," Ambrose said with a smile, a reference to the gambling debt he had incurred when his Renfrew team was defeated by the Wanderers. "I made it all back, and then some, with the win last night." They talked about the game for a while, then Ambrose came to the point of his visit.

"We're having a party at the house tonight," Ambrose explained, uneasily. "I thought, considering last night's impressive showing, that it would be nice to invite the team over, too. Sort of a victory celebration. But I wanted to check with you first, Lester. Would it be all right?"

It had not gone easily when Ambrose spoke to his father about Lester's request that the team cut down on parties.

"No more parties!" O'Brien bellowed. "As long as I'm paying their salaries those boys do what I say — not the other way around!"

"But father . . . "

"Son, do you know why I agreed to all this hockey business?"

"For the good of the town," Ambrose said. "To bring the Stanley Cup to Renfrew."

"Oh yes," O'Brien said dismissively, "for the good of the town. But for my good, too! What the hell do I care who wins the Stanley Cup? But having these boys on the payroll is good for business —"

"Not if they don't win," Ambrose interrupted.

The same argument Lester had used on him now worked on Ambrose's father. Still, O'Brien was not willing to give in completely.

"Very well," he said. "There will be less partying. But I insist on an affair to mark their first victory. And it had better come soon."

Lester's first thought, when Ambrose mentioned the party, was of Stella. This would be his first chance to see her in a social setting since

Ambrose had let it slip that she was fond of him. Lester smiled, but the smile quickly faded as a second thought came to mind. It had only been five days since he had announced, after the defeat in Montreal, that the social season must come to a close. Is that what he had said? He tried to remember. No. All he had said was that there must be less socializing if the team was to be successful.

Stella came to mind again. Was he about to agree to this party solely to see her? Was he putting his own selfish interests ahead of the team? Would he lose credibility in the eyes of the other players if he agreed to this party?

No, he decided. He had made his point with what he had said in the dressing room, and that was enough. The team couldn't please the O'Briens in the drawing room and the arena as well. Everyone agreed with that. Everyone understood. But one party in honour of their first victory would do no harm. Still, he wondered, was he giving in because of Stella? And what about Grace?

All of these thoughts swirled through Lester's mind for what seemed to him a very long time. It was, in fact, only a matter of seconds.

"Certainly it will be all right," Lester told Ambrose. Only a nervous smile hinted at his uncertainty.

Though he had been to many of these O'Brien functions by now, Lester was still amazed by the sight of the dining room table. His own family had become quite wealthy, but even that had not prepared him for anything like this. The O'Brien dining room table was so big! And the place settings! Three silver forks glistened in the candlelight to the left of his gold plate. They never actually ate off the gold plates, for the servants always removed them when they were about to begin serving. To the right of the plate was a large rounded soup spoon, and next to it, moving towards the centre, was a smaller teaspoon. Then a flat-edged butter knife, and, next to that, a serrated knife for cutting meat. Above the plate was yet another spoon for dessert, and above that a half-moon-shaped glass salad plate. Next to that was a crystal wine glass and a water goblet.

Suspended from the ceiling above the dining room table was a small chandelier with glass light bulbs. But electric light had never been used at any of the O'Brien affairs the hockey team attended, because Jennie O'Brien didn't consider electric light conducive to fine dining. Candle-light was. In the centre of the table stood a huge five-branched candelabra. More traditional three-branched candelabras were placed at regular intervals along the long dining room table. Candles in wall sconces added more light and an air of festivity to the dining room.

This party was smaller than the ones that had been held during the team's training camp. Ambrose had been careful to invite only the family's closest friends and business associates. Those with wives or sweethearts had brought them along as well.

As he was ushered into the dining room along with Frank and Taylor, Lester eyed the place at the table where Stella O'Brien usually sat. Her chair was empty. Lester glanced over frequently during the long meal, but Stella never arrived. He couldn't decide whether he felt disappointed or relieved. After the final course had been served, the women retired to the drawing room, while the men's talk turned to the previous evening's hockey game.

"Yes, I'm quite proud of my boys," Ambrose bragged when asked about the game. "Not only did they win, but they sold out the rink and I won back the money I lost betting on them in Montreal. My father and I are going to need that money if we are to continue paying these high salaries!"

Everybody laughed.

"Why do you have a bandage on the side of your head?" somebody asked Frank.

The younger Patrick brother related the tale of his battle with Newsy Lalonde, of how he had come to Lester's aid and been slashed for his troubles.

"But you should see the other guy!" Lester interjected with a laugh.

"That Lalonde is one tough player," Frank added. "Maybe he plays dirty, but he's very talented too. I think we'll be hearing more from Newsy before this season is over."

"I've heard enough from him already," Taylor muttered.

"I understand there was quite a disturbance before the game," someone said. It was an obvious reference to the singing of the "Chant Nationale" and the protest banner, but before the pleasant discussion could degenerate into yet another argument over the Naval Debate, Stella O'Brien entered the room.

"Gentlemen," she said with a smile, "if you're ready, there will be dancing in the upstairs ballroom." A murmur of agreement met her announcement. "Mr. Patrick," Stella said, spying Lester across the room, "would you care to escort me upstairs?"

Lester was surprised to see her. He had assumed that Stella's absence at dinner meant she would not be present at all. "Certainly, Miss O'Brien," he heard himself say, as mixed feelings of pride and embarrassment washed over him.

"Uh, Miss O'Brien?" Lester said uneasily. The two had been dancing together to the live music for a couple of songs now, but Lester was not enjoying it as he had imagined he would. Instead, he was racked with guilt. "Is there someplace we can go and talk? Alone?"

Stella led Lester out of the ballroom and down the stairs to a landing between the second and third floors. "This should be as good a place as any," she said.

"Miss O'Brien — Stella," Lester began, "I was attracted to you the very first time I saw you, but I never thought someone like you would care for someone like me. I mean, I'm sure you could have any man you choose. But then Ambrose said . . ." he searched for the right way to put this. "Well, your brother let it slip on the train the other day that he thought you might be interested in me."

"That brother of mine never could mind his own business," Stella said lightly.

"The thing is," Lester went on, "I have a girl back home." A faraway look came over his face as he conjured up an image of Grace. "And, well, I love her," he finished. It was the first time he had ever said those words out loud.

"I know," Stella said quietly. "I can see it in your eyes."

"I hope you don't feel that — that I've misled you in some way."

"How could I, Lester," responded Stella, gently. "But now let me tell you something. I will admit I asked my brother a lot of questions about you, but I never told him I was sweet on you. Lester, I think you are a very handsome man. And you are a delight to be around — so witty and well-spoken — but I could never fall for a man I know so little about."

Stella paused, summoning up the courage to say the rest of what she was thinking.

"Do you have any idea how difficult it is to be the daughter of M.J. O'Brien? Father and Ambrose bring dozens of men through this house as they conduct their business. Many of them show an interest in me, but I can never be sure if it's because of the person I am or if it's because I'm the daughter of the rich and powerful man they're trying to curry favour with. And the people here in Renfrew are worse —

they're in such awe of my father that they seem nervous to even look at me."

She stopped for a moment and looked into Lester's eyes.

"All I want is a friend," she said. "Someone to take me to dances. Someone to sit at my side at these parties. It can be awfully lonely when you're all by yourself."

A friend? thought Lester. Obviously Stella wasn't attracted to him in the same guilty way he was attracted to her. Was it possible for them to be just friends? he wondered. Well, at least Stella had made it clear that she wanted nothing more than friendship from him. And his thoughts about her were — his own thoughts. He knew now that he wouldn't act on them. But why shouldn't he enjoy her company, take her in his arms while the music played? Lester smiled at Stella and offered his arm to her. "Would you care to dance?" he asked.

Frank and Taylor were not at the dance. They had remained downstairs and were talking to an O'Brien business associate when Ambrose approached them.

"Cyc, I hear you're headed to Ottawa tomorrow."

"Yes," Taylor said. He was going to see Thirza Cook, whom he had not seen since leaving the Capital before Christmas. "I'm planning to spend the day there, then catch up with the team in Montreal for the game Saturday." The January 22 game would be the team's third in eight days — a tough pace considering that the quirky schedule provided almost three months in which to play just twelve times.

"Would you allow me," Ambrose asked, "to wire Fred Whitcroft and Hay Millar that you will be in Ottawa?" Their Edmonton squad had been unsuccessful in its Stanley Cup challenge, dropping the second game of the series 13–7, and the two players were now ready to join the Renfrew club. "I'd appreciate it if you would accompany them to Montreal. As sort of an envoy for the team. I was going to do it myself, but I won't be able to get away before Saturday."

"Be glad to do it," Taylor replied. "Now where were we?" he asked, turning to Frank and the other man.

"I was saying," the business associate and ardent Liberal repeated, "that you're letting your anger over the Naval Bill cloud your overall impressions of the Prime Minister. Laurier has done more for this country than any leader since John A. Macdonald.

"I would imagine," the Liberal continued, "that you're both too young to remember the doom and gloom predictions of twenty years ago. There were many in the 1890s who saw no future for the Dominion of Canada. They said the country was nothing more than an artificial blend of four separate geographic regions. Now we truly have a Dominion that stretches from sea to sea. And prosperity? New railways criss-cross the country, giving life to new towns and cities, binding the provinces together. It would seem to me that the past decade has justified the Prime Minister's boast that the twentieth century will belong to Canada. Certainly there have been problems along the way, but Laurier has always taken the middle ground, and it has always served him well."

"I would take it, then," Frank reasoned, "that you see the Naval Bill as Laurier offering up another compromise solution to a difficult problem."

"And a damn good one, I think."

"I wouldn't want to lay money on Laurier's chances of surviving the next election," was all Taylor offered to the conversation.

INTERMISSION

XXIII

LAURIER'S SURVIVAL WAS VERY MUCH ON THE MINDS OF other people in other places, who expressed sentiments similar to those voiced by Cyclone Taylor in the drawing room of the O'Brien home, but with more sinister intent.

"If you want Laurier killed," Richard Lawrence said to Sean Mitchell, setting down his beer mug on the sticky table top, "why not let me do it?" They were in the same Ottawa tavern where, a few weeks before, their one-time partner had been strangled.

"This isn't like getting rid of Harris," Mitchell said, referring to the dead man. "We can't simply lure the Prime Minister into a tavern and kill him."

Lawrence shrugged. "So why can't I just shoot him?"

"Because whoever shoots Laurier will be caught and hanged for it. That's why we need an outsider to do it, someone who has no ties to us whatsoever. That's where David Roberts comes in."

"David Roberts," Lawrence repeated, with a frown. "What do we know about him, anyway?"

"He's the best at what he does," explained Mitchell simply.

"And what, exactly, is it he does?"

Mitchell smiled and ran his fingers back and forth across the gold chain of his pocket watch. It was typical of Lawrence that he cared more for the "how's" of a crime than the "why's." Indeed, Mitchell had chosen wisely when he selected Richard Lawrence as his personal assistant.

Sean Mitchell's great-great-grandfather had come to Canada in 1784, fleeing the persecution in the United States of those who had remained loyal to Britain during and after the American War of Independence. Alexander Mitchell had been among the roughly 14,000 Loyalists who helped to establish the city of Saint John in the newly created British colony of New Brunswick. With its many rivers and abundant supply of lumber, New Brunswick quickly became one of the most important shipbuilding regions in the British Empire, and Mitchell became a shipbuilder — as did his descendants. His grandson helped design the *Marco Polo*, considered for many years after its launch in 1851 to be the fastest ship in the world. As a reward for his efforts, the grandson was given a share in the ownership of the company that had built the ship.

The fast passage made by Canadian ships, their great size, and their innovative design made them popular among British shipowners, and contributed to Britain's commercial conquest of the sea. Canada itself, by 1878, had developed the fourth-largest merchant fleet in the world. Thomas, Alexander Mitchell's great-grandson and Sean's father, built upon his father's shares in the company until he became its principal owner.

Thomas Mitchell worked tirelessly at making his shipbuilding company the best in the Maritimes. Often, his hard work came at the expense of those who loved him. But he believed that the financial security he would leave for his family would be a far greater legacy than the love he had neither the time nor, if truth be told, the desire to provide, and Thomas Mitchell did indeed guide the family business through its most profitable era.

Like his father before him, Sean Mitchell lived only to make the company great, but circumstances he could not control conspired to thwart his dreams. By the time he inherited control of the company, just after the turn of the century, Canada had fallen behind in the big business of shipbuilding. Iron- and steel-hull ships, like those being built in Britain, Denmark, and Germany, had made Canada's wooden sailing vessels less desirable. Thousands of woodworkers, designers, and other labourers were put out of work by the slump in the Canadian market. Still, Sean Mitchell was driven by the desire to succeed as his father had succeeded. It was an intense, unquenchable desire that shaped everything he did.

Richard Lawrence had left Listowel after the end of the Boer War in 1902, determined to become a soldier. He never made it. Lawrence, it transpired, was more determined simply to fire a rifle than truly to become a soldier. He had little use for marching or army discipline, so the army had little use for him. After countless run-ins with his superiors, he was paraded before the Colonel and discharged as being unsuitable for the service. Afraid to return home a failure, Lawrence fled eastward, determined to put his home town and all of its inhabitants out of his mind forever. He settled in Saint John, and, in need of work, took a menial job at Sean Mitchell's shipyard. He had only been working a short time when, once again, he found himself in trouble. He shattered a man's jaw with a mallet after the man had inquired about his decision not to pay his union dues.

Lawrence would likely have been carted off to jail had Sean Mitchell not taken an interest in him and summoned him to his office for a meeting.

"Trouble seems to follow you around, doesn't it, Mr. Lawrence?" Mitchell tossed a copy of Lawrence's army record onto his desk as a means of proving the point. "Why did you hit that man in my shipyard?"

Lawrence, sitting across the desk from Mitchell and assuming he was about to be fired, spoke his mind freely. "I have no desire to join anyone's union," he said. "I work only for my own benefit."

A calculating smile appeared on Mitchell's face. He had, for some time, been searching for a man to handle a problem for him. With the hard times that had befallen his industry, he was in need of some effective cost-cutting. Rather than simply being thankful they still had jobs, Mitchell's employees had been looking for guarantees of greater security. Union demands had been forcing expenses way up, at a time when revenue was way down. Mitchell had been looking for a union buster, and now he believed he'd found his man.

Leaning forward in his chair, Mitchell made an elaborate display of clasping his hands together, each of his fingers interlocking slowly as he placed his elbows on the desk. Resting his head on his knuckles, he again addressed Lawrence. "How would you like to work for me?" he asked.

Lawrence shrugged. "I already work for you," he said.

Mitchell chuckled. "That's not what I mean. You work for my company. I'd like you to come to work for me."

After a short discussion, Sean Mitchell and Richard Lawrence had shaken hands on a partnership that would serve both men well over the next few years. Murder had not been part of the original job description, but, occasionally, when intimidation was not enough, it had become necessary. Lawrence had grown fonder of the task with each kill, so that it caused him little more than logistical concerns when Mitchell first mentioned the plan to assassinate the Prime Minister.

Sean Mitchell's reason for wanting Laurier dead was related to the Prime Minister's Act Respecting the Naval Service of Canada, but had nothing to do with the French-English debate over the Naval Bill that was taking place throughout the country. In fact, the roots of Mitchell's murderous resolve could be traced back to 1897. In that year, Queen Victoria had celebrated her Diamond Jubilee. To mark the occasion, Wilfrid Laurier and the leaders of Great Britain's other self-governing colonies had been invited to the motherland by British Colonial Secretary Joseph Chamberlain for a great meeting of minds — the first Colonial Conference.

With his monocle screwed into his eye socket, and the ever-present orchid in his lapel, Joseph Chamberlain looked to be the living embodiment of British Imperialism. "I believe in the British race," he was fond of saying. "I believe that the British race is the greatest of governing races that the world has ever seen, and I believe there are no limits to its future."

Joseph Chamberlain also believed the Imperial enthusiasm generated by the Jubilee year must be turned to Britain's advantage, and he intended to use the Colonial Conference to lay out his plans for the colonies. Chamberlain believed that the Empire's self-governing colonies should not be encouraged towards further autonomy, but should instead be given a share in running a more centralized Imperial Government. Chamberlain paid flatteringly close attention to Laurier while the Canadian prime minister was in England, since it was important to have the leader of Britain's largest and most prosperous colony on his side. With Canada in favour of an Imperial Government, "Pushful Joe," as he was called, was sure he could easily convince the other colonies to follow suit.

Based on the favourable speeches Laurier had made when he first arrived in England, Chamberlain expected to find in the man a charismatic ally who would champion the cause of Imperialism; but once the Colonial Conference began, the British Colonial Secretary was faced with a Wilfrid Laurier he had not seen before. No longer was Laurier the charming guest intent on saying all the right things and captivating his audiences with what he knew they wanted to hear. Chamberlain did not yet know what Canadian political opponents had come to learn, that beneath the warmth and charm of Wilfrid Laurier, there lay another man — a wily and well-seasoned politician.

Laurier was fifty-six years old in 1897, and had long since lost the thick, dark, wavy hair of his youth. It had receded from his high forehead, and what remained was now almost completely grey and swept back from his face. Yet advancing age had not taken its toll on Laurier's handsome features. Tall, thin, and distinguished-looking, Canada's first French Canadian Prime Minister carried himself with an air of dignity, yet rarely appeared arrogant or condescending. A lawyer by profession, Laurier was a gifted speaker, fluent in both of Canada's official languages. He was elegantly dressed in frock-coated suits, double-breasted vests, and knotted ascots. His top hat and tails were the height of fashion. Laurier's wide, infectious smile and gracious charm had won him the trust of the Canadian public, and the admiration of political friend and foe alike.

Despite the speeches he had made in England, Laurier believed that the natural destiny of Canada, and, in fact, of all the British colonies, was independence. He was not yet ready to push for that future, but he in no way intended to back away from it, either. When it came time for a decision at the Colonial Conference, Laurier took the lead in rejecting the plan to unite the Empire. A stunned Chamberlain, unable to push through what he had wanted, was further shocked when Laurier refused to make contributions to the British Navy, always the backbone of England's military might and the key to the defence of the Empire. The rift between Laurier and Chamberlain did not become public at the time, but it did become known to a few insiders, including Thomas Mitchell.

Sean Mitchell's father was in the Canadian delegation which went to England with Laurier to attend Queen Victoria's Diamond Jubilee celebration. He wasn't concerned that Laurier had not wanted to support Chamberlain's call for an Imperial Government, but he was incensed that the Prime Minister had refused to help fund the British Navy. Mitchell had, in fact, gone so far as to warn Laurier against such a decision. "The British are the most important buyers of Canadian ships," Thomas Mitchell had told Laurier. "Action such as this will cause irreparable damage to that relationship."

Indeed, the damage was done. The early 1900s — the years when Sean Mitchell assumed control of the family business — proved to be the worst on record for Canadian shipbuilding. Now, in 1910, Laurier planned to take action that would prove fatal to Mitchell's enterprise. Mitchell's business agents in England had confirmed it, advising him that if Laurier went ahead with his plans to build a Canadian Navy rather than contribute money to the British Navy, Canadian commercial shipbuilders would bear the brunt of the British Government's wrath. Mitchell would be ruined. He could not let that happen. The Prime Minister had not listened to his father more than a decade before and he would not listen now. This time, Mitchell decided, Laurier would have to pay for his decision.

"Roberts finds murderers," Mitchell said, answering Lawrence's question about David Roberts' role in the plot. "Or, rather, he recruits them."

"Right," agreed Lawrence. "I know that. But he's an American, isn't he?"

"He is," Mitchell confirmed. "He's from Chicago."

"So why does he care about Laurier?"

"Because I pay him to care," Mitchell stated. "He doesn't need a better reason. He arranges murders for money. And he's the best there is at doing that."

While Sean Mitchell and Richard Lawrence sat in a tavern in Ottawa discussing Wilfrid Laurier and David Roberts, Anton Petrovic sat in a union hall in Winnipeg.

Four years had passed since the streetcar strike had spurred Petrovic to take action against the injustices he saw in Winnipeg. Four years of frustration and growing anger.

Few options had been open to him once he made the decision to get involved in political life. A poor man like Petrovic was effectively excluded from active participation in Winnipeg's local politics. A citizen was required to own property valued at a minimum of $2000 before he would be given the vote. Women had won the right to vote in municipal elections since before the turn of the century, but, from Petrovic's point of view, votes for women had merely served to give the elite commercial class even more influence within the city. The poor immigrants he knew rarely, if ever, met the property qualifications themselves, so their wives didn't benefit from women's suffrage. But for the affluent business class, it meant that both husband and wife had a voice in civic affairs.

Petrovic had turned to his union and the socialist groups as a means of combating the injustice in his city. How funny, he would sometimes think, that not so many years ago his cousin had told the border guard he had lost his papers while running away to escape socialism. And now here he was, encouraging his co-workers on the loading platform to attend their union meetings, and taking to the streets to spread the socialist dogma among his fellow citizens of the North End.

At first, Petrovic felt reborn in the action he was taking and was filled with a hope he had not known since his earliest days in Winnipeg. He no longer felt as though he were a victim of his own existence. But his euphoria did not last. Although Winnipeg had a long history of organized labour, it was far from a cohesive movement. Petrovic was quickly demoralized by the actions of labour leaders who used as much energy in their quarrels among themselves as they did in confrontations with capitalist politicians and local business leaders. As the bitter infighting raged on, Petrovic came to the conclusion that he would have to search for other, more forceful means of expression. He became more and more obsessed with the idea of finding a way to make his life matter, wherever that search might take him.

SECOND HALF

XXIV

CYCLONE TAYLOR, FRED WHITCROFT, AND HAY MILLAR boarded the train in Ottawa on Saturday morning for the short journey to Montreal. Taylor, acting as the team's envoy as Ambrose O'Brien had requested, had met his new teammates the previous day at the Windsor Hotel, where Ambrose had arranged rooms for each of them. But Taylor hadn't spent much time with them; instead he had spent most of his brief stay in Ottawa with Thirza Cook.

Taylor called on Thirza at the Immigration Department late Friday afternoon, and took her to dinner. Later, when he walked her home, Taylor was disappointed to find that, while Ottawa was enjoying unusually balmy weather for January, Amelia Cook had not thawed in the slightest. Despite his hockey stardom, Thirza's mother still regarded him as little more than a hooligan, not worthy of her daughter's love. Fortunately, Thirza refused to let her mother's harsh judgment affect her own opinion. She was very much in love with him.

Despite the frosty stare of her mother, whom they could see watching them from the top of the stairs, Thirza led Taylor to the sitting nook where they could be alone for a while. Taylor hoped he would be able to persuade Thirza to make the trip to Montreal with him for the game against the Shamrocks.

"No Fred, I can't," Thirza told him, trying to come up with a valid excuse. "It's mother," she said. "She's having her ladies over for tea tomorrow. She wants me to help."

Taylor sighed. "She doesn't need your help," he protested. "That's what people like her have maids for."

"That's not a very nice thing to say!"

"I know why you don't want to come," Taylor said. "You're afraid I might get hurt." Thirza had not seen him play since the night in

Ottawa the season before when he had suffered the cut foot that had nearly forced him to miss the Stanley Cup contest. "You don't have to worry about that," Taylor assured her. "I can take care of myself out there."

Thirza said nothing. Taylor didn't know it, but she had simply used the injury as a convenient excuse to stop attending his games. As she had found herself more and more attracted to him, she had found his hockey games less and less enjoyable. The violent nature of the sport seemed so out of keeping with the man she knew.

"I don't want to go to the game in Montreal," Thirza said at last. "Nor any other game.

"I love Fred Taylor the man," Thirza continued hesitantly. The man she had first gotten to know on the Rideau Canal two winters before. The man who was so good to children. The man who had gone to Renfrew for his love of her. Not the man who turned a hockey stick into a weapon, charging up the ice with a furious intensity that unsettled her. "Not Cyclone Taylor the hockey hero," she finished, feeling that the rest was better left unsaid.

It was Taylor who was quiet now. No response seemed appropriate. When Thirza kissed him, he realized just how much he had missed her. The next day, as he travelled to Montreal with Whitcroft and Millar, he decided he would make the short train trip from Renfrew to Ottawa more often.

As the players rode along on their eastbound voyage, their conversation quickly turned to hockey and the just-concluded Stanley Cup series between Edmonton and Ottawa. Though the team had undergone quite a few changes since his own Stanley Cup triumph with the Senators just a season ago, Taylor was anxious to hear about his old teammates. Four of them still remained — Marty Walsh, Bruce Stuart, Fred Lake, and Percy Lesueur — but three newcomers had been added. Hamby Shore, who had played with Ottawa back when the team was known as the Silver Seven, had been enticed back to take over Taylor's position at cover point. Bruce Ridpath, who had played two seasons with Toronto in the Ontario Professional Hockey League, had been signed to play right wing, and rookie Gordie Roberts had been recruited to play the left side.

"I'm sure they miss you, Cyc," Whitcroft said, assessing Ottawa's play during the Cup challenge, "What team wouldn't? But jeez, they looked good!"

Ridpath and Roberts had blended into the Ottawa attack as if they were born to play with Marty Walsh as their centre. And rover Bruce Stuart hadn't suffered from the new lineup either. Stuart and Roberts had each scored seven goals in the two-game series with Edmonton. Ridpath had counted five goals while Walsh had tallied two. The speed and combination play they had shown during the series gave no hint at all of the short time they had spent together. Ottawa had played seven games so far in 1910, two each against Edmonton and Galt in a pair of Stanley Cup matches, two in the Canadian Hockey Association, which had started the season before being swallowed up by the new league, and one more since joining the NHA. The Senators had won all seven games, most by lopsided scores that included a twelve-goal victory and a pair of ten-goal decisions. There was no doubt in anyone's mind that, despite the loss of Cyclone Taylor, the defending Stanley Cup champions were in top form.

If the three new Renfrew teammates had not been so caught up in their discussion, they might have noticed that with every passing mile, there was less and less snow on the ground. Taylor had noticed that it was warmer than usual in Ottawa, but the mild spell there was nothing compared to the unseasonably warm weather just 120 miles to the east.

The players became aware of the unusual climatic conditions the instant they stepped off the train at the Montreal station. They were greeted by a warm breeze, and then they suddenly realized that, though it was the third week in January, there was almost no snow. No one said anything, but their thoughts turned immediately to that night's game. What would the ice be like?

The Montreal Arena, where the Shamrocks played their home games, was almost twice as large as the 3000-seat Jubilee Arena that the Wanderers and Les Canadiens called home. The Montreal Arena ranked second only to the Laurier Avenue Arena in Ottawa in its grandeur as a hockey palace. Cyclone Taylor arrived at the rink hours before game time, but he was not alone inside the building. The sight that greeted him as he walked through the double doors leading from the lobby into the playing area might have been comical if it were not for the serious repercussions it could have. Taylor took a seat in the stands to watch the unfolding drama.

Down on the ice, the rink manager and a team of attendants were trying to salvage a playing surface ravaged by the uncommonly warm weather. They scraped the surface with shovels, removing the top layer of ice (which was now little more than thick slush), in an effort to get down to a more solid layer that they hoped lay below. Taylor watched them work for over an hour until it finally appeared that they had beaten the weather. The sheet of ice appeared flat and hard . . . but not for long. Soon, small pools of water began to gather and the process of scraping and re-scraping started again.

As game time drew nearer, other players arrived and joined Taylor in staring glumly at the slushy ice. Lester, meanwhile, had another problem on his mind. The addition of Whitcroft and Millar to the Renfrew roster meant that, for the third time in three games, the Millionaires would be making changes in their starting seven. Ambrose had wanted to see both his new men in uniform, but Lester knew that the reports on Millar from the Ottawa series had not been favourable. The newspapers had blasted him for showing a lack of training and conditioning. The Millionaires had first-hand experience of how much that could hamper a hockey team, so Lester argued against his suiting up. He convinced Ambrose, and Alf Smith agreed, making the decision unanimous.

There was no discussion necessary when it came to Whitcroft. The longtime Ontario amateur star had never shone as brightly as during his years in Edmonton, where the previous season he had scored an astounding total of forty-nine goals. He had been a standout in the Ottawa series, scoring five times during the two games and displaying an abundance of all-around skills. It was decided that Whitcroft, normally a rover, would play right wing against the Shamrocks. Bobby Rowe would move across the ice to play on the left side. The rest of the lineup would remain the same: Taylor at cover point, Frank at point, Lester at rover, Herb Jordan at centre, and Bert Lindsay in goal. Larry Gilmour and Jack Fraser, who had split time at left wing for the first two Millionaires games, would dress as substitutes. Hay Millar would watch from the stands.

At ten minutes to game time, Lester slapped his stick on the dressing room floor, indicating to his teammates it was time to go.

Throughout the first half, attendants scrambled onto the ice during breaks in the play to scoop up bucket after bucket of water from the mushy ice surface. They scraped and scraped at the layers of slush but to no avail, as the pools of water spread. Skates stuck in the soft ice, sending the players sprawling headlong onto the watery surface. Their wool sweaters and hockey socks were quickly soaked through, making them as heavy to slosh around in as they were uncomfortable to wear.

The mush and slush made combination play almost impossible. Passes were slowed, sometimes even stopped, by the puddles. That was clear on the game's very first play, when Herb Jordan beat Shamrocks centre Don Smith on the opening face-off. The Renfrew centre attempted to draw the puck back to Lester but it never arrived, sticking, instead, in a pool of water. Smith moved around Jordan and scooped up the puck before Lester could reach it, but the fates were playing no favourites. Smith's skate blades sank into the soft surface, sending him skidding along the ice.

Only Cyclone Taylor seemed immune to the horrible conditions. He darted across the ice as always, initiating rushes, setting up plays, and hustling back on defence. Taylor got little help from his teammates as he sped along, kicking up sprays of water, but by the same token he received little resistance from the opposition. He would race ahead and then, discovering that none of his teammates had been able to keep up or that a Shamrocks player had fallen in his path, would suddenly double back with the puck. It was not a move that resulted in many scoring chances, but the tactic exasperated his opponents while bringing appreciative cheers from the usually hostile Montreal fans.

Ironically, while Taylor's play was far superior to that of the others, it was a blunder on his part that resulted in the game's first goal. While doubling back into his own end after an aborted attempt to carry the puck up ice, Taylor was unable to shake the tight checking of Tom Dunderdale. With Dunderdale on him, Taylor spied Frank open across the ice and attempted to slide the puck over to him. His weak pass didn't make it through the heavy slush. Joe Hall pounced on the loose puck and broke in on Lindsay all alone. He wristed a shot towards the Renfrew goalie. The puck flew through the air, obscured by a spray of water off the end of his stick. The slippery hunk of vulcanized rubber bounded into the Renfrew net off Lindsay's hands. This proved to be the only goal of the first half. But, while no more goals were scored, there was plenty of other action.

Frustrated by their inability to perform properly, the players took out their anger on each other. The trouble began when Lester hit Joe Hall with a fair check, only to receive a gash over his right eye in return, courtesy of the butt end of Bad Joe's stick. Though Lester was quite capable of taking care of himself, Frank rushed to his aid, just as he had when Lester was attacked by Newsy Lalonde in the game with Les Canadiens. Play continued around them while Frank and Hall exchanged words.

"You wanna start something, too?" Hall growled.

"That was a clean hit, Joe. You cut my brother for no reason."

"Who the fuck are you," Hall snapped back, "my mother? You just look out for yourself from now on or I might slice you up, too!"

With that, Hall wheeled away and skated back into the play. It wasn't long before he found Fred Whitcroft in possession of the puck. Hall slashed Whitcroft in the back of the leg with a vicious two-hander. The newest Renfrew player spun around quickly and swung at Hall's head with a gloved hand, landing a hard blow to Bad Joe's cheek. The two players dropped their gloves and went at it. It looked like a wrestling match, as each man grabbed hold of the other's sweater and tried to force him to the soggy ice.

Referee Tom Hodge and Judge of Play Rod Kennedy broke up the confrontation and ruled both men off for five minutes. After that, the players continued to mix it up at every chance. When the bell finally rang to end the first half, the dripping wet Millionaires dragged themselves to their dressing room, trailing the Shamrocks 1–0.

The rink attendants may not have been able to do much for the ice surface, but fortunately they had been able to round up some extra towels, which they'd left in the dressing rooms. Many of the Renfrew players stripped down completely, removing their sodden woollen sweaters and socks, the sparse padding they wore under their uniforms, even their long johns, and towelled their chilled bodies.

Bobby Rowe stood in the middle of the room, wearing nothing but a towel around his waist, holding his sweater over a metal garbage pail and wringing it out with his hands. He laughed at the amount of water he squeezed out. Herb Jordan found nothing funny about it. "Shut up, Bobby," he mumbled, more as an expression of frustration than anger.

The ten-minute intermission provided only a brief respite. The team carried no spare uniforms, so the players looked almost as wet and miserable returning to the ice for the second half as they had leaving it after the first. It wasn't long after the second half's opening face-off that the frustration which had been building up boiled over into violence.

Joe Hall had continued to go after any and all of the Renfrew players, but Bad Joe reserved his nastiest slashes and elbows for the Patrick brothers. Frank gave as good as he got, opening a gash over Hall's left eye with a butt end of his own. Finally, near the midway point of the second half, the smouldering feud between Frank Patrick and Joe Hall ignited.

Trouble began when Joe Hall picked up a loose puck, which had been stuck in a puddle of slush near centre, and carried it into the Renfrew end. Streaking down the far side, Hall was met by a stiff check from Frank that sent him sprawling. The hit was well within the rules, but Bad Joe took exception to it. He picked himself up and went after Frank, striking back with his stick and slicing open a long cut on Frank's cheek. As Frank brought his hand to his face to inspect the damage, Hall went at him with his fists. Frank ducked the blow and swung back, landing a fist flush on Hall's forehead. Blood sprayed out of the re-opened wound above the Shamrock player's left eye.

The crowd roared as the two bloodied players battled on for several minutes before they could be separated. While Taylor clutched at Frank's sopping sweater, Don Smith, the Shamrocks centre, held Lester pinned against the boards to keep him from going to the aid of his brother. Tom Dunderdale tried to hold Hall back, but Bad Joe, still in a rage, managed to break free and rush at Frank again. He was grabbed by Judge of Play Rod Kennedy before he could get near Frank. Hall was blinded by anger, as well as by the blood that was spilling from the cut on his forehead. He had no idea it was Kennedy who held him. Hall wriggled his arm free and lashed out with a wild punch that connected with Kennedy's face, just below the eye.

Officials were often taunted by partisan home crowds and threatened by players, but no one had ever seen such a violent attack on a game official before. The crowd gasped, and almost all action on the ice stopped. Only Bad Joe himself, apparently unaware of what he had done, continued to blunder around the ice, looking for someone else to fight. Catching his skate in the soft playing surface, he fell into the water and lay there until three of his teammates dragged him off the ice.

Frank was penalized five minutes for his part in the fight, but Hall was banished for the rest of the game. It was rare for a player to receive such a harsh penalty, but anyone who witnessed the melee felt the crime deserved the punishment. Just over fifteen minutes remained in the game, which the Shamrocks still led 1–0, when the two players were sent off. The teams played six men aside until Frank's five-minute sentence was up.

Because no substitution was allowed during penalties of any length, the Millionaires enjoyed a man advantage for the last ten minutes of the game. Unfortunately, its usefulness to Renfrew was limited by the solid goaltending of Jack Winchester and the increasingly awful ice conditions, although a heated effort in the game's final minutes produced the tying goal. Frank, creeping in from his point position, took a drop pass from Whitcroft and slammed the puck into the Shamrocks net. When the bell sounded to signal the end of regulation time, the Montreal players headed back to the dressing room for another welcome ten-minute break before the action resumed with an overtime period. National Hockey Association rules did not recognize a tie game.

The Renfrew team remained on the ice. There were matters Lester wanted to see settled before they left.

"Mr. Hodge," Lester called out as he approached the referee. "I believe there are a few things we need to discuss. Joe Hall, for instance." First and foremost, the Renfrew captain wanted to know if Bad Joe's banishment from the game would carry over into the overtime session.

"Mr. Patrick," the referee said, his weary tone matching the exhausted look on his face, "I wish to take advantage of this time to write up the report I will send to the league while all the events of this contest are still fresh in my mind. Mr. Kennedy and I will discuss what to do about Joe Hall and advise both teams before we continue. Now get your boys off the ice."

Once again the Renfrew players stripped out of their dripping gear and towelled off, barely saying a word. Near the end of the intermission, someone knocked on the dressing room door. It was Rod Kennedy, the judge of play and a former teammate of Lester's from his days with the Wanderers. The area under Kennedy's right eye was now swollen and purplish.

"Uh, Lester," he began, "we're having a bit of a problem — "

"What kind of problem?" Frank interrupted.

"It's not something I wish to discuss in front of all of you," Kennedy responded. "Mr. Hodge and I are at odds over an interpretation of the rules and we wish to discuss it with the coaches and captains."

He looked back at Lester. "Would you and your coach please follow me to the officials room?"

Lester, Kennedy, and coach Alf Smith made the short walk down the corridor to the officials' dressing room. Referee Tom Hodge, Don Smith of the Shamrocks, and W.P. Lunny, an executive with the Montreal squad, were already there. The six men were cramped as they sat in the small quarters.

"The problem we're having," Kennedy explained, to no one's surprise, "is what to do about Joe Hall."

The judge of play paused for a moment, then continued. "Mr. Hodge believes his penalty should expire with the end of regulation time. I feel it should not. His banishment, after all, was for the rest of the game."

"You're just saying that because it was you that got hit!" Lunny objected.

"Mr. Lunny!" Kennedy shot back, fixing a steely glare upon the Shamrocks representative. "I resent that remark! My interpretation of this situation is based solely on the bylaws of the National Hockey Association." He reached for his rule book and opened it to Section 3. "Listen to this," Kennedy said: " 'In the case of a tie after playing the specified two half hours, play will continue until one side scores, unless otherwise agreed between the captains before the match. It being understood, however, that any extra period played shall be considered part of the match.' "

"What's the problem, then?" Lester asked. "It seems to me that if the overtime period is to be considered a part of the match and a player has been suspended for the rest of that match, then his penalty must be carried over. I think the rule makes that clear."

"Well, a precedent has already been set for such a situation," Lunny interjected, "in a Stanley Cup game between Montreal and Winnipeg in 1903."

Lester looked confused.

"I'm afraid he's right, Mr. Patrick," Tom Hodge explained. "During that game, Billy Kean of the Winnipeg team was ruled off for the balance of the match for putting a Montreal player out with a broken collarbone. The match ended in a tie, and Kean was allowed to come on in overtime. Using that game as a precedent, I feel I have no choice but to rule Hall eligible for the overtime session."

"I remember when that happened," Alf Smith said, rubbing his chin.

"But what's it got to do with us?" Lester demanded. "That game was seven years ago in a league that no longer exists. Who knows what the rules stated about such a situation then? The rules that govern our league today make it clear that Joe Hall must be declared ineligible."

"May I remind you, Mr. Patrick," Lunny offered sarcastically, "that you are merely a player in this game. You are entitled to your own interpretation of the rules, but the rest of us are not required to play under the rules as you see them. The referee has the final authority on matters such as these, and it seems clear to me that Mr. Hodge feels Joe Hall should be allowed to play."

Lester looked at Alf Smith, who returned the gaze with a nod of his head, as if to tell Lester he would back any decision he made.

"If Joe Hall suits up for the overtime period," Lester stated flatly, "the Renfrew team will not continue the match."

"Then you forfeit the game!" Lunny declared.

"I think we should let the league decide," Kennedy said.

There was silence for a moment, as the other men in the tiny room looked towards the judge of play.

"I'm inclined to agree with you," Tom Hodge said, after giving the notion some quick consideration. "We've seen enough blood spilled in this game already, gentlemen. I'm going to declare it a draw and leave the final decision as to what should be done up to the league."

"Fine with me," Lester agreed. He was convinced that his own understanding of the rule in question was correct and was confident the league decision would bear him out.

"I'm prepared to abide by your ruling as well," Lunny declared. With or without Joe Hall, there was no guarantee his team could continue to hold off the powerful Renfrew squad, and a tie was better than a loss. Besides, if the league ruled that the match had to be replayed, it would add another game, and another game's gate receipts, to the team's bank account.

"Pack up your stuff, gentlemen," Alf Smith announced as he and Lester returned to the Renfrew dressing room. "We're going home."

When Lester explained to his teammates what had gone on in the officials room, they were all solidly behind him, although there was some concern that they were now three games into the season and had won just one. However, as other scores from the busy hockey night trickled in, they helped to alleviate that worry. The Montreal Wanderers had travelled north to Haileybury to start a two-game road trip and were beaten 4–2, a surprising upset that saw the Montreal team drop to 1 and 1 for the season. Meanwhile, Ottawa had beaten Les Canadiens 6–4, improving their NHA record to a perfect 2 and 0, but though they had won the game it was still considered something of an upset. Backers of the defending Stanley Cup champions had expected their squad to have little trouble in running up a big score and had bet accordingly. Canadiens supporters took quite a few dollars away from Ottawa fans that Saturday night.

XXV

No one knows exactly what is in the minds of the German Government, but everybody knows that between the people of England and the people of Germany there is no cause for war. They have always been fast friends so far back as contemporary history goes. In the Seven Years' War England and Prussia were fast allies; in the Napoleonic wars Germany and England were fast allies. And there is another feature: democracy is coming to the front in all countries of the world, and all the democracy of the world is opposed to war, because it is well known that war falls upon the masses of the people. War may come, I do not say it will not come, but . . . for my part, I do not see any cause of danger to Great Britain at the present time.

Sir Wilfrid Laurier,
Prime Minister.
Naval Debate, 1910

IT WAS A BATTLE-SCARRED COLLECTION OF HOCKEY heroes who rode the train back to Renfrew Sunday morning. Lester had a nasty gash and some swelling above his right eye. Frank had a long, thin cut on his cheek. Fred Whitcroft was minus a tooth, and Bobby Rowe was also marked up. Most of the players could thank Joe Hall for their injuries. They wondered if he would be fired out of the league before the Shamrocks got to Renfrew for a rematch on Friday night. Only Taylor spoke in defence of Bad Joe.

"Come on," Taylor said, as the bad-mouthing of his former protector became more than he was willing to listen to. "You guys were all praising Newsy Lalonde for the same kind of play after Wednesday's game."

"He didn't slug a referee," Frank pointed out.

"I know, I know, I know. But we all saw after the game that he shook Kennedy's hand and apologized. You heard him explain that with all that blood in his eyes he didn't know who he was hitting."

"And you believed him?" Whitcroft wanted to know.

"Yes, I believed him," Taylor answered testily, and he did. "You guys don't know Joe like I do. His reputation as a dirty player is overrated."

"Didn't look that way to me," Frank said, amid nods of agreement from the other players.

"OK, he is a dirty player," agreed Taylor, with a snort of laughter. "But a lot of it comes from having to face other rough players who keep trying to test him."

"Well, as I recall," Bobby Rowe put in, "Hall was the one who started all the trouble last night when he butt-ended Lester. Nobody provoked that."

When the other players voiced their agreement, Taylor realized he was outnumbered. He let them continue the discussion while he buried his head in the newspaper he had brought along for the ride. With no one left to take up the opposing point of view, the conversation quickly subsided. The players remained quiet until the train reached Renfrew.

Lester awoke Monday morning with a throbbing pain in his forehead. He lay in bed a little while longer, hoping the pain would subside. When it didn't, he decided to get up and have breakfast, in the belief that some food in his stomach might stop the pounding in his head. He sat up slowly, fearing that any quick movement would make his pain worse, then swung his legs off the side of the bed. He winced as his feet hit the cold floor. The warm spell, which had been felt particularly in Montreal but had engulfed the Ottawa Valley as well, had snapped overnight. In its place was clear cold weather in keeping with the season.

Getting out of bed, Lester pulled on his robe, put on his slippers, and plodded slowly across the room to the window. Drawing back the curtains, Lester winced again as the brilliant sunlight shocked his eyes. He raised his hands to wipe away the sensation, then pulled them away quickly. The pain in his right eye as he pushed his palm against it was intense.

"Jeez, Lester, you look terrible," Frank greeted him as he made his way into the kitchen. The cut over Lester's eye, courtesy of the butt end from Bad Joe Hall, had puffed up so much overnight that his right eye was almost swollen shut. In the centre of all that black and blue swelling was a crooked cut threatening to burst open its stitches.

"And good morning to you too, Frank," Lester answered sarcastically. He put the iron kettle on the wood-burning stove to boil up his morning cup of hot water, scooped up a bowlful of porridge, and sat down to breakfast.

"Good morning, Frank," Taylor called out as he entered the kitchen. "Good — Lester, you look awful."

The captain of the Renfrew Millionaires nodded, winced at the small movement of his head, and continued eating without saying a word.

Because so many players were nursing aches and pains after Saturday night's encounter with the Shamrocks, Lester and Alf Smith had decided to give the team the day off on Monday. Lester's own injury kept him from practicing the rest of the week as well. By Friday's game, the swelling around his eye had subsided to the point where he felt he probably could play, but considering that he had not worked out with the team all week, and that another few days of rest could only do more good, Lester decided not to suit up. Fred Whitcroft dropped back from right wing, where he had played in the first game with the Shamrocks, to fill Lester's spot at rover. Hay Miller would take over at right wing. His play at practice all week had been outstanding and Lester concluded that the negative reports on him from the Ottawa-Edmonton Stanley Cup series had been exaggerated. The rest of the lineup for the rematch would remain the same: Taylor at cover point, Frank at point, Herb Jordan at centre, Bobby Rowe at left wing, and Bert Lindsay in goal.

Lester took advantage of his week of inactivity to cultivate his friendship with Stella O'Brien, accompanying her to a dinner to welcome home her father after a business trip. Lester's evening with Stella provided a rich resource for playful ridicule from his teammates. He was teased for having issued the directive earlier in the season to cut down on socializing, only to be spending his nights with the boss's daughter. Mostly he was accused, in jest, of trying to curry favour with the millionaire by winning over Stella. The fact was, M.J. O'Brien already admired the handsome and articulate young man who seemed, in his opinion, a notch or two above the average hockey player.

"Mr. Patrick," O'Brien pronounced, spotting Lester across the room after dinner, "it's a pleasure to see you here this evening."

The tall, thickly bearded O'Brien strode the length of the room to greet the captain of his hockey team, and shook Lester's hand with a firm grip.

"That's quite a nasty looking bruise you've got there."

"Yes, sir, I guess it is."

"Well hockey's a tough business, isn't it, Mr. Patrick?"

"It is indeed, sir."

"No tougher than the railway business, though. I could tell you stories about men who'd have been happy to escape with just a black eye."

O'Brien laughed when he made the statement. Lester laughed too, though he wasn't sure exactly what O'Brien had meant.

"Wish the team good luck for me in the game Friday," O'Brien added, before Lester could think of an appropriate response. "I won't be here to see it, but I'll be thinking about you gentlemen."

M.J. O'Brien was not the only one thinking about the rematch between the Millionaires and the Shamrocks. Tickets to the January 28 game had disappeared quickly as fans snapped up seats in anticipation of the grudge match. Expecting a rowdy crowd to welcome Bad Joe Hall to town, Ambrose O'Brien hired Barney McDermott to head a security force and maintain order at the Renfrew Rink.

Barney McDermott was loved and feared in equal measure by most of the citizens of Renfrew. He had served as Renfrew's Chief of Police for almost twenty years before retiring in 1909, and had enforced the law without fear or favour. Even leading citizens had been charged for driving their horses-and-buggies too fast along the town's streets or for driving over a bridge at faster than a walk. One of the town's biggest taxpayers had been hauled into court by the Chief of Police for failing to maintain the grounds around his home. A prominent local merchant had been forced to appear before the magistrate for the crime of selling tobacco on a Sunday.

Public drunkenness was a transgression for which Barney Mc-Dermott had particular disdain. If a man drank too much and created a disturbance, the crusading cop was there to take charge, sometimes employing a wheelbarrow to cart off the inebriated transgressor to the local lockup, where he would be held until he dried out.

Ambrose was sure the presence of Barney McDermott and his hand-picked security staff would be enough to maintain order among the Renfrew faithful, but as it turned out, the theory never had to be tested. In the days leading up to the rematch with the Shamrocks, a special meeting of the National Hockey Association executive was held to deal with the outcome of the first game. They announced, on January 25, that Renfrew would not have to forfeit the match because, as Lester had correctly interpreted, according to league bylaws a player ruled out of a game must remain out if that game was extended into overtime. The league executive further stated that the tie game would be replayed at the end of the season if it had any bearing on the final standings; otherwise it would remain a draw. As for Joe Hall, he was fined $100 and suspended until the end of the month for his attack on Rod Kennedy. Bad Joe did not even accompany the Shamrocks to Renfrew. It was a move that kept the fans in line, but a blow to the Montreal side.

The second game between Renfrew and the Shamrocks couldn't have been more different from the first. Whereas the warm weather in Montreal had turned the ice to slush and rendered the game little more than a brutal battle for survival, the return of the cold in Renfrew meant hard and fast ice, which brought speed and skating skills to the forefront. The checking was hard, and the teams indulged in some stickwork now and then, but the rough play many fans had gone to the rink expecting to see never materialized.

The game was close only for the first few minutes, as the Shamrocks showed early indications that they might be able to hold their own against the Renfrew players. Soon, though, the Renfrew forwards, as-sisted greatly by the rushes of Frank and Taylor, were attacking the Shamrocks' net with regularity, as the Creamery Town squad finally appeared to be hitting its stride. The 10–2 victory left the fans filing out of the rink wildly enthusiastic about the improved play of their home team.

Most of the reporters who witnessed the game shared the feelings of the Renfrew faithful. Newspapermen were far from impartial in their coverage of sports, using their columns unabashedly to root for the home team. Like fans, they were lavish in their praise after good games, bitter in their criticism after bad ones. After the one-sided victory over the Shamrocks, even the Ottawa scribes wrote:

> The Renfrew hockey team tonight put itself right in the
> running for the National Association championship.

Haileybury was the next squad on the Millionaires' schedule. The silver town team arrived in Renfrew on February 4 — the Friday following the big win. Lester, after missing the Shamrocks game because of his injured eye, returned to the lineup for the match with Haileybury, meaning that once again the Millionaires iced a different seven-man alignment. The latest arrangement called for the Edmonton players, Whitcroft and Millar, to man the wing positions. Lester was restored to his spot at rover. The rest of the lineup remained intact.

Lester's childhood pal, Art Ross, served the dual role of coach and point man with Haileybury. The club, despite its surprising win over the Wanderers, had not been faring well early in the NHA season, but Ross had the team well prepared for the game with Renfrew. He did not wish to be shown up in the contest against Lester, his longtime friend and rival, and, as a result, his team gave the Renfrew side all it could handle.

The Haileybury squad pressed the play from the very start, firing several shots at Bert Lindsay in the early going, but he proved equal to them all, making spectacular saves with a gloved hand or padded leg, and clearing dangerous rebounds into the corner with his stick.

For the next twenty minutes, the puck was carried from end to end as the two teams exchanged scoring opportunities, but to no avail. The situation finally changed after Lester scooped up a loose puck in his own end. As the Renfrew captain streaked up ice, he heard his brother calling out from behind the play.

"You've got Whitcroft to your left," Frank shouted, "and Millar on the right."

Lester glanced around quickly, spotting the former Edmonton stars, but elected to hold onto the puck himself. By this time, Taylor had raced up the sheet as well and Lester spotted him across the ice. Using Millar as a screen and Taylor as a decoy, Lester split the Haileybury defence and moved in uncontested on the opposing goaltender. He beat Paddy Moran with a high shot to the stick side.

Cheers rained down from the stands as Lester accepted congratulatory slaps from his teammates. A similar scene was repeated just a minute later, after a goal by Herb Jordan. There was no further scoring in the last minutes of the opening session, and the Renfrew players climbed the stairs to their dressing room with a 2–0 half-time lead.

"Good effort, boys," coach Alf Smith enthused, as he followed his players into the dressing room. No one was really convinced, though. The team had looked listless, particularly in the opening minutes, and was displaying little of the fine combination work they had shown in the impressive win over the Shamrocks a week before.

As if to prove that the Millionaires were not really playing a strong game, Haileybury's Horace Gaul cut the Renfrew lead to 2–1 just seconds into the second half. The Haileybury team, inspired by the fast start, kept the pressure on as they fought to get back on even ground. Bodies were sent crashing to the ice as the Haileybury players fought for possession of the puck, chopping with their sticks and throwing elbows at the Renfrew men. Referee Doc Cameron sent off several players from both sides with one, two, and three-minute penalties. Renfrew did manage to score the next goal, but Haileybury scored again to cut the lead to 3–2. It was then that the Millionaires finally came alive. With a late flurry of activity, they emerged with a 6–3 victory, but though they had won again, the papers were much less generous in their appraisals this time. As one reporter concluded:

> If it takes the "great and only" Renfrew team all of the first
> half and part of the second to get going, what sort of chance
> have they got against Ottawa?

February 12, 1910, was a date circled on the calendar of many a hockey fan in the Creamery Town. It was the date of Renfrew's first game with the powerful Ottawa Senators, the Stanley Cup champions. The Renfrew fans saw it as a chance to get even with the big-city team for years of insults against small-town hockey. What sort of chance did Renfrew have against Ottawa? The answer was just eight days away.

XXVI

All roads lead to Winnipeg. It is the focal point of three transcontinental lines of Canada, and nobody, neither manufacturer, capitalist, farmer, mechanic, lawyer, doctor, merchant, priest, nor labourer, can pass from one part of Canada to another without going through Winnipeg. It is the gateway through which all commerce of the East and West, and the North and South, must flow. No city, in America at least, has such absolute and complete command over the wholesale trade of so vast an area.

William E. Curtis,
American Reporter.
Circa 1910

DAVID ROBERTS WAS IN WINNIPEG FOR SOME TIME BEFORE he found Anton Petrovic. Roberts needed to find a solitary man so embittered by the society in which he lived that he would be willing to sacrifice his own life to end the life of another, and yet a man who, despite such obvious instabilities, would be able to formulate such a plan of terrorism and carry it out virtually unaided.

Leon Czolgosz had been the perfect man for the task, but Roberts had received a lot of help in locating him. Throughout his career as a man who "eliminated problems," the words he euphemistically used to refer to his chosen profession, he had built up an extensive network of spies and informants, but, like himself, they were all from the United States, and they knew very little of Canada or Canadians. Roberts had considered using an American, but decided against it. The death of the Canadian Prime Minister at the hands of an American assassin would be too dangerous politically. A Canadian, Roberts decided, must carry out the deed.

Roberts had gone to Winnipeg in December of 1909, shortly after Mitchell had first contacted him. Why Winnipeg? Certainly not just because of its nickname, though Roberts had smiled to himself after hearing that the city was called the "Bull's Eye of the Dominion." Where better to find an assassin? But there were solid reasons for the decision to begin the search in Winnipeg.

The capital of Manitoba was the fastest-growing city in Canada. Rapid population growth, Roberts knew, puts strains on a city. Winnipeg had more than its share of tension, particularly between the city's established Anglo-Protestants and its immigrant newcomers. The deeply prejudiced majority saw the Jews and Slavs of Eastern Europe as a threat to their values. Newspapers in Winnipeg often reminded their readers of that fact:

> There are few people who will affirm that the Slavonic immigrants are desirable, or that they are welcomed by the white people of Western Canada. Those whose ignorance is impenetrable, whose customs are repulsive, whose civilization is primitive, and whose character and morals are justly condemned, are surely not the class of immigrants that the country should seek to attract.

Roberts was pleased when he read the *Winnipeg Telegram* editorial, not because he agreed with it but because he knew it was a symptom of the social ills he hoped to exploit. Roberts cared little about the colour of a man's skin or his ethnic background. In his coldly calculating mind, people fell into only two categories: those he could use and those he could not. It just so happened that the racially, socially, and culturally oppressed — dirt-poor immigrants in a thriving city, deprived of adequate schooling and proper health care — were people he could use.

Roberts' first step was to study the local newspapers for information on upcoming political lectures or social forums. He attended several such functions in an effort to determine whether there was any anarchist presence in the city, but he had no luck. The meetings he sat in on had all been socialist, urging the workers of the city to join the unions in the fight for industrial organization.

As his understanding of the political atmosphere in Winnipeg came into sharper focus, Roberts decided that he had a better chance of finding the man he was looking for by infiltrating the ranks of organized labour rather than by attending lectures. He began to turn up at local union shops, asking questions. It was not a process Roberts enjoyed, and in the past it had usually been carried out by his spies and informants. It was also dangerous. Political dissidents, labour unionists, and other social outcasts did not, as a rule, take kindly to strangers asking questions.

Roberts was careful how he went about his business. He never spoke to more than three or four men in a single visit, and rarely visited the same place more than twice. It made for slow going, but Roberts knew that it was much better to be safe than sorry. Still, he had his frightening moments.

The evening began as most others had. Roberts arrived early for a scheduled meeting at a small union hall. The building was plain, as most of the others had been — a one-storey, one-room rectangular structure built completely of wood. The planks covering the outside walls had once been painted white to give the building a less drab appearance, but the paint had since faded and flaked off in places, so that the hall now looked worse than if it had been left alone. Inside, the union hall was equally shabby. Rows of battered benches extended from the back wall to the front of the room where a rough wooden dais had been built. The worn floor was grooved and rutted.

Roberts always arrived early at union meetings, so that he could examine the members as they turned up. He looked for men who came alone. He had little use for those who liked to congregate in groups. Such men were less likely to speak their minds. They tended to take on the personality and attitude of the group. A solitary man, if questioned correctly, was more likely to give answers that revealed the true workings of his mind.

Few men attended these meetings alone, which was fine with Roberts. The fewer men he had to choose from, the less likely he was to make a mistake. He made it his practice to speak briefly to the handful of lone men, in order to pick out one on whom he would concentrate his efforts. He would sit next to that man during the meeting and pump him for information. It was usually pretty simple, but on this night he ran into trouble.

"This man's a spy or something!" shouted the tall man who sat to Roberts' right. A rumbling of indignation spread through the room.

Fear gripped Roberts, but it quickly gave way to anger. Anger at himself, for he knew he had been careless. He had been so involved in his questioning of the man on his left that he had not even noticed there was anyone on his other side.

The tall man, easily a foot taller than the tiny Roberts, clamped his hand on the shoulder of the man he had just accused and stood up. The man was not only tall but strong, and his action yanked Roberts to his feet as well.

"I heard what you been askin' this guy," the tall man growled, jerking his head in the direction of the other man. "You workin' for the railroad? You tryin' to bust this union?"

"Leave him be," said the man to Roberts' left. He spoke with a thick accent. "This man don't ask me nothing out of line and I don't tell him nothing I don't want him to know."

"Yeah?" shot back the tall man. "Well, I don't want him in here."

"Maybe it is best you leave," said the man Roberts had been questioning. "I leave too." Although his accent was heavy, he was not difficult to understand.

Something about the man who walked out of the union hall with David Roberts brought Leon Czolgosz to mind. At first, Roberts was unable to put his finger on what it was. There certainly wasn't any physical resemblance; this man was much more powerfully built. Then it came to him: the eyes. Both Czolgosz and this man had the dark, sunken eyes of the downtrodden. These were the eyes of men who had seen only the worst in life, who had every reason to have lost all hope and yet, in both cases, Roberts could see something different in them. Despite the misery these men had known, he sensed an innocence behind those dark, hollow eyes. To Roberts, innocence was like a blank slate begging to be written on, or a lump of wet clay aching to be sculpted. In the hands of a skilled artist such as himself, innocence could become dangerous.

Roberts knew that he could not let the connection he had made between Czolgosz and this new man influence his decision. First impressions were usually lasting, but not necessarily accurate. Still, something told him this could be the man.

"I want to thank you for sticking up for me in there," Roberts said, as a means of initiating conversation.

The man just nodded.

"No, really. I'd like to thank you. How about if I buy you a drink?"

"Don't see why not," the man answered.

Good, thought Roberts. Very good. Now he could move on to the part of his job he truly relished — the process of bending another man's will to suit his own purposes.

"I'm Nick Armas," he lied, believing the man would be more likely to speak freely to someone with a more foreign-sounding name. He extended his hand to the man in a gesture of friendship.

"Petrovic," the man said, shaking his hand. "Anton Petrovic."

Portage and Main. The heart of the city of Winnipeg. The core of the city's commercial focus. Around the intersection of Portage and Main were most of the city's banks, brokerage houses, and business head-quarters. Within a few blocks along Main Street, on either side of Portage Avenue, there were no less than sixty hotels. These hotels were more than just the temporary homes of business travellers on their way in and out of Winnipeg; these hotels were social gathering points. More than anything, they were places to drink.

The area was not one Anton Petrovic frequented. That was a fact David Roberts counted on. He preferred to study a man outside his normal environment. The central core of Winnipeg was basically a white-collar business district, to which Petrovic's station in life rarely gave him access. Roberts led Petrovic into the bar of one of the area's many hotels.

"We don't want no boloney-eaters in here," the man behind the bar informed him. With his floppy felt cap, his plain, loose-fitting coat, and his well-worn boots, not to mention his hollowed cheeks and generally haggard appearance, Petrovic had been instantly recognized as "a foreigner." In this great metropolis of the West, a foreigner meant anybody who wasn't of British ancestry.

"Boloney-eater." Petrovic cringed when he heard those words. They had taunted him many times before. At first, he had not understood. It had even sounded funny to him. Slowly, he had come to realize the subtle, hateful, meaning behind it. Rich men ate steak. Poor ones ate bologna. All he found miserable about his life was held up to him by that simple, cruel epithet.

"He's with me," Roberts informed the bartender, flashing a thick wad of bills he had tucked inside a gold money clip. He led Petrovic to a table. "What'll you have?" Roberts asked his guest.

"Vodka," he answered.

"Bartender, a vodka for my friend. Just some soda water for me." Roberts didn't drink when working.

The bartender kept his eyes on Petrovic as he brought the two men their drinks. Anton ducked his head, eluding the unfriendly stare. No sooner had the bartender poured the vodka into his shot glass than Petrovic drank it down in a single swallow. He tapped his glass on the solid wood table, indicating he was ready for more. The bartender shook his head disapprovingly: foreigners were known to drink too much, but he poured Petrovic another round.

"Why don't you just leave the bottle here," Roberts advised, peeling off some bills from his roll of money. "And have the kitchen fry us up a couple of steaks."

Petrovic was obviously uncomfortable amid the unfamiliar surroundings of the hotel bar. His eyes continually darted around the room, checking out Roberts, the bartender, the handful of customers seated at other tables. Occasionally, Petrovic would make direct eye contact with someone. He noticed the way their eyes shifted up and down as they gave him a quick going over. A look of disgust would cross their faces. At first Petrovic turned away, as he had from the bartender, ashamed of the reaction his presence caused, but, as the alcohol lessened his inhibitions, he no longer looked away. He would stare down these other people until they were finally forced to shift their gaze. When they did, a smile of almost wicked pleasure spread across his lips. It gave Petrovic a feeling of pride to know he could make these other people look away — no matter what the reason.

Roberts noticed the change that came over Petrovic. Roberts had been sipping his own drink slowly, watching Petrovic quietly. There were two reasons for his silence. First, he wanted to study the man. Second, Roberts wanted Petrovic to be uncomfortable. He wanted to see how the man would handle himself under strange circumstances. Roberts was pleased with what he had observed.

"You could have that feeling of pride all the time, you know," Roberts said softly. "I can help you."

Petrovic stared at Roberts. How had this man known what he was thinking? Before Petrovic had a chance to respond, the bartender returned to the table with two steaks. The delicious aroma and enticing sizzle of the steak drove all other thoughts from Petrovic's mind. He had never seen such a large slice of meat. Smothered in onions, the steak dinner was the most exquisite meal Petrovic had ever beheld. His mouth started to water.

Petrovic grabbed his fork and knife and began sawing into the piece of beef, cutting up the entire steak into bite-sized bits before stuffing the individual morsels into his mouth. He would not even finish chewing one piece completely before greedily jamming in another. He only put down his fork long enough to break off a piece of biscuit, which he used to sop up the steak's juices before popping it into his mouth as well.

"I trust the steak was to your liking?" Roberts inquired, once Petrovic had downed his final bite.

Petrovic only nodded, noticing with slight embarrassment that Roberts was barely halfway through his own meal.

"Good," said Roberts, smiling. "I'm glad to hear it." Now it was time to get down to business.

Roberts had already learned enough to know that, like Czolgosz, Petrovic was a socialist unhappy with his local socialist movement. He knew that Petrovic was a loner and, from what he had observed in the hotel, Roberts figured that the man would prove quite capable of adapting to unaccustomed circumstances. But was he a man who would be willing to kill for a cause? Roberts had to find the answer to that question.

"I could have that feeling of pride you spoke of," Petrovic said in his thick accent, "if only I was treated as equal.

"Look around this room," Petrovic continued. "I am so different from anyone in here? I think no. They have more money. Nice clothes. But underneath? We are not so different. They are just men, same as myself."

"Men," Roberts responded, borrowing a line from Emma Goldman, whose anarchist ideals he hoped to pass along to Petrovic, "under the present society are products of circumstance."

"I think you are right, Mr. Armas," agreed Petrovic. "Many times I am trying to change those circumstances. I leave my home as a boy to come to this country. I work hard at my job. I struggle to learn new language. Nothing changes. It is not so different here as I once think. I join union. Fight for workers' rights. Still nothing changes. I am not born English. That don't change, so nothing else changes."

"It's more than just that," Roberts pointed out. "The men who hold power, not just in this city but everywhere, hold it because they control the economy. The ones with the money are always the ones who call the shots. They control the government."

Roberts paused at this point and looked at Petrovic. Convinced that he was getting through to him, Roberts continued. "Under the galling yoke of government," he told Petrovic, quoting again from Emma Goldman, "it is impossible for the individual to work out his career as he could wish."

"Again, Mr. Armas, I believe you are right. That is why I join the labour party —"

"Socialism isn't the answer," Roberts interrupted, before Petrovic could go any further. "It's not enough to simply challenge the capitalist system. Whoever they are who form the government, they will impose their own set of beliefs on the people and that will always alienate someone."

Again Roberts paused to study the effect of his words on Petrovic. The man was completely caught up in what he was hearing. "Only by eliminating all forms of central authority," Roberts concluded, "will the individual be free to live his life as he sees fit."

It never ceased to amaze Roberts how eagerly the socially oppressed accepted anarchist ideology. To him, the ideas were outlandish. The thought of a society that would dispense with all laws and found its authority on the individual conscience was ridiculous. He expounded the virtues of anarchism because its outrageous theories attracted the type of people he needed, and, even more importantly, because anarchists provided easily identifiable scapegoats in any political assassination.

Roberts knew he had reached Petrovic with his anarchist propaganda. He could see that the man was willing to embrace the cause. He still did not know, however, if Petrovic could be convinced to kill for it. Roberts knew it wasn't a subject he could bring up for discussion. Petrovic would have to reach such conclusions on his own.

"I've taken up enough of your time, Mr. Petrovic," Roberts announced, after checking his pocket watch. "I want to thank you again for defending me in the union hall. I've enjoyed talking with you."

"I have also enjoyed talking with you," Petrovic said as he got up to walk to the door with Roberts. "Will I see you again, Mr. Armas?"

It was the question Roberts had been hoping to hear. "I'm leaving town for a few days," he told Petrovic. This was a lie. Roberts merely wanted to test the man to see if he had truly been hooked. "I'll be back at this same hotel next week. I'd be pleased to have you join me for dinner again then, if you can make it."

Anton Petrovic did make it back to the hotel the following week, and he and Roberts had dinner, this time in Roberts' hotel room. The man who arranged murders for a living preferred it that way. They could speak more freely if there was no fear of being overheard. The two men met for dinner again the night after that. And the night after that. By the end of the week, David Roberts knew Petrovic would be his man.

"I'm going to murder the mayor of Winnipeg," Petrovic told Roberts. "That will help to bring changes, yes?"

"That would help, indeed," Roberts said calmly. "But I think you're setting your sights too low."

"What do you mean?" Petrovic asked, disappointed that his pronouncement had not been met with greater enthusiasm from the man he had come to regard as his mentor.

"You want to do something that will serve as an inspiration to the working people everywhere, don't you? To show everyone that government is wrong?"

Petrovic nodded.

"Think about it," Roberts continued. "If you kill the mayor of Winnipeg, that will lead to changes in this city. But what else will it do?"

Petrovic had no response.

"Nothing," Roberts stated. "It won't even do much to help you. You'll no doubt have to flee the city after a crime like that, so you won't even be able to reap any of the benefits of the changes here."

Petrovic nodded slowly. He was beginning to see that Roberts was right.

"Now what could you do that would really cause people everywhere to take notice?" Roberts asked, beginning the final process of steering Petrovic towards the decision he wanted him to make.

"Let me see now," Roberts said musingly, as if he were thinking out loud. "If you feel the current form of government in the country is all wrong, what can you do to change it?"

"The Prime Minister," Petrovic said finally. "I'm going to shoot the Prime Minister."

XXVII

THE SUBJECT WAS WITHIN HIS SIGHTS, BUT IT WAS A struggle to line him up.

"Would you quit squirming, Cyc!" Lester laughed. "How can Gus take your picture with you moving around like that?"

"But it's hot under these lights," Taylor protested. "Especially with all my hockey gear on."

"We both survived," Frank pointed out. He and his brother had posed for pictures, too.

Gus Handford came out from behind the large box-like contraption that was his camera. "Cyc, I just need you to hold your head up a little higher," he instructed.

"That should be easy enough," quipped Frank. "It's not as if he's got much hair weighing it down!"

Everyone laughed, though Taylor shot Frank a menacing glance in jest. Frank had the utmost admiration for Taylor, but he liked to needle him every now and then, just to keep him from getting too cocky.

"And remember," Frank added in a knowing tone, "the quicker you get done in here, the quicker you get to Ottawa."

Frank was referring to Taylor's desire to see Thirza, but Gus was not aware of such things. Ottawa meant only one thing to the hockey-loving photographer: the big game with the defending Stanley Cup champions, which was now only one day away.

"Do you think you guys can beat the Senators?" Gus asked. "You know they've won twelve games in a row. Six straight since joining our league. Some people say they're unbeatable."

"No team is unbeatable, " Lester replied automatically, though he didn't answer Gus's question. It was not Lester's style to speculate on the outcome of games. Not all of his teammates felt the same way, though. Some of the Millionaires, Lester knew, had bet on the game. Ambrose O'Brien had money on it, too. It seemed strange to Lester that Ambrose wagered so much money on hockey games. Ambrose, though he liked his parties, didn't strike Lester as a playboy. And he was too able a businessman to be dismissed as the spoiled son of a wealthy father. Perhaps that was why he made the bets? Newspapers speculated that the O'Briens were losing one thousand dollars a game on their Renfrew hockey club, since revenues couldn't meet their extravagant expenses. Maybe Ambrose was just trying to cut his losses. Of course, Ambrose and the players always bet on themselves to win, but, although there was nothing in the rules to prohibit it, Lester felt that such wagering could place a person in a precarious position. What if someone found himself in so much debt to gamblers that his only way out was to fix the outcome of a game? It could happen, Lester thought. And what would that do to the sport?

"I don't know if we'll beat them," Frank told Gus, when it became apparent his brother wasn't going to answer. "But I'll tell you one thing: we're sure going to give them one hell of a battle."

"Hold it, Cyc!" Gus called out, his mind suddenly turning from hockey to photography as he noticed Taylor striking the pose he wanted. "Perfect," he pronounced, after snapping the shot.

It was just before three o'clock on Friday afternoon when Cyclone Taylor arrived in Ottawa. The short train ride from Renfrew got him to the city a little too early to call on Thirza at work, so Taylor decided to pay a visit to the newsroom of the *Ottawa Citizen* to renew acquaintances with the paper's sports reporters.

"Cyc, I've never seen such excitement surrounding a regular season game so early in the schedule," said Tommy Gorman, the *Citizen* sports editor. "It's like a Stanley Cup game or something. We've got two special telegraph wires running from the arena to the office so that people can telephone in for reports. The *Evening Journal* has a wire running up to Renfrew to give the fans there detailed score updates. You know as well as I do that people around here always take a keen interest in their sports, but this eclipses anything I can remember."

There were many reasons for the excitement. By the townsfolk in Renfrew, the contest was seen as a chance to pay back the residents of the big city, and gentlemen of the press in cities like Toronto as well, who had always dismissed their past hockey teams as bush league. In Ottawa, the game was seen as a chance to knock the small town back down a notch by defeating its famous team of all-stars. For hockey fans in general, the game was seen as the first true test for the Stanley Cup champs, since the Senators had only beaten up on the league's weaker sisters — the Shamrocks, Les Canadiens, and both Cobalt and Haileybury twice — in running up their 6 and 0 record. It was also the first opportunity to see how much the Millionaires had improved since their opening-game loss to the Wanderers.

"What kind of a reception do you think I'll get tomorrow night?"

That this was Taylor's first game back in Ottawa since his defection to Renfrew was yet another reason for the excitement.

"It'll be interesting to find out," Gorman said. "The fans here had really taken to you. Many of them still think of you as one of their own, and I'm sure they'll be cheering. But others were pretty offended when you bolted for the bush leagues. I don't think they'll be as kind."

Just then, Percy Lesueur walked into the office. "Who won't be as kind?" the great Ottawa goaltender asked.

"Tommy was just telling me," Taylor explained, "that a lot of the fans here didn't take too kindly to my signing with Renfrew."

"Oh, is that all?" Lesueur said dryly. "I thought you were talking about something important.

"As far as I'm concerned," the goalie added, getting in a friendly dig at his former teammate, "our defence has never been better."

"Oh yeah?" Taylor countered, responding with the same lighthearted banter. "Well, tomorrow night I'm going to score a goal by skating through the Ottawa defence backwards!"

All three men had laughed at Taylor's wisecrack, but Cyclone wasn't laughing late Saturday afternoon when, as the first person to arrive at the arena, he opened his newspaper to pass the time and saw a headline asking "WILL TAYLOR SCORE?" Surprised, he read on:

> Fred Taylor made a crack while in the *Citizen* office, Percy Lesueur being present at the time, that he would skate through the Ottawa defence backwards and score a goal. Although he was joking it seems to have got around and been taken seriously. At any rate a fan has posted $100 at the King Edward Hotel, to bet that Taylor doesn't score in any way, shape, or form.

As Taylor sat inside the arena reading his newspaper, fans were already lining up outside for the chance to see if he would make good on his boast. The line in front of the Slater Street entrance, which opened towards the rush seating sections, had begun to form at four o'clock. By six o'clock, the line extended to Albert Street, a full city block to the north. At seven they were as far along as Queen and at seven-thirty, when the doors were thrown open, the snakelike chain stretched three blocks to Sparks Street.

Back in Renfrew, a similar though smaller scale scene was being played out. The *Evening Journal* had done more than just set up a telegraph wire to provide fans in the Creamery Town with a way of following the game. The newspaper had secured the use of Temperance Hall and hired a reader, so that the townsfolk could gather in the public auditorium to listen to free reports from Ottawa. As game time approached, the hall filled quickly with eager fans.

Meanwhile, in Ottawa, the opening of the doors to the Laurier Avenue Arena had set off a fierce scramble for seats. The swelling crowd threatened to turn ugly, but police and arena officials managed to maintain some semblance of order. By eight o'clock, with the rush seat section filled beyond capacity and those in standing room lined three and four deep, the doors to the Slater Street entrance were closed. Hundreds of fans had to be turned back, but some, still determined to catch the action, climbed the outside walls to the roof. There, craning their necks uncomfortably, they peered in through open windows in an effort to see.

All the Renfrew players had arrived at the arena long before the doors to the building were opened. Their quiet, businesslike approach contrasted with the bedlam going on in the rest of the building. This was the biggest match of the young season, and everyone understood its implications. A victory by Renfrew in the game with Ottawa would certainly set up a three-way race to the finish between the Millionaires, Senators, and Wanderers.

Although the season was just reaching the halfway point, none of the other four teams in the league looked like serious contenders. The current standings found the Senators sitting atop the league with a 6 and 0 mark, while the Wanderers were a close second at 5 and 1. Renfrew was next at 3 and 1, not counting their tie game. A win by the Millionaires was needed to keep pace with the two top teams. A loss would not be fatal to Renfrew's Stanley Cup aspirations, but it would likely mean the Millionaires would have to win all of their remaining games, especially the rematches with the Senators and Wanderers later in the season, in order to claim the prized trophy. A loss would also mean that the team would require some help along the way: someone else would have to beat Ottawa for Renfrew to be able to win the Stanley Cup. The knowledge of these facts kept the usual pregame chatter to a minimum. Finally the silence was broken by the sharp crack of wood against concrete as Lester slapped his stick on the floor. It was time for the team to take the ice.

Nearly 7000 Ottawa fans, decked out, as was their custom, in the red, white, and black colours of their team, crammed every inch of the arena. The exuberant crowd quieted somewhat when Lester led the Millionaires onto the ice. All eyes turned to the opening behind the Renfrew bench, watching for the appearance of the red-toqued figure who had once been their hero but was now the enemy.

"Here he comes! Here he comes!" Taylor heard some young fans shout. The telegraph operator dashed off an update for those back in Renfrew:

TAYLOR GREETED BY APPLAUSE MINGLED WITH A CHORUS OF GROANS AND HISSES.

Taylor wasn't bothered by the mixed reaction. He had suspected that a cool reception was coming and realized his crack about scoring a goal backwards had probably made things worse. He accepted the situation with a smile as he got ready for the game. The telegraph operator got the fans in Renfrew prepared as well.

LINEUP FOR THE SENATORS: LESUEUR — GOAL; LAKE — POINT; SHORE — COVER POINT; STUART — ROVER; WALSH — CENTRE; RIDPATH — RIGHT WING; ROBERTS — LEFT WING.

LINEUP FOR RENFREW: LINDSAY — GOAL; F. PATRICK — POINT; TAYLOR — COVER POINT; L. PATRICK — ROVER; WHITCROFT — CENTRE; MILLAR — RIGHT WING; FRASER — LEFT WING.

"They changed the lineup again," pharmacist Dom Ritza said to Gus Handford, after the report from the telegraph wire was read to the large gathering at the Temperance Hall.

"Well, Whitcroft has been working out at centre all week," Gus pointed out. Herb Jordan had been absent from most of the week's practice sessions, still putting his off-ice job with the O'Briens ahead of his job with their hockey team. It was a decision his teammates respected, but they were not going to let it hurt them; if Jordan didn't practice, he didn't play.

WHITCROFT AND WALSH CALLED TO CENTRE ICE FOR OPENING FACE-OFF.

Whitcroft was first to line up, with his stick pressed hard to the ice. Walsh took his time, skating in tight little circles before finally gliding into position.

"Marty," said Whitcroft, nodding once as he spoke the name.

"Fred," Walsh replied in the same noncommittal tone, indicating neither friendship nor animosity.

The referee was Russell Bowie, who had been chosen to officiate the big game because he was considered the best in the business. He put the puck down between the sticks of Whitcroft and Walsh. "Play!" he shouted, and the game was on.

Walsh won the draw and fired the puck into the Renfrew end, where Taylor scooped it up. The receipt of the puck by the star cover point set off a chorus of boos. Apparently those angered by Taylor's jump to Renfrew outnumbered those who were still loyal to their hockey hero, or at least they made up the more vocal contingent among the huge crowd. But Taylor didn't hear the boos. His concentration on the game blocked out any distractions as he carried the puck up ice. He could hear Frank, though, as his defence partner called out instructions.

"Dump it in, Cyc! Dump it in!"

But Taylor didn't want to dump it in. He wanted to make something happen. He cut towards the sideboards, but the Ottawa players were ready for him and blocked his path. They knew, better than any other team in hockey, how effective Taylor was when given the opportunity to roam the ice freely. The Senators were determined not to give him any room at all. Cyclone was forced to spin to his right to avoid an Ottawa player, then move back towards the middle of the ice.

"Watch out, Cyc!" Frank called from behind the play. The warning came too late. Taylor was hit hard by Bruce Stuart and sent to the ice. The check brought forth a tremendous cheer from the Ottawa faithful. Although the hit had been within the rules of the game, with no high elbows or hidden butt ends, the Millionaires did not take kindly to their star player being knocked around. Whitcroft gave Stuart a shove just to let him know the attack had not gone unnoticed. Soon, though, the Renfrew players had more to be concerned about: within seconds after the hit on Taylor, Hamby Shore scored for the Senators and Ottawa had a quick 1–0 lead. Their concern mounted less than a minute later:

RIDPATH TAKES PASS FROM WALSH. BEATS LINDSAY ON STICK SIDE. OTTAWA 2; RENFREW 0.

There was shocked silence in the Temperance Hall. The game was little more than two minutes old and already the Senators were taking control. Was this game to be yet another procession of goals for the seemingly invincible Stanley Cup champions?

Not if Lester could help it. He summoned his teammates around him for a pep talk. "This is no time to let up, gentlemen," he warned, noting the dejected expressions on some of the players' faces. "A game is sixty minutes long and there'll be plenty more goals scored before this one is through. We'll get our share. Don't you worry."

"Mr. Patrick," barked referee Russell Bowie. "Get your team lined up for the face-off or I'm going to have to give you a penalty for delaying the game."

"All right, fellows," Lester said, "you heard the man. Let's get ready. And let's get the next goal!"

Lester backed up his words with action, and less than five minutes later he put the Millionaires on the scoreboard when he backhanded a blast past Percy Lesueur. Renfrew now trailed 2–1.

Walsh again beat Whitcroft to the draw, and the Senators wasted no time in returning to the offensive. But Lindsay handled an Ottawa shot easily and cleared the rebound behind the net, where Taylor scooped it up.

Emerging from behind the goal, Taylor moved up ice along the sideboards. He was just gaining speed when he felt something whiz by his head. It was a lemon, and as it splattered to the ice it set off an avalanche of garbage from the rush seats. Lemons, oranges, and a variety of other objects were hurled at Cyclone as he scurried along the boards. The fans in the cheap seats screamed with delight, and play had to be halted.

"Who brings old fruit to a hockey game?" Taylor asked, trying to maintain his sense of humour.

"Never mind that, Cyc. Just get out to centre ice," Bruce Stuart urged. "You have to get out of range!" Taylor heeded the advice of his old friend and former teammate.

Players from both teams helped sweep up the mess, but as soon as play resumed, another shower of rotten fruit, copper coins, and other trinkets rained down, accompanied by more boos and hisses. When play once more got under way and Marty Walsh scored to put Ottawa up 3–1, Taylor was again assaulted, but this time he was thankful to be hit only by a barrage of insults:

"Go home to Renfrew, Taylor . . ."

"You're going back, Taylor . . ."

"Back to the Bush League . . ."

Taylor was not only receiving abuse from the Senator fans, he was also getting special checking attention from the Ottawa players, so the job of leading the Renfrew attack fell upon Frank. Time after time Frank led the forwards into the Ottawa end and set them up for good shots on goal, only to have these turned aside by Lesueur's quick stick, gloved hands, or padded legs. Lindsay was equally sharp in the Renfrew goal.

RIDPATH TAKES PASS FROM ROBERTS. LINDSAY LUNGES TO HIS LEFT TO BLOCK RIDPATH'S SHOT. CLEARS RE-BOUND TO TAYLOR.

"Great save, Bert," Dom Ritza shouted amid the cheers of the Renfrew fans in the Temperance Hall. He could almost picture it.

No sooner had Taylor picked up the puck from Lindsay than Bruce Stuart was on him again. Circling in his own end, Taylor was unable to shake the tight checking.

"Drop it back, Cyc!" Frank directed, as he moved into position to take the pass. Taylor slid him the puck and Frank was off again. He quickly moved past Stuart, whom Taylor had managed to keep busy long enough to put his teammate in the clear, and swooped towards the sideboards. Moving with the short, choppy strides he had used since childhood, Frank needed more steps than many players to reach his top speed, but once he got up a full head of steam he was faster than most. He moved uncontested into the Ottawa end.

With a few swift dekes, Frank found himself in alone on goal, but the puck had slipped agonizingly out of reach. Percy Lesueur moved out to play it and reached the puck just as Frank did. A collision seemed unavoidable.

F. PATRICK SWERVES BY LESUEUR. POKES SLOW SHOT INTO OPEN NET. OTTAWA 3; RENFREW 2.

Cheers greeted news of the goal, not only at the Temperance Hall in Renfrew but all across the Ottawa Valley. Fans in towns like Pembroke, Almonte, Arnprior, and Perth stood in the cold outside telegraph offices at local train stations, bundled up in warm woollen sweaters and raccoon coats, to hear news from the big game in Ottawa. Details were few and impatiently awaited.

"Renfrew scores," a man in the office would announce to the gathered crowds, then he would chalk up the score on a blackboard for all to see. As many as ten minutes might pass before any more news from the game would make it down the line. There was rarely any more information than the fact that a team scored, yet the crowds came, hungry for any word they could get and anxious to talk hockey between bulletins. All the small towns were for Renfrew in the struggle with Ottawa; their victory would be a victory for all the towns whose teams had struggled for years in the shadow of the great hockey clubs from the capital city.

Though Renfrew had definitely gained the upper hand in play, the score was still 3–2 Ottawa when the bell rang to end the first half. Lester and Taylor were the last two players to leave the ice for the intermission, Taylor enduring boos from the crowd right to the end.

"At least they've stopped throwing things," Cyclone said with a chuckle. But he spoke too soon. An empty whiskey flask came hurtling down from the upper seats and crashed to the ice at his feet.

"Let's get inside! Quick!" Lester exclaimed, as he hurried Taylor off the ice. Once inside the dressing room, Lester was livid. "Close the damn door and lock it," he barked. "I don't want any of those crackpots out there trying to get in." Lester seemed more upset by the incident than Taylor. The team captain slammed his stick down in front of his locker and dropped angrily to his stool. "Dammit, that bottle nearly hit you in the head."

"What happened?" Frank asked.

"Nothing much," said Taylor matter-of-factly. "Some crank threw a whiskey bottle on the ice."

"It almost hit you, Cyc!"

"But it didn't, Lester," Taylor said with a shrug, "so let's just try to forget about it." Only the slight shaking of his hands as he unlaced his skates hinted that Taylor wasn't feeling quite as calm as he appeared.

Nothing much was said about the stormy first half during the ten-minute intermission. Nothing much was said about anything. Play had been strenuous. The checking had been hard, and, on more than a few occasions, the slashing and other stick work had found areas unprotected by the sparse padding the players wore, so the break was a welcome rest.

The Millionaires opened the second half even more strongly than they had closed out the first. They stormed the Senators' end of the ice, pushing for the tying goal, but the Ottawa tandem of Shore and Lake refused to crack. Aided by the back checking of the forwards, Lesueur and the Ottawa defencemen withstood wave after wave of Renfrew attacks. Not until an Ottawa penalty gave Renfrew the man advantage did the Millionaires finally net the equalizer, Taylor rushing the length of the ice before sliding the puck to Whitcroft, whose blast trickled past Lesueur. The score was even at three goals apiece.

A minute after Whitcroft's goal, Hay Millar scored to give Renfrew its first lead of the night. Now it was the Senators' turn to play catch-up, and catch up they did — not just tying the game but moving ahead 5–4 with just under ten minutes to play.

Trailing again, the Renfrew players poured all of their efforts into getting the tying goal, while the Senators pushed for another score to put the game away. Both teams were attacking hard as play moved quickly from end to end. Then, suddenly, the advantage swung in Renfrew's favour. With just over eight minutes to go in the game, Bruce Stuart was issued a five-minute penalty for throwing his stick at Jack Fraser. A minute later, Hamby Shore got five for slashing Lester.

The Temperance Hall faithful came to life when the telegraphed report detailing the two-man advantage was read aloud.

"That makes it seven men to five for four full minutes," Gus Handford pointed out excitedly.

"You can't ask for a much better opportunity than that," Dom Ritza agreed.

With the ensuing face-off deep in Ottawa territory, the Millionaires players prepared to throw themselves into the attack. Once again Whitcroft was the first man to line up. Walsh took his time getting set as the four Ottawa skaters and their netminder braced for the defence.

"Come on, Marty," referee Russell Bowie growled, certain the Ottawa centre was stalling so that he and his teammates could catch their breath.

Whitcroft beat Walsh to the draw cleanly and fed the puck back to Lester. "I'm with you," he heard Taylor shout, as he raced towards the middle of the ice. Lester dropped the puck for him.

"Shoot, Cyc! Shoot!" Frank called out.

Taylor rocketed the puck forward with a sweeping motion of his arms and a snap of his wrist. A low, hard shot was on its way towards the Ottawa goal.

Percy Lesueur was crouched down in front of his net, his head bobbing from side to side trying to spot the puck through the maze of players who stood in his way. He saw it at the last possible second and was able to clear the shot aside with his stick. Whitcroft corralled the loose puck.

"Point! Point! Point!" Lester instructed.

Whitcroft spun and fired a pass back to Frank. He played it easily, and slid the puck across to Taylor who fired another blast at the Ottawa goal. Again Lesueur blocked it.

As Stuart and Shore sat in the penalty box, the Millionaires launched shot after shot at Lesueur, but the goalie proved equal to them all. Finally, Ottawa was able to get possession of the puck and clear it the length of the ice.

"I got it," Taylor hollered as he sped back to the Renfrew end. Scooping up the puck behind his own goal, Taylor spun around quickly and headed up ice, gaining speed with each stride.

Only a few minutes were left in the game, though neither the players nor the fans were ever sure of exactly how much time had gone by. Time was kept on stop watches by men appointed by the two teams, and they were the only ones who ever know for sure how much time remained.

The booing started again as soon as Taylor touched the puck, but he was oblivious to it. He was in his own world. All he heard was the rhythmic "swish, swish, swish" of his skate blades as they cut into the ice. All he felt was the cold rush of air against his cheeks. Streaking up ice at top speed, Taylor was suddenly in alone on Lesueur. Moving to his left, then back to the right, Taylor pulled the goalie far out of position. But Taylor, too, had been taken too far to the side of the net. At the last moment he noticed Lester gaining ground from the rear and dropped the puck to him. The Renfrew captain jammed it into the yawning cage.

"Yes!" Frank shouted, punching the air in jubilation at his brother's goal. He rushed forward to join his other teammates, who were already crowded around Lester and Taylor, revelling in the goal that tied the score at 5–5.

"OK," Lester urged, as the Millionaires broke up their celebration to line up for the face-off, "let's put these guys away!"

Only about five minutes remained in the game when Russell Bowie put the puck back in play, and, with Ottawa still two men short for a couple of those minutes, the Millionaires were moving in for the kill. Suddenly all eyes were attracted to the strange goings-on near centre ice. Bruce Stuart had jumped the boards and was rushing to the aid of his imperilled teammates, but was being chased by a well-dressed man in a derby hat who was struggling to maintain his balance. The man was George Martel, the Renfrew hockey official who had been selected by his team to be their timekeeper. Referee Russell Bowie immediately called a halt to the action.

"What the devil is going on, Mr. Martel!" Bowie thundered.

"His penalty hasn't expired yet," the Renfrew hockey official explained breathlessly.

"Is this true?" Bowie asked Stuart.

"Not as I understand it," the Ottawa captain explained.

"What the hell kind of answer is that?" Bowie demanded.

"Well, according to our timekeeper, my penalty is up."

Bowie checked with the Ottawa timer, then took a look at Martel's stopwatch. "There's a five-minute difference, fer crissakes!"

To settle the heated argument that followed, Bowie decided to take control of the timekeeping himself. He ordered Stuart off the ice for another minute, and, splitting the difference on the two watches, declared three minutes remaining in the game as he called the teams back to centre ice for another face-off.

Renfrew again attacked the Ottawa goal relentlessly, but to no avail. Stuart's tactics had given his teammates a much-needed rest and they put up a strong defence. A wild roar of delight from the partisan crowd greeted Stuart when he finally jumped legally into the play, followed by Shore a minute later. One minute after that, referee Russell Bowie rang the bell to signal that time had expired. The Senators had averted what, for a time at least, had appeared to be certain defeat.

Before the game, it had been decided that, if the contest were tied after sixty minutes of play, a full ten-minute overtime session, split into two five-minute periods, would follow. Without a moment's delay, the two teams switched ends and continued the battle. Less than a minute into overtime, the Senators scored. Trailing now, the Million-aires had to open up their play and were more vulnerable than ever to further Ottawa attacks. Twice more in the game's final minutes the Senators found the net, and when the bell rang for the final time, Renfrew had been handed an 8–5 defeat by their greatest rivals.

There was little time to sulk over the loss to the Senators. The team was in the midst of a gruelling four-game road trip that took them to Montreal next, then to Northern Ontario's silver country to take on Cobalt and Haileybury, all within a span of eleven days. The loss in Ottawa meant that the next three games were now must-win matches if Renfrew was to keep its Stanley Cup dreams alive.

XXVIII

How could it be possible for any man in this country to imagine that Canada could be at peace with any great naval power in the world if that naval power at that very moment was at war with Great Britain? The thing is absolutely inconceivable. The nations of the British Empire are separated by great stretches of ocean; the Empire covers every continent in the world and the great nations are divided by vast distances, but, upon the sea, any British Navy, any Imperial Navy, must be one.

Robert Borden,
Opposition Leader.
Naval Debate, 1910

"RICHARD? RICHARD LAWRENCE?"

"Fred Taylor? My God!"

Taylor walked the length of the platform at the Ottawa railway station and shook hands with his childhood friend.

"It's got to be at least seven years since I last saw you," Taylor said. "You left Listowel even before I went to play hockey in Portage La Prairie."

"You still play?" Lawrence asked, looking down at Taylor and smiling to himself to see that he stood almost nine inches taller than his boyhood companion.

"Well . . . yes. Of course I do." Taylor was surprised, and more than a little disappointed, that his old friend didn't know of his fame. "I'm Cyclone Taylor . . ."

Lawrence shrugged. The name meant nothing to him.

In 1910, the names of sports stars were well known to their fans, but not to those who didn't read the sports page of their newspaper. And Lawrence certainly hadn't bothered to keep up with the activities of those from his home town. He had left everything about his life in Listowel behind when he fled to the Maritimes.

"I was with Ottawa last year," Taylor told Lawrence, thinking it might make some difference. "We won the Stanley Cup."

In Ottawa, or at home in Listowel, it would have been impossible for Lawrence not to know of Cyclone Taylor, but in New Brunswick, someone who did not follow hockey would never even hear the name.

"Well, I guess we all knew you'd make good," Lawrence said, though he really didn't care.

"What about you?" Taylor asked, raising his voice over the puffing and clanging of a train pulling into the station. "What are you doing these days?"

"I work for the Army," Lawrence told Taylor. It was a lie, but he certainly wasn't about to admit he was a professional thug.

"A soldier, huh?" Taylor laughed. "I guess that's not much of a surprise, either."

Lawrence forced a laugh. "I guess not," he agreed. Lawrence knew that the boys he grew up with would never forget the time he tried to run away and join the soldiers training to fight in the Boer War. He had packed his bags and walked down to the train station, intent on travelling to Regina to join up with the Strathcona Horse Brigade, only to be told that the two dollars he carried with him would not pay the fare. When no amount of pleading lowered the fare, Lawrence had gone back home and endured the teasing of the other kids until he left again, for his actual, unsuccessful, stint in the army.

"Do you remember how we used to parade around using our hockey sticks as rifles, pretending we were fighting the Boers to save the Empire?" Taylor smiled as he thought about it.

"I remember."

"And can you believe what's going on today?" The smile disappeared from Taylor's face, replaced by a scowl. "Can you imagine Canada remaining at peace with some foreign naval power if that same country is at war with Britain?"

"It's inconceivable," Lawrence agreed. "But listen, Fred," he continued, lowering his voice, "I know some people who won't let Laurier get the bill passed."

"Yeah?" said Taylor, his curiosity piqued. "Have you got some sort of protest movement planned?"

"Something like that," Lawrence confirmed with a sly smile. He was at the train station to meet David Roberts, who was coming back to Ottawa to tell Lawrence and Sean Mitchell about the man he had found for them.

"Would it help to have me speak out for the cause?" Taylor asked, still thinking his old friend had some sort of formal protest in mind. "I'd be more than happy to get involved."

"Still as modest as ever, I see." Lawrence smiled, but there was an edge to his voice. He was thinking back to Taylor's flashy entrances to those boyhood games at the Piggery, and how he had envied Taylor's skill and popularity. "We don't need any more help, thanks. It's all taken care of."

"All aboard," Lester called out to Taylor, leaning from the window of M.J. O'Brien's private railcar.

"Well, I guess I'd better get going," Taylor said, as he bent down to collect his belongings. "It was good to see you again."

"Good to see you too, Freddy." Lawrence put just enough stress on the childhood name to be insulting, but Taylor was already moving away from him with his mind on other things. Taylor also missed the expression of contempt that twisted Lawrence's face. Lawrence had not enjoyed the memories of the people and places brought to mind by his unexpected meeting with Taylor.

"Losing to the Senators is one thing, they're the Stanley Cup champs, they've won thirteen games in a row, and we battled them right to the bitter end. But losing to this team? There'll be no excuse for that!"

Lester was angry. Every player on the team knew they had to win every game remaining on this road trip if they were to have a chance at the Stanley Cup. So why had they come out so flat against Les Canadiens? A bit of a letdown was only natural after the struggle in Ottawa, but this was worse than that. The team was slow and stiff, and the fast skating and close checking of the French Canadian team had them completely bottled up.

"It's only fifteen minutes into the first half and we're trailing 4–1," Lester fumed. "We'd better shape up, I'm telling you, or we might just as well stay on the road forever. No one in Renfrew will let us back into town! Now line up for the face-off and let's start playing hockey!"

"Jeez, that Newsy Lalonde's something, isn't he?" Frank whispered to Taylor as they dropped back to their defensive positions. The flashy Frenchman had scored all four goals for Les Canadiens. "If we had him, nobody could beat us."

Taylor just grunted. He didn't like Newsy, but there was no denying he was an immensely talented player.

As had been the case early in the game with the Senators, Lester backed up his words with actions, netting a goal to cut the lead to 4–2. Soon the whole team was functioning as it should, skating fast and smoothly, passing the puck with precision, and checking effectively.

Renfrew fought to wipe out Les Canadiens' lead, while the French Canadian team was intent on widening the gap. The action raced from end to end. But the defence on both sides refused to crack. Time and again, bodies were thrown to the ice as the rival points and cover points took their men down hard, breaking up rushes.

"I've got Newsy," Frank cried out, shouting defensive instructions to Taylor as Lalonde led another raid on Renfrew territory. "You pick up the other man."

"Lalonde's mine," Taylor said defiantly, his eyes staring straight ahead at his old nemesis. "You take care of the other guy."

The fiery Frenchman tore up the ice, his skates flashing, the wild look in his eyes providing clear evidence of his fierce temper. Taylor, who could play the game with an equal intensity, readied himself as well.

Skating backwards and retreating further into his own end, Taylor kept his gaze riveted on the large "C" on Newsy's chest. Fast as he was when going forward, it was Taylor's ability to skate backwards that really set him apart. He had mastered the art at a very young age, challenging his friends on the pond in Listowel to try and beat him by moving forward while he backed up, and he had rarely lost. Moving backwards now, his weight shifting from side to side as he pushed off from his toes, his skates crossing over occasionally to keep himself in line, Taylor's movement appeared effortless.

As Lalonde raced into the Renfrew end, he took a quick look around and found he had no one with him who was open. Frank had picked up his man and Lester, doing good work back checking, had tied up another. Lalonde considered circling back to wait for the rest of his teammates to make it up ice but, seeing Taylor ahead of him, he changed his mind and decided to push on alone.

"I'm coming at you, Taylor!" Lalonde growled as he sped towards his rival.

The great Renfrew cover point merely showed Newsy the back of his gloved left hand and, bending only his fingers, beckoned with a wave. The flippant, taunting gesture fuelled the flames of Lalonde's anger and he raced on.

When the two men were nearly face to face, Lalonde slipped the puck between Taylor's legs. He had hoped his adversary would be distracted by the move, watching the puck and trying to play it while he stepped around him and picked it up on the other side, but Taylor never took his eyes off the Frenchman. When Newsy tried to go around him, Taylor sprang forward, bringing his hands up in front of him. He barrelled into Lalonde, striking his opponent chest to chest and then, pushing out with his hands, drove him backwards with great force, knocking him to the ice. Lester scooped up the loose puck and took it up ice. Taylor fell in line behind him, but not before giving Newsy one last look. He smiled triumphantly as the fallen player grabbed for his stick and scrambled to his feet.

With hard hitting on both sides throughout the first half, it was surprising that only one player was forced to leave the game with an injury. Three minutes before half-time, Jack Fraser was carried off the ice after being shaken up in a collision with Lalonde. Bobby Rowe lined up in his place and, immediately dispelling concerns that he might have gotten rusty while sitting out since the 10–2 romp over the Shamrocks, he set up Frank for a goal to cut Les Canadiens' lead to one. With the score now 4–3, the two teams went to the dressing room knowing it was anyone's game to win or lose.

"It's hard to believe," Taylor said, as he slumped to his seat, "that this team is only 1 and 5. They sure play us tough."

"It's hard to believe," Frank added, "that a team with Newsy Lalonde would only be 1 and 5." Heads nodded in agreement.

Les Canadiens' poor record had kept many fans away from the game that night. The small crowd in the tiny Jubilee rink after the large and boisterous gathering at the Laurier Avenue Arena in Ottawa had probably contributed to the Millionaires' slow start, but the minimal attendance had its advantages as well. Only real fans of the team had shown up, and they were there to watch hockey, not to make political statements. As a result, there were no incidents like the singing back in Renfrew.

Lester was relieved to see that the Naval Debate didn't seem to promote as violent a reaction as the Boer War had in his boyhood days. "Well let's just make sure they drop to 1 and 6," he said of Les Canadiens, forgetting thoughts of "the French problem" and joining in the current conversation. "There's no way this team is as good as we are."

Lester was right. The overall superiority of the Renfrew team proved to make the difference after intermission, and the Millionaires escaped with an 8–6 victory. Dreams of the Stanley Cup were still alive.

XXIX

My Right Honourable friend the Prime Minister speaks
eloquently of the perfect security afforded to Canadians in
foreign lands by the talisman of the British flag. What gives

that flag in distant seas and under alien skies its talismanic power? I saw a great British fleet last summer arrayed in the River Thames preparatory to its subsequent review by His Majesty, the King. . . . There was the power, there was the might which gave the British flag its talismanic virtue, and it was not a proud thought for a Canadian surveying that mighty fleet to remember that all the protecting power which it embodied was paid for without the contribution of a single dollar by the Canadian people. . . . Yes, the flag is the protecting talisman of every Canadian. That flag represents the power and the might of that great fleet and the Prime Minister proposes to sustain and support its talismanic virtue by ineffective proposals for petty cruisers which . . . would go to no war unless the Parliament of Canada chose to send them.

Robert Borden,
Opposition Leader.
Naval Debate, 1910

ON WEDNESDAY, FEBRUARY 16, 1910 — THE DAY AFTER THE victory over Les Canadiens — the Renfrew players were sitting in M.J. O'Brien's private railcar. They were waiting to pull out of the Montreal train station and begin the trip to silver country for games in Cobalt and Haileybury on February 19 and 22. It would be a long journey. From Montreal, the team would travel to Ottawa on the Grand Trunk Railway, a trip of about two hours. At Ottawa, the private railcar would be hooked up to a train on the Canadian Pacific Line and would roll into Renfrew about one hour later. From Renfrew, it was a six-hour ride north along the CPR line to North Bay, where once again the private railcar would have to switch tracks, this time to the Timiskaming and Northern Ontario Railway line, for the final two-hour trip north to Cobalt.

All in all, the trip to silver country would take about fourteen hours, and already it was getting off to a bad start. The train was late leaving Montreal.

"What's the delay?" Taylor asked Lester, who sat in front of him.

Taylor did not really expect Lester to have the answer and Lester, indeed, did not.

Just then, Ambrose O'Brien boarded the train. He was trailed by a very familiar figure.

"Sorry for the holdup, gentlemen," Ambrose apologized. "I had a little business to take care of first," he said, gesturing in the direction of the man he had brought with him.

"What's he doing here?" Taylor demanded. This time the question was not rhetorical. Taylor expected an answer.

"Gentlemen," said Ambrose, "I'd like you to meet the newest member of our hockey club — Newsy Lalonde."

"Bonjour, Newsy!" Frank said excitedly, leaping from his seat to shake the Frenchman's hand as the train finally pulled out of the station. "It's great to have you on our side."

"Welcome aboard," Lester greeted him, getting up from his seat to shake Lalonde's hand.

One by one, Lalonde shook the hands of all his new teammates until he came to Taylor.

"I hope we can put our differences behind us," Newsy said quietly, as he offered his hand to his longtime rival.

"You might help this team win," Taylor said, "and that's good. But it doesn't mean I have to like having you around." He turned, without shaking hands, and went back to his seat.

Taylor's teammates knew he didn't like Lalonde, but they were stunned by his refusal to shake the man's hand. Lalonde was more than stunned. He was outraged.

"*Va te faire foutre*, Taylor!" he shouted. "Fuck you!" He started to go after Cyclone, but Frank stepped in his path.

"Let him go, Newsy," Frank said quietly. "He'll come around. Eventually."

Lalonde sat down. The flash of rage passed but he stayed angry. Just as he had been that night in Renfrew when Frank had invited him back to the boarding house, Lalonde was surprised by Taylor's animosity. Intimidation was a part of Lalonde's game, and because Taylor was the best player he had ever seen — the only one he'd ever encountered who might be even better than he was — he naturally went after him that much harder. But off ice, he didn't take their rivalry personally. Not the way Taylor seemed to.

"*Je m'en fiche!*" Lalonde decided, as the train gained speed. "I'm on this team to play hockey. Not make friends." The harsh words he and Taylor had exchanged would not cause Newsy to rethink his decision to join Renfrew. As the top star on a struggling team, he had enjoyed the attempts by two of the NHA's top clubs to lure him away from Les Canadiens. The Senators had promised him $300 per week for the remaining five weeks of the season if he would come to Ottawa, but they were outbid by Ambrose O'Brien's flat-rate offer of $2000. Newsy obtained his release from Les Canadiens — a simple procedure since the O'Briens owned the team — and happily agreed to become a Millionaire.

By the second leg of the long journey, Taylor was ready to be sociable once again.

"When I was living in Ottawa," he said, as the train left that city for Renfrew, "I loved walking on Parliament Hill. It filled me with such a sense of . . ." He paused for a moment, not sure if there was a word to convey the feeling properly. "It was pride, I guess, but more than that — knowing this was my country's greatest symbol of the British Empire. I remember the first time I walked into the Parliament Buildings. My boyhood dreams of fighting to preserve the Empire all came flooding back to me. That's why this Naval Bill really burns me up."

"I can appreciate your strong feelings for the Empire, Cyc," Lester said, "but I still don't see what's wrong with Laurier wanting to give Canada the right to take responsibility for its own naval defence."

"Your father," Taylor asked Lester, "is in the lumber business, isn't he?"

Lester nodded.

"He owns all his own timberland?"

"He does."

"Well then, let's say, for argument's sake, he owns 3000 acres of land and gives you a holding of about 200 acres somewhere in the middle of his property. You go on to improve that land. Make some money off it. You pay no rent. No taxes. Everything you make goes right into your bank account. You don't assist your father or the rest of the family in any way. Then, one day your father runs into difficulty. An animal is eating his crops . . ."

Frank couldn't pass up the chance to give Taylor the needle. "What kind of animal eats trees?" he asked.

"How am I supposed to know?" Taylor spluttered, momentarily

flustered. Once he realized Frank was only trying to tease him, he quickly regained his composure.

"All right then," he began again, "let's say it's not your father. It's just some man who owns a farm and a wolf is eating his sheep." He looked at Frank as if to say, "got any problems with that?"

"The father approaches the son," Taylor went on. " 'My boy,' he says, 'I need a little help. I'm going to build an eight-foot fence all around this big property. What can you do to help me?' The son thinks about it a bit, and then he says, 'I will assist you by building a miserable little two-foot fence all around my own lot.'

"It seems to me," Taylor continued, "that's what's happening with the naval situation. England is in trouble and we're only offering token assistance. The power and the might of the British Navy has been this great big fence protecting us in Canada. We can't see it, but it's there. It helps keep the peace in good times and gives us security in bad times. What good will Laurier's little navy do in the defence of the Empire? Wouldn't it be better if the son said 'Yes father, I will do something for you. If a wolf can jump over your fence, then any fence I build around my farm will be no good to me so I'll help you to build your fence bigger and stronger.' "

"But, Cyc," Frank countered, entering the conversation on a serious note this time, "Laurier himself has used the example of a parent and grown child for Canada's relationship with England. Only he's saying that as a grown child, Canada must have the right to decide for itself. 'The ripe fruit falling from the parent tree' I think is the way he put it."

"But not falling that far!" Taylor and Lalonde countered, speaking out almost in unison. The men stared at each other in surprise. Taylor meant that Canada should not fall so far from England that it would radically alter the relationship between itself and the mother country. Newsy, on the other hand, meant that a policy placing the Canadian Navy under British rule during the time of war did not really constitute much change at all.

"Canada," Taylor said with conviction, "cannot refuse to participate in any war involving England."

"Canada," Lalonde said quietly, "shouldn't have a navy if the only reason for having it is to fight British wars."

"Cobalt," said Lester, deciding it was time to change topics, "is playing fine hockey. They beat the Shamrocks 11–4 last night."

Lester's statement was greeted with silence. It was obvious no one felt like talking about hockey, but Lester was glad that he had succeeded in ending the players' own version of the Naval Debate. As the train continued along the tracks to Renfrew, only the rumbling sounds of the engine and the occasional blast of the whistle disturbed the silence.

During the third, and longest, leg of the train trip — the journey from Renfrew to North Bay — some players stared out the window at the bleak landscape, noting the increase in snow as they travelled further north. At least the cold weather guaranteed that the ice wouldn't be soft. Others filled the hours by playing cards or sleeping. Taylor sat with Ambrose O'Brien, passing the time in conversation.

"Ambrose? How does it work when you bet on our games?"

Other than the time he had watched Thirza play, Taylor had never been to a hockey game he wasn't taking part in. He'd been thinking for some time that a few well-placed wagers might help him build up his $10,000 marriage fund, but he knew little about gambling.

"It's not much different from the fans in the stands, Cyc."

There really wasn't much secrecy surrounding the process of betting on hockey. It was never difficult to find people willing to wager. Someone would make it known he had some money he'd like to place on a team, usually by flashing a thick wad of bills. Someone else would agree to support the other team, and they would haggle over the terms. Supporters of the weaker team would usually hold out for odds of two or three to one. When one team was clearly superior to the other, the bets would usually be on whether the favoured team could double up the score, like 6–3, 8–4, or better. Sometimes the newspapers published a betting line to establish the odds.

"Who do you bet with, when you put money on our games?" Taylor asked Ambrose.

"Usually with the people who run the other teams. Sometimes with the business associates I have in the cities we visit."

"Not with a bookmaker?" Taylor asked.

"Oh no," responded Ambrose. "These are just friendly wagers."

"I heard you lost $5000 making 'friendly wagers' on the Ottawa game," Taylor said bluntly. "Is that true?"

"Not exactly," Ambrose replied. His ease in discussing such large sums of money was something Taylor found quite remarkable. "I did have $5000 riding on the game, but even though we lost, I didn't lose all of it. Some of the more reckless Senators supporters were willing to bet they'd double the score on us. I won those bets."

Taylor nodded his understanding.

"Then again," Ambrose sighed, "I lost money on the game last night betting we'd double the score on Les Canadiens."

Taylor shook his head. Ambrose, he realized, had likely lost more betting on those two games than he was being paid for the entire season. Nothing was ever a sure thing. For Taylor, gambling his savings wasn't worth the risk. "But if I had your money," he said to Ambrose reassuringly, "I'd keep on making those bets." Lowering his voice he added, "Don't let it get around I said this, but now that we've got Lalonde, I don't see how we can lose."

XXX

IT WAS WELL PAST DARK WHEN THE TRAIN CARRYING THE Renfrew Millionaires pulled into Cobalt. It was just as well — there was little to see in the silver boom town. Cobalt, Haileybury, and nearby New Liskeard had sprung up on the shores of Lake Timiskaming after the discovery of silver back in 1903. While Haileybury and New Liskeard had developed into attractive communities, catering to the wealthy mine owners rather than the rough-and-tumble mine workers, Cobalt, as the centre of the actual mining activity, had attracted tough, hard-working young men. The town reflected its rugged inhabitants, and, though it had begun to clean up its image by banning the sale of alcohol and building more schools and churches, Cobalt still wasn't much to look at.

Early reports had made it sound as though silver could be found lying loose throughout the entire region. It couldn't. Stories made it seem as if one only had to dig and blast at random to unearth buried treasure. Not so. It was necessary first to find a vein, and then go down. Silver had sometimes been uncovered near the top, but usually such a discovery required digging through solid rock for 100 feet or more, and even then there was no guarantee of success. Many men had spent their last dollar searching for silver and given up heartbroken, only to learn later that just one more shot would have made their fortune.

A great many mines circled the town of Cobalt. A tall shaft house on each site, and tall stacks billowing out black smoke, made every mine easily visible. The shaft houses were usually surrounded by a ramshackle cluster of smaller, barn-like buildings. Huge mountains of useless rock dug up from beneath the earth in the frantic search for silver further marred the landscape.

There was little for the visiting hockey players to do during the day on a trip to Cobalt — especially when the mercury dropped to well below zero degrees Fahrenheit — so much of their time was passed in practice at the hockey rink. The Renfrew players spent both Thursday and Friday afternoons working out at the local arena in preparation for the Saturday night game. The extended practice sessions provided ample opportunity for Newsy Lalonde to get used to playing with his new teammates. He lined up at centre, replacing Herb Jordan. Hay Millar and Bobby Rowe flanked Lalonde at right and left wing. Lester was at rover, while Frank and Taylor manned point and cover point. Bert Lindsay was in goal. By the time Saturday's game rolled around, the latest Renfrew lineup was more than ready to play great hockey.

The Saturday night contest was close for only a short time. Lester scored first, four-and-a-half minutes into the game, but the Cobalt Silver Kings evened things less than three minutes later. Lalonde won the face-off after the tying goal and immediately carried the puck into the Cobalt end. As he neared the Cobalt goal, Lalonde heard Lester calling for a pass.

"I'm with you, Newsy! Drop it back!"

Lalonde spun sideways, shaking the man who was on him, and was about to play the puck back to Lester when he saw a Cobalt player knock the team captain to the ice. No penalty. Play went on. Lalonde, who by now almost had his back to the goal, continued sliding sideways, cradling the puck carefully as he looked to make a pass. The Cobalt players scrambled to pick up their checks and suddenly the middle of the ice opened up. Without breaking his deceptive sideways stride, Newsy fired a shot on goal and beat the surprised netminder.

The Silver Kings were never really in the game after Lalonde's pretty play, with Newsy adding another goal, Lester scoring three more, and Frank tallying once as the Millionaires took a 7–2 lead into intermission. The onslaught continued after half-time, as Lalonde scored twice more to up the lead to 9–2. Cobalt threatened to make a game of it at last, with two quick goals, but Lester's fifth of the night ended any such hopes for the home town faithful. The Silver Kings put up a good fight in the game's final minutes, but additional goals by Taylor and Bobby Rowe kept the outcome from ever being in doubt, as the Millionaires rolled to a 12– 7 victory.

The Renfrew players were celebrating the win in their dressing room when Ambrose came in with more good news.

"Word just came in from Montreal," he said excitedly, waving the piece of telegraph paper he held in his hand. "The Wanderers beat Ottawa 7–5!"

All the players cheered. It was the best possible news. "So now we're right back in the race for the Stanley Cup!" Newsy said.

Newsy had spent the first half of the season with a team mired hopelessly in last place, but he was immediately aware of the significance of the score Ambrose read. The Millionaires had lost two games, the Wanderers just one. Ottawa had been undefeated but now they had one loss as well.

"That's right," Lester agreed, picking up on what Newsy had said, "and if we beat Haileybury on Tuesday, then go home and beat the Wanderers and Ottawa in our next two games, we'll all be even with two losses."

The Senators and Wanderers were scheduled to meet one more time during the season so, if everything went as the Renfrew players hoped, at least one of those teams would have three losses. If the Millionaires kept winning, they'd be assured of no less than a tie for first place with the other team. Then the league would have to arrange a playoff to break the tie and decide who would win the NHA championship and get the Stanley Cup.

"Of course, if we lose to either Ottawa or the Wanderers," Frank pointed out, "we're out of the running."

"So we'd better keep on winning," Newsy said.

Sunday morning, the day after the win in Cobalt, the Renfrew players found themselves riding the rails again. This time, however, the trip was much shorter: fourteen minutes from Cobalt to Haileybury. The team would spend Sunday and Monday in Haileybury, preparing for Tuesday's second outing of the two-game road trip to silver country, then travel back to Renfrew on Wednesday.

There would be little time to rest after the long road trip. On Friday, February 25, the Millionaires were scheduled to play the Wanderers. The Senators would arrive in the Creamery Town the week after that. The whole season would come down to those two games — unless Haileybury pulled off an upset on Tuesday night.

The members of the Renfrew Millionaires hockey club were not the only out-of-towners in Haileybury that Sunday morning in late February. Anton Petrovic was there as well.

Petrovic was en route from Winnipeg to Ottawa to assassinate the Prime Minister. He had chosen a meandering route east — a route that wound up taking him through Haileybury — because of the nagging feeling that he was being followed. There was good cause for that feeling; he was being followed. Before returning to Chicago, Roberts had assigned a man to trail Petrovic. There were two reasons for this. The first was to make sure Petrovic got to Ottawa by February 24, the date Mitchell had planned for the assassination. The second reason was to keep track of Petrovic's whereabouts at all times.

The task of putting a tail on Petrovic was the last one Roberts had performed for Lawrence and Mitchell before collecting his fee and disappearing back to the United States, going into hiding until his deadly assistance was needed by someone else. There was, however, something about Petrovic that Roberts did not know.

Sean Mitchell did not intend to let a man he knew nothing about, no matter how highly recommended, attempt the Laurier assassination alone. Although Mitchell had said he needed an outsider to commit the crime, what he really required was a scapegoat to draw attention away from him. Now it was time to make one other person aware of his true plan. He summoned Richard Lawrence to his Ottawa hotel room.

"Roberts assures us," Mitchell told Lawrence, "that this man will do every bit as good a job as Leon Czolgosz did in the assassination of William McKinley. I'm certainly glad he feels that way, but I see no reason to take chances. Not when I have you working for me." Mitchell smiled slyly at Lawrence.

"I don't understand — you want me to shoot Laurier?"

Lawrence was confused. He remembered what Mitchell had told

him: that they needed an outsider because whoever shot Laurier would be caught and hanged for it. Lawrence wondered if Mitchell now expected him to sacrifice himself for the cause.

Mitchell anticipated Lawrence's unspoken concern. "Don't worry," he said. "I've thought this through very carefully. No matter who fires the fatal shot, Petrovic will be blamed for Laurier's death." He then gave Lawrence the details of the plan.

On February 24, the Governor General would be giving a dinner party at Rideau Hall for the Prime Minister and seven members of his cabinet. Many other guests would be there too — including Sean Mitchell. Petrovic, as the driver of Mitchell's carriage, would be placed so that he could shoot Laurier at point-blank range as the Prime Minister left the dinner. But Lawrence would be present, too, armed with a rifle and planted among the soldiers of the Governor General's Foot Guard.

"At the very least, I want you to take care of Petrovic as soon as he has shot Laurier," Mitchell continued. "As the only soldier who understands what's happening, you'll be the first to react. I'm sure you can see why it's absolutely essential for Petrovic to die before he can say a word that would link him to us. And it won't be difficult for you to get away in the confusion that will surely follow.

"But if Petrovic hesitates at all as he approaches Laurier – then you'll have to shoot them both." Mitchell looked at Lawrence intently. "I know you won't let me down, Richard."

A cold snap had settled in across the silver region of Northern Ontario. The temperature outside the hockey rink in Haileybury on Tuesday night plummeted to a bitter −25° Fahrenheit. A howling wind made it even colder. The wooden walls of the Haileybury hockey arena provided little protection against the elements, so it was almost as cold inside as it was outside.

"You know," Frank said to Lester, as the Patrick brothers skated circles in their end of the ice, trying to warm up for the upcoming game, "it amazes me how the fans stay through a game like this."

"Or that they come out at all," Lester said. Like Frank, he had been staring up into the crowded stands where the spectators were bundled in rugs and blankets. "At least we can keep moving."

All the fans had to keep themselves warm was hot coffee, brewed in giant vats under the stands and sold for a nickel a cup. Of course, there were some who took repeated nips of scotch or whiskey from a flask to keep from freezing. The players also took additional precautions against the cold, wearing woollen mittens under their hockey gloves. Art Ross, the Haileybury captain, wore a pair of fur-lined gloves and a woollen toque that he rolled down over his face, with holes cut out for his eyes and mouth.

"Art looks like the devil himself in that outfit," Lester said with a laugh.

"No doubt he'll play just as mean as he looks," Frank chuckled.

Ross dressed as he did to guard against frostbite — a serious threat to a hockey player in Haileybury — but there was another danger to playing hockey in extreme cold, and there was no special attire that could combat it. Intense cold made ice so brittle it could crack and chip. A narrow fissure might easily catch the blade of a skate, causing the wearer to fall or, worse yet, twist a knee or break an ankle.

Despite the bitter cold, over 3000 fans filled the tiny arena for the game between Renfrew and Haileybury. It was standing room only, with many spectators pressed right up against the wire screen that extended above the boards around the playing surface. Hockey was a great attraction in the mining centres, where drinking, gambling, and the game were the favourite pastimes. Rumours persisted that $58,000 in bets had exchanged hands when Cobalt had visited Haileybury back in January, though no one was sure how much of it had been cash and how much had been mining stock. Newspapers had installed the Millionaires as 3-to-2 favourites for the game this night, and betting was brisk.

The game with Haileybury marked the first time all season that Renfrew had iced the same starting seven two games in a row. Lalonde, Millar, and Rowe again composed the forward line; Lester manned his usual rover position; and Frank and Taylor were point and cover point with Lindsay in goal. As in Cobalt three nights earlier, the Millionaires started quickly. Newsy scored just a minute-and-a-half into the game, beating goalie Paddy Moran with a hard shot from long range. Millar increased the lead to 2–0 just thirty seconds later, on a shot that bounced in off Moran's padded leg.

The unhappy rumblings of the Haileybury faithful quickly turned to cheers as Ross rallied the troops with a goal that halved the Renfrew lead. But almost as quickly, the cheers were silenced as a sickening scene was played out on the ice.

The play started innocently when Ross picked up the puck near centre ice and carried it to the Renfrew end. As Taylor moved forward to check him, Ross dropped the puck for right winger Horace Gaul. Gaul whipped a hard shot on goal, low along the ice. Bert Lindsay shifted his weight to his left and, with his knees bent slightly while leaning forward from the waist, he held his gloved hand down low and kept the blade of his wide goalie stick pressed flat against the ice. He was all set to make an easy stick save when the puck struck an ice chip and ricocheted into the air. The unexpected deflection caused the puck to strike Lindsay directly above the right eye, opening a wide gash. Lindsay, dazed by the blow, slumped to the ice. Blood flowed freely from his forehead, gathering in a pool in front of the net.

Frank was first to arrive at the goalie's side. "Bert! Bert!" he shouted frantically. "Can you hear me, Bert?"

The injured goalie just moaned.

"Let's get him to the dressing room," Lester directed, taking charge as he and the other players gathered around.

Frank, Taylor, Lalonde, and Millar carried the fallen goaltender off the ice, while Lester went to talk to the referee.

"It might take some time to get this taken care of," Lester said.

"League rules give you fifteen minutes to attend to an injured player, Mr. Patrick," the referee told him. "I'm afraid I won't be able to give you any longer than that. If Mr. Lindsay isn't able to continue, you'll have to put one of your other players in goal." The referee frowned sympathetically. "I'm sorry," he said.

"I understand," said Lester, nodding his head slowly. "Rules are rules, after all."

Inside the dressing room, trainer Billy O'Brian attended to Lindsay. The goaltender had regained consciousness, but winced in pain as the trainer pressed a damp towel against the wound in hopes of stopping the flow of blood. The area around the eye was already badly swollen.

"Hold this in place and press as hard as you can handle," the trainer instructed, as he handed Lindsay a fresh towel wrapped around a block of ice. "It'll help stop the swelling as well as numb the area a bit so that I can put in some stitches."

Lester was relieved to see Lindsay sitting up by himself when he arrived in the dressing room. "Will he be able to continue?" Lester asked.

Lindsay answered before the trainer had a chance to respond. "Who else have we got?"

"Well . . ." Lester paused. "Me," he said finally. "I guess." Then, looking around the room, he added, "I'm the captain of this team. I can't ask anyone to do something I wouldn't be prepared to do myself."

"That's awfully heroic of you," Lindsay teased, pretending to dab at a tear under his good eye. "But if you go in goal, does that mean I have to play rover?"

It was obvious to everyone that Lindsay would be able to continue.

There was polite applause from the Haileybury crowd when Lindsay skated back into position and turned back a few soft warm-up shots. When the Renfrew players broke away to line up for the face-off, Lester addressed the troops.

"No one gets in to shoot at Bert from close range," he instructed. "We'll play tight defence and force them to take their shots from a distance so he'll have plenty of time to react."

The face-off took place at centre ice. The puck was placed between the sticks of Lalonde and Nick Bawlf, his Haileybury counterpart. When the referee shouted "Play!" Newsy sprang into action. But instead of going after the puck, he chopped his stick into Bawlf's stick, knocking it from his opponent's cold hands. Newsy then drew the puck back easily, and, spinning to avoid an angry punch, headed up ice. A wicked smile flashed across Lalonde's lips. Newsy did not plan the moves he made on the ice; he improvised them as he went along or as the inspiration suddenly struck. "How can the other guy expect to know what I'm going to do," he was fond of saying, "if I don't know myself what I'm going to do until I do it."

As Lalonde dug hard into the frozen sheet and sped into Haileybury territory, tiny flakes of brittle ice broke off the playing surface, causing snow to spray from his skate blades. Looking around, he saw Millar with him on his right. Bobby Rowe began to move up along the boards on the left side, but something held him up. Lalonde couldn't tell what. With only Millar at his side, Newsy continued to push into the opposing end.

Ross and his defence partner Skene Ronan saw the play developing in front of them as they backed up in their own end. They saw Horace Gaul and Art Throope, the Haileybury wingers, coming back quickly to aid in their effort to break up the rush. Millar was effectively taken out of the play by the back checking of Gaul and Throope, leaving Ross and Ronan to concentrate on Lalonde. With two men covering one, the odds seemed in favour of the rush being thwarted, but when that one man was Newsy Lalonde, things had a way of evening out.

Lalonde charged straight ahead, his eyes jumping from Ross to Ronan and back to Ross again. He decided to take on the less experienced Ronan. He snarled without even being aware of it.

Ronan swallowed hard as he watched Lalonde bear down on him. He tried to keep his eyes fixed upon the scripted "R" on Lalonde's chest, but his gaze was drawn upward into Lalonde's icy stare. He never had a chance. Newsy bobbed his head to the right, then to the left, and then, jiggling his shoulders a bit, bobbed his head back to the right. Ronan was completely confused by the head fake, and Newsy, turning on an extra burst of speed, stepped by him easily. Art Ross wouldn't be so easy to fool. Newsy slowed down, hoping the action would force Ross to commit himself to moving to one side or the other. The move backfired, though, when not only did Ross refuse to budge but Ronan also had time to get back into the play.

Lalonde cursed under his breath when he realized what he had done. Looking around and finding no one to pass to, he went wide and carried the puck behind the net. Ross chased him while Ronan took up a position in front of the goal, ready to cover anyone who might try to move in for a pass. With no options open to him, Newsy fired the puck into the stands to force a stop in play. The manoeuvre brought a rousing chorus of boos from the large crowd. Deliberately delaying the game was not against the rules, but it was a tactic that never failed to infuriate the fans — especially when used by a member of the visiting team.

"Where the hell were you guys!" Lalonde hollered, as his teammates finally moved up ice to line up for the ensuing face-off.

"Playing defensively," Taylor shot back, reminding Lalonde of the words Lester had spoken when the team returned to the ice after Lindsay's injury. "I think the better question," Taylor continued, mocking Lalonde's French accent, "is what 'da 'ell' were you doing?"

"The best defence is a good offence," Lalonde snapped, then turned to set up for the face-off. As he lined up, Newsy noticed Bobby Rowe

staring back at the boards near centre. "What's bothering you?" Lalonde growled.

"Somebody in the stands tried to poke me with a stick or something
as I was skating up the side," he said, shaking his head.

Lalonde stared at Rowe as if he were crazy.

For almost twenty minutes, the defensive effort the Renfrew team put
forth seemed to be working. By forcing the Haileybury players to shoot
from long range, they made it possible for Lindsay, who could now
only see out of one eye, to keep the puck out of the net. Employing
Lalonde's offensive strategy sparingly, the forwards occasionally went
on the attack but, as the first half wore on, the Renfrew players drifted
further and further away from the boards near centre on the left side.
Just as Bobby Rowe had said, there was a man sitting there with a
long, pointed stick. He jabbed it through the wire screen every time
a Renfrew player passed by.

With just three minutes left in the first half, a crack finally developed
in the Renfrew defensive armour. Gaul took a pass from his centre,
Nick Bawlf, and, using Throope as a decoy, managed to squeeze between Frank and Taylor. Rushing in alone on Lindsay, Gaul beat him
with a shot over his right shoulder. With almost no sight in his right
eye, Lindsay never had a chance. The score was now tied 2–2. But it
didn't remain tied for long.

Lalonde won the face-off that followed, beating Bawlf cleanly this
time, and fed the puck back to Lester. Lester, with Newsy at his side,
carried the puck all the way into the Haileybury end. Faking a pass
to Newsy, Lester instead fired a fast shot on goal. The blast beat Moran
between the legs and when the bell signalling half-time rang a minute
later, the Millionaires retired to their dressing room with a 3–2 lead.

When the ten-minute intermission was near its end, Lester picked up
his stick and was about to give the signal to return to the ice, when
all of a sudden Lalonde leaped to his feet.

"What's wrong with you guys!" Newsy shouted. "Even when I was
with Les Canadiens we beat this team nine-to-five. And for damn sure
we didn't need that win to stay in contention for the Stanley Cup!"

Taylor was about to yell something back when he noticed Lester looking at him disapprovingly.

"Bert," said Lester, before Taylor could respond to Lalonde's tongue-lashing, "how's the eye?"

"Swelling's not getting any worse," the goalie said with a shrug. "It's nothing I can't handle."

"All right then, gentlemen," Lester announced. "Let's turn on the offence." And turn on the offence they did.

There was a change in the lineup to start the second half. Fred Whitcroft was at left wing. He'd taken over late in the first half when Hay Millar slipped in a crack on the ice and hurt his leg. Whitcroft, who hadn't seen action since the big game in Ottawa, didn't miss a beat. He scored the third goal in a six-goal outburst that put the game out of Haileybury's reach by the halfway mark of the second half. Unfortunately, he also took an opponent's stick in the face, which knocked out several of his teeth and left his upper lip badly cut.

Whitcroft was not the only casualty in a second half that saw the Millionaires blow open a tight 3–2 game en route to an 11–5 victory. Late in the game, just after he had scored Renfrew's tenth goal, Taylor picked up the puck behind his own net and headed up ice with it. Making a series of short, sharp turns, he zigzagged past Gaul and Throope. Heading into open ice near centre, Cyclone was in full flight.

"Lester's right behind you, Cyc," Frank called out. "Newsy's on your right."

With a quick look around, Taylor spotted both his teammates but elected to keep the puck himself as he continued to race further into the Haileybury end. Seeing Ross and Ronan backing up hurriedly in front of him, Taylor tried to split their defence. He didn't make it. Ross hit him from the right and Ronan from the left. Sandwiched between the two players, he went down hard, and the back of his head hit the ice with a terrible crack. As he lay face up, blood trickled from behind both his ears.

A hush fell over the crowd as the great Cyclone Taylor remained motionless on the ice. Then the silence was broken by a loud rattling coming from the wire screen above the boards near the spot where Taylor was lying, followed by shouting.

"Get up, Taylor, you yellow-bellied bastard!"

The man screaming curses was the same man who had been trying to gouge the Renfrew players with his pointed stick. He was standing on top of the boards now, holding onto the screen with both hands to keep his balance, causing it to rattle as he swayed back and forth. The smell of alcohol on the man's breath was clearly detectable even from a distance.

"You're nothing but a gutless, chicken-livered coward," the man screamed. "Get up and fight, Taylor. You son of a bitch!"

The attention of the players on the ice was divided between their concern for Taylor and their astonishment at the scene going on in the stands above him. Finally, as the man continued to heap abuse on the fallen hockey star, Frank could take it no longer.

"Why don't you just shut up!" Frank shouted, skating towards the man in the stands.

"Why don't you make me!" the man taunted.

Frank skated right over to the screen, lifted his stick and slammed the butt end through the wire mesh and into the man's face. Blood gushed out of his nose and spurted over the boards. The man slid out of view.

"The bum had it coming to him," Art Ross assured Frank, as the younger Patrick brother stared in disbelief at what he had just done.

The postgame scene in the Renfrew dressing room was not in keeping with the impressive 11–5 victory which had put the team in solid contention for the Stanley Cup. The injuries to Taylor, Whitcroft, Millar, and Lindsay kept the celebrating to a minimum.

Frank sat quietly on his stool for a long time before stripping off his gear and heading for the showers. He soaked under the water for almost as long. He was thinking about the spectator he had hit when Lester came to him with some bad news.

"Uh, Frank," Lester said reluctantly. "There's a policeman waiting for you outside the dressing room."

Frank wasn't surprised. He'd almost been expecting it. He knew hockey players had, on occasion, had criminal charges laid against them for their actions on the ice. Visions of spending the night in a jail cell immediately came to mind. He took plenty of time getting dressed, putting off what he thought was inevitable for as long as he could.

"You're going to have to face the man sooner or later," Lester said sadly, as he watched his brother stall. "Might as well get it over with."

Frank nodded in agreement, but still didn't hurry.

When he finally went outside, the constable did not arrest him. Much to Frank's surprise, he shook his hand. The constable told Frank that the entire town had been embarrassed all season by the antics of the man he had hit, and that he was in need of shutting up.

"Where's the fellow now?" Frank asked.

"In hospital," the constable said, grinning. "Resting. Quietly."

The next morning, the team arrived at the train station at eight o'clock sharp to embark on the long trip home. Frank, Lester, and Ambrose were standing on the platform waiting to board the train when Frank was again visited by the provincial constable.

"I'm sorry to have to inform you of this, Mr. Patrick," the constable said to Frank in an embarrassed tone, "but the man you hit at the game last night has decided to press charges. I'm going to have to hold you here until he can be convinced to change his mind."

"You can't hold him here," Lester protested. Like Frank, Lester was well aware that players had been charged for their on-ice actions, but he also knew that the charges were not usually brought up until the next time the player came to the city. "We have a game back in Renfrew Friday, officer. We're going to need Frank in town before then."

"I think this can be taken care of in plenty of time for that," the constable said. Neither he nor any other town official wanted the incident publicized. In fact, the constable had already sent someone to the hospital to try to talk the man out of taking legal action.

"Then we'll all stay here in Haileybury until this is taken care of," Ambrose declared. "I'll have somebody unhook our railcar."

"There's no need for everybody to be inconvenienced by this," Frank protested. "Take the team home, Ambrose. It's been a long enough road trip already, and some of the boys are pretty banged up. We've got a tough game coming up, and they can use all the rest they can get. If this can be cleared up as easily as the constable says, I'll catch an overnight train for Ottawa this evening and be back in Renfrew Thursday."

"Are you sure, Frank?" Lester and Ambrose asked together.

"Positive."

With that, Ambrose, Lester and the rest of the Millionaires boarded the train for home, while Frank accompanied the provincial constable to the local courthouse.

XXXI

What has the Royal Navy to do before a declaration of war has taken place in Great Britain? It may be attacked by the enemy, and it would repel an attack, but for all that I do not think it would precipitate an attack. . . . And so it is with regards to the Canadian Navy. The Canadian Navy will repel an attack, but will not attack until there is the authority to do so.

Sir Wilfrid Laurier,
Prime Minister.
Naval Debate, 1910

HAILEYBURY'S COURTHOUSE WAS TINY. AT ONE END OF the building was a large desk where the judge would sit when court was in session. In front of the desk was a small table where the defendant would sit while pleading his case. Next to that table was another table for the prosecution. Behind the two tables were several rows of benches for spectators. A low wooden railing separated the spectators' section from the rest of the courtroom. A small room at the back of the courthouse functioned as the police office.

"I'm sorry to have to put you through all this," the constable told Frank as the two men sat inside the small office. There was a desk, with a chair on either side, and a bookshelf. In one corner was a Union Jack. A portrait of the King and a printed reproduction of a hand-drawn map of the silver region hung on the wall behind the desk. There was also a clock with fancy Roman numerals and a set of brass chimes. The clock, Frank thought, looked much too elegant for its spartan surroundings. A small stove sat in the middle of the office, used for cooking and, more importantly, for warmth. Along the back wall, a row of bars formed two small prison cells.

The constable sat in the chair behind his desk, and invited Frank
to sit in the other chair. Frank was relieved that the constable had not
felt it necessary to put him in the lockup. One of the cells, he noticed,
was already occupied. A man was sleeping on the uncomfortable looking bunk which was the tiny enclosure's only furnishing. Probably a
drunk who'd gotten too boisterous and was snoozing off his bout with
the bottle.

"Coffee?" asked the constable, as he took a pot off the stove and
poured a cup.

Frank accepted it gladly. It was early in the morning and, even with
the warmth of the stove, Frank felt the chill of the walk over from
the train station.

"Hey," the constable shouted, as he left Frank to attend to the man
in the lockup. "Hey, you. It's time to get up!"

When the man didn't move, the constable grabbed his club and ran
it back and forth against the bars of the cell. The awful clanging woke
the man with a start.

"Good morning," the constable said, as the man in the cell looked
up at him blearily. "Drink this," the lawman added, sliding a cup of
coffee between the bars. "It'll make you feel better."

When the constable sat down again, Frank motioned with his head
towards the man in the cell. "What's that fellow here for?" he asked.

"Had a little too much to drink," the constable said, confirming
Frank's suspicions. "We picked him up in the bar of a hotel late last
night. He was going from table to table telling people that no man
can work out his career as he would like to with the government the
way it is. Then he started shouting about being an anarchist and eliminating all forms of authority."

Frank shook his head. He'd never heard such talk before, and didn't
like the sound of it. Curious about what kind of man would say such
strange things, he looked back over his shoulder towards the cell and
straight into the eyes of the caged man. Frank had never seen such
dark, sunken eyes.

"The more he drank," the constable continued, "the more he shouted.
It got so that he was making such a disturbance the saloonkeeper had
no choice but to have him arrested."

"He's not from around here?" Frank asked.

"Never seen him before in my life," the constable responded.

"Where'd he come from?"

"I don't know," the constable said. "He says he's on his way to

Ottawa, though. And he sure has a large stack of bills with him, but not a single piece of identification.

"Hey, you," the constable shouted, "What's your name?"

"Petrovic," the man said, rolling the "r" with a thick accent. "Anton Petrovic."

Petrovic felt no need to conceal his identity. Soon, he thought, when I shoot the Prime Minister, the whole world will know who I am.

"What are you going to do with him?" Frank inquired.

"He's got more than enough money to pay his fine," the constable said. The penalty for public drunkenness was three dollars or three weeks in jail. "But I'm still going to hold him here all day. At least until I can get him on the next train to Ottawa."

"And what are you going to do with me?" Frank asked.

"Well," the constable said with a sigh, "I guess we'll have to wait and see about that."

It was well into the afternoon before Frank heard any word on his case. The town clerk sent to talk to the man Frank had hit arrived at the courthouse with some good news.

"He says he won't press charges," the clerk told the constable, "providing the hockey team is willing to reimburse him for his medical expenses."

"That shouldn't be a problem," Frank said with relief. He checked the fancy clock on the wall and visualized the route of the Millionaires' railcar. "Our train must be getting close to Pembroke by now. You can telegraph the station there, constable, and leave word for Ambrose O'Brien."

By six o'clock that evening, everything was taken care of. Ambrose arranged to send the money, the man agreed to drop the charges, and Frank was free to go. And all in plenty of time to catch the eight o'clock train to North Bay, where Frank could connect with the overnight train for Ottawa.

"Listen, Frank," the constable said when he let him go. "I know I have no right to be asking you this, but since you and Petrovic are both headed for Ottawa, would you please keep an eye on him? Make sure he stays out of trouble? And make sure he gets on that train in North Bay?"

"Sure," Frank said, though he really didn't want to, "I'll watch him."

"We've got some time before the train leaves," Frank said to Petrovic after they bought their tickets. "I don't know about you, but I'm pretty hungry. I noticed a café across the street. Would you care to join me for dinner?"

Petrovic didn't answer, but when the strange man followed him out of the station Frank took this as a yes. They found a table inside the small restaurant, ordered their meals, and then sat in silence, each man eyeing the other suspiciously.

"You're headed to Ottawa," Frank finally said, no longer able to stand the silence. "Is that where you're from?"

Petrovic shook his head. "Winnipeg."

The one-word answer was uttered in a tone which clearly indicated that the man was not in the mood for talking, though Petrovic did continue to stare at Frank. His hollow-eyed gaze made Frank feel uncomfortable, and he was glad that, when the food finally arrived, Petrovic lowered his eyes to his meat, which he cut into hurriedly.

Now it was Frank's turn to stare. He'd never seen a man attack his food the way Petrovic did. He didn't even finish chewing one piece of meat before he took another bite. Frank guessed Petrovic hadn't seen too many good meals in his life and it came as a surprise when the man pulled two dollar bills from a large roll to pay for the food. Then he remembered what the constable had said: the man didn't have any identification on him but he did have a whole lot of money. How was it, Frank wondered, that a man with that kind of cash gave the appearance of being so poor? The contradiction in Petrovic's character puzzled him. Who was this strange man?

"He's boarded the train for Ottawa," Richard Lawrence told Sean Mitchell. It was a little before 11:00 PM. Lawrence had just received a telegram from North Bay, from the man Roberts had assigned to trail Petrovic, and had gone to Mitchell's hotel to give him the news. "He'll be here tomorrow morning."

"Excellent." Mitchell had been sitting at a desk in his room reading a newspaper when Lawrence came in. Now he sat with the chair pushed back, rocking it gently on its rear legs. The thumb and index finger of his left hand pulled thoughtfully at his chin. "Excellent," he repeated. "Just in time for the Governor General's dinner at Rideau Hall."

Mitchell closed his eyes and envisioned the scene in his mind.

"There's something else," Lawrence said.

"What is it?"

"It seems Petrovic has picked up a travelling companion."

Mitchell stopped rocking, his eyes opening slowly. "What do you mean, 'a travelling companion'?"

"The telegram says a man was seen boarding the train with Petrovic in both Haileybury and North Bay."

"So who the hell is this man?" Mitchell asked angrily, bolting from his chair and reaching for the telegram.

"I don't know," Lawrence said defensively. He had thought, for a moment, that Mitchell was going to hit him. "It doesn't say," he added, handing the piece of paper to Mitchell.

"Well, we'll just have to grab them both at the train station tomorrow morning," Mitchell decided, taking the telegram and turning away.

"It'll be good to finally sleep in my own bed again," Taylor said through a yawn, as the kitchen clock chimed eleven times. Except for a brief stopover on the way from Montreal to Cobalt, none of the players had been in Renfrew for almost two weeks. Taylor was glad to return to his winter home. So glad, in fact, that he hadn't even objected when Lester invited Newsy to use Frank's room for the night. The latest addition to the star-studded Millionaires lineup had not yet had time to arrange for accommodations.

"How are you feeling?" Lester asked, as Taylor headed off for his own room. Lester knew drowsiness could be a sign of a concussion, and he was concerned about the head injury Taylor had suffered late in the game with Haileybury.

"I'm perfectly fine," Taylor said reassuringly. "Just a bit of a headache."

"And you're still planning to go to Ottawa tomorrow to see Thirza?"

"Yup."

"What time?"

"Probably catch the noon train," Taylor said. "Why?"

"I thought maybe you'd meet up with Frank."

"His train gets in real early, doesn't it?"

"About eight in the morning," Lester confirmed.

"Send a telegram to the station for him before you go to bed to-night," Taylor said. "Tell him if he wants to spend the day in Ottawa he can meet me at the station at noon and we'll make plans. We can catch the train back together at night."

"We're less than an hour outside Ottawa, sir. It's time to get up."

The porter was gently nudging Frank on the shoulder as he made the announcement.

"I'm awake, I'm awake," Frank mumbled, as he sat up and rubbed the sleep from his eyes.

"We're less than an hour outside Ottawa," Frank heard the porter tell Petrovic, who was sleeping in the berth above him. "It's time to get up."

Only because he had been so tired after a tough road trip and the long day in the courthouse had Frank been able to sleep soundly. The constant shaking and rumbling, as well as the cramped sleeping quarters, normally left him tossing and turning, but this time he had slept like a baby. The same could not be said for Petrovic. The knowledge that morning would bring him face to face with the final phase of his mission had made him too nervous to sleep.

Frank rolled out of his little bed, pulled on his robe and squeezed down the narrow corridor on his way to the washroom. He bumped into the walls occasionally; the train's movement made walking in a straight line almost impossible. Entering the tiny washroom, Frank poured a little water out of a ceramic jug and into the small wash basin. He splashed some water on his face and ran a comb through his hair to improve his just-awakened appearance. A shave would have aided greatly in that endeavour, but Frank didn't dare risk putting a sharp blade next to his skin in such a shaky environment.

By the time Frank emerged from the washroom, Petrovic was standing outside, waiting to get in.

"Good morning," Frank said.

Petrovic just grunted and pulled the door closed behind him. Frank shrugged his shoulders and walked away.

"Five minutes to the station," the porter called out as he made his way through the passenger coach. "Five minutes to the station." His voice became fainter as he made his way down the train.

Right on time, the train from North Bay pulled into the Ottawa station, its wheels screeching to a halt.

"It's been a pleasure," Frank said sarcastically, as he and Petrovic stepped down to the station platform. He had a bad feeling about Petrovic and had not enjoyed the task of keeping an eye on him; nonetheless, he offered him his hand. Frank didn't really expect the sullen man to shake it, but to his surprise Petrovic, filled with a sudden exhilaration at finding himself in Ottawa, grasped his hand as if they were old friends.

The display did not go unnoticed by Sean Mitchell.

"That one's Petrovic," he told Lawrence, cocking his head in the direction of the man he recognized from David Roberts' description, "and that must be the man he's travelling with." He looked Frank up and down.

"You know what to do?" Mitchell asked.

Lawrence nodded.

The two men had revised the impulsive plan Mitchell had made the night before. Grabbing Petrovic and his unknown travelling companion at the station was too likely to cause a commotion. Instead, they would simply trail them for a while. Mitchell would follow Petrovic; Lawrence would tail Frank. If the two men were cooking up something, he and Lawrence hoped to find out quickly.

Petrovic left the station first and Mitchell set off after him. Meantime, Frank was checking the schedule for the trains back to Renfrew when he heard a boy call out his name.

"Telegram for Mr. Patrick," the boy hollered. "Telegram for Mr. Patrick."

"I'm Mr. Patrick," Frank told the boy, and tipped him a dime as he took the message. Frank read it, smiled and started to leave the station, tossing the message in a garbage pail.

Lawrence had brought a magazine to use as a cover and was observing his quarry from a bench across the train terminal. He was pleased to learn the man's name so easily, though the Patrick name meant nothing to him. But what about that telegram? As he got up to follow Frank, Lawrence fished the message from the garbage in hopes of finding a clue.

CYC ARRIVING ON NOON TRAIN STOP
MEET AT STATION TO MAKE PLANS STOP
(Signed) LESTER

"What sort of plans?" Lawrence mumbled as he tucked the telegram into his pocket. Who was Lester? And what was a Cyc? He hoped the answers would become clear at noon. In the meantime, he would follow this Patrick fellow.

Meanwhile, Mitchell was trailing Petrovic. The man who had come to Ottawa to murder the Prime Minister had no clear plan in mind, so he wandered the streets aimlessly. Leaving the train station, Petrovic had walked northeast through Lower Town and found himself in the By Ward Market.

The oldest section of the city of Ottawa reminded Petrovic of Winnipeg's North End. The narrow streets were lined with shops and echoed with the chatter of numerous accents, dialects, and languages. But unlike the North End, the By Ward Market was not a foreign ghetto. It was a thriving working-class community in the heart of the city and there was little of the filth and decay associated with Winnipeg's North End.

Petrovic wandered south out of the By Ward Market and soon found himself in Ottawa's fashionable Sandy Hill district. Again he was put in mind of Winnipeg. The opulent homes of Sandy Hill were like those of South Winnipeg, the section of the city that had once tantalized Petrovic with its promise of riches but had since served only to taunt him, flaunting its wealth in the face of his own appalling poverty.

As he walked through Sandy Hill, Petrovic remembered the words David Roberts had spoken to him the first night they met. "The men who hold power, not just in this city but everywhere, hold it because they control the economy. The ones with the money are always the ones who call the shots. They control the government. Only by eliminating all forms of central authority will the individual be free to live his life as he sees fit."

By the time they left Sandy Hill, Mitchell, who had now been following Petrovic for almost two hours, sensed a change in the man.

Any lingering doubts Petrovic had concerning his plot to assassinate the Prime Minister had been put to rest by his walk through arrogant Sandy Hill. He was reassured that he had finally found the means of expression he had long been searching for. The assassination of Laurier would give him a way to make his mark on history.

Petrovic's new-found resolve found expression in his movements. Up until that time, he had sauntered absentmindedly through the streets, head hung low, feet shuffling aimlessly, arms falling almost limp at his sides. Now he held his head high; he walked with long, purposeful steps and his arms swung confidently in rhythm with his stride. Mitchell, of course, had no idea what had produced the change in Petrovic. Nor did he care. All he wanted to know was what Petrovic had told the man on the train.

Lawrence was having no better luck in uncovering the connection between Frank and Petrovic. After leaving the station, Frank had stopped at a restaurant for breakfast. He also purchased a newspaper — one filled with stories of the Millionaires' upcoming clash with the Wanderers, as well as a report on the Naval Debate and a story about the Governor General's dinner for the Prime Minister and Cabinet that night — and then returned to the depot to await the arrival of the noon train from Renfrew. Lawrence waited too, checking the clock on the wall frequently and wondering who, or what, was going to be on that train.

Although he was watching the clock almost constantly for the last few minutes, Lawrence still jumped when the piercing blast of the train's whistle caught him by surprise. His surprise was much greater a few minutes later when he discovered it was his old boyhood friend Fred Taylor whom Frank had been waiting to meet.

"Hiya, Cyc," Frank said, as Taylor stepped down from the train. "How's your head?"

"Well that's a real warm welcome," Taylor teased. "My head's fine. How's yours?"

"Not bad at all," Frank said with a straight face, "considering the whack I took during the prison riot in Haileybury!" A concerned look flashed across Taylor's face before he realized it had been a joke. Frank smiled when he saw the look. "Gotcha!" he said.

Taylor shook his head in mock disgust. "Just for that crack, I'm not going to invite you for lunch."

"You know what I could use more than lunch," Frank said, as he rubbed the itchy growth of stubble on his face, "is a shower and a shave."

"The rooming house where I used to live when I was playing for Ottawa is close by," Taylor said. "I'm sure the gentleman who runs the place would let us have a room for you to get cleaned up in."

"Sounds good," Frank said. "Lead the way."

"Don't I always?" Taylor replied with a grin. "And while we walk over, you can tell me about what really happened in Haileybury. You know, I've never had a friend who spent the day in jail before!"

Frank laughed.

Lawrence looked on in amazement as Frank and Taylor talked on the train platform. Though he desperately wished he could get close enough to hear them, Lawrence didn't want to take the chance that Taylor would recognize him. As he studied the two men from behind his magazine, Lawrence remembered his own conversation with Taylor ten days before.

"I know some people who won't let Laurier get the bill passed," Lawrence had said slyly, as he and Taylor talked about the Naval Debate. He had delighted in his own cleverness, hinting at the crime he and Mitchell planned. And Taylor had been very interested. He had even volunteered to help out.

"He couldn't have known what I was really talking about," Lawrence assured himself. But was it possible that Taylor had found out about the plot to kill Laurier? It seemed so unlikely, and yet there he was making plans with the man who had ridden the train into town with Petrovic. What did these two men know? Had they been enlisted by Petrovic to aid him in the assassination attempt? Or were they trying to stop him? Lawrence would have to find out.

Soon after leaving Sandy Hill, Petrovic had realized he did not yet have a place to stay. Before his walk through Ottawa's most affluent neighbourhood, such a thought might have panicked him. Now, more confident, he decided he would begin his search for lodgings by returning to the only landmark in the city he recognized — the train station.

Petrovic arrived back at the station just as Frank and Taylor were leaving it. Frank saw Petrovic first, and tried to turn away. But it was too late. Petrovic had seen him and was walking over.

"The man coming towards us —" Frank started to explain. But

Petrovic was too close now for him to finish. "Leaving town so soon?" Frank said weakly, as Petrovic stopped in front of him.

"No," said Petrovic, surprising Frank with his direct response. "I am needing a place to stay."

"Well, you're in luck," Taylor told him. "We're on our way to the best boarding house in the city. They'll probably have room for you, too."

Frank just sighed. What could it hurt to find Petrovic a room, he thought. Still, he would be glad to see the last of this man.

Lawrence and Mitchell, reunited at the station, had both witnessed the brief exchange between Taylor, Frank, and Petrovic, and followed them as they left. Mitchell felt sure that they were up to something. He believed his suspicions to be confirmed as he watched all three men enter the boarding house together.

Leaving Lawrence out front, Mitchell, too, went inside. He heard Petrovic being given room 302, and watched him climb the narrow, winding, wooden staircase until he disappeared from sight. Unsure of what his next move should be, Mitchell left the boarding house. He spied Lawrence waiting for him across the street.

"My man's named Patrick," Lawrence told Mitchell. The two men had not had time to exchange information since their surprise meeting at the station. "The other one is Taylor." He couldn't bring himself to add that he'd known Taylor as a young boy and had recently spoken with him.

"Good work," Mitchell said.

He and Lawrence had no idea these men were celebrated hockey teammates. Mitchell was a Maritimer who knew little of central Canada's sports heroes. Even their faces were not recognizable, since photographs of hockey players rarely found their way into the newspapers. Mitchell only saw these men as potential allies or potential enemies. He had to find out which.

Remembering he still had Frank's telegram in his pocket, Lawrence showed it to Mitchell.

"What do you make of this?"

"How very interesting," Mitchell said, convinced now there must be a plot. "You go get Taylor and Patrick," he told Lawrence. "I don't care what you tell them, or what you have to do. I'll get Petrovic.

We'll take them all to the warehouse in Hull. Then we'll get to the bottom of this, one way or another!"

XXXII

TAYLOR WAS SITTING ON THE BED IN HIS OLD ROOM AT the Ottawa boarding house, reading Frank's newspaper and waiting for his teammate to emerge from the bathroom. Naturally, he flipped to the sports page, where a large headline caught his eye:

OTTAWA AND RENFREW HAVE BEST
CHANCES FOR STANLEY CUP

———

Wanderers will likely lose at Creamery Town tomorrow night

"It is difficult to see where the Wanderers can beat Renfrew," the article went on to say. "The Creamery Town boys, in fact, should double the score."

Taylor smiled. "According to *The Citizen*," he said, as Frank came out of the bathroom, one towel wrapped around his waist and a second hanging off his shoulders, "all we have to do is show up tomorrow night and we'll beat the Wanderers."

There was a knock at the door before Frank could respond.

"Who could that be?" Taylor wondered aloud, getting up to answer. "Richard!" he said, in surprise, as he opened the door to find his old friend Richard Lawrence standing there. "What are you doing here?"

Lawrence did not respond to Taylor's friendly inquiry; this was not a reunion. Instead, he came right to the point. "What do you know about Anton Petrovic?" he demanded, barging into the room.

"The guy from the train station?" Taylor said.

"Why?" asked Frank. "He's not in trouble again is he?"

"Why ... yes," Lawrence said slowly, realizing he had been presented with a simple way to handle the situation. "Yes. He has gotten himself in trouble again, and I need to know how he's connected to you."

"We came in from up north on the same train," Frank said.

"Then I'm afraid you'll have to come with me," Lawrence announced.

"Why?" said Frank. "Who are you? I don't see a badge or anything."

Suddenly Lawrence felt a lot less smug, but again he got lucky.

"It's all right, Frank," Taylor told him. "His name's Richard Lawrence. He works for the Army. We grew up together."

"I think it would be helpful, Freddy," Lawrence added, speaking as matter-of-factly as he could, "if you came along, too."

After Frank had dressed, Lawrence led him and Taylor down the staircase to a back alley. He had brought along a horse and carriage to transport the two men, and had hitched it up in the alley instead of out front, just in case he had to sneak them out. He hadn't expected it would all be so easy.

"Didn't you say this guy is with the Army?" Frank asked Taylor, after Lawrence seated them in the back of the carriage and went up front to drive. "Why isn't he in uniform, then? And why isn't this some sort of official Army vehicle?"

"I don't know," Taylor replied. He didn't share Frank's concern. He had no reason to doubt what his old friend had told him. He did, however, have a question of his own. "How much do you know about this Anton Petrovic?"

Frank shared the little information he had as they rode through the streets. Before long, they found themselves on the Royal Alexandra Bridge.

"I wonder why he's taking us to Hull?" Taylor asked.

Frank decided he would find out, and moved up front to ask. "Where are we going?" he said to Lawrence.

"Don't worry," Lawrence told him. "We'll be there soon."

"Yes, but where are we going?"

Lawrence didn't answer.

When the carriage came to a halt a short time later, outside what looked to be an abandoned building, Frank's suspicions grew.

"What is this place?" he asked, as Lawrence let him and Taylor out onto the street. He took a few reluctant steps forward. "This certainly doesn't look like an Army building," Frank said. "Who are you, anyway? What's going on?"

Lawrence decided he'd heard enough questions. Producing the Luger he always kept with him, he cracked the gun butt across the back of Frank's head, then turned the weapon on Taylor.

"I'd shoot you in a minute, Freddy," Lawrence warned, "so don't move a muscle." Taylor was too stunned to try anything. He stared at the gun, then at the man who held it, then at Frank, who had slumped to the sidewalk.

"You've killed him," Taylor mumbled.

"He's not dead," Lawrence said. "Help me get him inside."

Frank's eyelids flickered as he began to regain consciousness. He found himself on the rough plank floor of a dank, dark room. The only light came from a small, barred window high up on one wall. The room had no heating, and Frank's first sensation was that of the cold, damp wood against the skin of his hands and face. The clammy feeling forced him to sit up quickly. As he did, a throbbing pain drummed through his head.

Frank had only been unconscious a few minutes, but he had no idea where he was, nor any recollection of how he had gotten there. Then he remembered Richard Lawrence.

It took a moment for Frank's eyes to focus, but as they did he saw he was not alone. Lawrence was sitting in a chair in a corner of the room, watching him. Taylor, however, was nowhere to be seen. As Frank slowly got to his feet, Lawrence pushed opened a small, creaking door and let in another man.

"Ah. I see he's awake," Sean Mitchell said, running his fingers along his gold watch chain as he entered the room. "Good."

"What have you done with — ?" Frank's voice was shaky and broke off in mid-sentence. The inside of his mouth was so dry it made speaking difficult, but Mitchell knew what Frank was asking.

"Your friend is safe for the time being," Mitchell said. "I would be more concerned with myself if I were you."

"Who are you?"

"Never mind who I am, Mr. Patrick," Mitchell replied briskly. "It's what I want that concerns you. Tell me everything you know about Anton Petrovic."

"Anton Petrovic," Frank repeated, remembering that the strange man he had met in Haileybury was somehow responsible for what was happening to him now. "I don't know anything about Anton Petrovic."

"I find that very hard to believe," Mitchell sighed. He pulled a tiny Colt .380 pocket pistol out of his jacket and looked at it thoughtfully. "I think it's time you told me the truth."

"I am telling you the truth," Frank protested. Staring nervously at Mitchell's gun, he slowly told the story of how he had met Petrovic in the Haileybury courthouse — though not the whole story. While his head might be pounding, it was still obvious to Frank that these men had no idea who he was. Yet it seemed to him that announcing his celebrity and demanding they release him might not be his best course of action, at least not until he could figure out what was going on. "Petrovic and I were both on our way to Ottawa," Frank said, as he reached the end of his abbreviated tale, "so the constable asked me to keep an eye on him. That's the only reason we were travelling together."

Mitchell was losing his patience with what he believed to be Frank's stalling. He waved the telegram from Lester in Frank's face.

CYC ARRIVING ON NOON TRAIN STOP
MEET AT STATION TO MAKE PLANS STOP
                                    (Signed) LESTER

"How did you get that?" Frank asked incredulously.

"It doesn't matter how I got it!" Mitchell snapped. "Just tell me what it means. What plans?" He felt that he was losing control of his emotions. So many thoughts were churning in his mind. The Naval Bill must be stopped. Laurier must die. Was this man for him? Or against him?

"What plans does this telegram refer to?" Mitchell repeated, trying to regain his composure. "You spent twelve hours on a train with Petrovic, you shook hands with him, then a few hours later you went into the same boarding house. I can't believe you don't know what he's up to. You're planning something! Tell me what!" He pointed the gun at Frank.

Frank could only shake his head. He needed to know more. "I — I — I don't know anything," he stammered. "I barely met the man — he wouldn't talk to me."

Again, Mitchell's anger got the better of him. "You're asking me to believe," he shouted at Frank, "that you had no idea Petrovic was on his way to Ottawa to kill someone?"

"What!" Frank gasped. If only the pain in his head would stop pounding, it would be easier to think — he knew he had to think, if he was going to save himself. What had Taylor said? That Lawrence was a soldier! Could it be that Lawrence and this man were somehow on the side of the law? It didn't seem possible, but Frank couldn't be sure. "Jesus," he groaned, "I can't believe this is happening."

"Spare me the theatrics, Mr. Patrick. Petrovic has to carry out my orders tonight. At Rideau Hall. Each passing day brings Laurier's tin-pot navy closer to reality. He must be stopped."

Kill someone? Stop Laurier? "My God," Frank thought. "Are they plotting to assassinate the Prime Minister?" There could be no confusion now as to which side these men were on. Frank had to get out of this room and get help! But how could he do it? Then blessedly his head seemed to clear, and an idea came to him.

"OK, Mr. — "

"Mitchell," the man snapped.

"OK, Mr. Mitchell," Frank continued, formulating in his mind the lie he was about to tell. "You're right. I know what Petrovic is up to. But you don't think you're the only one who doesn't want the Naval Bill passed, do you? It's tearing the country apart! I agree with you. It must be stopped. And I wish Petrovic well — if I had more guts I'd do it myself. But risks like that aren't really my line. Still, I like to keep an eye out for good business opportunities. Petrovic had a big secret he was bursting to tell, and a big bankroll to go with it. I wanted to make a deal with him. I'd keep his secret — for a price."

Frank looked earnestly at Mitchell. He'd been afraid to mention Laurier by name, although it seemed obvious to him that the Prime Minister was the target. Was the man buying his story?

Mitchell appeared stunned. "Blackmail," he said finally, mulling over what Frank had told him. It was an angle he hadn't considered. He had been so caught up in trying to determine which side Frank was on that he had completely overlooked the possibility there might be yet another side. Patrick, Mitchell thought, isn't for me or against me. He's in this for himself.

"Blackmail," he repeated. Frank's lie had made sense to him. "And you persuaded Petrovic to pay you off?"

"No," said Frank, feigning disgust. "Your friend here," he cocked his head in Lawrence's direction, "burst in on us before we had a chance to make a deal."

Mitchell nodded. He couldn't dispute that.

"There is one more thing," Frank said. "My brother," he lied, "the one who sent the telegram from Renfrew, will be telephoning me at the boarding house to confirm our plans later this afternoon. If he doesn't reach me there, who knows what he might do. He might even suspect something has gone wrong and go to the police."

There was a lingering moment of silence. Frank tried to conceal his nervousness, as he waited to hear whether his ruse had succeeded.

"It's ten minutes to three," Mitchell announced, after checking his pocket watch. "At what time will your brother be calling?"

"Between four and five."

"All right, Mr. Patrick," Mitchell said slowly. "I see no reason why you can't go back to the boarding house." He put his gun down. Frank exhaled a long sigh of relief. "There's just one thing I'd like you to see before you leave," he added. "Richard, will you take Mr. Patrick next door?"

Lawrence led Frank out of his dark, musty room and into another equally gloomy chamber. There he saw Taylor, sitting in a corner. He was gagged and tied to a chair with thick ropes. Before either of them had time to react, Mitchell entered the room and nodded at Lawrence. Frank watched, terrified, as the man pulled out his Luger and fired. The shot missed Taylor by inches, striking the wooden wall behind him with a sharp crack, splinters spraying like ice chips off a skate blade.

"He won't miss next time," Mitchell warned, fondling the chain of his pocket watch. "I trust you'll keep that in mind when I let you go. And I want you back here no later than six o'clock. If you're late — or if I see anyone who even looks like a policeman — your friend will be shot."

"I checked on Petrovic," Lawrence said. Once Frank had left, Lawrence had gone to the upper floor of the warehouse, where Mitchell had taken their assassin, to check on Frank's story. "He says he didn't tell this Patrick fellow anything, but he didn't sound very sure of himself."

Mitchell just nodded. "Did you give him the gun?" he asked.

Lawrence grunted his response. "Yeah." He had given Petrovic a .38 calibre Colt revolver with the serial numbers filed off.

"What's the matter, Richard? We have nothing to fear from him."

Mitchell, when bringing Petrovic back to the warehouse, had told him that he and Lawrence had been sent by his friend Nick Armas to help him commit his crime. The lie had worked wonderfully. "Petrovic trusts me completely."

"I'm sure he does," Lawrence said. "But I'm not sure I trust him."

"Petrovic is not a concern," Mitchell snapped. "He's a pathetic fool. He'll do as he's told. And then he'll be dead."

"And what about Taylor and Patrick?"

"I think they'll be useful, too. At least until the end of the night."

"What happens then?" Lawrence asked, although he knew the answer already.

"Then you'll shoot them."

It was three-thirty when Frank got back to the boarding house and put a panicked phone call through to his brother.

"Lester, we've got big trouble, Big trouble. Grab any of the guys you can find and get on a train for Ottawa. The four o'clock train!"

"Why, Frank? What's wrong?"

"Just do it, Lester!"

Frank was too upset to go into details over the phone. Although the pain in his head had subsided to a throbbing headache, the bizarre events of the afternoon were still too fresh in his mind. He had calmed down by the time Lester arrived in Ottawa at five o'clock.

"So what's this all about?" Lester asked. Newsy Lalonde stood at his side. Lester had not had time to round up any of the other players. Newsy's expressive face reflected the concern and confusion both he and Lester felt.

Frank told them what he knew. He told them about Petrovic, and how the constable in Haileybury had asked him to keep an eye on him. He told them how he and Taylor had been taken to the abandoned warehouse. He told them about Lawrence and Mitchell and their plan to kill somebody that night. Likely Laurier. "Probably at the dinner for the Prime Minister the Governor General is giving tonight," Frank reasoned. "They have no idea who we are, and I was able to convince them that Cyc and I are in favour of their plot. They think we're trying to blackmail Petrovic. They want me back there by six o'clock."

"Have you called the police?" asked Newsy.

"Where's Cyc now?" Lester said at the same time.

"That's just it," Frank exclaimed, trying to answer both questions at once. "They've still got him and they told me they'd kill him if I went to the police. I've seen these men in action and I believe they'd do it!"

"Then we should go to the Prime Minister," Newsy reasoned, "and tell him he must not go there tonight."

"How will we get to him?" Lester wondered.

"And besides," Frank said, "if it is Laurier they're after and he doesn't show up, these guys might suspect something and kill Cyc anyway."

"But we have to do something!"

"You're right, Newsy," Lester said. "And I think I know what." He smiled reassuringly. "We're going to pay a visit to the Governor General."

"How can we get to him any easier than the Prime Minister?" Newsy asked.

"Lord Grey is an admirer of mine," Lester said proudly, recalling the time back in Nelson, B.C. when he had met the Earl. "And a big hockey fan. I'm sure he'll consent to an audience with us."

"So we warn the Governor General and he warns Laurier!" Frank said excitedly.

"That's right," Lester said, though without the enthusiasm of his younger brother. There were two parts to Lester's plan. The second part was far riskier. "But while Newsy and I are doing that," Lester told Frank, "you have to go back to the warehouse just as they ordered. Find out as much as you can about them. Try to get them to take you along tonight. That way nothing can happen before you get to Rideau Hall, and we'll be able to get help when we see you there."

It was a dangerous plan, yet Lester could think of no other way to save Laurier without getting Cyclone killed — even if it meant risking his own brother's life.

XXXIII

"HIS EXCELLENCY WILL BE WITH YOU SHORTLY, GENTLE-men. You may wait for him in the study. Follow me."

Lester and Newsy were led up a short stairway that went from Rideau Hall's entrance into the lobby, then down a long corridor that ran to the back of the house, where the offices were. The Governor General's residence was indeed an impressive structure, appointed with polished oak furniture and many paintings and statues. It had been built in 1838 by Thomas MacKay, a stonemason from Scotland who had emigrated to Montreal in 1817. MacKay came to what would later be Ottawa in 1826, when he contracted to construct the Rideau Canal for Colonel John By. The massive stone house he built on his hundred-acre estate overlooking both the Ottawa and Rideau rivers was dubbed MacKay's Castle by his contemporaries, but MacKay himself chose to call it Rideau Hall.

More than twenty-five years later, in 1864, with the Parliament Buildings nearing completion and Ottawa almost ready to assume its duties as Canada's new capital, Rideau Hall was leased by the government for $4000 a year, to serve as a residence for Viscount Monck, the Governor General. Four years and several renovations later, the house was purchased outright by the government for $82,000. Many more renovations followed, so many that by the time Lester and Newsy were led through it, the original Rideau Hall was almost lost among the numerous additions.

The study had been built for Lord Grey himself just a few years before. Wood panelling rising almost to the ceiling lined the walls of the circular room. Large windows, a large fireplace, an even larger bookshelf, and a roll-top desk were the most striking features of the study. Yet the study, like Rideau Hall itself, was not ostentatious but comfortable and welcoming. It crossed Lester's mind that the O'Brien house in Renfrew, though not nearly as large, was much more obviously a rich man's home.

Newsy paced the study nervously as he and Lester awaited the arrival of Lord Grey. Lester sat on the couch, apparently quite calm. Only the uncontrollable bouncing of his right leg hinted at his apprehension. The silence in the thickly carpeted room added to the uneasiness both men felt. Fortunately, the silence did not last long. The Governor General arrived after only a few minutes.

"Mr. Patrick. How good to see you again."

"It's good to see you again as well, Your Excellency." Lester rose from the couch and shook Governor General's outstretched hand. Then he turned toward his new teammate. "Lord Grey, may I present Edouard Lalonde."

Lester chose to introduce Newsy by his given name, feeling that a nickname, no matter how common its usage, would not be appropriate when meeting a representative of the British Crown. The Governor General, however, had no such concerns.

"Newsy Lalonde needs no introduction," Lord Grey told Lester. He moved towards Newsy and shook his hand. "I've seen you in action, Monsieur Lalonde. You play a most spirited game, indeed. It's quite exciting to watch!"

"Thank you, Sir," Newsy said quietly, at a rare loss for words. He had no idea his fame had spread to such high places. Lester was not surprised, however; he had counted on Lord Grey's love of the sport to get them in to see him.

Albert Henry George Grey, the Fourth Earl Grey and the ninth Governor General of Canada since Confederation, came from a long line of British aristocrats. His grandfather had been Prime Minister of Great Britain. His uncle had served as Colonial Secretary. His father had been Private Secretary to Queen Victoria. He himself had served his country in both the House of Commons and the House of Lords.

Lord Grey was almost completely bald, having lost his hair early in life after suffering sunstroke on a trip to India, and his thick moustache was flecked with grey hairs, causing him to look older than his fifty years. Still, he was a handsome man. He was tall and lean, and his love of life twinkled in his eyes. He was a gifted speaker and had a warm personal charm that endeared him to the public during his time in Canada. His wide-ranging interests embraced travel, agriculture, the arts and — like a great many British aristocrats of his day — sports. He had been a good cricket player as a boy in England and fell in love with the sports he discovered in Canada. His first official act as Governor General had been to face off the puck that opened the Stanley Cup challenge match between Dawson City and the Ottawa Silver Seven back in 1905.

"I want to thank you, Your Excellency, for allowing us to see you on such short notice," Lester said after the introductions.

"It is always a pleasure to speak with the most proficient players of Canada's splendid winter game," the Governor General assured him. "Is there something in particular you wish to discuss with me?"

"I'm afraid, Sir, it's some very bad news."

"Then you had better tell me at once," he said.

Lester explained, as clearly and concisely as he could, how Frank had stumbled onto what they believed was a plot to assassinate the Prime Minister, and that it was to unfold sometime that night.

"Why haven't you gone to the police with this news, Mr. Patrick?"

"We can't, Sir. You see, these men are holding one of our teammates. Fred Taylor —"

"Cyclone Taylor!"

"Yes, Sir. And they say they'll kill him if they see any policemen."

"Frank also thinks they might kill Taylor if the Prime Minister doesn't show up here tonight," Newsy added. "That's why we've come to you."

The Governor General shook his head sadly. He understood the predicament the players were in. "And where is your brother now?" Lord Grey asked Lester.

"He's back with the assassins, trying to uncover more of their plot."

"Isn't that extremely dangerous?"

"Yes, Sir. But Frank has managed to convince these men to take him into their confidence, so we really didn't see any other choice."

"I suppose you're right," Lord Grey agreed. "In any event, I must warn Monsieur Laurier immediately."

"That's right," Lester said. "Advise him to take whatever precautions necessary, but explain to him why he still must come up here tonight."

The Governor General nodded his understanding.

"With your permission," Lester continued, "Newsy and I will attend the party tonight as well."

Frank stood outside the warehouse in Hull, preparing to face Mitchell and Lawrence once again. He raised his hand to knock, but hesitated for a moment, taking a deep breath and letting it out slowly as he got his story straight in his mind. Then he rapped on the door.

"See who it is," Mitchell ordered.

Lawrence took out his gun and went to a window. "It's Patrick," he said. "And he's alone."

Mitchell smiled, then checked his pocket watch and went to the door. "Come in, Mr. Patrick. You're right on time."

"I want to see Taylor," Frank said as soon as Mitchell opened the door.

"Your friend is fine, Mr. Patrick."

"Look, I've kept my end of the bargain. I want to see him right now!"

"Fair enough," Mitchell said. He turned towards Lawrence. "Richard, Mr. Patrick and I are going downstairs to see Mr. Taylor. Would you come along, please?" Mitchell wanted Lawrence close to him in case there was trouble.

"You see, Mr. Patrick," Mitchell told Frank a moment later, when they entered the tiny room to find Taylor unharmed — though still bound to the chair, "your friend is quite all right."

When Taylor saw Frank, he tried to speak but, gagged as he was, he could only make unintelligible sounds. Frank watched Taylor struggle with the ropes around his wrists and ankles, and wished he could say something reassuring. But that was impossible with Lawrence and Mitchell in the room. He could only hope that as he spoke to Mitchell, Taylor would realize he had a plan in mind.

"And what about your brother?" Mitchell asked Frank. "I trust you got your telephone call."

"I told him everything was proceeding as planned."

"Very good," Mitchell praised. "I must say I'm pleased you haven't tried anything foolish."

"I have no desire to interfere with your crime, Mr. Mitchell. As I tried to explain to you, I'm only looking to profit from it."

"You're more like me than you know in that regard," Mitchell said with a smile.

"How so?" Frank asked.

"Let's just say my interest in killing Laurier and stopping his Naval Bill relates more to the business empire than the British Empire. I think you and I both understand that, in the end, everything's about making money."

"Well, of course making money is not my greatest concern at the moment," Frank said, surprising himself with his ability to sound so calm, "since my life seems to be at stake. But I still have hopes of getting something out of this. I realize I'm no longer in a position to bargain, but I have a proposal for you."

Frank paused to see Mitchell's reaction. The man seemed receptive, so he went on. "I will help you any way I can," Frank said, "if you will let my friend go free."

"How very noble of you," Mitchell said dryly. Frank waited anxiously for him to speak again. "All right, Mr. Patrick," he said at last. "Mr. Taylor will go free. But not until the job is done. I'll release him to you at the end of the evening, as long as you continue to do as I say."

"All right," Frank said. "What do you want me to do?"

"It's very simple," Mitchell explained. "I am to be one of the guests at the Governor General's dinner party tonight. You will be my driver. I was going to use Petrovic, but it will be better if he can hide inside the carriage. You will drop me off in front of Rideau Hall and then guide the rig directly to the stables, where you will wait with the other drivers. All you have to do after that is keep your eye on the Prime Minister's driver. When he brings his carriage to the front entrance at the end of the evening, that will be your cue to deliver Petrovic to the scene of the crime. I'll be out front as well. That way, it will look as if you're doing nothing more than picking me up."

"What about Mr. Lawrence?" Frank asked, again hoping to uncover as much information as he could. "Where does he fit in?"

"Mr. Lawrence will remain here," Mitchell lied. He saw no reason to tell Frank that Petrovic would not be acting alone. But Mitchell's lie did more than simply keep Frank from learning the truth about the assassination plot. Frank now believed that Lawrence would kill Taylor if someone was sent to free him. With Lawrence at the warehouse, any chance to rescue Cyclone was gone.

Parties had long been a tradition at Rideau Hall. Thomas MacKay had received nearly all the eminent visitors to Bytown during the 1840s and 1850s. Since it had become the residence of the Governor General in the 1860s, social functions had become even more frequent. Lord Grey's term of office proved no exception. There were dances at Christmas, levees at New Year's, and a State Ball at Easter. Skating and tobogganing parties were held every Saturday afternoon in winter, garden parties during the summer, and musical plays throughout the year. Dinners were given frequently, especially during sessions of Parliament.

Dinner this night would be served just past nine o'clock, but some guests began arriving before eight. A small orchestra provided entertainment for the early arrivals as they made their way into the lavish ballroom where the dinner was to be held. Despite the cold of the February evening, Lester and Newsy stood in front of Rideau Hall, watching the carriages come up the circular driveway, and studying the well-dressed men and women. They were searching for anyone who might fit the descriptions of Lawrence, Mitchell, and Petrovic that Frank had given them, but mostly they were looking for Frank himself.

Mitchell's carriage was among the last to arrive. Frank spotted Lester and Newsy first, as he brought Mitchell's vehicle up the driveway. Although he was encouraged by their presence, hoping it meant that the Governor General and Laurier had been alerted, he didn't dare let them see him. Who could say how Mitchell would react if he noticed Frank making contact with them? Mitchell had a gun. There were other people around, and he might shoot any one of them. Frank shuddered at the thought.

Only the Prime Minister had not yet arrived when Lester and Newsy heard a clock inside chime nine times. Lord Grey was now outside as well.

"You haven't yet spotted your brother?" the Governor General asked Lester. He was dressed in ceremonial garb: navy blue jacket and trousers with gold trim down the legs and a gold leaf design on his wide cuffs and high collar. A red-and-white sash was draped over his right shoulder and bunched together above his left hip. Numerous medals and ribbons were pinned to his chest.

"No, Sir," Lester said.

Lord Grey checked his watch. "Mr. Laurier is scheduled to arrive at five minutes past nine," he said. As the Governor General spoke, the soldiers of his private guard marched into view. They were an impressive sight, adorned in their full-dress scarlet tunics, dark blue trousers and tall bearskin hats. The three men watched as the soldiers, rifles on their shoulders, lined up as if to form a human wall that would protect the Prime Minister.

Five minutes later, the Prime Minister's carriage arrived. The driver brought it to a halt in line with the soldiers. Lord Grey, Lester, and Newsy held their breath as Laurier got out. Each man could feel his pulse racing. Hear his heart beating. Only when the Prime Minister had safely passed through the line of soldiers and was securely inside Rideau Hall did the tension ease.

"You gentlemen might as well come inside, too," Lord Grey said to Lester and Newsy, as he prepared to re-enter the building. "My soldiers will remain stationed outside and one of my aides will be posted at the door. He has been instructed to notify us when Frank arrives. There is nothing more we can do."

Richard Lawrence checked his watch. Five minutes past nine. It was time to get ready.

Lawrence went to the upstairs washroom in the warehouse and filled the small sink with water. After stripping down to his underwear, he began applying shaving soap to his face with a soft, white brush. Next, he reached for his razor. He snapped the blade open with a sharp flick of his wrist. Then, staring hard at his reflection in the mirror, Lawrence pressed the razor against his skin and began shaving.

Even if Lawrence did not have to look neat in order to play his part in Mitchell's scheme, he would have shaved anyway. He always shaved before going to work. The simple familiarity of the task helped to relax him, not that he needed much help in relaxing any more. Killing a man had become almost second nature to him — and the fact that the man might be the Prime Minister made no difference. Richard Lawrence disappeared into a world of his own when he was committing a murder. He was distracted by nothing that went on around him. His concentration on the task at hand was more than intense. It was all-consuming. That was what made him so good at what he did. Still, he always liked to shave first.

After rinsing the excess lather from his face, Lawrence went into a small room, where he found the package containing the outfit Mitchell had promised him. Lawrence took the package over to a table and removed the lid, smiling like a child on Christmas Day when he saw what was inside.

The box contained the soldier suit Lawrence would wear that evening. It was identical to the uniform of the Governor General's Foot Guard. The big, black bearskin hat lay on top of the other clothes. Lawrence lifted it carefully out of the box. It stood nearly two feet tall! He stroked the soft fur, which looked so much like his own black hair, as he placed the hat on his head. The brass chin chain felt cool against his freshly shaven skin. After taking a few seconds to get used to its weight, Lawrence removed the hat and placed it on a cot behind him.

One by one, Lawrence removed the rest of the contents from the box: the shiny black boots, the stiff white gloves, the red leather sword sling, and the white leather waist-belt. As he pulled on the dark blue trousers, he ran his hands down the scarlet welts on the outside seam.

He enjoyed the feel of their military crispness, but not until he put on the scarlet tunic did he truly begin to feel like a soldier.

With exaggerated care, Lawrence put his right arm in first, then his left, and pulled the tunic carefully up over his shoulders so as not to disturb the twisted gold shoulder cords. Gold braid also decorated the dark blue collar and the long, pointed cuffs. Slowly, deliberately, he pushed each of the eight brass buttons through the small slits in the fabric, fastening the tunic into place.

Not until he was completely dressed did Lawrence allow himself to look in the mirror, studying his reflection with steel-grey eyes.

"A soldier at last," he said in an awed whisper. His mind conjured up images — not of his own failed military experience, but of the boyhood days playing war games by the Piggery.

Lawrence spent a few minutes admiring himself, then began to laugh bitterly. He knew he wasn't a soldier. He was a soldier's worst fear come true! Dressed as he was, he would have no trouble infiltrating their ranks. He raised a gloved hand in front of his face, and slowly squeezed an imaginary trigger.

"Bang!"

Frank climbed down from the driver's seat and peered in at Petrovic, who sat alone in the back of the carriage. Frank was bundled up in a driver's warm attire, while Petrovic wore an expensive dress coat and suit selected by Mitchell so that he would look like any other guest. Frank was worried. He had to leave the carriage to join the other coachmen, so that he could keep his eye on the Prime Minister's driver, but he still had no idea what he was going to do.

Frank had considered trying to overpower Petrovic, but that, he realized, would not be easy. Not only did Petrovic appear powerfully built, but he also carried a loaded gun. And even if Frank could subdue Petrovic, what then? If Mitchell didn't see him out front at the proper time and place, what would happen to Cyclone?

Despondent, Frank stared silently at Petrovic. The strange air of confidence the man exuded contrasted with his sullen moodiness the day before. Petrovic appeared very much at ease with what was about to happen. That Petrovic was so calm enraged Frank. Perhaps he would be better off sitting among the other drivers. Away from Petrovic, maybe he'd be able to come up with a plan.

Leaving Petrovic alone to hide in the carriage, Frank took a seat inside the small room reserved for the drivers. He tried to clear his mind. What if Newsy and Lester had not yet been able to warn the Prime Minister of the danger he was in? Should he seek out the Prime Minister's driver and warn him? But what would he say? That he was transporting Laurier's assassin in the back of his carriage?

"He'd think I was crazy," Frank told himself. Or worse. The driver had no reason to trust him. What would keep the man from thinking Frank was the killer? "He'd probably go to one of the soldiers and have me hauled away." Mitchell would soon learn that Frank had betrayed him, and that would mean the end for Cyclone.

Trying to come up with another alternative, Frank continued to watch the Prime Minister's driver, looking away occasionally to check the clock at the far end of the room. When it struck ten, Frank saw the driver head back to the stable.

"Why is he going so early?" Frank wondered. He'd thought he would have at least until midnight to figure out some way to foil the crime. But he quickly answered his own question. It only made sense for the Prime Minister to leave the party early if he'd been warned. Laurier would not wish to remain at Rideau Hall any longer than he had to.

Frank, too, got up to leave, knowing that whatever he did, he must do it now.

"You still haven't seen your brother?" Lord Grey asked Lester.

"No, Sir. I haven't."

It was just after ten o'clock and Lester was back at the driveway, watching for Frank. Newsy was still inside, close to the Prime Minister, in case Frank somehow showed up in the ballroom. Dinner had just ended. It had gone off without incident. Even if anyone had noticed the soldiers out front, it would have caused no concern; soldiers in dress uniform were always a part of the experience of visiting Rideau Hall. Laurier, ordinarily so charming on such occasions, had been unusually quiet, but the other guests attributed that to the ever-toughening battle in Parliament over the Naval Bill. That might also excuse his early departure.

Music and dancing in the Tent Room were scheduled to follow dinner, and the party wouldn't break up until after midnight, but Lord Grey felt it would be best to get the Prime Minister out as soon as possible. Leaving right after dinner, the Governor General decided, would be the least likely time to arouse suspicion. He was right. Even Sean Mitchell wasn't worried when he saw Laurier preparing to leave early. He would simply move up his own departure time, too, and be ready out front when the Prime Minister made his exit.

"Where could your brother be, Mr. Patrick?" Lord Grey wondered aloud.

"I don't know, Sir," Lester said, his voice full of worry. One thought played over and over in his mind. No matter how he tried to put it out of his head, he could not get rid of it. "My brother is dead," Lester thought. "And it's my fault. I'm the one who sent him back there."

The Governor General could see the concern on Lester's face. "Don't worry. My soldiers are ready. Nothing will happen." He pointed down the long trail leading to the driveway. "Sir Wilfrid's carriage will be along any minute. The Prime Minister will be safe, and so will your brother. I'm confident of it."

Lester didn't share the Governor General's optimism, but his mood lifted when he saw Newsy appear at the front door. He stared at his teammate hopefully, but Newsy could only return his gaze with a shrug and a slow, despondent shaking of his head. Lester's hopes sank and, as Laurier prepared to leave Rideau Hall, he was overcome with a feeling of helplessness.

With their thoughts focused on finding Frank, neither Lester nor the Governor General noticed the new soldier who had taken up a position at a point further down the driveway. Why would they have noticed? He looked just like the rest.

Standing beyond the other stonefaced soldiers, their eyes fixed, staring straight ahead, Richard Lawrence watched for the Prime Minister's carriage, and for the second rig only he knew would be following it. This was the time he enjoyed most: the last few minutes before a crime when he was the only one who knew what was about to happen. It was at this moment that Lawrence began to disappear into that world of his own. His entire being became focused on himself and his victims.

He saw nothing else. He felt nothing else. No sympathy for his victims. No remorse for his actions. He was ready.

Frank arrived back at the carriage knowing there was no time left to think. He felt he had to stop Petrovic. Even if the Prime Minister had been warned, and Frank was now confident he had been, who knew what would happen if Petrovic was allowed to approach Laurier. His only chance to stop Petrovic was to try and convince him not to go through with it.

"Why do you want to shoot the Prime Minister?" he blurted.

Frank's sudden outburst caught Petrovic off guard, but he recovered quickly with a ready-made explanation. "Only by eliminating all forms of authority," he said, reciting, as if by rote, the words David Roberts had spoken to him, "will workers be free to live as they want to."

When Frank said nothing, Petrovic went on.

"Government is wrong. I strike a blow for workers of the world by shooting the Prime Minister."

"I don't understand," Frank said. "I thought this was all about business and money." Mitchell had made that point very clear to him. Petrovic's answer didn't make sense. But then, almost instantly, Frank understood. If Petrovic shot the Prime Minister, and gave those reasons for doing it, no one would ever connect Mitchell to the crime! Petrovic was being framed!

"Listen to me," Frank said. "Murder is not the answer. You can't go through with this!"

"But I must go through with this," Petrovic said calmly.

"No," Frank cried. "You don't understand! There's more to this than you realize! He's just using you! You're nothing but a patsy!"

Petrovic said nothing.

"You'll be killed if you do it!"

Still Petrovic did not respond. Frank's words were too much for him to absorb so quickly.

Frank mistook Petrovic's silence for indifference. "Dammit," he shouted, "you don't care, do you!" He grabbed Petrovic by the shoulders and shook him. "Say something, you dumb bastard!"

Angry and frustrated that he could not articulate an answer, for the first time in his life Petrovic pushed back. He shoved Frank so violently that he was knocked off the carriage seat. Frank struck his head on the door handle and collapsed on the floor.

For a moment, Petrovic was not sure what to do. Was it possible that even now he was being cheated of his chance to make his actions matter? He pushed the unbearable thought from his mind. Climbing up to the top of the carriage, Petrovic grabbed the reins. With Frank lying dazed on the floor, Petrovic would have to guide the carriage to the front entrance himself.

Carefully, Petrovic manoeuvered the carriage out of the stable, down the driveway, and into position, bringing it to a halt about ten yards behind the Prime Minister's. He had already left the carriage and begun to stalk Laurier by the time Frank had regained his senses.

Frank stumbled from the carriage, looking around frantically. Though his head and his heart were pounding, Frank could see everything clearly — just as he could on the ice during games. He saw the portico that extended from the front entrance of Rideau Hall into the driveway, and the four sets of pillars that supported it. He saw the large electric lanterns that were attached to the last two pillars, casting their light on Lester, Newsy, Lord Grey, and the soldiers. He spotted Laurier approaching his carriage. Frank saw Mitchell coming towards him, but he could not find Petrovic!

Suddenly, Frank did see Petrovic, edging around Laurier's carriage, but was it too late? He was reaching for his gun.

Then Petrovic froze.

A wave of relief flooded over Frank. Had his words gotten through to Petrovic? Then he saw a soldier further up the driveway raising his rifle. "He's spotted Petrovic," Frank thought. "The Prime Minister is safe!" Now it would be up to him to get Mitchell into the carriage and away from there as quickly as possible in order to save Cyclone.

Frank had begun to climb up to the driver's seat when the horrifying reality of the situation hit.

That wasn't a soldier!

It was Richard Lawrence!

He was going to shoot Laurier!

There was no time to worry about what Mitchell would think now. Frank leaped from the carriage and hit the ground running. But he knew he would never outrun a bullet. There was only time to shout a warning.

"THE ONE ON THE DRIVEWAY! HE'S NOT A SOLDIER!"

Lester recognized the voice immediately. With the strong bond of teamwork between them, forged through hundreds of hours of hockey, no more words were necessary.

Lester lunged at Laurier as the first shot was fired.

The Prime Minister collapsed to the ground.

A second shot rang out.

More gunfire filled the air as Frank reached Petrovic, and Frank yelped in pain as a bullet nicked his arm. Spinning around as he grabbed his coat sleeve, Frank saw Petrovic on his back, blood escaping from a wound in his chest.

"No!" Frank cried. He dropped to his knees beside the fallen man. Petrovic barely had the strength to raise his head. Still, he looked up at Frank with a weak smile. He seemed about to speak, but as Frank leaned closer to hear him, Anton Petrovic died. Sickened, Frank turned his head away, and saw Richard Lawrence drop his rifle.

Lawrence had known instantly that something had gone wrong. His first shot had been aimed directly at Laurier's chest. It couldn't have missed! But it had. Lester had reached the Prime Minister in time and tackled him to the ground. Lawrence's second shot also missed, as Lester rolled the Prime Minister to safety under his carriage.

When his first two shots failed, Lawrence's self-control snapped and his strange world disappeared. He awoke, horrified, to the confusion all around him. He fired wildly, killing Petrovic with one of his random blasts, then dropped his gun and fled in terror, ignoring commands to halt. A bullet from one of the Governor General's soldiers struck him in the side, but, panicked as he was, Lawrence barely felt the blow. A second bullet struck him in the leg, breaking it and throwing him to the ground. Still he struggled to get away, until a third bullet shattered the back of his head.

"Are you hurt, Sir Wilfrid?" Lord Grey asked, as Lester and Newsy helped the Prime Minister out from underneath the carriage.

Laurier wiped the dirt and snow from his pants and coat and checked himself for damage. "Not at all," he said. "Thanks to these men."

"You were all very brave," Lord Grey said. Turning to shake hands, he noticed blood on Frank's coat.

"Good Lord! You've been shot!"

Frank didn't hear the Governor General's words. He had just spotted Mitchell boarding his carriage. As Mitchell whipped the horses, Frank pointed at the escaping carriage and shouted, "Stop that man! He's going to kill Cyclone!"

"Your friend has double-crossed me," Mitchell told Taylor breathlessly, as he began to cut him loose from the ropes that bound him to the chair. "I'm sure they'll all be here any minute," he said after cutting the final knot, "but you're going to get me out of here." He jammed his gun into Taylor's ribs. "On your feet!"

Taylor rose slowly. His legs had gone numb and he could barely stand up. His wrists and ankles ached, bruised from the tight knots and cut from hours of rubbing as he had struggled to free himself. His head throbbed, the stress of the day aggravating the injury he had suffered in Haileybury.

As Mitchell led Taylor out of the tiny room that was so much like a prison cell, he heard the sound of footsteps coming from above.

"They got here even sooner than I thought," Mitchell muttered. He pushed his captive ahead of him, and bound Taylor's hands behind his back. "You go first. And not a sound," he cautioned in a hoarse whisper, pressing his gun into the small of Taylor's back as they reached the stairs. For the first time all day, Taylor thought he detected a note of nervousness in Mitchell's voice.

Up on the main floor, Frank led Lester and Newsy to the back of the building and to the head of the basement stairs. Taylor, slowly climbing the steps from the basement, reached the top just as Frank got there.

"Cyc!" Frank hollered. "You're alive! You're all right!"

"Of course he's all right," Mitchell snapped. He had come up the stairs right behind Taylor. "I told you before, Mr. Patrick, as long as you do as I say, he won't be killed." As Mitchell spoke, he brought the gun from behind Taylor's back and jammed it into his ribs where the others could see. "However," Mitchell continued, "you no longer do as I say, do you?"

Again Taylor thought he heard a quaver in Mitchell's voice. He believed he now heard fear, and he was right. Mitchell had never even fired his gun, much less shot a man in cold blood. Lawrence had always taken care of that end of their partnership. Taylor could sense Mitchell's vulnerability as he continued talking.

"But I'll give you one more chance, Mr. Patrick . . ."

Cyclone's eyes darted around the room.

". . . if you and your friends will just stand back . . ."

Taylor spied a broom leaning against the wall behind Newsy.

". . . and give me clear passage out of here . . ."

Taylor stared hard at Lalonde, trying to attract his attention. His brow furrowed with concentration as he tried to steer Newsy's gaze toward the broom, using only his eyes and an ever so slight nod of his head.

". . . no one has to get hurt . . ."

The word "hurt" had barely left Mitchell's mouth when Cyclone and Newsy sprang into action, moving with the lightning-fast reflexes that made them so dangerous on the ice. Though his hands were tied, Taylor shoved Mitchell aside with a shoulder to the chest, knocking him off balance. As Mitchell tried desperately to regain his equilibrium and fire a shot, Newsy, who had grabbed the broom in the blink of an eye, smashed it hard into his chest as if he were cross-checking a hated opponent.

Newsy's vicious stickwork drove the man backwards. Windmilling his arms in a futile attempt to regain his balance, Mitchell tumbled down the basement stairs. His panicked cry was silenced the instant he hit the floor. From the awkward angle of his head as he lay sprawled below them, the hockey players knew, even as they dashed down the stairs, that Sean Mitchell was dead.

XXXIV

This House agreed by unanimous resolution upon the line of our policy of 1902, and in order that there may be no misgivings or misunderstandings upon that . . . I shall once again read this motion . . .

This House fully recognizes the duty of the people of Canada, as they increase in numbers and wealth, to assume in larger measure the responsibilities of national defence.

This House is of the opinion that under the present

constitutional relations between the mother country and the self-governing dominions, the payment of regular and periodical contributions to the Imperial treasury for naval and military purposes would not, so far as Canada is concerned, be the most satisfactory solution of the question of defence.

. . . This was in 1902, nearly eight years ago, and for eight years this policy of the present government has been before the country. From this policy the present government has never deviated. This policy was affirmed again at the Imperial Conference of 1907. We affirmed it again last year in this House when the question came up for concrete and immediate action. This policy is embodied in the [Naval] Bill now before this House, and by this policy the present government stands or falls.

Sir Wilfrid Laurier,
Prime Minister.
Naval Debate, 1910

AT A LITTLE BEFORE EIGHT IN THE MORNING ON Friday, February 25, 1910, Frank, Lester, Newsy, and Cyclone returned to the Ottawa station to catch the train home to Renfrew. To Frank it seemed incredible that only twenty-four hours had passed since he had arrived at the station on his way home from Haileybury. Now the big game with the Wanderers was just twelve hours away.

Though the game with the Wanderers seemed less important after the events of the night before — it was, after all, only a hockey game, even if the Stanley Cup was at stake — all four players wanted to get back to the boarding house and rest up. None of them had gotten any sleep the night before. They had spent a few hours at the hospital, where Frank and Taylor had had their injuries attended to, but most of their time had been spent in meetings at Rideau Hall, where government officials wanted Frank to tell them all he knew — little that it was — about the men who had plotted the failed assassination. The

Prime Minister and Lord Grey were also at the meeting, and it was the Governor General who had the final word on the subject.

"Gentlemen," said Lord Grey, after the few bits of available evidence had been sifted through again and again, "it seems likely to me that all the men who wished to commit this horrible act are dead. There is no one left to be brought to trial and so there is no reason to launch a public investigation. We may never really know what provoked these people to plot such a crime, so I suggest we all simply go about our lives as if this terrible event had never occurred. None of the other dinner guests observed this incident tonight. My soldiers have all taken an oath of silence. I myself will handle any inquiries from the press. I hope never to hear of this incident again, gentlemen, and I trust that you will put it out of your minds and never breathe word of it to anyone."

A few hours after the Governor General swore them to secrecy, the four hockey players were on their way back to Renfrew.

When Taylor heard the clock in the kitchen of the boarding house in Renfrew chime two o'clock, he decided to get out of bed. Tired as he was, Cyclone had been having trouble sleeping. Mostly, he had lain awake staring at the ceiling. Whenever he closed his eyes, visions of the tiny room in Hull haunted him. On the rare occasions when sleep finally overcame him, it was fitful. His mind would conjure up images of boyhood hockey games at the Piggery. The game would break up, as it often had in those days, into a re-enactment of the Boer War. Hockey sticks in hand, the boys would playfully shoot at each other. But Richard Lawrence was using a real rifle. With real bullets. And he was shooting at Freddy Taylor. As the bullets tore into his body, Taylor was jarred awake, in a cold sweat. Better to get up than go through that again, he decided.

Taylor went down to the kitchen and found himself some milk in the icebox. He drank it right out of the glass bottle.

Frank walked in. "Couldn't sleep either?" he asked.

Taylor shook his head, but didn't speak.

"You mind if I have a drink of that?"

Again Taylor said nothing. He passed the bottle to Frank.

Frank wiped the mouth of the bottle with his sleeve before taking a swig. As Frank swallowed, Lester entered the kitchen, and Newsy followed a few minutes later. None of the players had been able to sleep.

The four Renfrew teammates sat around the kitchen table in silence. None of them knew what to say to each other.

"I'm going for a walk," Taylor said finally.

"Mind if I tag along?"

"Thanks, Frank, but I just want to be by myself for a while."

"Sure, Cyc. I understand."

But Taylor was never alone when he walked the streets of Renfrew. Everyone who saw him that afternoon wanted to shake his hand and wish him good luck in the game with the Wanderers. The significance of the match that night was lost on no one in the small town. A win would put the team in solid contention for the Stanley Cup, while a loss would end all chances. It was the kind of big-league excitement the townsfolk had been craving for years. It was all anybody wanted to talk about. The enthusiasm of those he encountered couldn't help but lift Taylor's sagging spirits. Still, he wanted to be alone with his thoughts, so he bought a copy of the *Ottawa Citizen* and headed for the rink.

"Jeez, Cyc. It's awfully early — even for you. The game's not for another five hours!"

It was Charlie McNab, the arena manager. He had a bucket of snow with him, and he was using it to patch up some ruts in the ice when he noticed Taylor climbing the stairs to the dressing room. The team hadn't played a home game in over two weeks, but the Renfrew Rink was always open for public skating, so the ice surface was in need of some repair.

"You're right, Charlie. But it's a big game." Taylor felt he owed the friendly man some sort of explanation, even if it wasn't a truthful one. "How's the ice?" he asked, changing the subject.

"It'll be hard and fast, Cyc," the rink manager said. "Just the way you like it!"

"Glad to hear it, Charlie," Taylor said, as he disappeared into the dressing room. He expected the room to be empty and the shock of seeing someone already there caused his heart to jump.

"Shit! You nearly scared me to death!" he shouted.

It was Larry Gilmour. He hadn't suited up for Renfrew since the second game of the season, when the addition of Fred Whitcroft and Hay Millar from Edmonton had left him and Ernie Liffiton without a position to play. Liffiton had left the squad, but Gilmour had stayed on, assuming the duties of club manager and overseeing the day-to-day needs of the hockey team.

"Sorry, Cyc," Gilmour said, laughing at Taylor's startled face.

"What are you doing here?" Taylor asked, a hint of anger in his voice.

"The new uniforms just arrived," Gilmour said mildly. He attributed Taylor's agitation to the pressure of the up-coming game. "I thought I'd unpack them and hang them up."

"What new uniforms?"

"The new blue ones," Gilmour said. "The Wanderers' colours are the same as ours, so we thought we should change them." Gilmour held up a sweater and some socks for Taylor to see. Their design was the same as the old red-and-white ones, but with blue instead of red. "Besides, you know Ambrose. He wants something special for the big game."

Taylor nodded as he sat down on the stool in front of his locker. When he opened his newspaper, the first article he saw was about the Naval Debate. He didn't read it. The anger he had once felt toward Laurier over that issue seemed inappropriate now. Turning the pages, Taylor searched for news of the night before. He found a tiny article which mentioned that gun shots had been heard at the Governor General's residence, but that Lord Grey himself had dismissed the sounds as the backfiring of a troublesome motorcar. The anonymous writer of the article accepted the explanation unquestioningly. It was over. Taylor would put it out of his mind, as Lord Grey had suggested. "Life goes on," he thought, and he turned to the sports section.

RENFREW OUTCLASSES WANDERERS ON DEFENCE
AND LINE

The headline caused Taylor to frown. The *Citizen* article made it seem like the Wanderers would be pushovers, but Taylor knew that wouldn't be the case. After winning the Stanley Cup in three successive years, they had lost to Taylor's Ottawa Senators by just one game last season, and Cyclone knew the Montreal players would like nothing better than to get their revenge on him by knocking his current club out of contention. Taylor thought they were capable of doing it, too.

"*REN*-FREW! *REN*-FREW! *REN*-FREW!"

The Millionaires faithful roared in anticipation of the upcoming clash. They were shouting, clapping their hands, stamping their feet. This was the moment they had long been waiting for. Nearly three-quarters of the population of the small town of 4000 had jammed the tiny Renfrew Rink. Hundreds more were milling around outside in the snow, unable to get tickets. They were all screaming for the Millionaires. About 200 Wanderers fans had arrived from Montreal on a chartered CPR train. Dressed in the red-and-white colours of their team, the Wanderers fans were easy to spot, but their cheers were drowned out by the shouts of the home-town crowd.

It was much quieter in the Renfrew dressing room. Those inside were aware of the cheering fans — it would have been impossible not to be, since their antics shook the entire building — but the players sat in silence.

With game time fast approaching, Lester reached for his stick. He was about to slap it on the floor, but he paused and looked around the room. The fates have not been kind to the Renfrew Millionaires, he thought. They could not have picked a worse time for such an important hockey game.

Many things were going through Lester's mind. The Wanderers had been given a much better break when the schedule was drawn up. In the past two weeks, the Montreal team had only been scheduled to play twice: both games at home and with a week between them. In the same period of time, Lester and his teammates had logged some 1000 miles, travelling from Renfrew to Ottawa to Montreal and then to silver country and back. They had played four tough games.

The Wanderers, Lester knew, were fresh and injury-free. The Millionaires were tired and hurting. Lester looked at Bert Lindsay. The swelling around the eye of the tough little goalie had gone down, but there was a dark bruise on his forehead and a long line of stitches, as well: souvenirs of Haileybury. Hay Millar's leg was still bothering him, but he had suited up. He had to, because Fred Whitcroft couldn't. The big man from Edmonton was laid up in the hospital. Not only had he cut his lip and lost some teeth as a result of the stick in the face he had taken in Haileybury, but his mouth had become infected and his entire jaw painfully swollen.

There were also the events of the night before to consider. Newsy, Frank, and Taylor had not had any sleep in the past twenty-four hours — nor had he himself. That wouldn't help matters. And Taylor's wrists and ankles were badly swollen. Rubbing against the stiff leather of his gloves and skates would surely be painful. There was also the injury Taylor had suffered in Haileybury to worry about. His head was still tender, and another such mishap would be dangerous indeed. Frank would be playing injured, too. There was the wound from the bullet that had grazed his shoulder, and an aching head as well. But worse than any physical problems were the emotional ones. He'd noticed that Taylor was jumpy, and he was sure the others were badly shaken too. They still hadn't been able to bring themselves to discuss the close call they'd had.

Lester sighed. This was not the way he would have chosen to be entering such a big game, but he couldn't let that bother him now. The team had a job to do.

"The Stanley Cup is on the line tonight, gentlemen. We need this win. You know it. I know it. The people out there know it. Let's give 'em all we've got."

Lester slapped his stick on the dressing room floor. It was time to go.

"*REN*-FREW! *REN*-FREW! *REN*-FREW!*"

The air in the arena was charged with excitement. The hockey-mad citizens of the Creamery Town revelled in the recognition their highly paid hockey heroes had bestowed upon them. After years of ridicule, the fans craved the respect a Stanley Cup would bring, and they let loose with an extra burst of noise when Lester led his teammates down the stairs and onto the ice. They booed with equal fervour when the Wanderers appeared a few minutes later. There was a constant excited buzzing in the stands as the two teams went through their warm-ups.

As the rest of the Millionaires loosened up, skating in circles and poking shots at Bert Lindsay, Taylor went through his own limbering up routine. His thoughts drifted back to the Stanley Cup clash between the Wanderers and Senators almost exactly one year ago. On that night, his injury — the deep cut in his ankle — had been headline news. Tonight, no one knew about his pain. His wrists and ankles ached more with every stride, and the game hadn't even started yet.

"How you feeling, Cyc?" Newsy asked. It was the first time he had called Taylor by his nickname.

"Pretty good," Taylor lied. "I feel pretty good." He smiled an unconvincing smile and started to skate away. Then he stopped and turned back. "You saved my life last night, Newsy. *Merci*."

The two men, bitter rivals for so long, stared uncomfortably at one another. A signal from referee Russell Bowie, calling the players to line up for the opening face-off, brought an end to the awkward moment. Newsy tapped Taylor on the butt with his stick, then skated to centre. Taylor smiled and took up his position, too. Bowie placed the puck on the ice. "Play!" he shouted.

The Renfrew faithful roared their approval when Newsy won the opening draw and played the puck back to Lester. Wanderers centre Ernie Russell tried to step around Newsy, but was unable to get by as the Frenchman drove his shoulder into his opponent's chest. Lester had taken only a few strides forward when he heard Taylor calling for the puck. Cyclone wanted to know right away how his injuries would affect his play.

"Drop it back, Lester. Drop it back!"

Lester passed the puck to Taylor. Gritting his teeth hard to block out the pain, Cyclone took off up ice.

The fans were on their feet. Shouts of "Cyclone!" filled the arena as Taylor gained speed. He stepped around left winger Jimmy Gardner and outraced rover Pud Glass, but, as he reached the other end of the ice, he couldn't beat the Wanderers defence. Cover point Moose Johnson poke-checked the puck off Taylor's stick, then point man Jack Marshall knocked him to the ice with a solid body check.

Taylor was slow to get up. He had to put his hands down to help support his weight, and was overcome for a moment by a sharp pain in his wrists. By the time he got to his feet, Johnson had carried the puck into Renfrew territory, where Frank was scrambling to try and stop him. With a snap of his wrists, Johnson fired a shot past Bert Lindsay. The Wanderers led 1–0.

"Dammit!" cursed Frank. He knew he had been slow to react. "Did I screen you?" he asked, as Lindsay fished the puck out of the net.

"Maybe a little," the goalie said. "But I should have had it anyway." The crowd was silenced by the Wanderers' quick goal, but the noise from the stands picked up again as the two teams lined up for the ensuing face-off. This time Russell beat Newsy to the draw, and fired the puck into the Renfrew end. Frank chased it down behind his goal. He looked up to see the Wanderers forwards — Russell, Gardner, and Harry Hyland — racing towards him. With all of his teammates up ice ahead of him, and therefore offside, Frank had only two options. He could give up possession by firing a long shot back into Wanderers territory or he could try to outmanoeuvre the oncoming Montreal players. He decided on the latter, and carried the puck towards Russell. Frank reasoned that the high-scoring centre was a less effective checker than his linemates and would be the easiest player to beat. He was right — he had no trouble stepping around Russell. The Wanderers centre, incensed that Frank had beaten him so cleanly, spun around and gave him a chop with his stick. As Frank went down, the referee's hand went up.

"Three minutes for tripping," referee Bowie announced.

"Come off it!" Russell protested. "I barely touched him! The son of a bitch took a dive! Are you blind? How could you miss that?"

"Perhaps you'd like to serve ten minutes more," Bowie said in the quiet but authoritative voice of hockey's best referee. Russell skated off in silence to serve his three minutes. Frank smiled weakly as he got up off the ice. It hadn't been a dive; he had really been tripped and the hard fall was painful.

The face-off that resumed play was held deep in Renfrew territory. Pud Glass moved up from rover to take the draw, and surprised the partisan crowd by beating Newsy to the puck. Glass fed the rubber disk back to Johnson, who carried it towards his own end, ticking time off Russell's penalty. When the Renfrew wingers, Hay Millar and Bobby Rowe, caught up with him, Johnson lofted the puck back into the Millionaires' end. The few hundred Wanderers fans in attendance applauded the efforts of their cover point, but soon it was the Renfrew fans who were buzzing again as their own cover point, Cyclone Taylor, picked up the puck behind the net.

Taylor stopped back of the goal and looked up ice. He saw Johnson retreating further into his own end, where his defence partner, Jack Marshall, was already setting up. Seeing Pud Glass and Harry Hyland rushing back as well, Taylor swung out from behind the net and crossed in front of Lindsay.

"Watch out, Cyc!" Frank shouted, but Taylor's mind was elsewhere. He didn't hear the warning. Nor did he see Jimmy Gardner. The pesky Wanderers winger had not backed up like the rest of his teammates. He was on Taylor before Cyclone knew what hit him.

Up in the pressbox, Taylor's friend, Tommy Gorman of the *Ottawa Citizen*, frowned. "It doesn't look like Cyc's head is in this game," he mumbled as he wrote:

> Fred Taylor attempted his hazardous trick of carrying the
> rubber in front of his own net. This time Taylor's luck in such

a daring move failed him, Jimmy Gardner knocking the puck
off Cyclone's stick and batting it into the twine for the second
goal of the match.

Again the crowd fell silent. The Wanderers' fast start had robbed the
home town fans of their enthusiasm. The contest was just five minutes
old and their heroes already trailed 2–0.

"What's the matter with them?" Dom Ritza wondered. The pharmacist was confused, as was everybody else who sat in the stands.
"How could they come out so flat in such an important game?"

Tommy Gorman asked himself the same questions as the first half
wore on. "I can't believe they're putting out such a listless effort," he
said to himself, as he continued his report:

> The next goal was a long time in coming . . . but eventually
> fell to the Wanderers, Gardner driving from the side, a long
> shot that flew past Lindsay and landed square in the side of
> the flags. At half-time the score was 3–0 Wanderers.

The Renfrew players dragged themselves up the stairs to their dressing
room. The disappointed fans filed out of the seating area and into the
lobby, where rumours spread like wildfire.

"I don't think they're trying to win!"

"I heard that gamblers got to 'em!"

"I think they're throwing the game!"

Poorly as their team was playing, few were willing to believe such
stories. The fans had seen their hockey heroes overcome slow starts
to win other games earlier in the season. They were confident it would
happen again. Tommy Gorman summarized the news for his readers:

> Coming out for the second half, the Renfrew team received a
> big ovation, hundreds being under the impression that they
> would quickly round to form and overcome the Wanderers
> lead.

"*REN*-FREW! *REN*-FREW! *REN*-FREW!"

The crowd was shouting as the two teams lined up for the face-off.
The Millionaires would start the second half with a man advantage
for three minutes — courtesy of a penalty to Pud Glass just as the

first half had expired. The fans knew this was an excellent opportunity for their team to get back on track.

The second half started just like the first, with Newsy beating Russell to the puck. He carried it into Wanderers territory with Lester, Rowe, and Millar rushing up ice behind him. Frank and Taylor moved forward as well. With the cheers of their fans ringing in their ears, the Millionaires were on the attack.

For almost the full three minutes, they worked the puck around. One player, usually Newsy or Lester, would try to carry the puck as close as he could to the Wanderers goal. Millar and Rowe ran interference, trying to place themselves between Lester or Newsy and the Wanderers' defence and create openings. If the wingers succeeded, the puck carrier would fire a shot at goalie Riley Hern. If there were no openings, the disk was dropped back to Frank or Taylor, who would move up for a shot through heavy traffic. The Millionaires' tactics kept the crowd on its feet, ooh-ing and ahh-ing at the close calls, but they couldn't put the puck in the net.

With the Wanderers' penalty nearing an end, Lester made one last attempt to capitalize on the man advantage. He picked up a loose puck in the far corner and circled behind Montreal's net, looking for someone out front. Seeing Newsy break free of his check, Lester was about to send him the puck when he heard Frank calling for a pass.

"Point! Point!" Frank shouted. He was slapping the blade of his stick against the ice, trying to get Lester's attention.

As soon as Lester played the puck, he knew it was a mistake. His concentration had been disrupted by the sight of Pud Glass leaping over the boards and back on the ice, his penalty over. As a result, Lester's pass was off line. Newsy hustled back to try and receive it. Frank moved forward with the same thought in mind. They collided with a thud. Both players fell to the ice as the puck skidded, untouched, towards centre ice. Frank was slow to get up. He had landed on his bad shoulder and the pain made it hard to move. Newsy, concerned for his friend's well-being, was slow to get up as well.

Meanwhile, Pud Glass pounced on Lester's errant pass near centre ice. There wasn't a Renfrew player within twenty feet of him as he cruised in on Bert Lindsay. Slowing down as he approached the Millionaires goaltender, Glass faked a shot to one side, freezing Lindsay momentarily, then tucked the puck past him on the other side. Wanderers 4, Renfrew 0. The cheering died. It was a goal to lend credibility to the rumours that the Renfrew players really weren't trying to win. The fans were starting to wonder.

"Why were they lying on the ice like that?" Gus Handford moaned, as he slumped into his seat. The photographer, like all others in the stands, had no idea why Frank had remained down so long. Maybe the game really has been fixed, he thought.

As the second half dragged on, Tommy Gorman continued to describe the Millionaires' poor play:

> They had dozens of chances to slip one past Hern, but they either shot high or wide or drove it so weakly that the Wanderers' defence quickly shoved it aside.

With ten minutes to go in the game, the Wanderers scored again. This time it was Harry Hyland who slipped the puck past Lindsay. The team from Montreal led 5–0. Dreams of a Stanley Cup season were dead. Tommy Gorman confirmed it in his column:

> As the game drew to a close, scores of disappointed spectators left their seats and filed slowly out, Renfrew's visions of the Stanley Cup having been snuffed out.

Gus Handford lingered outside the Renfrew Rink for a while before beginning the sad walk home. Dom Ritza was there as well.

"I heard a fella from Montreal say Ambrose O'Brien sold the game," Gus told Dom. "He said Ambrose has lost so much money on the team that the only way he could make it up was to convince the players to throw it."

"I heard the same sort of thing," Dom confirmed sadly. "You don't think it's true, do you?"

"I hope not," Gus answered. "But they sure looked bad, didn't they?"

He didn't know what to believe. Only one thing was certain: there would be no Stanley Cup in Renfrew this year. Could the game really have been fixed? Tommy Gorman didn't think so. He said as much in his game report:

The showing of the Renfrew team on the whole was a keen disappointment. The usual rumours consequent upon such surprising reversals of form, such as "throwing the game," "not trying to win," etc., were soon in circulation, but they were as nonsensical as they were numerous, Wanderers emerging victorious on their merits.

But why, he wondered privately, had the Millionaires looked so bad?

Tommy Gorman stopped Ambrose O'Brien on his way out of the rink after the loss. Coach Alf Smith and manager Larry Gilmour were with him as well.

"There's a rumour going around," Gorman said bluntly, "that your team is going to throw in the towel now that a Stanley Cup title is no longer possible." There were many rumours going around. This was the only one that Gorman considered somewhat credible, and he wanted to confront Ambrose with it.

"That's completely untrue," Ambrose responded. "I'm as disappointed as anyone by our poor showing tonight, but we absolutely intend to play out the rest of the season. Our next game is scheduled against Ottawa, and we've got a score to settle with the Senators."

"That's right," Alf Smith agreed. "The boys have played a lot of hockey the past two weeks, but we've got ten days off before the Ottawa game. I think you'll see a different team then. The real team."

"Are you saying that was the problem tonight?" the newspaperman asked. "Too much hockey?"

"The boys looked awfully tired to me," Larry Gilmour said. "I'd say they were stale after a long road trip and four tough games."

Gorman nodded. The explanation made sense. Renfrew had played more hockey during the past two weeks than any other team in the NHA. "Thank you, gentlemen," Gorman said. He went back inside to the telegraph room to finish his report of the evening's events:

> After the game it was rumoured that the Renfrew team would drop out of the league and throw up the sponge, but such is far from their intention. They announced that they intend to stick to the game and will endeavour to repay old scores by beating the Ottawa team here on March 8.

Renfrew officers were as mystified as anyone over the poor form displayed by their galaxy of stars, Coach Alf Smith and Manager Larry Gilmour attributing their downfall to too much hockey and staleness. The team did not get working at any time.

Despite Gorman's report of the game, and other articles like it, rumours persisted that the match with the Wanderers had been fixed. Gus Handford didn't want to believe the stories — Lester, Frank and Taylor were his friends. But he wasn't sure. When he saw Taylor walking the street outside his photo studio a few days later, he waved him inside.

"What can I do for you, Gus?" Taylor asked.

"I hate myself for asking you this," the photographer said, "but I have to know." He took a deep breath and blurted his question. "Did you throw it, Cyc? Tell me you didn't and I'll believe you."

"The game was on the level, Gus. We didn't throw it." How Taylor wished he could tell him the whole truth. He wanted so much to explain what had happened. That there had been a plot to assassinate the Prime Minister. That Frank had been shot trying to prevent it. That he himself had been held hostage all day, bound to a chair in a tiny, dark room. That Newsy and Lester had spent many anxious hours as well, as they tried to prevent the crime. Gus can be trusted, Taylor thought. I can tell him what happened. But he had given his word to remain silent.

"It was just an off night," Taylor said. "That's all."

PART IV
POSTGAME

XXXV

*In the Senate Chamber, His Excellency the Governor General
was pleased to give Royal Assent to . . . An Act Respecting the
Naval Service of Canada.*

— Hansard

*I am glad to relieve you from further attendance in Parliament
after a session which has been marked by legislation of the
most important character . . . . The measure for the
establishment of a naval service, which has become of pressing
necessity, in view of the extraordinary advances, within recent
years, of Canada as a nation within the British Empire, is the
crowning development of a policy which was anticipated from
the earliest days of Confederation.*

Lord Grey,
Governor General.
May 4, 1910

THOUGH THEY WERE OUT OF THE RUNNING FOR THE
Stanley Cup, Frank, Lester, Newsy, and Cyclone were not about to
let their Renfrew teammates just play out the string. It had truly been
circumstances beyond their control which led to the disappointing
defeat by the Wanderers, but the talented foursome still felt they owed
something to the people of Renfrew. A win over the Ottawa Senators
would be a start.

The game with the Senators had no bearing on the Stanley Cup —
the Wanderers had followed up their win over Renfrew with a 3–1
victory in Ottawa to clinch the league title — but the players knew a
win over the big-city team would be almost as sweet to residents of
the small town as a championship trophy. They gave it everything they
had. The result was a crowd-pleasing 17–2 rout.

Cyclone Taylor was the star of the Ottawa game, providing the fans with their biggest thrill on a night of thrills when he made good on his boast of a few weeks earlier to score a goal backwards. With the outcome already well beyond doubt, Taylor took a pass from Lester, spun around while going at full speed and, with his back to the net, hoisted a shot over the shoulder of Ottawa goalie Percy Lesueur. Newsy was the hero three nights later, when the Millionaires closed out their season with a 15–4 thrashing of Cobalt. He scored nine times to overtake the Wanderers' Ernie Russell for the National Hockey Association scoring title, with thirty-eight goals in eleven games.

The big finish to the season helped take the sting out of losing the Stanley Cup, but the best was yet to come. An exhibition match between the Ottawa Senators, Stanley Cup champions of 1909, and the Montreal Wanderers, Stanley Cup champs for 1910, had been arranged for the artificial ice surface at New York City's St. Nicholas Street Arena. Since the Renfrew Millionaires had stolen the late-season thunder from the two Champion teams, the team was invited to come to New York to take on the winner. The Millionaires avenged their bitter loss to the Wanderers, beating the Montreal team 9–4 to win the tournament, and were declared World Champions by the American press. That victory in New York was as close as Renfrew ever came to the Stanley Cup.

Frank and Lester Patrick left the Creamery Town after the 1910 season and returned to British Columbia, where, a year later, Lester married Grace Linn. In 1912, with the financial support of their father Joe, who had sold his lumber company to a syndicate for $500,000, the two Patrick brothers revolutionized their sport with the formation of the Pacific Coast Hockey Association. Frank served as president of the league; Lester was the league director. Both brothers also owned, managed, coached, and starred on league teams: Lester in Victoria, Frank in Vancouver. The Patrick brothers introduced over twenty pieces of legislation in their new hockey association that eventually found their way into rule books everywhere, including the tabulation of assists as an official statistic, the painting of lines on the ice to mark out separate zones, and the development of the forward pass. When economic pressures forced them to disband their league in 1926, Frank and Lester went on to enjoy careers as hockey executives in the NHL. Even then, though, the on-ice heroics were not quite complete. In the spring of 1928, Lester, then forty-four years old, donned the pads as an emergency replacement in goal for the New York Rangers during a Stanley Cup game. The Patrick brothers passed away within four weeks of each other in June of 1960.

Cyclone Taylor had joined his friends the Patricks on the West Coast in 1913, when he signed on with Frank's Vancouver squad. His great talent seemed to improve with age, as Taylor led Vancouver to a Stanley Cup championship in 1915 and won back-to-back scoring titles in 1918 and 1919, before he finally retired in 1923 at the age of thirty-nine. Taylor and his wife, the former Thirza Cook, whom he married on a trip back east in 1914, stayed on the West Coast. Taylor was ninety-five years old when he died in 1979.

Newsy Lalonde also left Renfrew after the 1910 season, and returned to Les Canadiens. After a season with the Patricks in the PCHA in 1912, he went back to Montreal again in 1913. Newsy was still starring with Les Canadiens in 1916 when they won their first Stanley Cup, and in 1918 when the NHA was reorganized as the National Hockey League. Newsy went his old rival Cyclone Taylor one year better, playing until he was forty, before retiring in 1927. He passed away in 1970.

Three other players left Renfrew after the 1910 season: Fred Whitcroft, Hay Millar, and Jack Fraser announced their retirement from the game. Herb Jordan left hockey as well that year, but remained in Renfrew, continuing to look after O'Brien interests in the Creamery Town.

Only three players from the star-studded 1910 Renfrew Millionaires were back with the team in 1911: Bert Lindsay and Bobby Rowe (who both later joined the Patricks in the PCHA), and Cyclone Taylor. As had happened the year before, the new mix of players in Renfrew got off to a slow start. Rebounding late in the season, the team could finish no better than second and watched the league championship and the Stanley Cup go to the hated Ottawa Senators.

Ambrose O'Brien's railroad contracting business had suffered during the 1910 season, so he found himself giving less of his time to hockey in 1911. His father, M.J. O'Brien, sold off the family interests in the hockey teams in Cobalt and Haileybury and relinquished ownership of Les Canadiens as well. The O'Briens had lost $20,000 dollars pursuing their Stanley Cup dream in 1910 — almost double the $1000-a-game deficit people had predicted. It became painfully obvious the next year, when Renfrew was the only NHA franchise not to turn a profit, that the tiny town simply could not generate large enough gate receipts to offset the team's expenses. Money-making business deals outside of hockey were demanding more and more of their time. After the 1911 season, Renfrew and the O'Briens withdrew permanently from professional hockey.

In the two seasons they were involved with the game, Ambrose and M.J. O'Brien failed to bring a Stanley Cup to Renfrew, but in their bid for the prized trophy they left a great legacy to the sport of hockey. The O'Briens truly ushered in the professional era in Canadian sports. Professionalism, which just three years before had been ridiculed as a detriment to hockey, was given an air of respectability by the O'Briens. More importantly, M.J. O'Brien's money and Ambrose O'Brien's initiative gave rise to a new league which would later, as the NHL, come to be recognized around the world as the greatest in the game.

At about the time the Renfrew Millionaires were playing out the 1910 hockey season, Sir Wilfrid Laurier's Naval Bill was finally passed in the House of Commons. At about the same time professional hockey was coming to an end in Renfrew, so, too, was the Laurier era. Laurier's Liberal Party, which had been in power since 1896, winning four elections in a row, and winning them handily, was defeated by Robert Borden's Conservatives in the General Election of 1911. Laurier's controversial naval policy was a major factor in his defeat.

During Laurier's fifteen years as prime minister, "The Dominion from sea to sea" ceased to be a mere geographic or political expression. It became a reality with the construction of two new transcontinental railway lines. It became a reality with the admission of Saskatchewan and Alberta to Confederation. It became a reality with waves of new citizens settling in the West, establishing population centres there that rivalled those of the East. But, after years of unparalleled growth and prosperity, a great era in Canadian history was coming to a close.

Times would not be as good during Robert Borden's years as prime minister. These were the years of The Great War, and, while Canada's soldiers served heroically in the Allied effort, the First World War proved to be the darkest episode in the young country's history. Over 60,000 Canadians lost their lives in battle. Almost 200,000 more were wounded. Conscription bitterly divided French and English Canada as no other issue had before — neither the Naval Debate nor the Boer War. Gone forever were the carefree days of a more optimistic era, an era when small towns like Renfrew could capture the hearts of a nation in their quest for hockey's most prized trophy, the Stanley Cup.

AUTHOR'S NOTE

Almost every character who appears in this novel, with the noted exception of the Laurier conspirators, existed in real life. Much effort was taken to present these characters, as well as the historical detail pertaining to their time period, as accurately as possible. There were occasions, however, particularly in the sections dealing with the creation of the National Hockey Association and its subsequent takeover of the Canadian Hockey Association, when it was necessary to omit or condense information for the sake of the story.

There are many people to whom I wish to express my thanks; first among them is Barbara Hehner. Barbara's early critique of my work provided the direction that turned a first-time writer's manuscript into a novel. Later, as my editor, she helped me complete that transition. Barbara not only was a good editor; she has become a good friend.

I also owe a great deal of thanks to Mike Cameron, whose help was invaluable to me. His offer to edit my earliest drafts, and willingness to listen to my ideas throughout the entire writing of this book are greatly appreciated.

Bev Cline, too, must be singled out for thanks for the time and encouragement she gave to me in the early going. There are others, as well, whose tidbits of information provided much-needed authenticity: Joseph Romain, formerly of the Hockey Hall of Fame, Serge Barbe of the City of Ottawa Archives, David Tomlinson of the National Firearms Association, Gary Toffoli and others at the Monarchist League, Ed Anderson of the Toronto Historical Association, and the people at the Bell Canada historical department. Thanks go also to the people I met in Renfrew, by whom I am probably long-since forgotten, but whose help I have not forgot, and to the staff of the Canadiana Room of the North York Public Library, who helped me uncover much information on what must have seemed to them to be an awfully strange assortment of seemingly unrelated topics.

Finally, I must offer my thanks to Eric Whitehead (*The Patricks: Hockey's Royal Family* and *Cyclone Taylor: A Hockey Legend*), Scott and Astrid Young (*O'Brien*), and Charles Coleman (*The Trail of the Stanley Cup*). I have never met these people, but their books provided me with invaluable research material.